Woven in Moonlight

Woven in Moonlight

ISABEL IBAÑEZ

PAGE STREET
PUBLISHING CO.

PAGE STREET
PUBLISHING CO.

Copyright © 2020 Isabel Ibañez

First published in 2020 by
Page Street Publishing Co.
27 Congress Street, Suite 105
Salem, MA 01970
www.pagestreetpublishing.com

Distributed by Macmillan, sales in Canada by The Canadian Manda Group.

24   23   22   21   20   2   3   4   5

ISBN-13: 978-1-62414-801-9 (hardcover)
ISBN-10: 1-62414-801-8 (hardcover)
ISBN-13: 978-1-64567-065-0 (special edition)
ISBN-10: 1-64567-065-1 (special edition)
ISBN-13: 978-1-64567-076-6 (special edition)
ISBN-10: 1-64567-076-7 (special edition)

Library of Congress Control Number: 2019935219

Cover and interior illustration © Isabel Ibañez

Printed and bound in the United States

TO MY FAMILIA:
Mami, papi, Rodrigo, and the entire Bolivian brigade

ANDREW,
who believed in me before I did

CAPÍTULO

uno

My banged-up spoon scrapes the bottom of a barrel that should've held enough dried beans to last for three more months.

No, no, no.

There has to be more.

Sickness churns my stomach, and my knuckles brush against bare wood as I coax a handful of shriveled beans into a half-empty bag. I wipe dirty hands against my white trousers and ignore the sweat dripping down my neck. The kingdom of Inkasisa is in the middle of her stifling wet season. Even though it's night, there's no escaping the muggy heat.

"Something wrong, Condesa?" asks the next person in line waiting for their ration.

Yes, in fact. We're all going to starve. Not that I can say this out loud. It goes against everything I know to do as their leader: A condesa should never show fear.

I school my features into what I hope is a pleasant expression, then turn to face the long line of Illustrians waiting for their evening portions. Drawn faces stare back at me. White clothes

1

hang off gaunt frames, loose and big like the tents the Illustrians sleep in next to the keep.

My whole life, I've trained for situations like this: manage expectations, soothe people's worries, feed them. It's the condesa's job.

We're standing in the round storage building with the door propped open, allowing for people to crowd around as I sort through the provisions. Luna's light casts rectangular patterns on the dozens of empty barrels piled on their sides, while a rickety wooden staircase leads up to the armory housing swords, shields, and bundled arrows. All we could carry when we fled for our lives the day La Ciudad Blanca fell.

What would Ana, our general, want me to say? *Manage them. You're in charge. Don't forget what's at stake. We need to survive until we can take back the throne.*

I glance at the door, half expecting to find Ana's broad shoulders leaning against the frame, moonlight reflecting off the silver wisps in her hair. But she's not there. Ana left four days ago on a mission to chase a rumor about Atoc, the false Llacsan king—a rumor that, if true, guarantees our victory.

She promised to be back by yesterday.

An arm brushes against mine. Catalina, silently reminding me of her presence. The knot in my chest unwinds slightly. I forgot she was standing behind me, ever helpful.

"Bring me the wheat, por favor." I gesture toward the wall the barrels of rations are lined against. "And the cloth bags over on that shelf."

She obeys, grabbing the supplies off the shelf first and handing them to me, her dark eyes lowered. Then she darts toward the barrel.

"Condesa?" a woman asks. "Is this all that's left?"

I hesitate; the lie waiting on the tip of my tongue tastes sour and wrong. My gaze returns to the dwindling piles of food at my feet: husked corn, a half-filled bag of rice, and an almost empty basket of bread. Not nearly enough.

A lie won't feed all these people.

"We're short on some supplies," I say with a tight smile. "No beans, I'm afraid, but—"

Next to me Catalina stiffens, pausing in her attempt to drag the wheat barrel to my side. Normally it takes the effort of two people, but somehow she manages by herself. Which means *this* barrel isn't full either.

The woman's mouth drops open. "No beans? ¿No hay comida?"

"That's not what I said." I force my smile to remain in place as I come to a split-second decision—our best and only option. "We have to be careful with what we have. So here's what's going to happen: Starting immediately, everyone will receive less than half their usual ration, per family. I know it's not ideal, but it's either that or we starve," I say bluntly. "Your pick."

Voices rise up.

"Less than half?"

"Not ideal?"

Another woman shouts, "How can there be no food left?"

A headache presses against my temple. "We do have *some* food—"

But the woman's words travel down the line, catching fire in the dark, until fifty people clamor for attention, wanting answers, wanting their rations. They wave their empty baskets in the air. Their loud cries boom like thunder in my ears. I want to duck for cover. But if I don't do something, I'm going to have a full-blown riot on my hands.

"Reassure them," Catalina hisses.

"I can't offer what we don't have," I whisper. Catalina shoots me a meaningful look. A condesa should know how to maintain control of any situation. "I'm doing my job. You do yours."

"Your job is my job," she snaps.

The people's cries swell, bouncing off the walls and threatening to strike me down. "¡Comida! ¡Comida!" The crowd stomps their feet and pushes in, hot breath brushing against my face like heavy smoke. I fight the impulse to step back.

Someone in the crowd yells for El Lobo, and I tense, hoping no one else sings that stupid vigilante's praises. Every time something goes wrong, someone inevitably brings up the man in the mask. The trickster.

"El Lobo can help us—"

"He steals from Atoc's coffers all the time—"

"He's the hero of Inkasisa—"

Oh, for goodness sake. He's a man in a ridiculous mask. Even my niñera could prank that puffed-up idiotic pretend king. And she was eighty the last time I saw her.

"We want El Lobo!" someone shouts.

"Lobo! Lobo!"

"That's enough!" My voice rings out, sharp as the edge of a blade. "No one speaks his name in my presence, understood? He's a scoundrel who plays pranks on the false king. That kind of reckless behavior could get us killed. The vigilante is dangerous and not one of us."

Someone throws a rock at a window. Glass shatters, and

moonlight-touched shards fly everywhere. Faces blur as my vision darkens and I can only make out hints of mottled cheeks and flailing arms as the crowd bellows for the vigilante. They press forward until Catalina and I are almost backed against the wall.

"Condesa," Catalina says, her eyes wide and frantic.

My mouth goes dry. The words don't come. I glance at the empty doorway, willing Ana to appear. But more people push into the building.

"I need . . . " I begin.

"¿Qué? ¡Más fuerte!"

"I need you all to remain calm," I say louder. "Shouting or throwing rocks won't fix the—"

Their protests grow louder and louder until I can't distinguish what they're saying. My legs wobble, and it takes every ounce of will left in me just to remain upright. It's not supposed to be like this. Ten years ago my people were the aristócratas of Inkasisa. But our way of life, our culture, is gone, like pages torn from a book. No more visits to the plaza to hear live music while strolling with friends in our long skirts and fancy leather shoes. Or walking Cala Cala, the prettiest path overlooking La Ciudad, where you can pick figs and peaches while enjoying the vista. Birthday fiestas are a thing of the past, existing only in my memory, but sometimes I can still taste my abuela's torta de nuez, a rich walnut cake smothered in creamed coffee and dulce de leche.

Another rock sails toward a window, jarring me from my thoughts. Shards of splintering glass ring in my ear. My nerves threaten to eat me from the inside out. An empty feeling in the pit of my stomach makes my head spin.

Catalina touches my arm and steps in front of me. "What the

condesa means is that we have a plan to get more food underway. For now we have plenty. Everyone will receive the usual amount."

I cut her a warning look, but Catalina ignores me. So does everyone else. Her words work like a balm over a blistering wound. The crowd quiets and holds out their baskets, mollified, shuffling around her like chickens clucking for feed.

"Why don't you all step back in line and I'll sort out the food? Have you on your way so that you can put your children to bed, and have something to cook for your families tomorrow, all right?"

They file into a straight line like obedient schoolchildren. I step away from Catalina, my shoulders slumping. They don't want me or the bad news I carry. I can't give them what they need, so I give them what they want instead—Catalina. Their friend.

Something I can't be as their supposed queen.

She knocks the lid off the barrel at my elbow and scoops up a handful of wheat. "Who's first?"

Catalina distributes heaping portions of wheat and bundles of husked corn until only a smattering of provisions remain. Then she reaches for the barrels that contain the last of our supplies—*for emergencies only.*

I stand off to the side, my fists clenched and my mouth shut. I can't manage a polite smile even if I try. Ana normally leads undercover raids to La Ciudad to steal food, but since she's not back, who knows how long it'll be before we get more supplies? At the rate Catalina's giving out rations, we have mere days left. And just who does she think they'll come after when everyone discovers how close to starving we are?

Certainly not to their *friend.*

Catalina spares me a brief glance, then she picks up a small bowl by her feet filled with a handful of dried beans, ground wheat, and an ear of corn. Her own ration she set aside earlier. She hands it to the next person in line.

"I need air," I say curtly. Without looking at her, I head toward the door. The remaining crowd parts so I can pass. Glass crunches underneath the soles of my leather boots. I avert my gaze from their watchful eyes, but I feel their disappointment anyway.

The condesa has let them down.

When I want to escape, I head to the top of the northernmost tower in the keep, the massive fortress that once housed the legendary Illustrian army before it was destroyed by Atoc's supernatural weapon. After the revolt, we sought refuge within this stronghold of massive stone towers and high arches. Mountains envelope the rear of the fortress, and abysms several hundred feet deep encircle those. It's as if our fortress stands on a floating island. A single bridge allows entry, enchanted by Ana's magic. Only Illustrians can cross.

But that hasn't stopped Atoc's priest from trying.

Outside the storage building, mosquitos buzz and toads croak in the sweltering night. The heat of my torch sends rivulets of sweat dripping down my face. The air hangs heavy with the smell of cooking fires drifting from the long rows of tents next to the keep. The scents are of simple dishes, beans over white rice, and nothing at all like how we used to eat in La Ciudad: plates piled high with silpancho or salteñas, grilled choclo and fried yuca, and then washed down with toasted cane sugar, ginger, and mango juice. Overhead, a full moon adorns the night like a bright jewel. Luna's looking her best.

I pass the stables and spot Sofía practicing drills with her mother's blade. A gift for her eighteenth birthday. Ana was so proud to hand over her most prized possession. That blade had saved us during the invasion. Now her magic saves us day and night. Ana is everything to everyone on this side of the bridge.

General and mother. Mentor and friend. If she's in danger— or worse—how long can we survive without her?

I open the double doors to the great hall, a square room filled with long wooden tables and a fireplace. Above the dirty fireplace is a shield that belonged to an Illustrian queen who ruled Inkasisa hundreds of years ago. Our battle cry *Carpe Noctem*—"Seize the Night"—is etched along the upper arch. The ceilings are tall, and tapestries I've woven over the years decorate the stone walls. Shooting stars are stitched across the length of them. Some with puffy clouds that look real enough to float away. The skies and heavens, moon and stars, Illustrian pride.

I climb the tower's spiral staircase, trailing my fingers against the rough wall. My boots thud against the stone. At the top, a small round room waits for me, empty except for a basket of white llama wool and a sturdy wooden loom, a gift from my Llacsan niñera. I haven't seen her since Atoc drove us out of our own city.

Ten years ago. A lifetime.

The loom sits near an arched window, close enough to bathe in Luna's moonlight, but not close enough for the heights to make me queasy. The room is far removed from everyone else, making it easier to weave without any distraction.

My fingers twitch. I want to weave. No, I *need* to.

With my heart thudding, I grab a bundle of the snow-white wool and tie knots on the top and bottom pegs. Once the loom is properly warped, I gather more wool. I start at the top, threading the strands over and under to create diamond-shaped lights peppering the evening sky.

As I work, moonlight glints around me, growing brighter, as if peering over my shoulder to watch me work. My fingers blur as I move from left to right and back again. When I finish dotting the tapestry with twinkly lights, it's ready for my magic thread. The one only I can make.

The one made of moonlight.

My fingers tingle, and I reach for a ray of silver light. Feel it glide over my hand, like putting an arm through a sleeve. The moonlight slants, turning supple and smooth, bending and twisting as it lengthens.

My breath catches. No matter how many times I use Luna's rays to make thread, it always manages to surprise me—the shimmer of magic courses through me, delighting the fabric of my soul.

I work the incandescent thread, over and under again, building a scene of the night sky. The moonlight turns to moondust as I weave, fluttering to the stone floor like falling snowflakes.

In what feels like minutes, a new tapestry winks back at me. A glittering silver work of art that lights up the small room. Pools of moondust gather at my feet, as if I've wandered into winter. My neck and shoulders stiffen—a telltale sign that I've once again lost track of time. The pain is worth it. While I weave, life's troubles melt away: worry about Ana, our lack of food, and the infernal Llacsans. I pick up the strand to finish the bottom row.

Footsteps shuffle behind me. I stiffen, bracing myself for the fight I know is coming.

"It's beautiful," Catalina says from the doorway. "One of your best, I think." Her voice turns wistful. "And that's saying something. The moon thread—"

I turn to face her. "Is the food all gone?"

She shakes her head as she steps into the room.

"How much do we have left?"

She avoids my gaze. "Enough for a few days."

I suck in a breath and hold it for a long moment. It forces my anger deep within me. A trick Ana taught me to keep my temper in check. She always keeps calm and thinks of practical solutions. I admire the way she handles bad news, however ugly. If it were me, I'd hit something with my loom. Preferably a Llacsan.

I let out my breath slowly.

Catalina bends closer to study the tapestry. The silver light flickers across her face. People say we look like sisters. Same wavy hair and dark eyes, olive skin and thick, arched brows. Some days I like to pretend we are. But right now I want to stay mad at her for putting us in the most impossible situation. Three hundred displaced Illustrians live near our fortress in rows and rows of tents. Their homes cover the grounds, leaving little room for growing food.

I sigh. I know her heart. She means well. But coño.

"We're going to starve, Catalina."

"I appreciate everything you're doing," she says in the same soothing tone she uses on overwrought children. "I really do. But you need to trust me—"

I throw my hands up, because really, I can't do a damn thing to fix our plight.

It's not my place. I'm not the real condesa.

Catalina is.

"You're the one in charge," I say. "I'm only *pretending* to know better." I grab the leftover wool and furiously wind the long strand into a tight ball.

"Ana will come back, and she'll lead another foraging mission into La Ciudad. You'll see. She'll steal enough to feed us for several months. I know what I'm doing, and you ought to trust her. She's always looked out for me. For both of us."

"Then where is she? Ana said three days. It's been four. You should have let me go after her, or at the very least let Sofía go." I raise my voice. "Maybe Atoc's priest got ahold of her. Did you think of that?"

"Stop it," Catalina says. "Just stop it. This isn't helping, Ximena."

Goose bumps flare on my forearms. I rarely hear my real name said aloud. When Ana first brought me into the keep ten years ago, she switched me with Catalina behind closed doors.

Back then, her protective parents limited public outings and kept her social circles centered around family. But they all perished in the revolt. When Ana had dressed me in the Condesa's fine clothing, Illustrians never questioned my identity. They believed I was their heir, their last hope to reclaim the throne, safely hidden from Atoc.

That's when Catalina became Andrea. Only Ana's two children, Sofía and Manuel, know the truth, and as a form of habit, they call me the condesa like everyone else.

"Atoc's priest keeps trying to cross the bridge with his underlings," I say. "You can't give away our emergency reserves. That's what they're there for—in case the Llacsans manage to cross, we'll have to wait them out."

Catalina's lips thin into a pale slash. "Keep your voice down. Everyone will hear you. Ana's shadow magic will hold against the priest."

As long as Ana's still alive. I slump forward on the stool, my fingers tangling in my hair. When Ana told me about her plans for this undercover mission to La Ciudad, I was against it. The city is crawling with Atoc's guards, and Ana isn't as young as she used to be. But rumors swirl that his greatest weapon—the Estrella—has gone missing, and if they're true, there won't be a more opportune time to finally strike the Llacsans.

I wanted to go with her, but she refused. It's an old argument. I already have a job. As a child, being the condesa's decoy seemed easier than living on the streets among the people who'd killed my family and ruined my home. But I didn't realize then what I'd be giving up—my very identity.

It's an honor to protect Catalina. To give up my life for hers should it come to that. And despite my duty, despite the long years of living as somebody else, I love her. As a sister, as my future queen.

Sometimes, though, that kind of love just isn't comfortable.

I send a silent prayer to Luna, asking for Ana's safe return. If the Estrella's missing, someone has to look into it. Ana knows the city better than anyone, aside from Manuel, who's off traveling to the ends of Inkasisa to secure allies. They are few and far between. Most tribes are loyal to the false king, and the ones who aren't don't dare rise against him. But still, Ana sends Manuel to every corner of the kingdom. She's stubborn that way. It's a trait that has kept us alive all these years.

Catalina is right. Ana will come through. There simply is no other option.

"I need to read the stars," Catalina says. "Maybe there will be something about Ana."

I force a smile. She needs every bit of encouragement. "Buena suerte. I'll be there in a minute."

After she leaves, I finish weaving the bottom row of the tapestry. I tie off the strands so my work won't unravel, then hang the tapestry on the wall. Next, I straighten up the place. The leftover wool goes back into my basket; the scraps go into my pocket. I scoop up the moondust shed from my weaving and dump the whole shimmering mess into a canvas bag I keep handy. When inhaled, the powder brings on a heavy, dreamless sleep. Sadly, I'm immune to it.

I sigh and head to the room I share with the condesa. We don't have much furniture in the keep, and what little we do decorates our room: a narrow bed and dresser, one nightstand, and a pillow. The white paint on the stone walls has faded to a dingy gray.

Catalina is leaning—practically falling—out the window, a dented bronze telescope in her hands. She leans out farther, and I suck in a breath, forcing myself to remain silent. She'd only laugh at my worry. Illustrian magic—magic from the heavens, the night sky—manifests in different ways and at different ages. For some, the magic is slight, like the ability to stay up all night. Manuel's Moonsight gives him clearer vision when the sun dips into the horizon. Sofía can illuminate darkened rooms. Others are masters of tides. Many who fight in our army become fiercer at night, dangerous like the creatures that hunt by the moon.

Mine is weaving with moonlight. But Catalina *reads* the stars, the constellations hanging miles above our heads. Deep in the night sky, she can see shifting, glittering lines. A trained and capable Illustrian seer can decipher each new message written in the heavens, but it takes years of dedicated learning and plenty of favor bestowed by Luna.

We used to rely on the seer's guidance for every major decision. The last person who could accurately read the stars died in the revolt. Now we have only Catalina left to guide us.

And her predictions rarely come true.

"Any luck?"

"Maybe." Catalina squints into the night. "I don't know. It's probably nothing."

That's a no, then.

She glances at me, her eyes drawn. "Why is this so hard? Even when I see something that might be useful, I'm too scared to share. What if I'm wrong?"

I lean against the arched doorway. "It'll get easier."

She wipes her eyes, yawning. "How do you know?"

"Because everything does with practice." I jerk my chin toward the door. "I think you've done enough tonight. Let's get some sleep. I brought you moondust."

Catalina tucks the telescope under her arm and smiles gratefully.

I plop onto the bed. "I'm sleeping in. Don't kick me in the middle of the night."

Catalina laughs and curls up beside me. "You always steal the blanket."

"You have the only pillow in the entire keep."

She nudges my shoulder sharply. I quickly snatch the pillow from underneath her head and smack her face with it. Catalina lets out a peal of laughter as she ducks away from my next hit. "Give me back my pillow, peasant."

I scoff and land another blow. Catalina grabs the pillow back with a dramatic huff and tucks herself under the blanket, pretending to be annoyed. Anything to forget about the roles we play. I'm not the only one who can't go by her own name.

She flings her arms wide, and I resist the urge to shove her off the bed. We settle into companionable silence. The pair of us staring up at the ceiling, lost in thought. I can't get the image of empty food baskets out of my mind.

"You're right," she whispers. "It's strange she's not back yet."

I turn toward Catalina and grab the small bundle of moondust from my pocket. "Try not to think about it." I hold up the bag. "Are you ready for it?"

"Don't waste it on me. I can try to sleep without it."

I give her a look. "It's not like I can't make more."

"How much time will you have to weave when you're managing what we're going to eat?" She refuses to meet my eye.

"Catalina . . ."

"I'm sorry." Her voice cracks. "I know I messed up. I just think the rations are paltry. Lo siento."

I understand how tempting it is to offer comfort in some way, however small. She can't *be* the condesa—not in public, anyway—so she makes up for it by helping and speaking for me, giving as much of herself as she can.

I throw my arm around her shoulders and squeeze. I don't

have the answers, but at least I can help her sleep. "Why don't you try to rest? Use the moondust."

She nods.

I blow a pinch of shimmering dust in her face. The effect is almost instant. Catalina's eyes shut as she snuggles deeper into the pillow.

She looks so young when she sleeps. I inch the blanket higher until it tickles the bottom of her jaw, and then I close my eyes. Thoughts of Ana and our low supplies crash around in my head, and I wish for the millionth time moondust worked on me. We depend on Ana for so much: to lead our resistance, to protect our fortress, to keep our people alive. And she's counting on us to keep things in order until she gets back.

It feels like my eyes have barely closed before a sharp knock jerks me awake. Next to me, Catalina sits up, rubbing her eyes. The heavy wooden door opens and Sofía pushes in, dressed for battle in a long-sleeve tunic and thick leather belt that stows her sword. On her feet are scuffed leather boots that I know hide slim blades in secret pockets.

"I hope you brought coffee," I mumble. "Lots of it. Con azúcar."

"We're out of sugar," Sofía says.

Of course we are. "Why are you up at dawn? Is there a training session I don't know about?"

Sofía motions toward the window, her face grim and serious. "The enemy comes. They're on the other side of the bridge."

CAPÍTULO

dos

I jump out of bed, flinging the sheets aside as if they're on fire. "How many are there? Have they crossed the bridge?" Has Ana's magic—

Sofía holds up her hand. "The Llacsans aren't warriors. They're asking permission to cross the bridge because they have a message from Atoc."

"Permission?" I ask.

In the years since the revolt, not one Llacsan has ever asked permission to enter the Illustrian stronghold. They've demanded entry, or Atoc's priest has tried to cross over with his blood magic, hoping to force an unsuspecting Illustrian to show him the way.

"Condesa, what do you want to do?" Sofía asks.

I open my mouth to reply before realizing she isn't talking to me.

Sofía is looking at Catalina.

My jaw tightens. I don't make the decisions. I simply uphold them. Catalina's voice is the loudest I hear in my head, governing what I think and sometimes even what I feel. I understand the role I play down to my bones, but that doesn't mean it's not hard. I want to be heard too. Sometimes, when my temper gets the best of me, I'm secretly pleased. That's the real me breaking through the mask.

Catalina's hands tug at the corner of the blanket. "Has your mother come back yet?"

Sofía's eyes darken. "Not yet."

I frown. This is bad. Really, really bad.

"No word from Manuel?" Catalina asks in a hopeful tone.

Sofía shakes her head. "My brother hasn't written in months."

"This is ridiculous. We need to send people to look for her—for *them*," I say. "How many went with her?"

"Four. I already gave the order to send out a search team." Sofía runs a hand through her dark hair in a gesture that mimics her mother.

"All right." Catalina takes in a deep breath. Her fingers drop the edges of the blanket, and she sits up straighter. Her voice doesn't waver as she speaks. "Take their weapons. Let them over the bridge. We'll hear their message, and when Ana returns, we'll decide what to do next."

"Are you sure?" I ask. A million things could go wrong. We've never let a Llacsan across the bridge. What if it's a trap?

"I want to hear that message." Catalina raises her eyebrow at Sofía. "Better to know what Atoc wants, right?"

Sofía nods. "There's more of us than there are of them. I think it's what my mother would do."

Catalina's expression clears at the mention of Ana. "See to it, then."

Sofía leaves at a full tilt and without a backward glance.

The idea of talking to the Llacsans twists my stomach. If the roles were reversed, Atoc would turn us away at the castillo gates. Or worse. Many Illustrian spies have perished in his dungeons. Death by hunger, loneliness, and darkness. No message is worth the risk of bringing them across.

But the condesa ordered it.

"Pick out what you want me to wear," I say. "Nothing too frilly."

"I wish I could meet with the messenger."

I consider pricking the condesa with one of her hairpins. "And unravel years of careful planning? I'm your decoy."

As soon as the words are out in the open, a flicker of unease sweeps over me. It *is* dangerous. That's true for her, but also true for me.

Catalina folds her arms across her chest. Deep down she knows every precaution matters. When the Llacsans overran La Ciudad, the usurper ordered a search for the last Illustrian royal that stretched the whole of Inkasisa. But by then Ana—captain of the Queen's Guard—had locked Catalina inside the fortress, hidden from prying eyes, Llacsan and Illustrian alike. Back then, Ana didn't trust anyone. We were all too desperate.

Anger courses through my veins. Atoc murdered Catalina's aunt—the Illustrian queen—along with my parents, by creating a powerful earthquake that destroyed the Illustrian neighborhoods of La Ciudad. Then he'd used the Estrella to summon *ghosts* who'd gone on a rampage. Illustrians died by the thousands, screaming, begging, helpless. The horror of the massacre hasn't dulled with time.

I want the condesa on the throne. I'll do *anything* to make it happen—fight, steal, lie, or kill. I'm not above it. Not if it ensures Catalina's future. Not if it brings me that much closer to the life I want, which involves something far different from pretending to be the condesa and swinging around my blade during training. I want to weave tapestries, learn how to cook, and explore Inkasisa.

Only Atoc stands in the way.

Catalina studies me, her head slightly tilted. "You look like you're about to kill someone."

"What do you mean?"

"You look . . . feral. What is it?"

I shake my head. I need to focus on today. On protecting our future queen.

Her dark eyes flick to mine. We've never talked about the cost of switching places, because I'm afraid of what would come out of my mouth. Does she know the anger I keep trapped inside?

"Wear the white skirt and woven belt." She sighs.

"I promise to tell you everything," I say. "Every word, every detail. But I need you to stay out of the way. You can go over your notes on the constellations. Perfect your craft—"

"Funny thing about my craft," she says sarcastically. "I sort of need it to be nighttime."

I search for something else. "Then think about ways to lure El Lobo to the keep?"

Catalina's eyes light up, and I sneer. Even she falls for that overhyped act. If the masked vigilante is on our side, why haven't we received a visit from him? For all I know, he's merely having a laugh at the king's expense. That's very different from the revolution we're planning. The revolution I've trained for every day of my life.

I change out of my trousers and knee-length tunic and pull on Illustrian-white garments. Catalina clasps a silver beaded necklace around my neck. I wrap the leather laces of the only sandals I own tight around my ankles.

The condesa turns me around so I face a chipped full-length mirror. She narrowly gazes at my reflection, the corners of her mouth turned down. I examine what she sees: unruly wavy hair, face clean of any makeup, shoulders slightly hunched. I try to imagine what I'd look like if I wore the simple clothing Catalina usually wears as Andrea, helpmate to Condesa. The person I might be if I weren't her decoy. Whoever that is.

I quickly wind my hair into a knot on top of my head, pinch my cheeks, and turn to face her. "This is the best it's going to get."

"You're not going to brush out the knots?"

She says it like I'm suggesting I greet Atoc's messenger naked. "It's already up."

I grab my sword propped against the dresser. It's not that I don't care about my looks—it's that I feel ridiculous dressing up. Maybe one day I'll be able to put on a skirt without trying to be somebody else. Maybe one day I'll look like myself.

I move toward the window to check on the progress of the messenger. The faded curtains whip in the breeze, and a smattering of rain sprinkles my face. The usual pull in my belly flares as I lean out of the window. We're three stories high and I feel every one of them.

I shield my eyes from the drizzle. The messenger rides a dapple-gray mare, flanked by twelve guards. I grip the handle of my sword, the weight a comfort in my palm. The group gallops confidently toward our fortress, an arrogant set to their shoulders, as if they own the land and the people on it.

Catalina stands next to me, hands on her hips. "What do you think he'll say?"

"Well, he's not inviting us to tea," I say dryly.

"At least Atoc didn't send the priest," she says, relief palpable in her voice.

The messenger and his companions ride through the iron gate and into our courtyard. They stop next to the fountain with exclamations of delight. The group dismounts their horses and creeps closer to the fountain, which is fed by an aqueduct carrying water from our coveted mountain spring. Ana destroyed the aqueduct's path to La Ciudad after the revolt. Because of her, all the fountains in the city dried up, contributing to the water shortage crippling the region. Her hope was to hit them where it would hurt most. Then cut them down at their weakest.

Our guards draw their swords and surround the Llacsans. The messenger, dressed in a vibrant striped vest and black trousers, tips his head back and peers up toward our window. I sidestep out of view, pulling the condesa with me.

"He looks like a brute," Catalina says.

"I'm going down. I'll send for you when it's safe." I dart around her and shut the door behind me. I don't want to see the forlorn expression on her face.

My feet somehow carry me down the two flights of stairs and toward the great hall. I keep my steps light on the stone floor, ignoring the sting from the leather laces wrapped too tightly around my ankles.

My heart thrums wildly. What does Atoc want? He doesn't have designs on peace, that's for certain. I take a deep breath, trying to slow my racing heart. The last thing I want or need is to reveal any weakness.

I straighten and push the double doors to the courtyard wide open. Droplets of rain patter softly onto my shoulders.

Everyone hushes at my entrance, Illustrian and Llacsan alike. Sofía steps aside so I can face the Llacsans, but signals for our guards to press closer, forcing the enemy into a cramped circle. Their spears lie at their feet in a neat pile. Every one of them wears sandals and loose-fitting tunics under brightly hued vests. None are dressed for battle. Thankfully, the courtyard is closed off to the rest of the Illustrians. Sofía's doing, more than likely. She doesn't have much patience for pesky questions.

Archers stand in the windows of the twin white stone towers guarding the entrance of our keep. I've never climbed to the top, but Catalina says that from them you can see La Ciudad in the distance.

Sofía comes to stand by my side. "Condesa." She nods and I return the gesture, thankful she's present.

The Llacsan standing at the front of the group steps forward. The messenger.

"Buenos días, señorita," he says. "King Atoc, His Majesty of the upper mountain and lower jungle and everything in between, sends you his greetings—and a message."

He pauses, eyebrows raised expectantly. He looks past me, toward the doors, as if he wants out of the rain and to relay his news within the keep. I scoff. I'll die before I let a Llacsan cross our threshold. Next he'll be wanting to see our mountain spring.

"Well? What is it?" I say, careful to keep my voice emotionless.

"His Royal Highness, the wondrous Lord of all the land and—"

"Spare me," I snap. "What's the message?"

One of the Llacsans murmurs disapprovingly. They throw uneasy glances at the Illustrians watching their every move. Some begin to whisper in their old language.

I don't care un pepino what these people think about me.

The messenger's brows slam together. "You're to be his wife."

I laugh.

Outrage erupts among our guards. They all step closer, snarling and cursing. Sofía glares at the Llacsan messenger and raises her sword until the tip is level with his heart. Another guard notches her arrow and aims it at the tallest Llacsan in the group. I can't help but glance over my shoulder to our bedroom window, hoping she heard that outrageous proposition. Though I probably shouldn't have laughed. It's the kind of behavior she disapproves of.

"You've traveled all this way for nothing," I say. "I'll never be his wife."

"That's not the entire message. You're to report to the castillo by sundown. Alone. Should you refuse, the Illustrians we've rounded up will be executed, one by one." He leans forward and adds conversationally, "I believe you're missing a certain general and her fellow soldiers?"

Ana.

The pain in my chest makes it hard to breathe.

My eyes snap to Sofía. She presses a fist against her mouth and lets out a high keen.

That bastard. I clench my fists, blinking back tears. "Where are they?"

"In the castillo dungeons. Or the prison. Or tucked away in

some remote estate." The messenger shrugs. "I honestly couldn't say. They are out of your reach, that's all I know. But their lives will be spared the moment you become His Majesty's wife."

The messenger turns to leave, signaling his companions to pick up their weapons. Our guards move out of the way to let them pass, but the messenger pauses. He looks over his shoulder at me and smiles again—catlike—his white teeth gleaming.

The smile snaps me back.

The words rip out of me. "Kill them all."

The Llacsans barely have time to register the command before the guards start hacking. I turn away, Sofía at my heels, and stride to the double doors, the sounds of clanging steel and horrified shouts bellowing in my wake.

I wish I could've given the order twice.

Catalina sits across from me at one of the rectangular wooden tables in the great hall, quiet and grim. The hall is empty and we're alone. I fidget on a stool, catching myself as it wobbles under my weight. She fiddles with the sleeves of her cotton shirt, refusing to meet my eyes.

"Out with it," I say.

She spears me with a glare. "What a time to lose your temper—you had them *killed*?"

I almost choke on my anger. "They kidnapped Ana and the others. What would you have done? Invited them in for breakfast? Have them sit down with us, serve them eggs and coffee—without sugar, by the way, because we're out—and eat together like we're all—"

"I wouldn't have acted impulsively," she says. "You have no idea who that messenger was. What position he held in the castillo. Do you understand what I'm saying? You may have just murdered members of Atoc's family."

I gather the frayed edges of my dignity. My words come out measured, my shoulders straight. "We are at war." Have been since the day Atoc came down from the mountain with his earthquakes and ghost army and killed everything and everyone I loved.

"Not every fight can be won with fists and swords," she says softly.

I don't have time for this. I didn't want to appear weak, so I met him with strength. I did the right thing.

"You'll take Sofía with you," the condesa says. "As protection. Luna knows what you'll be walking into, especially after what you did today."

"It's too dangerous," I mumble, trying to hide my blush. Maybe I had been a bit reckless.

"Ana would want her to go with you." She tugs on the ends of her long hair. "But it's your choice. I can't believe this is happening. There are too many unforeseeable outcomes. The stars will be impossible to read."

My fingers tap the table and I continue to fidget on the stool. The space between us seems to grow as if the table stretches for miles. "It's the best move we have," I say gently. "I'll be situated in the castillo."

"You'll be a spy—like Ana," she says.

"So?"

"It's risky. What if you end up *married* to the false king?"

I wave my hand dismissively. "He's a peacock! The wedding will take months to prepare. He'll want a ceremony, weeks-long festivities, and visits from foreign dignitaries to see all of his riches. There're the invitations and food, making space for all

28

the guests. The new queen will need to be crowned. We have at least six months. Maybe more. We've never had this kind of access before."

"Six months isn't a long time."

"It's long enough." I reach across the table for her. "And with the Estrella missing . . ."

Catalina grabs my hand. "Ximena. I saw it."

"¿Qué?"

Her voice drops to a soft hush. "I think the stars have been trying to tell me about the Estrella. It's still in the castillo, but Atoc isn't wearing it anymore—why? To keep it safe?"

I exhale slowly. If the Estrella is still in the castillo, but not on Atoc's person, I might be able to find out what happened to it, or even take it. If we have power over the ghost army . . . Hope surges like a weed, taking root within me. But I quash the feeling. This isn't the first time her predications have given me a false sense of hope.

"I'm sorry." Catalina shrugs helplessly, letting go of my hand. "I wanted to say something last night, but I didn't know for sure if what I read was real. I still don't know." She resumes tugging at the ends of her hair, eyes squeezed tightly as she whispers, "It should be me going."

I stretch my hand across the table and touch her wrist. She smiles—a sad sort of smile that doesn't reach her eyes. It dawns on me that she's afraid *for* me. I want to reassure her that I'll be fine, that I'll come back alive and with the Estrella, but I keep silent. We both know I'd be lying.

This mission isn't about me, anyway. It's about Inkasisa. Our people. Her.

"You're our people's hope," I say. "You *know* this. Stay out of sight until we can clear a path to the throne."

"Marrying the pretender gets me to the throne."

My jaw drops.

"It does," she says. "Once there I could—I could—"

"What? Kill him?" I ask, my voice sharp. *Her.* This is the girl who still practices with a wooden sword. *A prop.* Because of Ana, she knows the basics of a sword. And by basics, I mean she knows to hold the blade upright and to point the tip away from her. She's always preferred to strategize and plan for the revolt: What supplies would we need? When would we strike? How could we take fewer casualties on our side?

The business of fighting and getting her hands dirty? She leaves that to me.

"Fine," she says. "Go."

I force my face into a neutral expression. Does she not believe in me? This is the *why* behind the long years of my pretending to be someone else. It's the reason I don't answer to my own name. The reason I've spent so many hours on the training field and why I accept the walls that cage me in. We'll never have a better chance. *I'll* never have a better chance to avenge my parents, to make Ana proud, to get to the other side of this war and finally, *finally*, have my own life.

I steady my voice. "I'll figure out a way to send word when I get there."

"Use your weaving," she says suddenly. "You stitch secret words into your tapestries all the time."

I didn't know she paid that much attention. "In what world would Atoc let me send a tapestry to the fortress?"

She blows out a breath. "I don't know—but there has to be a way."

Was there? I think about it, discarding one idea after another until I land on something that might work. I could, perhaps, slip the tapestry somewhere our spies could read it. "You're going to have to keep a close watch on the castillo. Assign someone to walk the perimeter, the market, even the front gates. I'll throw the tapestry out the window if I have to. It's a good idea."

Catalina's gaze snags on one of my tapestries hanging in the hall: a scene depicting a shooting star escaping dense, puffy clouds, my favorite scene to weave. "You've come really far with your weaving. Luna's given you an incredible talent."

The way she says it makes me wonder if it's meant to be a compliment, but her tone sounds forlorn, as if my magic cheapens hers. Which doesn't make any sense. She can *read* the stars, whereas I merely copy them. Catalina holds the fate of Illustrians in her hands.

I hold wool.

Silence balances between us, tilting and tensing with each breath, until she finally sighs. "All I want is to make things like they used to be. The Llacsans are ruining everything. I feel like La Ciudad is tainted. Madre de Luna, I *hate* them. How will I ever get it back to the way it was?"

"You'll have help," I say. "And this time we'll drive out the Llacsans for good."

For a moment Catalina only stares at me until she gives a little nod. She heads to the door, shoulders straight, and places her hand lightly on the handle. "I believe you. And, Ximena?"

"¿Qué?"

"Pack my hairbrush."

I head straight for our room to pack. I don't have much, but it all goes into my bag: tunics, pants, a couple of belts made of llama wool, and one worn leather jacket. I'll have to leave my loom behind. There's no way I can squeeze it into my bag, but I'm not worried. A Llacsan sits on the throne; he's bound to have one in the castillo. The Llacsans prize their weavers and their skill for creating beautiful tapestries that tell the story of Inkasisa. Tapestries are often given as gifts, and it's quite an honor to receive one.

Underneath Catalina's skirt and tunic I slip on my scuffed leather boots and hide four slim daggers in sewn-on pockets. The ritual calms me for a moment.

I settle onto the narrow bed and think about my mission: discover what happened to the Estrella and figure out a way to communicate with the spies.

I pray to Luna I can do both without giving myself away.

The door to the room opens, and Sofía barrels in. She moves like a bull, her footsteps heavy and her chest pitched forward as if she's moments from charging.

She eyes my small bag. "That's it?"

"All I have," I say.

She tucks a strand of hair that's escaped my bun behind my ear. "I think what you're doing is incredibly brave."

I duck my head, surprised by the sudden prickling feeling at the back of my eyes.

"Has Catalina seen your hair?" she asks. "Were you going for a tilted side bun?"

I half laugh, half groan.

"I can fix it." She tugs at the knots until my eyes water. I've spent countless hours at her hands. Not just help with my snarls, but with combat training and discussing which boys among our guard to stay away from. She's older, faster, and tougher, but I've never held it against her. It's nice knowing someone has my back.

"Catalina suggested you come with me."

Sofía stops braiding. "Do you want me to?"

I waver between anger and impatience, and then move to crippling fear. The kind of fear that quickens the beat of my heart and makes my breath come out in shallow puffs. The kind of fear that makes me want to hide underneath my bed. Madre de Luna. Am I willingly riding to my death? I want to be brave. Like Ana, who risks her life so we can have something to eat. But even she takes people with her whenever she ventures into La Ciudad.

I swallow. "I don't think I can go alone."

Sofía finishes braiding my hair. "Then I'll come and help kill the bastard who took my mother. I'll go as your maid. Let me do the fighting, should it come to that. You want them thinking the condesa is weak, body and mind."

I nod. "They could hardly expect the condesa to travel without her personal maid."

"Don't lose your temper," she warns. "I don't care how many of those slingshots they point at us—"

"They're called huaracas." I hand her a pin to secure the braid at the top of my head.

Sofía's eyes light up. "Didn't you try using one at some point during training?" She claps her hands. "Yes! You broke five windows! And someone's nose."

"It was someone's foot, actually," I mutter.

Sofía's shoulders shake with mirth. "That's right!"

I cover my face with my palms. "Can't you just forget about that?"

She lets out a hoot of laughter.

It's not *that* funny. I move my hands away so I can glare at her.

"Just trying to make you smile"—she reaches over to give me a hug—"or get angry. Better than being afraid. For a minute you looked like you were going to be sick."

Warmth floods my cheeks. "I did not," I grumble, untangling myself from her arms.

"You did too. I'm-going-to-throw-up sick."

"I think your vision needs checking." I stand, impatient to get on the road. I grab my bag and race down the tower, through the great hall, and out into the courtyard, Sofía at my heels.

And I gasp.

Everyone, and I mean *everyone*, is standing outside in the courtyard. Their faces are pinched, lips tight and eyes drawn. I read the confusion, the fear, etched into their faces. They believe their condesa is leaving them, and it would jeopardize Catalina to tell them otherwise. Twilight casts the white stone of the keep in a golden glow. At the front of the crowd is Catalina, who looks like she's desperately trying not to cry. She steps forward and embraces me. I'm rarely affectionate with her in public, but I don't mind this last goodbye. Who knows when I'll see her again? If I'm honest, I need the moment just as much as she does.

"It's up to you, Ximena," she whispers in the dying light. "Say something to reassure them. They need to hear you're all right."

I nod, my face warm. "I will, and I won't let you down."

"I know." She takes a step back, giving me room.

I turn to address the assembly. They're oddly silent, standing with tense shoulders and worried expressions. Fear mingles in the air, hovering close like a dense fog. I didn't expect to make a speech. It's the worst part of pretending to be the condesa.

My throat goes dry, and I pull at the hem of my tunic. "Thank you for the send-off," I say, and even to my own ears my voice sounds stiff. I clear my throat. "I know many of you are afraid of what might happen to me. Please don't be. Everything . . . everything will be fine."

Catalina clicks her tongue impatiently.

"I want . . ." Madre de Luna, what do I want? I want them to survive. "I want you all to remember there's very little food in the storage building—please be mindful of what you're consuming while I'm gone."

Catalina steps forward and clears her throat loudly. "The condesa wishes to make Inkasisa safe for all of us. Being in the castillo will give her extraordinary access to our enemy and his secrets. She'll discover his weakness, and we'll use whatever means necessary to make him pay for what he's done to Inkasisa," she says, her eyes bright and shining. "What they've done to our homes, our way of life—but more than anything, we will make them pay for what they did to our families. She has a plan for our survival and with it we'll rise against the usurper!"

Half-hearted cheers follow. There are a few who clap, but I sense their unease. They might be a little mollified, but after

35

years of hunger and hiding, I can understand their caution.

Sweat trickles down my back. Shifting my feet, I glance at Sofía, who winks at me. She knows how much I want to be on my way.

I nod in the general direction of the crowd. To get to the stables, I have to walk through everyone and past the cinnamon and papaya trees Ana helped me plant when I first came to the keep. With a deep breath, I take my first step and the people shuffle aside, making room for me. The guards hold their swords upright to their faces, the blades flat against their foreheads.

The gesture demonstrates profound respect.

But it's respect for someone else—for the condesa they think I am.

Sofía trails behind me as we pass the upturned dirt of fresh graves, the last resting place of the messenger and his companions. All thirteen of them. We climb onto our horses and gallop toward the towers, kicking up dust in our wake.

Ana's shadow magic envelopes us as we cross the bridge—a sign that she's still alive, somewhere. Her gift from Luna shrouds the bridge from view. Only an Illustrian can see the glimmering outline. Even so, the ride to the other side makes me dizzy. I have a clear view to the bottom of the ravine.

"Even the horses are used to the magic!" Sofía yells as she passes.

"Cállate," I say, clutching the reins.

We ride through the once public farmlands. Carts piled high with stalks of the koka leaf are silhouetted against the dusky sky. Chewing just a little bit helps with the altitude and upset stomach, but more than that brings on hallucinations, and too much means you never wake up at all. The tops of the plants have feathery bushes, like the ends of a llama's tail. Wide, flat leaves stick out from their thick stems. It's an eerie sight, as if large spiky Boraro monsters dot the empty landscape. They're everywhere.

"I can't believe it," Sofía's voice carries back to me. "Using the farmlands to grow a drug? Not *food* for his people to eat and survive on, but a *product* to export?"

My ears pound as I clutch the reins. It takes everything in me to keep the horse moving toward the castillo and not the fields. Rage turns my vision to blood red. My fingers itch for my sword. The usurper has taken everything from us.

Our families.

Our homes.

Our queen.

And now the damned farmlands.

"Ándate a la mierda, Atoc!" Sofía shouts. We whoop in agreement, knowing such words will have to be swallowed in the coming days.

We gallop on, the city materializing on the horizon as dusk settles into darkness, the moon rising, the stars peeking out. Goose bumps mar my skin. The night promises danger.

Luna, give me strength.

We travel through the walnut trees, around the village neighborhood, and past La Ciudad's outer wall. Now, instead of Illustrians living in the city, it's the infernal Llacsans. Murals of the usurper and his entourage—particularly of Atoc and his younger sister, Tamaya—besmirch the once white walls. As if Atoc needs to remind everyone who won the war.

We pass a pair of Llacsans huddling on tattered blankets

against the city gate. They peer at us with red-rimmed eyes, their noses blotchy and bleeding. These are the unfortunate souls trapped in addiction. Ensnared by the deadly promises of Atoc's favorite export.

We ride silently, leaving the city walls. As we approach the castillo entrance, I grip the reins tighter and grit my teeth.

"Take a breath," Sofía murmurs as we ride up the pathway to the iron gates.

The castillo looms ahead of us, its white walls gleaming, simple and austere. The windows are narrow and arched, mere slits. Like prison windows. I can't imagine what my life will be like living inside. What horrors await me? Images of a dark dungeon buried beneath the castillo swim in my head. Of long, drawn-out days without food and cold nights without any hope of warmth.

My anger morphs into dread.

I'd agreed to this plan and jumped without thinking, the same way I'd jumped at being Catalina's decoy all those years ago. That impulse brought me to the home of my enemy, where I'll be scrutinized for any show of weakness. Once inside, I can never be Ximena. What if I mess up and they catch the lie? I clench my eyes and fight to remember why I'm riding toward the ugly and terrifying unknown.

How far am I willing to go for my queen?

I open my eyes again as we reach the front of the path. Tall iron gates block our way. A poster depicting El Lobo hangs from one of the bars. It offers a reward for information regarding the masked vigilante.

I pull back on the reins. And wait. Sofía follows my lead, quiet and alert.

The night hangs heavy and silent, as if hushed by something sinister, lurking on the other side of the castillo walls, like a hidden snare waiting for a fox.

"I see movement," I whisper to Sofía. "Upper wall. Left of the gates. Damn it, *put your weapon away*. You're supposed to be my maid."

Sofía frowns, but sheaths her sword. "I don't like this."

That makes two of us.

I tilt my head back and look up to where I'd seen someone creeping along the edge. Two men squint down from the watchtower. Only the moon and stars illuminate our upturned faces.

"Who are you?"

My heart hammers in my chest. No turning back now.

"The condesa," I say, loud and clear. "I'm here by At—the king's demand."

The sound of a rattling chain slashes the air and slowly the door rises, foot by foot, like the jaws of an anaconda before swallowing its prey whole. I nudge my horse forward, Sofía on my left. Thank Luna I asked her to come. My body is trembling so hard, I'm half amazed I haven't spooked the damn horse.

The courtyard is as I remembered—only more colorful. I'm expecting a white building, but the exterior walls are painted a vibrant shade of green. Murals depicting the false king wearing a crown of sunflowers sully every inch. The yard is in the shape of a square, with white archways lining each side. Giant potted plants are strewn about and stone benches line the walls. The stables, if memory serves, are off to the right.

A pair of doors blocks the main entrance—tall, formidable, and made of iron, designed to keep intruders out. They swing open and a man around Ana's age walks out to meet us. He studies me coldly. He's stocky, wearing amulets at his throat and wrists, and dressed in an eggplant robe that ripples as he approaches. His nostrils flare as he continues his assessment.

"Condesa." He says the title condescendingly. "I am the priest Sajra."

My heartbeat thrashes in my ears and I instinctively reach for the handle of my blade. Sofía sucks in a deep breath. This is the man behind the king. The loud shadow responsible for some of Atoc's most unthinkable edicts. The torturer who uses his blood magic to ruin lives.

He stops in front of my horse and runs an index finger along the horse's neck. I keep still, my attention on his hands.

"You were supposed to come alone," he says in a neutral tone.

I clench my jaw, my body coiling tight.

The priest steps away from the horse. A prickle of warning makes the hairs on my forearms stand on end, and a glint of silver arrests my attention, turning it to a darkened window.

I gasp.

Something long and thin blurs past me.

My mouth drops open as the force of an arrow catapults Sofía off her horse. Her head cracks against the ground.

Blood gushes from the hole in her chest, staining the white stone.

CAPÍTULO

cuatro

I keep blinking. My eyes tell me one thing, my head another. This isn't real. It can't be.

Shaking, I slide from my horse and fall to my knees beside Sofía. Her eyes watch me. Blood trickles out of her nose and mouth; long, snakelike streaks slither down her cheeks and neck. Her body convulses as her blood soaks through my skirt and sticks to my shins. She's losing too much. The arrow pierced her chest, near her heart. Pulling the arrow will only kill her faster. But maybe I can stop the bleeding? I reach for the shaft.

"Don't," she says, panting. "I'm already dead."

I grip her hand. It's icy. "No."

"Condesa," Sofía whispers, her voice thin, as if she's already a ghost. "Save my mother—"

Rough hands jerk me away. A rattling gasp comes from Sofía, but I don't see the moment she dies. That's taken away from me like everyone and everything I've already lost. My parents and home, the city I loved before it was corrupted, the chance to wholly be myself. It was my decision to bring Sofía. This is on me.

Instinct takes over.

My heels smash toes, my elbows drive into stomachs. I claw and kick as the Llacsan diablos pull me farther away from Sofía. The world is awash in blood red. I flip soldiers onto their backs, crush windpipes, and break arms. My hits are imperfect, sloppy, fueled by rage and grief. More of them come. I'm surrounded. My small daggers are hidden in my boots and thanks to Ana, I know that a well-placed thrust can cause as much damage as a sword. I bend and reach for my right boot.

The priest steps forward and everything slows.

"That's enough, Condesa," he says, giving an arrogant lift of his jaw, his eyes careful.

By now I have a dagger in each hand. I have two more hidden deep within my shoes. My chest rises and falls in tune with my breath. Then suddenly my throat tightens, as if someone has wrapped their hands around it, squeezing. A subtle constriction that makes my toes curl. The priest holds up a single index finger. That's all it takes for him to block the air from my lungs.

I freeze.

"That's it," Sajra says with a cold smile. "You're done now."

I shut my eyes. Something sour tickles the back of my throat.

The priest loosens his hold and I suck in air, the smell tainted from all the blood staining the cobblestone.

My heartbeat slows, shock and hurt melting away, leaving dread and guilt tangling together like unattended balls of wool. When I open my eyes, the scene before me is so depressing, I almost laugh. Twelve men encircle me, arrows notched at the ready. Their stunned faces spell out their horror. The men I've taken down half crawl, half limp away.

I made a mistake. I'm supposed to be the condesa—not a resistance fighter. Not Ximena the rebel. Catalina wouldn't have fought. She would have been expected to cry furious tears while remaining dignified.

Fool that I am, I've given *the priest* of all people a reason to suspect me. Even after Sofía had warned me not to lash out and show strength. As Catalina's decoy, I'm her greatest weapon against Atoc. He's supposed to think I'm docile and subservient.

The priest stands close enough to touch. Close enough to destroy me with his blood magic. I know he won't. I'm here to marry his king. I control my breath, and my heart slowly stops thumping painfully in my chest. The daggers go back into my boots. Sofía's sword is collected off the ground by one of the guards, the blade soaked with her blood. Her vacant expression will haunt me forever. I press my hand tight to my mouth. That weapon belonged to Ana, and I'll be damned if I allow a Llacsan to wield it. Slowly, I let my hand drop to my side in a tight fist.

"I want that back," I say to the priest.

His gaze flickers to the sword clutched in the guard's meaty paw. "Are you done showing off?"

I hiss. Showing off? Is that what I was doing? Sajra regards me with his lifted chin and ugly smirk. I clench my jaw and nod once.

"Then come with me, and maybe I'll make sure it's not lost."

It's a lie. I'll never see Ana's sword again. It's gone like Sofía, and my heart feels as if it's been ripped away, leaving a jagged hole in its place.

The priest turns on his heel. As if by their own accord, my feet follow the evil Llacsan. They follow because of Catalina—

my future queen, my best friend, the sister I never had, and the only person left living who knows the *real* me.

The guards keep their pointed arrows trained on me. Not once do any of them lower their weapons.

I know, because I watch.

The castillo doesn't look at all like I remember it from the time I visited as a child. Gone are the calming white stones I trailed my fingers along. Gone are the empty spaces. Instead the Llacsans have painted everything in vivid colors that make my head spin: One hallway, the bright yellow of the maracuya fruit lashes out; another, it's a raw meat red that threatens to overwhelm me. If the castillo's exterior is sober, then the interior is drunk on cerveza.

Nearly every inch of space displays paintings of Llacsans, tropical flowers, parrots, or llamas. Potted plants in every corner, candles burning vanilla and orange and eucalyptus blend together and attack my nose. Dogs and cats and a mule cross my path.

I want the white back.

It gives space to breathe.

The guards press into my sides. The priest snaps his fingers and motions toward a hunched boy leaning against a door frame just inside a massive foyer.

A guard yanks my elbow, pulling me to an abrupt stop, and I let out a sharp hiss.

"Get the condesa ready for court," Sajra says to the boy, then heads off to wherever priests go in this forsaken place. Half the guards follow him. Three remain, their arrows notched and aimed at my heart.

The boy's eyes flicker to mine. His dark heavy-lidded gaze betrays a careful alertness, instantly replaced by a flash of contempt. He straightens, assuming responsibility as easily as if he's donned a shirt.

I study the face of my jailor.

He's not handsome. All sharp angles and lines. A blade-like nose, thin lips, and a razor-edged jaw. His rich brown skin, a blend of copper and the tawny rock from a mountain cliff, sets off his shoulder-length black hair. It curls slightly and softens his pronounced cheekbones. He's wearing beige trousers, a black shirt opened at the collar, and the common Llacsan leather sandals that leave the wearer with dirty feet.

"Do us both a favor and hand over the daggers in your boots," the boy says, his arms crossed. He asks me to give up my weapons the same way an attentive host might ask if I'd like something to drink.

The guards shift uneasily on their feet, waiting for me to obey—or not.

Without taking my attention off the boy, I bend and pull out two of my four daggers, throwing them at his feet. He doesn't bother to retrieve them.

"What else?"

"That's it," I say. "I'm not an armory."

The boy lifts an eyebrow.

Images of Sofía fill my vision, and angry retorts burn on my tongue. My temper wants release. "I hate what you've done with the castillo. Just because there's a lot of colors to choose from doesn't mean you actually have to use them all."

He blinks. "I don't have time to talk about paint, Condesa. His Radiance is waiting."

The way he says *His Radiance* with such devotion turns my stomach.

"I think you have more," he presses.

I splay my hands. "I'm all out."

He stares at me for a moment then slowly shakes his head. "I don't think so."

"Believe what you want, Llacsan."

His black brows pull into a swift frown. I guess he doesn't like it when I say *Llacsan* like it's a dirty word. One guard growls. The boy raises a single hand, and I step forward, ready to heave another insult—

The boy shoves me backward.

My head hits the castillo wall, and his arm presses hard against my throat. I hadn't thought he was particularly tall, but now he towers over me. I try to push his arm away, needing to breathe. His other hand grabs my left thigh, yanks it up, and he deftly removes the dagger hidden there. He tosses it over his shoulder and eases the pressure on my throat. I suck in air.

He stares down at me, hatred radiating off him like boiling water threatening to escape a pot. I see it in the way he curls his lip. I feel it in the way his fingers dig into my skin.

The scent of dirt and herbs coming from his clothes hovers between us. An odd smell that reminds me of burnt leaves. I gag against his forearm, my eyes watering from the pungent odor. It makes me weirdly light-headed.

"Now the right," he says coldly. "Or am I getting it for you?"

I fight against the impulse to spit in his eye. Abruptly, he steps away as if he can't stand the idea of being near me for a second longer. The feeling is mutual.

The boy hunches his shoulders again and leans against the wall. I bend forward, my hands on my knees, and gulp in air, free of his awful scent. When my breathing returns to normal, I straighten and shoot my jailer a glare. I take out my last dagger. I'm tempted to launch the blade into his heart. He stiffens, as if guessing my intention. His hand hovers near his pocket.

Common sense takes over and I toss the knife at his feet. It clatters against the stone, and he relaxes.

"You'll be meeting with His Majesty," he says. "Try to contain your delirium."

I keep silent.

"A word of advice, Condesa. A little humility before my king will go a long way. His Radiance might put you in a room with an actual bed in it." He straightens away from the door. "Or he might decide he doesn't want you after all, and you'll spend the rest of your life in the dungeon."

The blood drains from my face. "He wouldn't *dare*—"

The boy's face shifts into a faintly pitying look. "It's terrible, isn't it? To be disrespected and mistreated? I can't imagine how that feels, my being a Llacsan and all."

What does he mean?

The Llacsans were never mistreated. It was their choice to stay up by the mountain, their choice to hold on to their old ways and not embrace the future. The Illustrian queen wanted them to assimilate. She wanted a unified country, and they ungratefully protested her rule.

They killed her.

The boy jerks his head in the direction of the massive double doors at the opposite end of the foyer. "Ready to meet my king, Condesa?"

The guards press around me, and I have no choice but to follow the boy's lazy strut across the open, square foyer. It's overlooked by balconies on all four sides. Guards on each end of the tall doors use long gold handles to open them, and as they swing inward, the boy bends his head closer to mine, his breath tickling the curve of my neck. "After you."

With my knees shaking, I take the first step toward my enemy.

Cinco

An empty gold throne sits on a dais between two large columns. I don't know why this surprises me. After the revolt, Atoc seized most of the Illustrians' gold. Family heirlooms were melted down so that His Royal Highness had a shiny place to rest his ass.

The long hall varies in earth tones: the orange-and-red blend of clay, the rich brown of the earth drenched in rain, the tawny gold of the sunlit mountain cliff.

The boy motions for me to wait. "You'll be called forward. Then you can stand in front of the king."

I try to refrain from rolling my eyes. What pomp! What ceremony! Does the king think to intimidate me with his traditions?

Am I intimidated?

My head says no, but the rest of me disagrees. My palms are slick with sweat. To my surprise, my knees shake. For once I'm thankful to have chosen a skirt. Bloody as it is from the hole in Sofía's chest.

The boy leaves my side, weaves through the assembly, and stands by the throne. The guards he leaves with me, each with a firm hold on one of my arms.

So I wait, casting an eye around the room.

Llacsans crowd the great hall, dressed in their traditional ensembles—solid color cotton tunics, trousers, and open-toed sandals. Their capes are woven masterpieces, varying in colors from jalapeño green to rose-petal red. Some depict the silver mountain, others the jungle. Several show llamas and condors. The women wear elaborate macramé shawls hemmed with fringe, and tailored blouses tucked into layered pollera skirts. Headdresses made of vibrantly hued gems, feathers, and gold adorn their braided hairstyles.

Though my people would disagree, I secretly think their use of color in their weaving is beautiful. I dye my wool various shades of neutrals to keep with Illustrian tradition. But sometimes I crave to pair colors together to see what I could come up with. There's only so much you can do with art when using white as the main color.

The chamberlain at the front of the room clears his throat. "Behold, majesty of the upper mountain and lower jungle, and everything in between. Son of the sun god, Inti, and faithful servant of Pachamama, King Atoc, ruler of Inkasisa!"

I steel myself for looking into the eyes of my enemy for the first time. Years of training have prepared me for this moment. But even so, my hands shake. I move them behind my back and lift my chin. Anger and fear both war within me. I pray to Luna that my anger will win.

From a door to my left, the usurper strides out. Short and squat, with a blunt face and deep bronze skin, dark eyes and hair. He wears a flowing cape knitted with gold strands over a red tunic and black trousers. I scan his wrists—no adornments. Ana said Atoc had fashioned the Estrella into a silver bracelet.

The priest leads a procession after the false king. I tremble with what I hope is rage at the sorcerer's presence. Next comes the rest of Atoc's family. The boy stands at the end of the line, his attention intent on Atoc, as if he's a sunflower and the king his sun. They form a curved line around the dais then turn to face the room as the usurper steps onto the platform.

The boy's eyes flicker over to mine.

As he stands among several men and women who all fairly resemble one another, the truth sends an icy chill coursing through my veins. He's related to Atoc. I ought to have known.

I search for Princesa Tamaya—the king's younger and only living sibling—but none of the women look my age or are dressed in the finery befitting a princesa. As the highest-ranking female in the court, why wouldn't she be here? Shouldn't she be trailing after her brother?

"Condesa," Atoc says coldly. "Come forward."

I square my shoulders and slowly walk across the long aisle, past the sneers and hurling insults, past the mocking stares, down the whole ostentatious length of it, until I stand in front of the pretender. Sweat beads at my hairline, but I don't wipe it away. I don't want to accidentally lower my chin.

Servants stand on either side of Atoc, fanning him with banana leaves. Gold glitters from the rings and bracelets adorning his throat and ears. His crown shimmers from the moonlight washing the room in silver light. I remember that crown. Remember how it used to sit on the queen's dark curls.

Back when my parents were alive.

Everyone drops to their knees, but I stay on my feet. The guards shove me down, forcing my head forward until my forehead cracks against the floor. My breath tickles the stone.

"Get up, Condesa," the usurper says.

Part of me wants to gag. The other half wants to laugh at the sheer ridiculousness. The false king with his cold eyes glittering and solemn, sitting stiffly in his imagined godlike persona, looking down his nose at me—an Illustrian.

Sofía's pale, shocked face flashes through my mind. I can never forget Atoc is dangerous—explosive, ruthless, and worst of all, entirely ignorant. He claims to want to help Llacsans and the Lowlanders, *his people*, then he plans for a road to cut through their territory, destroying homes and wildlife, all to easily export the koka drug to neighboring countries. Gratification, wealth, and notoriety are his real gods, and his greed invites dangerous criminals from powerful countries into Inkasisa who worship at the same altar.

I'm afraid of what his ignorance may cost me—my life, my mission, or Catalina herself—if I ever let it slip I'm her decoy. I don't want to be afraid, so I cling to my anger.

"You're the niece of our oppressor," he comments. "You don't look a thing like her. Tyrant that she was, at least you could say she was beautiful."

I don't flinch. He wants to demean me in front of his subjects? Fine. A small price to pay for revenge. "My deepest apologies for disappointing you."

He ignores my sarcasm.

"Provided you don't in the future, I'll forgive your unfortunate appearance. After all, you will be my wife."

I stand in stunned silence. I'm prepared for this, or so I believed. But looking at my enemy, at the power radiating off him, I suddenly want to sit before I fall over. Dimly, his words circle me and none of it makes any sense. I can't silence the roaring in my head.

". . . married at Carnaval. We'll—"

I startle. "What did you say?"

A collective gasp erupts behind me. He regards me coldly, a muscle in his jaw twitching. He leans forward. "Never," he says, "interrupt me again. *Nunca*."

My mouth goes dry.

He settles back, his fingers drumming against the seat. "I said the wedding will be during Carnaval."

I sway on my feet. Carnaval? That's a mere . . . eight, no *six*, weeks from now. I thought I'd have more time. I have to find the Estrella, have to figure out how to get my tapestries out of the castillo. Ana needs to prepare our troops.

A cold reality hits me. Ana isn't at the keep. Sofía is dead. Manuel is away on his mission. The only person left to lead the Illustrians in the battle to win back the throne is . . . Catalina.

The high priest marches to Atoc and whispers something in his ear. Sajra fastens a hard gaze on me, probing and invasive. Time slows as it did at the castillo gates and I struggle to remain on my feet.

He bends and whispers once again, and Atoc nods.

"An excellent idea, Sajra."

My heart thunders painfully, slamming against my ribs.

"Until the wedding," Atoc says, "you're not to leave the

castillo grounds, and a guard will be with you at all times. Should you try to leave, or inflict harm on any of my subjects, I'll burn down the bridge. All Illustrians will be rounded up and sacrificed to Inti."

My lips thin. An empty threat. Ana's magic will protect my people—

I nearly faint.

If Ana's safety isn't guaranteed, our protection will disappear. Even worse, our bridge will become visible. She must be released and returned to the fortress. The walls of the Illustrian keep are nearly indestructible. Without the Estrella, Atoc would lose a sizable chunk of his army trying to tear down the fortress.

"I want complete access to the fort," he goes on.

"You'll be given access after the wedding." I keep my expression firm. "Not a moment before."

The room quiets, but I don't care. He can't be allowed inside the Illustrian fortress. As far as I know, none of these Llacsans understand how the protection spell on the bridge works. They don't know it's Ana who weaves it. To them, the only way inside the keep is with my word.

He stands, his fists on his hips. "I'll have it now."

"If you're serious about peace between our people, then you'll accept my terms," I say. "How do I know you won't try to murder me before the wedding?" I make my voice softer, almost coaxing. "Once we're wed, the fortress is yours—along with the spring."

The words are out in the open and until I say them, I don't realize how true they are. If I fail, my people will not only lose their future queen, but their home as well. Cielos, even their lives.

This is our only chance to reclaim what belongs to us.

"It's only six weeks," I say. "In the meantime, I'm here as your guarantee."

He appears mollified and sits again. "As a gesture of goodwill, I'll be lenient."

Atoc snaps his fingers, beckoning to the boy standing at the end of the line. The boy who took away my weapons. The boy who smells like burning ragweed.

"Rumi," Atoc says again, louder this time. "Quit daydreaming or whatever in diablos you're doing."

The boy jerks in surprise and laughter ripples through the crowd. He pushes his way through until he stands in front of his king. The people around him give him a wide berth as he sinks to his knees. A few snicker when the boy lays a hand over his heart.

"High King of Inkasisa," he says. "I am your faithful servant. How may I—"

"Take the condesa to her chamber," Atoc says impatiently. "See to it she is bathed, and her garments burned. She can wear Llacsan clothing." He doesn't glance my way. "Leave a guard outside her door. The girl is your responsibility, primo."

"It will be my pleasure, Your Majesty. May the ruler of Inkasisa live forever," Rumi says with a winsome smile, all simpering charm and polite manners. A sharp contrast to my earlier treatment. He remains kneeling, as if transfixed.

Someone chuckles.

"Rumi," Atoc says, exasperated. "Do it now."

He springs to his feet. "Yes, Shining One. Por supuesto."

His king rolls his eyes and turns to face me. "You're dismissed."

I frown. He never mentioned the Illustrian prisoners. "A moment, Atoc."

Atoc bends his head and examines his fingernails.

"I want your assurance that the Illustrian prisoners will go free. That was part of the deal, right?"

"It was," he says mildly. "But you see, one of my cousins never made it back to the castillo."

My feet twitch as if preparing for flight. "Primo?"

Atoc's lips curl into a satisfied smile that could have belonged to a jaguar. "The messenger."

I'm cold all over. He's going to hurt Ana because I'd been reckless. Sofía's mother. My friend, who always made sure to save me a cup of coffee after lunch. Who baked cuñapes on my birthday and taught me how to plant cinnamon trees. "I didn't know. Por favor, the Illustrians must go free," I say, hating how my voice cracks, sounding like a plea.

He stares at me, hand still raised as if he finds what's under his fingernails more interesting than our conversation. I wait, holding my breath.

Something in his expression shifts, as if an idea has taken root. "All right, Condesa. They will be permitted to leave the castillo."

I nearly sink to my knees in relief. My thanks burns on my tongue, wanting to be said, but I hold on to the words. He never should have taken Ana and the soldiers to begin with. Why should I thank him for their release?

Rumi ambles down the steps of the dais. The guards grab my arms again and haul me back up the aisle lined by the disdainful faces of the Llacsan nobility. Such as they are. We're almost to the tall doors when Atoc's voice echoes in the throne room: "Oh, and, Condesa?"

I turn, wary, his men still holding on to both arms.

"You belong to me now. Never forget that I can round up more Illustrians if you don't fall in line. On this, do not tempt me. I *own* you."

His words skid along my flesh, creating goose bumps. The guards push me forward; the doors slam shut behind me and the sound reverberates in the hall. I'm conscious of Atoc's cousin standing behind me, the guards crowding me, and my jaw clenches.

"How does it feel being His Radiance's possession?" Rumi asks. "I imagine the loss of control is devastating."

"I belong to no one," I say quietly.

Rumi silently stares back at me, his expression inscrutable.

I raise my chin, wanting a fight, but he doesn't give one. Atoc wants to humiliate me, bend Illustrians to his will, amass power and legitimacy, and force us into compliance. If the condesa becomes his queen, Illustrians will have to fall in line.

It's fortunate, then, that the false king will marry her decoy instead.

CAPÍTULO

Seis

The guards maintain their tight grip on my arms as we follow Rumi's lazy strut.

"I can walk on my own," I snap.

"I have no doubt," Rumi says over his shoulder. "But you're not allowed to."

That's right. I'm their wild animal not allowed loose in the castillo. I clench my jaw and forcibly remove their hands from my body. When one of the guards reaches for me again, I snarl. He retreats a step and glances at Rumi.

"If they touch me again," I say, "I'll break their noses. Watch me."

Rumi throws his hands up in the air. "You're a menace."

I smile at his turned back. It's a small victory, but a victory nevertheless. We walk down a long corridor and up one staircase then another. The helplessness of my situation gnaws at me. Searching for the Estrella will be impossible if I'm constantly guarded. Is there a way to get Atoc's primo to talk?

"So you're the king's cousin," I say, stepping over a chicken. Yes, a *chicken*. On the third floor. They belong in a pen, not a castillo.

These people.

Rumi makes no comment.

"You must be proud," I say, after turning down another corridor, chicken-free this time. "If he dies, are you next in line for the throne?"

He whirls to face me, thunderstruck. "Is that a threat to the king's life, Condesa?"

And because I know it'll annoy him, this *Llacsan* who worships the usurper, I smile. "It was just a question. Or are those not allowed either?"

"Gods, you're going to be insufferable throughout this, aren't you?"

"All signs point to it, don't you think?"

He mutters something about spoiled idiots and turns away.

I don't know what's come over me, or where this sudden impulse to sass the king's cousin stems from, but I enjoy annoying him. Perhaps because the only thing I can control at the moment is what comes out of my mouth. Without my daggers or my sword, it's the only weapon I have left.

"Am I allowed to leave my room?" I ask as we pass narrow window after narrow window. "How do you keep warm during the winter if none of these windows have glass?"

I've only visited the castillo once and it was during the wet season—hot and unforgiving temperatures amid stormy afternoons that feed the earth and turn it green.

A flash of bewilderment crosses his face. "Why do you want to know about the windows?"

"Making conversation," I say. Each annoyed expression

that crosses his face is a small triumph. A triumph that can't be measured, but it bolsters my confidence nevertheless. "I suppose we could talk about El Lobo."

Rumi scowls. "The human wart, you mean."

I have my reservations about the vigilante, but upon hearing Rumi's dislike, my respect for him soars. "He's not so bad. And since you don't like the subject, you can think of something to say next."

"Generous of you," he drawls. Another beat of silence, and then he adds, "Who trained you to fight?"

I frown. "How did you know I could fight?"

"Do you often carry around daggers as adornments?" His sarcastic tone feels like a smack. "I saw you fight in the courtyard."

I wince. My accursed temper will be the death of me, no doubt. But at least word will spread that the Illustrians and their condesa aren't to be underestimated. "We all learn to fight, Llacsan. Or did you think we sat around all day admiring ourselves?"

Rumi stops at a heavy wooden door, the middle in a long line. I wonder who else sleeps on this floor. He turns to face me. "It certainly wouldn't surprise me."

As if we lazy aristocrats are capable of only climbing in and out carriages. As if we aren't capable of surviving. "I don't even own a hairbrush," I mutter.

The corners of his mouth deepen, as if he fights a reluctant smile. Or a smirk. Then it's smoothed away by hostility. "This is you," he says. "You're not to leave unless escorted—"

"I remember."

"Fine," he says, waspish. He gestures to the guard on his left.

He's almost Rumi's height, with long hair that brushes past his shoulders. They look about the same age, but this one smells better. Woodsy with a hint of mint. "This is Juan Carlos. If you need to find me, ask him. He'll be outside your door all night."

I stare at the guard. "Nice to meet you."

Juan Carlos's lips twitch at my sarcasm.

"I'll come for you mañana." Rumi opens the door, and Juan Carlos ushers me inside.

The lock slides into place.

Someone has done a thorough job of going through my bag. Everything has been dumped on the floor. All of my clothes, gone. My boots and strappy sandals remain. They let me keep my llama wool, a knotty mess that'll take hours to untangle.

Looking around, I curl my lip. My room is the color of pigskin. It's a narrow rectangle, with one big window at the end that leads out to a balcony. The bed has a woven striped blanket and a *pillow*. A real, honest-to-Luna pillow. I haven't slept on one since I was a child.

There's a handsome wooden dresser with knobs painted in turquoise—of course—and a reading chair propped in the corner. A matching striped rug covers the floor.

Throwing open the balcony doors, I let the evening air in, not caring if fat mosquitos wander through. The balcony looks sturdy, but even so, I don't venture out. I'm on the third floor. High enough to unsettle my nerves. But the fresh air feels nice, and it gives me a glimpse of La Ciudad. The bell tower strikes the seventh hour. I look for home, but it's too dark to see the fortress, even with all of Luna's stars.

They're no doubt settling in for the night. Making do with the food on hand. Bowls of quinoa and several pitchers of jugo de lima on the table, Catalina at the head, smiling and beginning the meager meal with a prayer to Luna.

I said goodbye to her only this morning and already I miss her. She'll expect some word from me soon. I have to find a loom, have to tell her about the wedding during Carnaval.

Carnaval. An Illustrian three-day festival honoring the moon and stars. Parades and costumes, sticky desserts sold on every street corner, dancing and music. It was my favorite time of year. But the Llacsans have claimed it as their own: Now during *our* holiday, they celebrate the Llacsan sun god and Mother Earth—Inti and Pachamama. The grand finale is a human sacrifice of someone around my age.

I take a deep breath, and another. I still have time—*weeks*—before then.

The door opens, and I spin away from the balcony. Servants carry in a metal tub. More follow with pails of water. I don't bother hiding my surprise. I'm allowed a bath? With the water shortage in La Ciudad, how is that possible? Is it special treatment? Perhaps Atoc wants to show off his wealth. I suppose it doesn't matter if he's "wasteful" anyway. In his mind, access to our spring is a guarantee.

The room teems with people. Two young girls come in bearing long skirts and floral stitched tunics with ruffles, frilled collars, and scalloped hemlines, the fabrics ranging from buttery yellow to lime green. The mantillas are lacy with fringed hems, and there are a couple of fajas, wide belts, in a deep red. Llacsan clothing. No one in the room openly acknowledges me, and those I catch looking in my direction twist their lips in disgust, as if they've found a cucaracha in their soup.

After they leave, the guard locks up and I'm alone except for a girl who stands, staring at me, her dark eyes unreadable, from the corner of the room. She might be my age, although a full head shorter than me. Her pollera, a pleated skirt that stops at her ankles, rustles in the night breeze sweeping the room. A cream-hued manta made of llama wool is wrapped around her shoulders.

"¿Sí?" I ask.

"Your new clothes are a gift from His Majesty," she says stiffly. "I'm to take your old things with me."

I gesture toward my bag. "I think you already did."

"Not the ones you're wearing."

Is she expecting me to strip in front of her? Do these people not know the meaning of the word modesty? "What if I refuse? I happen to prefer what I'm wearing."

Her face shutters. "To refuse a gift would be an insult. You must accept."

"Fine, then I'll give them to you after my bath."

She shakes her head. "I'm not waiting until you're done washing, Condesa."

I was in a completely new world. How did we manage to live side by side with the Llacsans for all these years? Loud and shameless, with gaudy tastes in paint and clothing.

We haven't lived side by side.

Before the revolt, Illustrians lived in the city; Llacsans stayed up by the mountain. Then they came down carrying spears and torches, with Atoc at the lead, wielding the power of the Estrella.

My boots come off first. I discard my bloodied skirt and shirt and throw everything at her. She catches the bundle calmly and knocks on the door twice. Juan Carlos opens it, and I quickly snatch the blanket off the bed to cover myself. I make a noise at the back of my throat.

The girl glances over her shoulder.

"I'm hungry."

She shrugs dismissively and heads out. Juan Carlos locks the door after her, and the way he looks at me is almost apologetic, but that can't be right. They're both leaving me in here without food. I furiously throw the blanket back on the bed to keep myself from breaking down the door. My eyes sting with pent-up fury. The room doesn't feel big enough for my frustration.

My skin crawling with humiliation, I head to the bathtub, but as soon as I dip my foot in the water, I let out a loud screech. It's frigid cold.

"Carajo." I'm dusty from the ride, sore from the fight in the courtyard, and sticky with sweat. I want to be clean. I still remember what it is to be dirty, unable to bathe as I dragged my battered loom around on the streets of La Ciudad. That was how Ana found me—left behind after the revolt. Alone without family, without friends. She took one look at me, an eight-year-old child with smudged cheeks, half starved, but who resembled her charge, Catalina, the rightful heir to the Inkasisa throne. Ana brought me to the fortress, where my life as a copy of someone else began.

I sink into the tub, letting the icy water engulf me. I don't care to remember what followed—the goose bumps and chattering teeth, the water swirling, mixing with Sofía's blood—but it's not until I'm all the way in, hair dunked and everything, that I realize the extent of my problem.

The Llacsans didn't bother to bring soap. I got in for *nothing*. Climbing out, I look around for something to wrap myself up in, only they didn't bring me anything to dry off with either.

With my hair dripping icy rivers down my back, I grab the bed blanket and manage to dry off. I don't have anything to sleep in, so I settle for the Llacsan clothing and layer everything until I'm as round as a stuffed pastry.

Cool air breezes in, rustling the curtains. I shut the balcony doors, but the chill sneaks in. Because of the high altitude, nights are always cool, no matter how hot it gets during the day. Scowling, I climb into bed and pull the sheet up to my chin. My stomach rumbles. The last thing I ate was a bland bowl of quinoa eight hours earlier. I burrow deeper in the bed, away from a world where I don't belong.

Sofía's face drifts into my mind—her last gasp of life, the hot blood spurting from her chest. I can't keep the sob from escaping, so I give in, releasing my tears and smothering the sound with the pillow.

My first night in enemy territory.

CAPÍTULO

Siete

The glow of a torch lurches me awake. I sit up, reaching for the dagger I always keep under my pillow—but come up empty. Where is my blade? I blink in the flickering dark, scrambling away from the heat of the fire. I don't recognize the room I'm in. Gone are Catalina's piles of books and clothes. None of my tapestries adorn the stone walls.

And I remember.

I turn toward the source of the light and meet the figure of a tall boy barely illuminated by the fire. Atoc's smelly cousin. I groan.

"Are you wearing—" Rumi squints at me, moving the torch closer to me. "Are you deranged? You're not supposed to wear everything at once."

"I'm cold," I snap, wiping the sleep from my eyes. "What time is it?"

"Time for you to head downstairs," Rumi says. "Congratulations. You get to be in a parade."

I sit up, fumbling beneath my layers of garments. "What do you mean, a parade?"

67

Rumi strides to the balcony and throws the doors open. Dawning sunlight floods the room. The sounds of whinnying horses and lively chatter filter inside as I squint at him.

"Atoc decided to announce the engagement with fanfare. Most of the castillo has been awake all night preparing a lavish procession to herald the news throughout La Ciudad. Your dress is arriving any minute." He pauses, a slight smirk framing his mouth. "It's very colorful. Lots of ruffles."

I pinch the bridge of my nose and focus on breathing. His smile is unsettling because I know it means something else. An insult. Judgment.

"Get out of bed."

"Un minuto."

"You don't have a minute," he says coldly. "We need to go. Ahora."

My hands itch for something to throw at his head. Instead I curl them as I look for my boots. Everything from the day before comes back to me in a rush: the ride to the castillo, Sofía, meeting Atoc, that frigid bath.

I start taking off the extra clothes but pause when I register his eyes widening. I turn away, surprised at the warmth spreading to my cheeks. I've never had a boy in my room before. Catalina had her flirtations among the aristócratas, but nothing ever came from those coy exchanges. I'd had no flirtations, coy or otherwise. It seemed cruel, considering my job. Why reach for a future that couldn't be counted on? Why give in to a longing that'll only cause pain? No one would really be flirting with *me*, but the condesa they thought I was. I am a decoy first. I trained, pretended to be Catalina, and tried to make Ana proud. That has been and will be my life until I can finally take my mask off and be me—Ximena.

"How could you possibly have fallen asleep in all that?" Rumi mutters. He's leaning against the wall, holding on to the flickering torch. Whatever shadows remain in the brightening room dance across his face. His clothing is a watered-down version of Atoc's from the day before, a well-made tunic of quality cotton, dark pants, and leather sandals. The faint smell of wet dirt and burnt ragweed attacks my senses. Does he ever *wash* his clothes?

Rumi lifts the corner of his mouth, as if my discomfort amuses him. I ignore him, and quickly step out of a skirt and pull the extra two tunics off.

The same girl who took the rest of my clothes the night before enters—without knocking—and holds up a dress that's yards long and outfitted in every color of the rainbow. It's clear the previous owner was taller than me since pollera skirts are supposed to stop at the ankles. Delicate white lace lines the hem, and I spot several ruffles decorating the short sleeves. All in all, the entire ensemble reminds me of the jam-filled pastries my mother used to buy in La Ciudad when I was a child. Puffed up and frilly. Catalina would have loved it.

"Do you need help dressing?" the girl asks stiffly.

"No," I say as Rumi says, "Yes."

I glare at him. He merely smiles again and leaves, calling over his shoulder, "Juan Carlos will take you outside. You have ten minutes."

That bastard. He *wanted* to wake me, wanted to see my expression while he gave me the news about the parade. I'm still fuming as the girl helps me dress, tucking me inside the gown, tying bows, and laying all the ruffles where they ought to be. She pinches my cheeks, adds rouge to my lips, and braids my hair. She hands me leather sandals, and I'm surprised to see they're a perfect fit. Her doing, most likely, given her satisfied smile.

Apparently pleased with my appearance, she leaves and Juan Carlos steps inside. "Ready, Condesa?"

"In a minute." I start to make the bed. Some habits are hard to break. Coming back to a clean room always makes me calmer. In control and organized.

The guard stands off to the side, leaning against the wall. He watches me silently fold the sheets, tucking each corner until they sit crisp and flat. I pull the blanket off the floor, finally dry, and smooth it over the bed. The top still needs to be folded down.

"I didn't expect you to handle chores meant for maids," Juan Carlos says.

"I think it's best if you keep your expectations to yourself from now on."

"Whatever you want."

The next minute we're out the door, the guard at my side. I can feel his gaze on me. He keeps pace, and despite Rumi's command to hurry, this guard doesn't rush me. I peek up at him. He's still watching me. I'm amazed how he's deftly avoiding trampling on a wandering chicken.

"Stop staring at me," I say through gritted teeth.

He sounds amused. "Sleep well?"

"Fine."

"Bed comfortable enough for you?"

He almost sounds like he's teasing me. "So, you're a friendly guard."

"Yes," he says dramatically. "One of those."

"Ugh."

That makes him laugh. His smiles come easy and free, unlike Rumi's. Juan Carlos shoots me a wink, coaxing me to engage with him. To grin or laugh. I force my expression to retain a careful blankness that reveals nothing, especially to a guard who might use whatever he can find against me. After all, I am a decoy.

Atoc leads a procession on horseback into the city. He's dressed and adorned in an elaborate robe with detailed stitching of various flowers found in the wild, and a headdress that wraps around his gold crown; on his wrists are gold bracelets. No Estrella. Horn blowers alert La Ciudad of his approach.

I follow yards behind his retinue, Juan Carlos next to me. Craning my neck, I try to spot Illustrian spies in the growing crowd outside the city gates.

"See anyone you know?" he asks.

"If I did, you'd be the last person I'd tell."

Neither my tone nor my words seem to bother him. He's all smiles, waving at the people as if he were the main event of this spectacle of a parade. And the people eat him up as if he were dipped in dulce de leche. After a few minutes of playing the crowd, he shifts in his saddle and tries to engage me in conversation. Again.

"So, tell me about yourself."

My lips thin. His affability is clearly a tactic to get me to trust him—which will never happen.

"Why?"

"Just making conversation," he says. "Next to Rumi, I'm the main person you'll be spending time with leading up to Carnaval."

"Lucky me."

He merely laughs and resumes waving at the crowd. "You should try smiling; it's fun."

Commotion bursts from a group of people ahead that keeps me from responding. How can he suggest I smile? I'm a *prisoner*. The commotion grows louder and Juan Carlos beckons to the guard riding behind him. "Possible threat. Watch the condesa."

He rides straight for the growing mob. I can't tell if it's a fight brewing or if the people are making such a racket because Atoc is within a few feet of them. I lose sight of Juan Carlos in seconds, and the replacement guard urges me along until we've passed the noisy group.

Juan Carlos doesn't return and the procession snakes into La Ciudad using the many winding streets that bleed into the heart of the city. A crowd of Llacsans waits for us in the Plaza del Sol. There are vendors selling sugared choclo and roasted nuts glazed in cinnamon and cayenne spices. A few are squeezing fresh jugo de mandarina into clay cups, passing them around for tres notas each.

The constant hum of chatter, the sound of animals and people and the wheels of their carts sloshing through puddles, remind me of life before the revolt. Merchants calling out prices for their wares, trying to coax someone into buying something they don't need, the tolling of the temple bells, the grunts coming from masons building towers and tall buildings that reach the heavens, set against the hazy lavender mountain.

I love the song of the city. After moving to the Illustrian fortress, I found that the sudden silence filled me with regret. It took me years to get used to it, but it still always unnerved me.

I peer at the crowds, reveling in the bustle and noise. All the buildings are decorated with streamers and potted flowers, and in the middle of the plaza stands a platform where a group of prisoners wait for their fates. My gaze narrows at the trio.

Ana stands bound and gagged on that platform.

I gasp and pull on the reins. Acid rises in my gut, sour and faintly tasting like tomatoes. "What is this?"

The guard yanks the reins from my hands. "Move."

I keep blinking, hoping what I'm seeing isn't real. But there's no mistaking Ana—head held high, graying hair fluttering in the morning breeze. On either side of her are bound Illustrians, lined up and waiting to be executed.

"Ana!" I scream. "Atoc! You *promised*. You said—"

Atoc whirls around in his seat, his brows slamming together into a sharp line. The guard riding next to me hauls me off the horse and drags me across his lap, his dirty hand slapping against my mouth to keep me quiet. I rage against his hold as his horse continues forward, pushing through the crowd.

I turn my head and catch sight of Sajra, his feet spread out, his fingertips lightly touching, giving an air of profound patience as the procession curls around the platform. The guard's hand presses harder against my mouth, but I bite a stubby finger and he yelps as I slide off his lap, falling to my knees on the hard rock. I barely feel the impact.

I duck around the horse and then scramble forward, dragging

my ridiculous dress across the dirty cobblestones and pushing onlookers out of my way to get to Ana.

Her shoulders stiffen and her gaze widens as she jerks her chin upward in warning. She's seen me. Rough hands grip my shoulders and waist, reeling me back until I'm surrounded by a tight circle of Atoc's men. I push and shove, but I might as well be fighting statues.

The chamberlain steps forward to announce the king, and everyone drops to their knees. I break off my attack, panting. Through the gaps of the guards' shoulders, several people gawk at my display. I don't give a damn. Atoc gave his word. He promised, he—

Luna. My eyes shut. He'd said the prisoners would leave the castillo. That's *all* he said.

I let out a hoarse laugh. He tricked me.

The usurper steps in front of the platform, blocking my view of Ana. "You may rise, Llacsans."

I scan the crowd with a mixture of hope and dread—half wanting to see a friendly face, and half hoping I don't. Guards weave through the crowd, spears at the ready. If anyone attempts a rescue, it'll be a massacre. There are too many of them. Atoc drones on and on, and the words scrape against my skin. He says something about flattening the last of the rebels, triumphing over his oppressors. Tears prick my eyes, a salty sting I don't want anyone to see.

The high priest Sajra walks onto the platform. The crowd hushes. I didn't realize Atoc had finished his ramblings, and now it's time. I'm not ready. Sajra yanks off Ana's gag.

"Ana, you are to be an example for all the Illustrians in

Inkasisa," Sajra says. "Let the condesa see what happens to her people should she not obey His Majesty, the faithful servant of our earth goddess and sun god, King Atoc!"

Ana looks in my direction. I can barely meet her gaze because of the guards blocking my view. This is the woman who brought me to the Illustrian keep. Who taught me how to defend myself. Who made sure I had enough water to drink and food to eat. This is Sofía's mother, who I vowed to save. Without her magic, we're near defenseless. The bridge will become visible and then only stone walls will be left to protect my people against Atoc's army.

I shove against the backs of the guards, but they don't move an inch.

"Condesa!" Ana calls.

I stop pushing. My hands are shaking, and I'm afraid to meet her gaze. I've *failed* her. Somehow we lock eyes. Her expression is soft and brave, resigned to her fate. It's in her furtive stare that I understand what she's trying to tell me. A last message—for her kids, Sofía and Manuel.

For *me*.

La Ciudad is ours. Inkasisa belongs to us. Never forget it. Fight for every stone, for every handful of soil. Do not show weakness, or you will lose it all.

Her words are as clear as if she had whispered them into my ear. These are the mandates I've grown up hearing. The truths that have guided my actions and governed my thoughts. We are the rulers of this great city, and every winding path in it, every building and home, every iron gate that stands at the barrier belongs to us. Illustrians.

Not to this fake king.

Rage blazes beneath my skin, lighting my body as if I were a torch. "Atoc!" I bellow. "You *liar!* Bastard, heaping pile of—"

Someone shouts in the crowd. For a moment I think it's the Illustrians launching a rescue. A whirring noise slashes the air, and something hurtles toward one of the guards standing next to an Illustrian prisoner. My breath catches as the guard is lifted off his feet and catapulted into the crowd.

There's a sudden silence. Another voice cries out, pointing upward toward the parapets lining the plaza. A lone figure dressed entirely in black stands along the edge, holding his telltale slingshot.

El Lobo. The vigilante of Inkasisa.

He lifts an arm in mocking salute to Atoc, who lets out a guttural roar. Mayhem descends in full force: people shouting, feet stomping in frantic escape, overturned carts filling the streets with dried beans and corn and smashed fruit. The ground trembles, cutting through the commotion. Everyone freezes.

Pacha magic. Atoc's earthquakes. I bend my knees to keep balance, but the sudden shaking forces me to the ground. I'm not alone—the tremor drives all the Llacsans to their knees. I catch sight of El Lobo holding on to a balcony rail as the building sways left to right and back again. The vigilante jumps, reaching an Inkasisa flag. His body spins in a wide arc, and then he lets go, landing onto the crowd and disappearing fully.

This is my moment. I lurch forward, the ground pulsating under my feet. People scramble out of the way, running in the opposite direction of Atoc. He's climbed onto the platform, seemingly oblivious and unafraid of the waking earth. His arms surge upward and another quake cracks the walls and splits stone. I push closer, trying to reach Ana. Someone trips over my dress, and I curse as we both slam onto the cobblestone. I heave the person off me, desperate to get to my feet.

El Lobo rushes onto the other end of the platform. A silver glint catches sunlight as the vigilante uses a sword to slice at the ropes binding the Illustrian prisoners. The first captive is free, scrambling off the platform, the second follows suit, jumping into the crowd, fastened hands and all, but Ana has fallen onto her side, bound at the wrists. Atoc stands above her, arms still outstretched.

"Lobo!" I scream. "Help her, please!"

The roar of the crowd drowns out my voice. Several guards surround him, and El Lobo is fighting them off with his thin blade. Atoc conjures another massive quake. This one splits open a wide crack near the platform, revealing the deep belly of the earth. Ana tries to crawl away, but Atoc laughs at her attempt and pulls her back by grabbing her hair.

Her eyes widen in terror.

Another earthquake fractures the plaza. The stones slap my knees and my teeth chatter. Before I can push onto my feet, Atoc shoves Ana toward the yawning hole in the cobblestone. Rolling out of control, her feet jerking wildly, she can't grasp anything because her wrists are bound.

Seconds later Ana vanishes into the earth, screaming the whole way down.

"*No!*" Tears stream down my face as the ground continues to shake. My fingers can't find purchase to push myself up. I'm not getting enough air. It hurts to breathe.

Ana is gone.

The earth swallowed her whole.

Somewhere in the madness, I've lost sight of El Lobo. He must have broken free of the guards because he's nowhere to be seen.

Atoc quiets the earth, and he's the only one left standing. Everyone is a mess of dusted cheeks and hair, skinned flesh and bloody gashes. The plaza is a war zone, buildings nearly toppling over, overturned food and flower carts spilling onto the street.

The memory rolls into my mind swiftly, the scent of smoke and metal strong in my nose. Bellowing cries pierced the black night. Not a single star hung in the sky. Dust and dirt and blood stung my eyes. I sat on the ruins of our house. And somewhere beneath me, my parents lie buried beneath cracked stone.

Atoc's men rise to their feet, and I shove the recollection from my mind. Horses are found, carts are righted. People slowly come back to life as the shock wears off.

Atoc stalks toward me. He stops when he reaches the tattered hem of my dress. His toes brush the fabric. I tip my head back, not bothering to hide the tears streaking my face. He stares at me, eyes bloodshot and furious.

"Get her out of my sight."

One of the guards ties my hands with a thick hemp rope. I barely notice. My vision blinks to black, and I taste salt on my tongue. The procession forms its long line—Atoc at the front— and we all travel back to the castillo in single file, battered and filthy. I bring up the rear, the rope yanking me along while I try to keep up on foot. The hemp bites into my skin, rubbing my wrists raw.

The last thing I want to do is cry, but the tears keep coming.

My grief pecks at me like a starving vulture, tearing deep into my flesh until I feel Ana's death in every part of my body.

We arrive at the castillo, but instead of the pink room, the guards drag me below to the dungeon. "You're to stay down here until the king changes his mind," one guard says.

He unwinds the rope from my wrists, rough and quick. I force myself not to wince. Another guard pushes me into the small barred cell. Guttering torches give enough light for me to see my bloody wrists, burning as if on fire.

"Can I have water?" I ask, my voice hoarse from crying.

"There's none," one of them says in a curt tone.

No water. Of course. Last night I'd received a tubful. Today not even a drop. "What's going to happen to me?"

One guard shrugs. "All I know is that you're to stay here."

My punishment for speaking out against the king. Their footsteps echo in the dim dark of my prison. The door clangs shut, ricocheting off the stone and ringing in my ears. But not loud enough to block out the memories of Ana's terrified screams as she vanished into the earth.

My second day in enemy territory.

ocho

There isn't much to do in a cold, dark place except count the stones that line the floor and walls—nine hundred and eight— and do exercises to keep warm. I stretch and walk around in circles, jump and practice my high kick.

Without a single window, I lose track of time. I think it might be morning, given the way my stomach rumbles with hunger. Maybe all that jumping was a bad idea. But if I don't keep moving, if I don't stay busy, then I'll only think about Ana and Sofía.

And my burning wrists.

I'm sick of my heart hurting. The pain goes deep, deeper than the fissures Atoc opened in the earth. It's been forged by long years of living without my parents, of nearly starving as I tried to survive in a city blown up after the revolt. The ache grew when Ana and Sofía died. I'm bleeding, and I don't know how to stop it.

I need Catalina. Not the condesa. Mi amiga. My friend.

My only visitor comes during the night to add more oil to the torches—one guard, who ignores my request for a blanket.

This is very bad. I can't do *anything* from down here. All I've managed to do so far is cause my friends' deaths. Reason tells me it's not my fault. I didn't shoot the arrows, and I didn't create a giant hole in the middle of the earth for Ana to fall into.

But my heart—my traitorous heart—whispers that none of my friends would have been in danger if it hadn't been for me. I shouldn't have executed that messenger. I ought to have expected an attack once we reached the castillo. I ought to have found a way to secure Ana's release. Or stopped her from leaving on that mission in the first place.

I could have pushed harder. Planned better. Done more.

But I'd been arrogant.

Catalina was right. The weight of the condesa's responsibility is tremendous.

My knees give out, and I slump to the stone floor.

There has to be *something* I can do. Maybe I can connect with the other Illustrian prisoners? But a quick glance around the dungeon proves to be a vain endeavor. I don't see or hear any other victims. My cell seems to be in an empty wing.

Think, Ximena. Use your head.

With Ana gone—I flinch at the thought—her magic surrounding the bridge has vanished. Finding the Estrella isn't just about safeguarding Catalina's reign; it's about ensuring the Illustrians' survival. Once Atoc realizes he can cross that bridge . . . I shudder. The fortress can withstand an attack, but with food scarce there's no way our people will outlast a prolonged assault.

I gently bang the back of my head against the cool stone. *Thud, thud, thud.*

Overthrowing Atoc is my priority. Finding the Estrella guarantees victory. But even so, I have to send a message to Catalina to let her know how much time she has to prepare for the attack.

And for that I need a loom.

The lock creaks and slides back, wrenching me from my thoughts. Heavy footsteps thudding in the dark make me lurch to my feet. A shape materializes. It's Rumi—his shoulders hunched, carrying a blanket tucked under his arm, a basket in one hand. I sniff. The basket definitely has food. Some kind of cheese and bread. It takes everything in me not to rush to the bars and snatch both out of his hands.

He stops in front of the door to my cell. "Congratulations, you've earned an extended stay down here. If that's what you were hoping to achieve with your antics yesterday, it worked."

I clench my fists. Intolerable idiot.

"If you've come to gloat," I say, "I'd rather not hear it."

He reaches for the key hanging on a rusty nail in the wall. "I'm here to do a job, Condesa. Observing your rash stupidity is just a perk, and my prerogative."

I don't expect sympathy from him. But his tone, sour like week-old milk, sends a sharp flare of annoyance coursing through my body. I welcome it. I prefer to have a target for my emotions instead of holding on to my grief.

"I don't think it's stupid or rash to stand up for a friend," I say. "But I guess that's where we differ." As a quip, it's not one of my best, but I'm reasonably proud of my tone—I sound stronger than I feel.

Rumi turns the key, opens the door, and forcefully throws

the blanket at my face. The basket with food he drops by the door. "Oh, I'm in complete agreement with you. We're certainly different."

"Fundamentally."

He runs a cold, assessing eye over my person, seemingly dismissing me, until his attention focuses on my wrists. I tuck them behind my back, wrapping them around my ruined dress.

"Let me see."

"Go away," I snarl.

He takes a step closer. "Show me where it hurts."

"Ándate a la mierda." Showing him my wounds feels wrong. They're raw, and they badly sting. I don't want him near me, let alone examining my injuries.

"Fine," he snaps when it becomes clear I won't give in. The door to my cell clangs shut behind him, ringing in my ears. "Someone will be down with a chamber pot."

My stomach twists at the thought of relieving myself in the room where I ate my dinner, but hunger wins, and I eat the marraqueta loaf, queso blanco, and plátanos in one sitting.

The chamber pot is delivered. The guards set up cacho, a Llacsan dice game, where they play by torchlight. Their hollering and laughing keeps me up for hours, so I sit in the corner of my cell, glaring in their general direction for most of the night.

Rumi returns sometime later. A full day may have passed. By now I've taken several hundred restless turns in the cell. I want to scream in frustration. I have to get out of here. Illustrians are depending on me; *Catalina* is depending on me. I still don't have any idea of how I can get a loom.

Then there's the not so small matter of my raw wrists.

They're getting worse—bubbling and oozing. Without proper care, infection will set in. The infection will lead to a fever, and I'll be useless if I get sick.

Nothing can jeopardize my mission. *Nothing*.

The loud clang of the lock sliding open makes me turn toward the dungeon's door. Rumi approaches, carrying another basket. I'd been fed earlier by one of the guards, and the blanket hasn't been taken away. What is he doing down here?

He takes the keys to the cell off the rusty nail and uses them to come inside my prison. "Let's get this over with, Condesa." He gives me a resigned look.

My fingers twitch as if reaching for my blades, but I have only my hurting hands to defend myself with. "Get ready for what?"

He pulls a carefully wrapped package slowly from the basket.

I frown. "What's that for?"

Rumi opens the folds, revealing pressed herbs. He means to treat my rope burns.

I back away. "You're not coming near my wrists." He'll be rough, and heaven knows what else he has in that basket. He might make things worse, then I'll be ruined. I need to be alert, to somehow find a loom so I can write my messages for Catalina. If he drugs me, or puts the wrong medication on my wounds, I'll have to recover and I don't have time for that. "I want to see a healer."

He lifts a dark brow. "I am a healer, you fool."

I purse my lips. "You?"

Somehow that doesn't fit. To heal people, you have to understand them. You have to take the time to listen and actually hear what bothers them. Rumi doesn't strike me as a good listener. It does, however, explain why his clothes reek of burnt leaves.

"Yes," he says. "Me. It's my Pacha magic. I don't have all day, and I will literally sit on you to get this done, Condesa. Don't fight me on this."

If he thinks I'm going to willingly submit to his treatment, he's in for a surprise, healer or no. I'm not going to risk my hands for nothing. I need to weave my messages.

He takes a step forward.

I take a step back. Glancing over my shoulder, I calculate how many moves I have left. About three more steps until my back reaches the cold stone. An idea streaks through my mind, bright like a shooting star. I hold on to it as if my life depends on it. And in a way, it does. "What's in it for me?"

Rumi blinks. "What?"

"You heard me."

"What's in it for you?" he repeats. "How about not having to deal with an infection? Not succumbing to fever? Avoiding death?"

I shake my head. "That benefits *you*. I'm your charge, right? What would it look like if you couldn't keep one girl alive? Will the king still trust you if his soon-to-be wife falls ill?"

A scowl rips through his face, sudden and fierce. "The mark of a true Illustrian. Always wanting more than their due. Well? What is it?"

"I want your promise that you'll bring me what I ask for."

"My promise?" he says, raising his voice to a near shout. "As if you have any room to negotiate—"

"I'll fight you if you take one step closer," I snap. "Hear this, Llacsan: I can make your life easier or much, much worse. Give me what I ask for, and I'll let my wrists be treated. That's what I'm proposing."

"What do you want?" His voice comes out in a growl.

"The promise first."

He rolls his eyes until the whites show. "I promise to bring what you ask for—*within reason*. I can't guarantee your release. At present, the king won't let anyone breathe your name."

I smile—a triumphant smile that spreads from ear to ear. "I want a loom."

Rumi takes a step back, stunned, his dark eyes widening. There's a long beat of silence.

"Well?"

"Why," he asks carefully, "do you want a loom?"

"I like to weave."

Rumi frowns. "That's not an Illustrian hobby."

I shrug. So I shouldn't like to weave because of who I am? That's ridiculous. I like creating with my hands. There's something rewarding about making art out of nothing. The tucking and untucking, the folding over and under. Repeating until a bright new thing winks back at me. I make tapestries with my own two hands. There isn't anything better than creating something beautiful, especially if it hides a message that can save my people. Who gives a damn if I'm an Illustrian or not? The loom can't tell the difference.

"You really like to weave?" he asks in a skeptical tone.

I shake my head. "No, I really *love* to weave."

A peculiar expression crosses his face, incredulousness mixed with surprise. I know what he thinks of me—or rather, the condesa, Catalina—spoiled, vain, and useless with a streak of cruelty. That's what all Llacsans say. It's how they define us. Illustrians are cruel. Monsters and oppressors. Harbingers of disease and misfortune.

We invaded their lands, sure, but they'd invaded the original natives of Inkasisa—the Illari. Driven them away until they disappeared into the Yanu Jungle, left to fight poisonous insects and snakes and the untamed wild. We aren't all that different from the Llacsans.

We'd just won.

Rumi studies me, his head tilted slightly to the side. Another beat of silence follows, my heart thundering in my chest. I need him to get me that loom. If he doesn't . . .

"I'll see if I can find one in the castillo," he says at last. "If not, I'll have to send for one."

My relief nearly sends me to my knees. *It worked.*

He holds out his hand. "Your wrists."

I hesitate. I have a profound respect for healers. They fix people. It's something to admire, the ability to make someone better and whole. I don't want to confuse Rumi for one of them. He's my enemy and always will be.

"I can do it myself," I say stiffly. "Just tell me what to do."

Rumi lets out an exasperated sigh. He drops the basket by my feet, snatches my hand, turns my knuckles downward, and drops the herbs into my palm. I let out a small yelp, but he ignores it. He steps away and leans against the bars.

"I brought several remedies," he says in a curt tone. "Use the vinegar to disinfect the wounds first."

"Vinegar?" My wounds already blister; adding something that acidic will feel as if I've stuck my hands in a fire.

"It'll heal faster," he says, a hint of challenge in his eyes.

That pushes me. I sit down, my legs folded over each other, and pull the basket closer. Holding up a glass vial with what looks like white vinegar, I wait for Rumi's go-ahead. He nods, and I find a cloth inside the basket then soak a corner of it.

I take a deep breath and press the rag against my burns. The intense sting makes me bite my lip. A cold, sharp ache follows a loud rushing noise in my ears that threatens to overwhelm my senses. I take away the cloth, eyes watering. I suddenly realize Rumi is sitting in front of me.

"I'll get this done in a moment," he says briskly.

I faintly nod, my wrist screaming. He pours more vinegar onto the cloth and cleans my wrist. He takes out a bandage and then presses the herbs—dried lavender—and wraps everything together, finishing with a tight knot. Rumi quickly cleans my other hand, and I try not to make a sound.

Once finished, he gathers his supplies and stands. I remain on the ground. My head swims, and I'm weirdly light-headed.

"We need to do that once a day," he says in that same brisk tone. "Don't sleep on your hands."

"I want the loom."

A muscle in his jaw jumps. "I said I'll get it, and I will."

He leaves without a backward glance. I crawl to the stone wall and lean against it, appreciating its harsh coldness. My wrists feel like they're on fire. I tip my head back, and my gaze snags on a word etched into the stone, just above eye level. I reach for it, sink my finger into the crevices, the edges sharp. *Courage*, it says, written in Castellano. Whoever carved this message must have been an Illustrian. I close my eyes, my finger tracing the word as if it's a lifeline, as if it connects me to the person who carved it.

My heart whispers a name, and I believe it.

Ana.

Rumi visits again. Instead of the loom, he brings that infernal medicine basket and a book.

A book.

I frown. What is this? Reading in the dim light will give me a headache. "That's not a loom."

He holds out the book in between the bars. "Take it."

I eye it warily. Studying is more Catalina's thing. At the keep, it's a normal occurrence to see her surrounded by piles of books in the library. Everyone is given access to these written tales, all the ones that survived the revolt. But it's Catalina who painstakingly keeps track of each page and tome. "I'm actually not much of a reader."

He stares at me, his hand still outstretched. And waits. I sigh, snatch the book, and glance at the title. *Historia de las Llacsans.*

History of the Llacsans. Wonderful.

"Why would I read this?"

"Consider it an education," he says testily. "You've got plenty of time for reading. And you need a bandage change."

Resigned, I let him pour vinegar onto my wrists again and

change the old bandages. It hurts a little less than the day before. I study him while he works. What if he breaks his promise? Maybe he has no intention of finding a loom. My attempts to ask him are met with curt dismissals. Unease sweeps over me. His cold indifference does nothing to soothe my nerves.

Rumi goes back up to his king, and I leave the book on the floor. I don't need to read about their history. I only care about tomorrow.

I stay in the dungeon. The guards play their dice game. Someone changes the oil in the torches. I sleep on the stone when I can get comfortable, but mostly I stare at the ceiling or stretch my sore legs. On the rare occasion the guards are gone, I practice my fighting stances.

Rumi notices the book by the door on his next visit. Other than his lips pressing into a flat line, he barely registers my presence. Even so, it breaks up the monotony. He makes sure I have food and water, changes my bandages, and leaves.

He doesn't bring the loom.

It's hard for me to admit when I've made a mistake. I thought I'd been clever in getting him to agree to the deal. But I wasn't clever—I was foolish. And naïve. I trusted a Llacsan to keep his word. Catalina isn't here to see me fail, but if I don't send a message soon, she'll know I failed anyway.

A group of guards descend on my cell. Weak from lack of sleep, I don't resist when a female guard, one of the few I've seen, lifts me by my armpits. I stumble and another helps her carry me from the dungeon. Moonlight cutting through the windows hurts my eyes, but I welcome the pain. The goddess revives me as if I'm drinking water after having none for days and days.

My head clears. My vision focuses. Small changes, but I feel them in my soul.

And when Atoc's guards deposit me onto the bed inside the pigskin-colored room, the first thing I see standing in the middle is a loom.

CAPÍTULO

nueve

It still hurts that I had to part with my own loom—a gift from my Llacsan nanny. Whatever I feel about the rest of *them*, I won't and can't tolerate a single thing against *her*. She helped raise me. It was her dedication to my early upbringing that turned me into the weaver I am today. She'd patiently sit with me for hours while I practiced making diamond and cloud patterns and learned how to create shapes and letters by weaving strands over and under the warp thread.

It's been a long time since I've thought of her.

The guards shut the door behind me and I step closer to the loom. This one, sturdy and handsome with contrasting light and dark wood, takes up most of the space in the center of the room. A small stool sits in front of it. Next to it are rolled-up balls of wool, varying in shades of yellows, purples, reds, and deep blues the color of blueberries. The loom is bigger than mine by probably half a foot, but that doesn't matter. It'll work.

Moonlight peeps through the curtains, giving my legs the energy to stand. Skirting around the loom, I fling open the balcony doors. Silver light pours in, transforming my room from something dark and claustrophobic into a livable space bathed in Luna's rays.

Food is sitting in a big bowl on the dresser—herbed quinoa, crispy papas flavored with black mint and smoked salt, and grilled choclo, a long ear of it. But even that doesn't tempt me from sinking onto the stool and thinking of a new design to weave.

My heart beats fast, and I grab some white wool. I loop the warp thread around the top and bottom wooden bars. As I work, my gaze snags on the basket filled with colors.

I should use Illustrian neutrals . . . but I've never had the chance to experiment. The basket is a riot, a parade, a *fiesta* of color, and I want to dive into it with both eyes open.

I bite my lip. Catalina will expect me to use my wool, I know that, but maybe it's wiser to hide the message in traditional Llacsan color combinations. Maybe Atoc and his priest will be less suspicious. Atoc might even appreciate the tapestry on its own merit. Or be happy that I can weave at all. Excelling in a Llacsan skill will only make him look better. A wife who can follow his traditions.

I reach for the wool in the basket and then thread a strand around my finger. A bright tomato red. I glance at the window and look for the moon. Will Luna be pleased? Will the moonlight still turn to thread in my fingers if I use dyed wool?

There's only one way to find out. I push aside my white wool, fighting off the stab of guilt, and weave the red thread, over and under, until I reach the other end. Next, I add a watermelon pink and an eggplant purple. Up, over, and down, up, over, and down, until the three colors cover the bottom third, making a thick stripe of each color.

Starting at the middle, I begin with a simple diamond pattern, weaving a red strand from the left to the right. I know countless techniques by heart, but this one is my favorite. It's the first one I learned.

"Under one, over three, under one, over two, under one, over two, and repeat," I say under my breath. Then I start from the other side and repeat the process.

As I work, the moonlight glints around me, growing brighter. My fingers blur as I move from left to right and back again. I finish with the red, start on the pink, and then I'm ready for my moon thread.

My breath catches in the back of my throat. No matter how many times I've used Luna's rays to make thread, each time the shimmer of magic courses through me, it surprises me. I can feel my wounds, internal and external, closing and healing. I am made whole. Not quite happy, but Luna's soft touch heals what she can.

With the moon thread wrapped around my index finger, I wind the strand around and around, forming a glittering silver ball. It lights up the whole room, and everything it touches shimmers and shines, awash in Luna's glow.

Now the real work begins. It takes all of my discipline, all of my energy, to weave my secret message into the tapestry. Hours pass. Moonlight winks and glitters and turns into dust as I work the thread. The dust flutters to my feet, sparkling brightly, like the stars peppering the dark night.

My shoulders and neck stiffen, my fingers cramp.

But at last, I finish.

The moon thread shimmers and touches ordinary strands of llama wool, blending the words into the diamond pattern. Only an Illustrian will be able to read them: WEDDING DURING CARNAVAL.

After some considering, I add a swarm of bees to the tapestry in a honey-hued string as a way to distract from the message. Or maybe because I want to use the bright yellow color. I weave in the moon thread to add a touch of sparkle to their wings then bend close to examine my work.

One of the wings twitches beneath my thumb.

Gasping, I bring the tapestry closer. The wing flutters again and stills. My fingers clutch the thread tighter.

¿Qué diablos? *Did I really just see the tapestry move?* I must be tired, or . . . I had really seen . . .

I lean closer. "Do it again," I whisper.

But the wing stays put.

I study the tapestry. Is Luna trying to tell me something? Weave more bees? Add something else to the message? Go to sleep, Ximena, it's nearly morning?

I stand, reaching high until my back cracks. I must have imagined it.

Quickly, I gather up the moondust. Cielos, if a guard—or worse, Rumi—finds it, what would they do? It's a relief to have some on hand again, but without a broom, I have to gather the dust with my hands. By the time I finish, my knees drag on the floor. I devour my cold dinner—still delicious, damn them—before I flop onto the bed, my eyes heavy with sleep. But a nagging thought prevents me from drifting.

How am I going to get the tapestry out of the castillo?

The Llacsan maid holds out a dress, trying to push the yards of fabric into my arms. I want to swat her advances away like she's a mosquito. But she prevails. I glare, staring at the ruffles and black lace tickling my chin.

Atoc demands that I attend court. And not just today, but *every court day in the foreseeable future*. I'm expected to dress in the finery of his choosing, my hair styled in the Llacsan fashion of two long braids down the back, and my lips painted a cayenne-pepper red.

Nothing I say or do changes the maid's mind. Sensing my dwindling protests, she begins braiding my hair. When she finishes, she points to my tapestry, draped over the chair.

I nod. "Yes, mine, I did it."

She seems surprised and maybe a little curious, given the way she stares at me, her head tilted and her eyes crinkling. She hands me a little pot of dyed wax for my lips. I let her finish my makeup and then at last, at long last, she gives me her idea of a look of approval.

By that I mean, she isn't scowling at me.

She finishes tying the black bow on my back. My dress is a dark yellow that reminds me of honey. The same color as the bees woven into my tapestry. I can't believe I thought they actually moved. How long has it been since I had a real Luna-blessed night's sleep?

The door opens—no one in the castillo seems to know how to knock—and the guard ushers Rumi in. The maid nods once in his direction and then leaves.

He stops short at the sight of me.

For a moment he appears stunned. Then his face resets to its usual haughty lines: His dark brows pull together with a sharp crease in between, and his lips press into a thin slash. "Who gave you that dress?" He sounds furious.

I haven't said a word and I've already done something wrong. It's not like I had a choice in what to wear. "I'm not changing," I say through my teeth.

"¿Qué?" he snaps, his hand on the doorknob. "Did I say you had to?"

"You didn't have to say it."

"That dress—" He breaks off, his mouth twisting.

"What about it?"

He shakes his head.

"¿Qué te pasa?" I ask, impatient.

"We're late. Forget I said anything. Can you walk and talk at the same time? King Atoc, ruler of the Great Lake, of El Altiplano and all the land in between—"

His voice hits a worshipping note that makes me snort.

"—wants you up front."

I grab a fistful of the dress—it's nearly a foot too long—and sweep past him. But as I do, he suddenly reaches out and takes hold of my upper arm.

"What," he asks, "is that?"

I follow his line of sight to my tapestry. It takes everything in me to keep my face perfectly neutral. To not react or stiffen or jerk away in surprise. The rest of me blazes. All of my senses are on high alert, crying out a warning.

"Did you meet her?" His eyes snap to mine.

I blink in confusion. "Who?"

Rumi leans forward, his eyes intent on me. "So you didn't?"

"I have no idea who you're talking about, Llacsan."

He releases me and walks toward the chair. I suck in a quiet breath and fight the impulse to cry out when he lifts the tapestry, poring over every detail. "You made this."

His tone suggests he doesn't think me capable of creating something this beautiful.

"Yes." I shift my feet, clasping and unclasping my hands.

What if he finds the message? It's impossible, I know that, but his intense study increases my apprehension. Luna *only* reveals herself to Illustrians. The message won't make sense to a Llacsan. He sees only the glimmer of light. A faint silver. A touch of magic. Only part of the picture.

"Aren't we late?"

He merely grunts and continues studying the work. "That's just something I say to get you out of my hands faster. You used several techniques in this, and they surprisingly work well together."

I'm not sure what to respond to first. The first insult or the second.

"I told you I was a weaver. It's why I asked for the loom."

"You'll forgive me if I don't automatically trust the word of an Illustrian," he says, finally looking away from the tapestry. His intense expression startles me. "I've never seen this color thread before. It's *glowing*. It definitely wasn't in the basket I sent up."

"No, it wasn't," I agree.

"Where did you get it?"

His scrutiny of the moon thread does nothing to settle my

anxiety. I don't want to share my magic with him. It's mine. It brings me joy and peace and *life*. It hides the truth in plain sight.

Rumi wears his usual scowl as he waits for my answer. Which I absolutely won't give.

Juan Carlos pokes his head inside the room. "Are you two coming or what? His Majesty hates when people arrive after him." When he sees what's in Rumi's hand, he walks in, his mouth slightly agape. "Who gave you this gift, Condesa?"

I blink, long and slow and annoyed. "No one. This is my work."

"Who knew you were so talented?" he says with a wink. "What do I have to sacrifice in order to get one?"

"I'm not wasting my wool on you."

He shrugs and leans forward to study the tapestry alongside the healer. A flutter of unease spreads through me. Now there are two Llacsans studying my secret message to Catalina.

It's taking all of my self-control to keep myself from ripping the tapestry out of their hands. I analyze both boys as they stand shoulder to shoulder, their heads bent toward the shimmering thread. Rumi and Juan Carlos share almost the same height, have the same long, curling hair and dark eyes. They could be brothers. One with an eternal smile, the other an intolerable grump. I like people who fall somewhere in the middle.

"Are you related?" I ask.

The question seems to amuse Rumi. They both remain silent, engrossed by the moon thread.

"This would make an excellent gift for King Atoc," Juan Carlos says, ignoring me.

My face blanches. That tapestry belongs to Catalina. It

absolutely can't be gifted to the usurper. "What? *No.* He hates me. He'd probably burn it or use it to wipe his—"

"What do you think?" Juan Carlos interrupts. "You've been so worried."

Rumi growls. "Stop talking."

"But you get what I'm suggesting?" He fingers the soft thread.

Rumi slowly nods. Then he picks up the tapestry and carries it out of the room, turning away from me as I try to reach for it. Anger sears me. What gives him the right to take my things? I used the majority of my wool on that message.

"Where are you taking my tapestry?" I ask. The healer ignores me. I stalk out of the room after him. "Who do you think you are?"

"You're his responsibility," Juan Carlos says, keeping in stride with me.

"So?"

"*Everything* you do reflects on Rumi." Juan Carlos shoots me a pointed look.

He's referring to my time in the dungeon.

"Not my problem." I stop walking. "I'm not taking another step until you give me back my tapestry, Llacsan."

Both of them pivot and reach for me, Juan Carlos on my left and Rumi on my right. They each grip an arm in a viselike hold that makes me flinch.

"Come along, Condesa," Rumi says.

Madre de Luna. He actually sounds bored.

"It's mine," I say, digging my heels in. I can't let them have it. I can't, I can't, I can't. "Give it back."

Juan Carlos locks the bedroom door. Working together, they drag me down the corridor, setting off for the great hall. I have no choice but to follow, stumbling over my long dress, cursing them both.

"My abuela would blush to hear you talk," Juan Carlos says mildly, rounding one of the corners.

I sidestep a squawking chicken, and their hold loosens enough for me to jump, my fingers just grazing the wool. Rumi spins around, somehow forcing me toward the wall. I pull up my hands in time to save myself from the crash. I barely notice the sting on my palms.

"Where are you taking my tapestry? I worked on it for hours—give it back!"

"You'll present it to the king," Juan Carlos says as we reach the stairs. "The giving of gifts is an important part of our culture. Understanding our traditions will help make you into a better partner for my king. The tapestry is a fine gift. It will put you back in his good graces."

"When have I ever been in his good graces?"

"You ask too many questions," Rumi says.

"It's because I have a mind."

He turns his head away but not before I catch the corner of his mouth tugging upward. "Don't you want to be in his good graces?"

Oh no, this has nothing to do with me and everything to do with *his* image. When Juan Carlos said Rumi was worried, this is what he meant. He's worried about his reputation in the castillo.

"More like put *you* back in his good graces," I snap. "You're a fool. Chasing after the king like a lovesick child, desperate for a scrap of attention. Everyone at court laughing at the spectacle you make."

Rumi scowls. "Do you have any idea—"

He stops, breathing hard through his nostrils. I wait, my hands on my hips.

"All eyes are on me," he says finally. "It's not a good thing. I'm not going to repeat myself. You'll take this tapestry, give it to the king after court, and all will be like it once was."

"Why isn't it a good thing?" I ask.

He gives me an exasperated look and strides on, still clutching my tapestry.

What was that about? For a moment something flashed in his eyes. It almost looked like . . . fear. But for what? His position in the castillo?

"I bet my time in prison didn't work wonders for your position in the castillo."

Juan Carlos shoots a quick look at Rumi. *That's it.* My jailor is in trouble with his king.

"You know nothing about what I do here, Condesa," he says tightly.

I open my mouth to let out a sharp retort but realize he's right. Other than being a relative of Atoc's and a healer, I have no idea who he is. What does he do all day? The question bubbles up, unbidden and unwanted. I squelch it, chalking it up to curiosity, and return to the important matter at hand.

Carnaval is a mere five weeks away. I've been in the castillo almost one week and Catalina knows nothing of my wedding date. That means one whole week lost for preparation. We thought we'd have more than enough time to find the Estrella, and that we'd have Ana to guide us. My stomach tightens into a knot. They'll know about Ana by now. How I've failed her and

Sofía. It's Catalina who has to take over. She's never had that kind of responsibility. I hope Catalina knows enough to fortify the newly visible bridge with soldiers. I hope she manages the provisions wisely.

We reach the tall double doors to the great hall. Rumi half turns in my direction, keeping the tapestry out of my reach. "Present the tapestry after court, Condesa," he says again. "Present it sincerely and privately. Remember what I said about flattery? It'll work wonders. Ready?"

"Of course not."

"Too bad," Juan Carlos says.

I make one last attempt to grab the weaving, but Rumi jerks away. The doors swing open, and I follow behind him, my attention on the silvery words that spell out my treason.

And my doom.

The false king stands on the dais, wrapped in an intricate woven cape and feathered headdress. As much as I hate to admit it, the piece certainly has flare. Catalina would love it if she could forget that it sits on the head of a Llacsan.

Color continues to dog my step wherever I venture. It's splashed on the walls, woven into their fabric, and painted on their faces. Back home, white and its cool crispness adorn every Illustrian. Even the children. And if I'm being honest—privately—it always made me sad to see them trying to keep their outfits pristine.

Rumi wears simple black trousers and a hat, a multicolored striped vest and leather sandals. He looks royal, matching the king's cool stare as we walk down the long aisle toward the throne.

Rumi drops to one knee. "May the High King of Inkasisa live—"

"Enough," Atoc snaps. "Move away, primo."

Rumi scrambles to join the rest of his family. Once again I frown at Princesa Tamaya's absence. She's old enough to be here. Unknowns are not what my people need right now. What is Atoc hiding with his sister? Something dangerous?

Atoc stares down at me as if I'm an araña to be stepped on. On his left stands the high priest, dressed in a long robe, his beady eyes watching my every move as I approach. I can't return his gaze, the cold fingers of his magic capturing my breath imprinted in my memory.

"Condesa," Atoc says coldly. His fingers curl tightly over the armrest of his gold throne.

"King Atoc."

He tilts his head at the empty gold seat to his right. "You're to keep silent."

I swallow a retort. I vowed to control myself, to play the part. Catalina and our people are relying on me. At least I called him king.

Rumi rushes to my side, awkward and bumbling amid laughter from the court, and places the tapestry into my hands. I expect Atoc to remark on the work, but he's already looking toward the doors. The healer walks to the side of the dais and gives me an expressive look that says something along the lines of, *Don't embarrass me.*

As if he doesn't do that enough to himself already. But I go and sit stiffly, the tapestry on my lap. Atoc frowns at the bundled fabric. I clutch at it protectively. He opens his mouth to say something—

"They're assembled outside, King Atoc," Sajra says, and everyone's attention turns to the tall double doors.

I breathe a sigh of relief.

"Allow the first petitioner inside," the false king says. His bronze arm rests near mine, and I scoot as far away as I can. He doesn't seem to notice. Instead he settles into his role—a solemn face, his posture cold and uninviting, a god in his gold seat. His throne is made of fuego and mentiras.

Unlike last time, there are only twenty people in attendance. Llacsans, dressed in their finery, sit on benches lining the aisle. Two guards open the doors, and a small group wearing the traditional garb of the Tierra Baja region—light tunic and trousers, and well-made cognac leather sandals—strides in.

Inkasisa has the Highlands—El Altiplano—and the Lowlands—Tierra Baja—a region of tropical land that forever stays humid and warm, even during the wet season. Atoc claims to rule the whole of Inkasisa, but there are several tribes in the Tierra Baja that have their own heads of state.

Of course, they all pay the king's tax. Everyone does, except the Illari living in the Yanu Jungle. Legend says that after the Llacsans drove them out of La Ciudad, they fled to the jungle and built a city made entirely of gold called Paititi. Only one person ever came back from trying to find it, hundreds of years ago, and when he stepped out from the tree line, he became blind and unable to return to the city. Manuel always dreamed of finding it.

A sharp stab lances my heart. *Has he found out about his mother? About Sofía?*

I shove the question aside and try to focus on the petitioners. Perhaps I'll learn something useful. They pay their respects, going on and on about the usurper's greatness and splendor. No wonder he has a puffed-up image of himself. I expect Atoc to demand a giant gold statue fashioned after his regrettable profile.

"What is your complaint, petitioner?" Atoc asks, buttered up enough that I could have stuffed him inside a furnace and baked him.

A Lowlander steps forward, his head appropriately angled downward, his hands holding a sombrero. His eyes flicker over to mine nervously. "Highest King of Inkasisa, my complaint is about the onslaught of Illustrians festering within La Ciudad."

I narrow my gaze and sit up straighter.

"Go on," Atoc says.

"They're causing a ruckus in the streets," the petitioner says. "Stealing food in El Mercado, sleeping under doorways. Some are even trying to reclaim their old—" He breaks off, clearing his throat. "Trying to steal *our* homes."

My eyes shut. Catalina. She must have run out of food after giving away too much, acting more like our people's friend and not the queen they need. Now Illustrians at the keep are taking matters into their own hands. Fed up, hungry, wanting leadership—they're rioting in the city, putting themselves in great danger.

What a mess. I can't blame the Illustrians who leave the keep to search for food. Hunger is a relentless taskmaster.

I remember the days of living under the doorways of La Ciudad after the city had fallen. My ability to hide in tunnels, dark alleys, and sprawling catwalks was my salvation, but Catalina never had the same education in survival. She was whisked away from the horror and kept safe and fed, adored child that she was. She never had to fight for a loaf of bread. Perhaps we'd done her a disservice by keeping her so sheltered? If we hadn't, she'd have at least learned how to be strong.

Because right now, her show of weakness could kill us.

"Certainly a problem," Atoc agrees, a cold smile bending his unforgiving mouth. I want to take his headdress and smack his face with it. "Tell me, what do you propose I do?"

I touch his arm with a single index finger. "Perhaps I can go—"

"Be silent," Atoc snaps. "Go on, petitioner."

"Round them up," the man says. "They're repeat offenders, greedy—"

"*What?*" I say.

"Done," Atoc says over me, gripping my wrist. "Capitán, see to it immediately."

His capitán is standing by the tall double doors. At Atoc's word, he nods and leaves, taking with him several of the guards lining the walls. My heart sinks. More Illustrians crowding the dungeons, their lives hanging over my head.

Why couldn't Catalina have made my job just a little bit easier? I slump in my seat. My feet tap against the stone floor, wanting to carry me out of this stifling room and into open air. The walls are closing in on me like strong currents, hitting me like a smothering wave. There's no escape. The role I play only compounds my anxiety. I don't want to look at the face of my enemy for another second, let alone several more weeks. I'm trapped behind this mask of my own choosing. Trapped by the walls I volunteered to live within.

One wrong move, one careless slip, and my life is forfeit.

I inhale deeply. Rising tides can't be held back, but they can be ridden. I have to ride this wave through. It's the only way I'll be free.

Court drags on as the king's plans for tomorrow's city outing are finalized. I'm not included, which will give me the perfect opportunity to explore the castle with fewer people present.

Then conversation moves swiftly to the new fields opening for the production of the koka leaf. My mood plummets lower than ever. Atoc expects everyone to take part in the planting and selling of the koka leaf, distorting and corrupting the plant until it becomes a drug. That's what he wants us to be known for. That's what he wants to base our entire economy on.

I sneak a glance at Rumi. His eyes are half lidded, as if profoundly bored. Gone is his intense scrutiny. It seems he can fall asleep where he stands. How annoying. Madre de Luna, doesn't he care?

Atoc doesn't want what's good and right for everyone, only his family and friends. He stole the lives and dreams of everyone else, consequences be damned. I'll make him pay for never looking back at the destruction he's left in his wake.

The next petitioner is called forward. This one is wealthy, judging from the amount of gold jewelry adorning his wrists and neck. "My king, last night while riding through La Ciudad, I was robbed by El Lobo. He took my bag of notas, the coat off my back—even my horse!"

Once I watched an oncoming thunderstorm roll toward the Illustrian keep. Blinding lightning streaked through menacing clouds. I remember the howling wind; I remember gripping the windowsill, bracing myself for the onslaught. The expression on Atoc's face reminds me of the storm. Terrible, dangerous, unforgiving.

"Say no more," Atoc says, and then he turns to face another guard. "What's being done?"

The guard rises from his seat on a long wooden bench and clears his throat.

"Well?" Atoc asks.

The man fidgets, shifting his weight from one foot to the other. "I regret to say that we have no new leads, Your Majesty. If we had more time—"

"¿Tiempo?" his king asks coldly. "You've had more than enough time to get me information. You're telling me we don't even have his name? Is he a Llacsan? An Illustrian?"

Atoc shoots me a glare.

"We don't claim the vigilante as our own," I say.

His forehead wrinkles. I don't think he believes me.

The guard shrugs helplessly. "He wears that black mask, it covers his entire face, my king, and we—"

"Last night he raided another one of our storehouses," Atoc says. "Four days before that he robbed *members of our court* on their way to Tierra Baja. He's making us all look like fools."

I clutch my sides to keep myself from laughing. The poor man who stands before his angry king turns purple.

"I expect better news by next court," Atoc says softly. "Get out of my sight."

The guard flinches before shutting the door behind him, and everyone starts speaking at once about the mysterious man dressed in black.

Sajra steps forward and quite abruptly descends upon the room like fire suffocated by a thick blanket. "Your Greatness?"

The Llacsan king nods toward the priest.

"Have you decided on who will be sacrificed during Carnaval? There is much to prepare."

"I have made my decision," Atoc proclaims, his voice booming. "Princesa Tamaya will be sacrificed to Inti during Carnaval. She is honored to have been chosen and welcomes the day when she'll be reunited with the sun god."

I gape at him. He means to kill his sister?

Low murmuring erupts, disbelief and cries of surprise. Once again Atoc demands attention by reaching out his arms, a silent gesture that everyone quickly obeys. "I believe I'm feeling charitable enough for one more petitioner. Send them in."

The next petitioner owns a stall in El Mercado. He has an argument with the stall owner next to his and wants Atoc to intervene in the dispute. Sajra answers for the king, and a solution is promised in seven days, during the next court meeting.

It's been a long time since I truly visited the market: ordered salteñas and walked past the long line of stalls, admiring the many kinds of woven wares—pouches and bags, blankets and capes. In another life, I might have set up my stall to sell alongside them.

The tapestry rustles in my lap as I shift in the seat. A salty taste crawls up my throat. I can't let Atoc have this tapestry. The message must reach Catalina. Perhaps the healer has forgotten all about it. Perhaps he—

"Now, what's that on your lap?" Atoc asks, squinting at my shimmering tapestry.

I deflate like a pastry left out in the sun. *Carajo*. I try to swallow, but my throat refuses to work. Everyone in the room focuses on me.

"Well?" He takes ahold of my arm. "Where did you get it?"

Sajra steps forward from somewhere behind me. He leans over my armrest in order to examine my work closely. His breath tickles my cheek and I shiver as he runs his finger along the silver thread.

Sweat beads at my hairline. Madre de Luna. Can the priest see the message with his blood magic? Is that even possible? I can't give the tapestry to Atoc, or my message will remain in the castillo *forever*. What happens if someone becomes suspicious?

I grip the tapestry with both hands. "I . . ."

The vendor turns to leave.

The word flies out of my mouth. "Espera."

The merchant looks back at me, a deep crease between his brows. "Are you speaking to me, Condesa?"

My heart thunders in my chest. Most of our spies get their information by hiding in the market. Catalina will have stationed spies at the castillo gates, too. We talked about it before I left. I can only hope she remembered.

Luna, please let this work.

"I have a gift for this man," I say loudly, my voice ringing in the hall. It's my best chance. Giving the message to the merchant ensures the tapestry will leave the castillo.

Atoc releases my arm in surprise. "What?"

I turn to the Llacsan vendor. "For your trouble at the market, I'd like to give you this work of art I wove myself. Please accept it as a gift. It would bring me much joy to see this tapestry decorating your stall. Perhaps I'll get to see it one day myself, on a visit."

I stand and hold my work for all the room to see. The merchant appears dazzled, mouth agape. He comes up on the dais, takes the tapestry, and says his thanks.

"I happen to enjoy weaving. Immensely, actually. What if I wove more tapestries? Perhaps you could sell them in your shop?"

The vendor blanches but covers his dismay quickly by looking to Atoc.

"The gift is plenty," Atoc snaps. "He doesn't need your help to fill up his stall."

But what about the other messages I have to send? "Are you sure?" I press. "I believe they'd fetch a good price. He might earn even more notas than he was planning."

"That's enough, Condesa," Atoc says, his tone cold. "I thought your gift was meant for me."

"It's essentially for you. It's a gift for your people."

The vendor turns and leaves, holding my tapestry as if it were a baby.

Relief floods my senses. I sit down, my knees shaking. Atoc turns to me, a speculative look in his eye. He doesn't say anything for a long moment. Then in a low, hard voice, he says, "What made you think to give a gift like that to a merchant?"

The priest leans in to hear my response.

"It's important that your people respect their future queen." I fight to keep my voice steady. "What better way than to send a gift for all Llacsans to admire?"

"And what about a gift for your king?" he asks. "I deserve one."

I swallow hard. "Becoming your wife isn't a grand enough gift?"

His eyes travel from my eyes to my mouth. "No."

Sajra snickers and sinks back to his place.

Bile rises quickly as I look away. "I'll be sure to weave you something special."

I feel his gaze, but I won't return it. When he shifts his attention back to court, I let out a slow breath. My heart continues to race. To keep from getting sick all over his gold throne, I focus on the positive: I managed to do my job. The first message has been sent. Our spies will spot the tapestry in the market and relay the message to Catalina.

As I settle back into the chair, I seek Rumi. Everyone else seems impressed by my weaving and generosity toward the Llacsan. Rumi's response sends a shiver down my spine.

His is a look of pure hatred.

CAPÍTULO

once

I freeze, unable to tear my gaze away from his stare. Usually, whenever I catch one of his expressions, it's by accident, and whatever I'd seen vanishes in the space of a blink, only to be replaced by a scowl. But this time, he keeps his cold attention on me. Not breaking his hold. I don't know how to respond, and a small part of me feels unsettled. Maybe a little surprised, too. Of course I know he hates me. Don't I hate him as well? An insistent voice reminds me that he'd brought me the loom when he didn't have to.

Dimly, I hear Atoc announce court is over, but all I can focus on is that nuisance of a healer. What difference does it make how that Llacsan looks at me? They're all going to look at me that way by the end.

Again, I quash the things I don't want or need to understand deep within me and hope none of them resurface. I have no room for such questions; I only have space in my life for the revolt.

My guards approach and I quickly step away from the throne. I crave fresh air, the chance to breathe in the eucalyptus trees surrounding the castillo. Madre de Luna, I want to be *alone*. I miss training. Miss swinging a sword.

"How do I get to the gardens?" I ask.

"We go with you," the guard says in a stern tone.

That wasn't my question. Annoyed, I open my mouth to repeat myself—

"I'll take her."

My face falls. I smell him before I see him. Slowly, I turn to face Rumi. His arms are folded, his lips turned down in a pronounced scowl.

Whatever it is I've done, it seems he wants to talk about it sooner rather than later. Not how I wanted to spend the last scrap of daylight.

"Fine," I snap. "But I just wanted a place to—"

"Don't care," he interrupts, and ushers me to a side door that opens up to a long hallway. Numerous clay pots clutter the stone floor. I have to skip and weave around giant stacks of them.

He pulls me along until we reach another set of double doors. Using his shoulder, he pushes one open. Outside, the smell of the eucalyptus trees kisses my cheeks. It's a pleasant scent that masks the odorous healer. Warm air gently sways through the trees' leaves. I squint, waiting for my eyes to adjust to the last fighting glare of the sun before it meets the horizon. Everything always seems sweeter in the minutes before darkness descends.

I inhale deeply. "Honey and mint."

Rumi glances down at me. Even slouching, he's really quite tall, unlike most Llacsans. I half worry I'll develop an ache from tilting my head back just so I can read his eyes. Surprise flickers in them.

"The trees," I explain.

He scowls and pulls me to a stone bench. I lean backward and look up at him, steeling myself against his oncoming assault.

"All right, Llacsan, let me have it."

His body goes rigid. "You were supposed to give the tapestry to the king."

That's why he's upset? Someone ought to tell this boy to grow a thicker skin.

"I bet he has thousands," I say. "Why aren't you pleased? A Llacsan—one of your own—has something valuable from the future queen of Inkasisa. Isn't receiving a tapestry a great honor?"

"It would be, coming from a *Llacsan*," he says in a deceptively calm voice. "Tell me something, Condesa. Do you have any idea how insulting it is for you to sit on that throne, preening like a peacock, showing off your weaving? You were meant to present it to King Atoc *privately*. Not flaunt your own skill."

"I—" My voice breaks off. I didn't do that. I wanted to give my message to the vendor. That's all I cared about. There was absolutely no preening.

I don't think. Damn it. Did I *preen*?

"You were the one who suggested I give it to Atoc—"

"*King* Atoc. Gods, show respect."

"*As I was saying*, it was your idea to give the tapestry as a gift."

"No. It was Juan Carlos's."

I roll my eyes. "Semantics. You went along with it, and now you're mad about it?"

"I didn't think you'd put on a show," Rumi fumes. "Have you ever given a gift before? It's about the receiver, you intolerable fool. This was supposed to be for him—not you."

I flinch.

"Weaving is our skill; it's *Llacsan*. For you to claim it as your own and act like it's the best thing ever made . . . *por Dios*." His voice rises with each word. Then it pitches higher, as if imitating me. "Why don't you take it, you poor Llacsan? In fact, why don't I provide all of your wares for you? Because I'm an Illustrian, I'm better at everything, even something your people have been doing for centuries. And you're—"

I jump to my feet, pushing him back. "You never should have brought it down!" He almost ruined everything. Thank Luna I had the wherewithal to think of a way for that message to be sent out. "Atoc asked me about it! What was I supposed to do? Ignore him? That would have gone well."

"How hard would it have been to tell him it was a gift you were planning on giving him after court was over?"

"You shouldn't have taken it," I repeat stubbornly. "You acted in the wrong first."

"You really can't see how your behavior is insulting?" There's an almost despairing note in his tone. I fight anger with anger, but this sounds different, and it gives me pause. I didn't do what he's accusing me of *intentionally*, but I see how it could look that way. If my enemy came into our keep and proceeded to read the stars better than Catalina, I'd probably feel the same.

The silence stretches. I don't know how to reply—because I still think he shouldn't have taken my tapestry to begin with.

Rumi pinches his nose. "I never dreamed you'd take it upon yourself to—Dios," he says while pacing. "And while wearing her dress."

"Whose?"

"The princesa," he says hoarsely. "It's her dress."

Realization dawns. I understand the look of fear I saw in Rumi's eyes before we entered the throne room. It doesn't matter if you're a relative of the king. He can do whatever he wants, kill whoever he wants, in order to solidify his control over Inkasisa. No wonder the healer doesn't want any undue attention on him.

My defense of Ana in the plaza endangered his life.

"I don't get to choose what I wear."

"I know that," he says. "All your clothing must be hers. It makes sense now. She won't need anything because she's to be executed."

Several things become clear: Rumi isn't happy about Atoc's newest decree, and a family member of his will die in the next few weeks.

"She's your cousin, right?"

He takes a step back in surprise. He'd been pacing farther away from me. "We're not related by blood. My aunt married into their family but was widowed after only a year. His Majesty has always acknowledged the connection, though."

"Ah," I say. "That explains it."

"What?"

"Why you become a sniveling buffoon in Atoc's presence."

"King Atoc," Rumi corrects me again, his gaze narrowing. "Sniveling buffoon?"

"You're trying to earn your place at court. And you look ridiculous. Someone ought to tell you. Or doesn't everyone laughing at your expense get through that thick head of yours?"

His expression hardens like the stone walls of my prison, granite and iron and fire. This is why he cares so much about his image. He's not really part of the family—they don't have the same blood. His position in court is a moving current under his feet. One wrong move, and he'll go under.

His response about the princesa is certainly telling too. He does seem incredibly distressed about her. I thought it was because she's family, but now I wonder . . . Is he in love with her? If I ever meet her, I'll offer my profound sympathies.

"It's horrible, what he's doing." I lean forward, my voice dripping with honey. "Can't something be done about it?"

"Whatever do you mean?"

The blandness of his tone brings me up short. I note the dangerous alertness in his dark eyes. A warning rings loudly in my head. But for what, I don't know.

"You seem distraught over her fate," I say carefully. "You weren't the only one upset by Atoc's announcement."

"You would like that, wouldn't you? Dissension in our ranks. Spreading distrust like wildfire in a dying forest. And you mean *King* Atoc."

I smile slowly, because of course I would. He may not be easily rankled, but I'm almost positive there are others who don't want the princesa to die.

"You wouldn't understand anyway," he says curtly. "Being chosen as a sacrifice to Inti is the highest honor anyone could ever receive. Of course it's sad, but His Radiance picked her out of everyone in Inkasisa. He saw how her beauty and grace would please our god." His voice drops to a whisper. "She's the perfect choice. A pure being."

He swings from despair to adoration in a matter of seconds. His loyalty for his king wins out over his distress for Princesa Tamaya.

"How will they murder her?"

A flash of distaste twists his lips, but it's gone a second later. "It's not murder."

"So you say. Well? What will they do to her?"

His shoulders tighten, but his voice is nonchalant, as if we're discussing what we ate for desayuno. "There will be a ceremony in her honor in the Plaza del Sol, and right after, she'll be led up to the top of Qullqi Orqo Mountain."

I hiss out a disgusted breath. "Where she'll be left to freeze to death."

"Where she'll be strangled."

I stare at him in horror.

"You wouldn't understand," he repeats.

No, I'll never understand. Our worlds have an impassable chasm between them. Their god Inti is brutal. Luna would never demand something so cruel from her followers.

"Then I guess I owe her my congratulations," I say sarcastically. "You'll be sure to pass them on to the princesa? I don't think the *king* wants us to be friends."

His lips tighten. "Well, I can hardly blame his judgment on that. Let me take you to your room. Dinner should be waiting for you."

As we leave, a guard I recognize catches my eye. He stands some twenty feet away on a grassy patch of land surrounded by vivid pink flores. He carries a giggling boy on his shoulders. The child attempts to use a miniature slingshot, but only ends up dropping rocks on the guard's head.

"One of your guards," Rumi says. "Pidru and his son. He's very ill."

I pull my attention away from the laughing child. "Who is?"

"Pidru's son, Achik."

"You can't heal him?"

"Do you care?" Rumi counters.

I grit my teeth. Insufferable Llacsan.

The corner of his mouth lifts into a faint smirk as he opens the door to the side entrance. We're silent the whole way up to the third floor. At one point, he absently takes ahold of my wrist, paying careful attention to the wounds from the rope. Rumi traces the raw puckered skin with his index finger. A shiver skips down my spine, and I shrink from his touch. From the odd smell of his clothes and his assessing eyes.

"Coconut oil will help lessen the appearance of the scars," he says. "Though they won't go away entirely."

"Fine," I say. He's switched on me again. His tone sounds mild and approachable. Rumi the healer wants to take care of my scars. Little does he know I have several up and down my body. Years of training guaranteed that. I don't mind the ones on my wrists. Every scar tells a story. The ones I have from that day in the square are part of Ana's life. Her last chapter. I don't want to forget how her story ended.

When we arrive at my room, Rumi opens the door and motions for me to go inside.

But I hesitate.

I used two generous rounds of wool on my tapestry last night. In order to write another message, I'll need several more yards. And I'll have to write another message—preferably once I've found the Estrella.

"What is it, Condesa?" Rumi asks, impatient.

"I need more wool."

"That's too bad." He crosses his arms. "You're not getting any from me."

Not after how I apparently "preened" earlier. There has to be some way I can slide into his good graces. Some way I can convince him I didn't mean any harm. At least, not in the way he thinks.

"I was only trying to help."

It's the wrong thing to say. He takes a step away from me. "You wanted to *help*?" He starts laughing humorlessly. "So says the Illustrian who kept us oppressed for hundreds of years. Were you listening to a word I said earlier?"

That's unfair. I didn't *personally* mistreat the Llacsans. It's not like I'd been cruel to my nanny. I cared for her. I gave some of my money to the homeless Llacsans I saw in La Ciudad—and that was *after* the revolt. After my parents died and I lost everyone and everything.

But an unbidden image assaults my mind. A memory long tucked away and witnessed by a younger version of myself. Llacsans protesting, blocking roads, and walking off their hard-labor jobs. No one could travel anywhere or buy anything because of their demonstrations around the city.

They wanted better pay.

Swallowing hard, I glance away from Rumi's scrutiny. That picture of the protest hovers in my head, and I can't escape it. I try to imagine what it must have been like living under an Illustrian queen.

"I didn't create the system—I was born into it," I say at last. It feels like a fair thing to say.

His face seems to be at war. A flash of anger, a sharp narrowing of his gaze, then a slight pull of his eyebrows—exasperation maybe, but smoothed away to make room for a clenched jaw. "Please stop talking before I do something I regret. Por favor."

"What did I say that was so terrible?" My hands fly to my hips. "If you don't explain it to me, how am I supposed to know—"

"I'm a little tired of explaining myself," Rumi says flatly. "Have been for years. And you all never listen. Do your own reading on the subject, why don't you? And then come back and we'll discuss whatever you like."

No one has ever spoken to me this way before. I wonder how I'd feel if I had to explain why I distrust the Llacsans. I wouldn't want to talk about my dead parents to strangers. I wouldn't want to share my hurt over and over again.

"Where's the book I lent you, Condesa?"

I shut my eyes. I'd left it in the dungeon.

When I open them again, a sad smile twists his lips. "That's what I thought."

Rumi turns and leaves me standing there thinking about that infernal book.

He doesn't look back.

The guards arrive as he rounds the corner. I scurry to my room, shut the door, and lean against it. I wish my thoughts would return to the wool and how to get more of it, so that I could weave more messages. But instead I think about that sad, twisted smile and about the book I never cracked open. Lying forgotten in that cold prison.

I slide all the way to the floor, feeling boneless. What just happened? I'm Catalina's decoy—her friend and confidante.

Rumi is nothing to me. What do I care about his opinions?

Stop it, Ximena. I shake my head. *Focus. Remember what's at stake.* Catalina's reign, the lives of all Illustrians. *You don't have time for this.* I stand, pushing away from the door.

Tomorrow I'll begin the search for the Estrella.

Nothing and no one will keep me from looking.

CAPÍTULO
doce

The bell tower rings, announcing the eighth hour. I curl over, flipping my pillow to the cool side and snuggling deeper under the covers. Today is the day. The pretender and his entourage are planning on visiting La Ciudad this morning.

I wait to hear the sounds of people gathering in the courtyard: a smattering of chatter, horses neighing, and carriage wheels clipping against stone as they're brought around to the castillo entrance.

I smile against the rough cotton of the pillow.

I'll have the whole castillo to myself.

Of course, I'll have my watchdogs hovering over my shoulder. But I can memorize the number of rooms on my floor, take stock of the castillo's layout, determine the number of sentries on rotation. If my guards don't let me wander around, then I'll use the moondust powder.

A couple of pinches is risky, but it'll get the job done.

The door snaps open, and the maid comes in carrying a tray laden with fried eggs, thick slices of bacon, and café con leche.

The aroma of the dark nutty roast swirls in the room and I inhale deeply. A slab of what looks like dark chocolate sits next to the coffee.

"From the merchant," the maid says, following my gaze. "His thanks for your gift."

My mouth waters.

"You're going to have to eat this fast," she says, pulling drawers open. "I'll pick out your clothes for the outing. His Majesty will want you in a full skirt, I think. Perhaps you'll wear the mantilla, too?"

She drops several tunics onto the bed.

I sit up. "What do you mean 'for the outing'? I'm not going."

The maid ignores me and shakes out the creases of a night-colored skirt.

I scramble out of bed and stalk over to her. "I'm not going to La Ciudad."

I can't leave the castillo today—not with everyone else. Why does Atoc want me there anyway? He won't notice my absence, not really. In response to my stubbornness, she grabs the cup of coffee and waves it under my nose.

"Why do I have to go on the outing?" I back away from the nearly overflowing cup. The last time I was forced to visit La Ciudad, my friend died. This could be another one of Atoc's tricks.

"His Majesty's orders are not for me to question. I have to get you dressed. Are you going to drink this or not?" She sets the cup on the dresser when I remain silent.

I sit on the bed and glare. "I'm not going to repeat myself."

She pauses mid-fluff on the skirt and stares at me. Waiting, as if the answer is obvious. Anger sprouts like prickly weeds in my chest. He only wants to show off his prize. He wants to demonstrate his ownership. My skin itches as if an army of hormigas have bitten me.

"You realize if I don't have you in a dress in ten minutes, I'll get in trouble?"

I feel a second's worth of sympathy, but I shove it away. I don't want to feel anything for these Llacsans. They are my enemy. "Not my problem."

She sighs. "Condesa."

For another moment I waver. Then the guard opens the door and Juan Carlos bounds in, all high energy and smiling. "You're not dressed? Everyone's waiting. Put on something suitable."

I open my mouth to argue and then shut it. What's the point? If these Llacsans don't get their way, they'll never leave me alone. Maybe if I exhibit exemplary behavior, Atoc will allow me some liberties—like exploring the castillo with fewer guards.

"Fine," I mutter.

The maid cheers and ushers Juan Carlos outside as he says, "Make sure to do something with her hair. It's a fright."

I throw him a peeved look.

"Now *that* only makes it worse," he says merrily before leaving.

She pushes a long rose-colored skirt and matching tunic into my hands. I dress and put on my boots. If I'm visiting El Mercado, I don't want to be wearing sandals. The Llacsans let their animals run wild in La Ciudad. There's no telling what I'll accidentally step in.

"Rápido, rápido," she says. "Here's a faja to go with that outfit. I don't have time to braid your hair. It will just have to be loose."

A few minutes later I'm out the door, following Juan Carlos down the hall and out into the bright sunlit courtyard, where most of Atoc's household waits in their finery. At my entrance, everyone turns and eyes my unbound hair; the other women wear theirs in elaborate braids and twists.

I joyfully wave as Rumi approaches, leading a mare.

"Dios," he mutters. "Can't you behave for at least an hour?"

I consider the question. "No, I can't."

He scowls, and I smile.

Atoc sits in an open carriage at the head of the procession, and his chamberlain whistles for everyone to mount their steeds. We travel to town in a single line.

La Ciudad Blanca. A city of white buildings glimmering gold in the sun's rays. Of cobbled roads that twist and curve around square plazas, lined by arches. Of clay-tiled roofs and wooden doors etched with flowers. A city that bows to the snowcapped Qullqi Orqo Mountain looming before it.

A city overrun by Llacsans. I used to love it.

We arrive at the Plaza del Sol and despite my initial protests, a sense of freedom washes over me—however false. I'll have to return to the castillo with everyone else. But for now I tip my head back and let the sun's warmth kiss my cheeks. Atoc waves at the crowd of Llacsans gathered in the plaza. The same plaza where Ana disappeared into the earth.

My smile fades, and I trace the scars on my wrists.

"We're supposed to walk around with His Radiance," Rumi says. "He'll want to go to El Mercado. They'll have orange rinds dipped in dark chocolate waiting for him in his favorite shop." Rumi jumps off his horse as the rest of court follows.

My stomach rumbles; I didn't have a chance to eat desayuno. "Can we stop for salteñas?"

"You like them?" He sounds skeptical as he offers his hand.

I ignore it and slide off the saddle. "Absolutely."

"Picante or dulce?"

"Spicy. Definitely spicy."

We trail behind Atoc as he makes his rounds, smiling and greeting the crowd. Several Llacsans press around our group, some gaping, others not interested. I walk past a plump woman standing in front of a vendor selling freshly squeezed jugo de mandarina, saying, "But where is Princesa Tamaya?"

Another whispers, "She didn't come—"

"I don't see her—"

"What do you think happened—"

They sound like they actually care. My ears burn to hear more about the missing princesa. Murals of her likeness are painted on many of the once white walls. Fresh flowers surround her images and several people kneel, seemingly praying for her—or *to* her. The princesa is like a goddess among the Llacsans.

Atoc veers toward El Mercado, where vendors line the streets, calling out their wares.

Quince notas for chicken feet!

Diez for a cow's tongue!

Tres for a horse's tail!

Three Llacsan children run up to our group, holding out their hands. Their clothing is grimy and tattered. Dirt is caked under their fingernails, dust smudging their cheeks. All three are barefoot.

"Por favor," one of them says. He barely comes up to my hip. "¿Notas? ¿Agua?"

I shift my feet. "Lo siento. I don't have water."

The children run off to another group heading toward the plaza, their hands pressed together to catch water. I sigh. This infernal pretender. What is he doing to Inkasisa? Making the koka leaf a legal export has certainly filled the coffers of the nobles loyal to Atoc, but what about the common Llacsans? The ones actually planting the seeds, living in La Ciudad, trying to eke out a living? Not one of them looks to have benefited from the increase in koka production.

We pass a shop selling sandals, and the scent of leather mixes with the spice of cinnamon ice cream sold across the street. The steps leading up to the temple entrance are crowded with Llacsans selling baskets woven from palm leaves, as well as beaded necklaces and fresh jugo de naranja. A group of merchants are outside their shop doors, girasoles in their arms and motioning toward a mural of the princesa.

I round on Rumi. "Do you hear the chatter about Princesa Tamaya?"

He shrugs, idly nibbling on pasankalla—puffed choclo topped with sugar—and reading painted signs hanging over shop windows. I didn't see him buy an entire bag. He catches my longing stare and grudgingly drops a handful in my waiting hands. I pop several in my mouth, enjoying the burst of sugar.

The court mingles with villagers crowding the cobbled streets. I never lose sight of Atoc. The guards surrounding him keep their long spears pointed to the cloudless sky.

Rumi nudges my arm. "Over here. Stay close, Condesa."

As if I needed the reminder. Sentries follow my every move. Dogging each step. Hearing every word. I pray I won't run into an Illustrian spy. It'd be too dangerous for them, considering the amount of guards surrounding me.

I follow Rumi to the salteña line. There're dozens of people waiting for one. The smell alone makes my mouth water.

"It's too long," I say.

He gives me a look and shuffles to the front. Loud cries of protest follow.

"We were next!" a man exclaims.

"Get in the back!"

"I'm on the king's business," Rumi says, squaring his shoulders. "Let me through."

I roll my eyes. But he returns carrying a bag full of almond-shaped pastries filled with diced meat and potatoes, peas, raisins, and a single black olive baked in a savory soup. We sit at one of the available tables and Rumi hands me a salteña, a spoon, and a clay plate.

I drop the pastry onto the plate and am just about to pierce the dough when Rumi makes a loud sound of disgust at the back of his throat.

"What are you *doing*?" he asks, sounding like I'm about to murder a baby alpaca.

I stare at him blankly.

Rumi makes more disgusted noises as he drags my plate away. "Condesa, let me teach you how to eat a salteña correctly." He picks one up, holding the pointed ends with his middle finger and thumb, and gently shakes it. "After you shake it, take a small bite at one of the ends. Then pour the soup into your spoon *first* so it doesn't spill all over your plate."

It takes several spoonfuls before Rumi eats all of the jugo.

Meanwhile, my stomach continues to rumble. I eye my food longingly.

"You're eating it wrong if you get even a drop of juice on your plate," he says in a serious tone. He bites into the pastry and proceeds to scoop the filling into his mouth. He eats the whole thing without spilling any of it.

Isn't he talented. I grab the plate with my salteña, my stomach still rumbling loudly. I try to eat the salteña the way he taught me, but some of the soup ends up on my plate.

Rumi smirks at me. "You know what they say about people who spill the juice, right?"

I eye him warily. "What?"

"That they're terrible kissers."

For some unfathomable reason my cheeks warm. I glare at him and grab another salteña.

This time I don't spill a drop. Somehow it tastes better. Probably because most of it gets to my stomach. When I finish, I stare at him as he devours his third salteña. He eats like a starving wolf. As if any moment the food will vanish into thin air.

"So," I say. "The princesa?"

Rumi grunts and reaches for another salteña.

I frown. Why doesn't he want to do something about it? The Llacsans living in the city certainly do. And if they care enough, they'll speak up. "I don't think anyone in La Ciudad has a clue about her execution."

He chokes on his first bite of his fourth salteña.

"What do you think the people will do when they learn the truth?" I ask loudly. Several Llacsans enjoying their food stare in my direction.

Rumi accidentally dribbles jugo onto his plate.

"Ha! Looks like you're a terrible kisser too."

He stares at me in impotent fury. "You don't get to ask or talk about the princesa. Stop spreading rumors and being dramatic." He shakes his salteña at me.

It seems Atoc is blithely unaware that his decision regarding his sister will have terrible consequences. Consequences that are better for us. An idea strikes me. Can the Llacsans loyal to the princesa come to our side?

"Will they revolt, do you think? Boycott tax day? Cut down trees and block the roads?"

"They'll do nothing," he says coldly. "We *all* obey the king and respect his leadership. And it's not an execution. It's an honor to be chosen—"

I wave my hand dismissively. "For the sacrifice. So you've mentioned."

His lips thin.

I think about the distress I heard in the crowd's voices as they wondered about the princesa's absence. I remember the murmuring at court when the king made his announcement. Rumi is wrong.

The Llacsans won't take her death lightly.

He eats the rest of his food in silence and doesn't speak to me the whole way back to the castillo.

Fine by me.

I need to focus. Distractions are mounting, and they only serve to confuse me and slow down my progress. How many times in training did I have to remind myself to block out everything except for the task at hand? Keep my eye on the target. Focus on my opponent. Stay alert.

The next day I avoid all conversation with Rumi. I don't want to clutter my mind thinking about the princesa—after all, what is she to *me*?

No one.

What do I care about her fate?

Not a damn thing.

Unrest among the Llacsans is a good thing. Let the princesa be executed, then. It might make a difference for Catalina's bid for the throne.

Thankfully, Rumi seems to be of the same mindset, as he doesn't talk to me either. I never press him for the wool I need. There has to be another avenue for me to pursue.

As the next three days blur together, I settle on a routine. In the mornings I eat desayuno sitting outside on the balcony, examining the comings and goings through the large iron gate to the side of the garden. All the servants enter and exit the castillo and into the city through that gate. Midafternoon, I study hallways and entrances, memorizing the castillo layout. In the evenings, the gardens have my sole attention. I know every corner, and I sit and observe members of the court as they flit around the tall plants. They're a wealthy and bored bunch. Their loud chatter ricochets off the stone walls as they lounge on couches. Most of the time their eyes are red-rimmed, and they act drowsy, as if bone-tired.

But they aren't dropping from mere exhaustion. Many of them are consumers of the koka leaf, made accessible thanks to our good and wise king. What a mess. The whole of Inkasisa will become addicted to the drug, Illustrians and Llacsans alike.

Though guards dog my every move, I also have the distinct feeling I'm being carefully observed by the priest and his followers. Signs like a tickle on the back of my neck. A creeping sensation that raises goose bumps on my arms. A flash of an eggplant-colored robe ducking around a corner.

Why are the priest's minions stalking me? Did the order come from Atoc? I start keeping moondust in my pockets, just in case. It helps knowing I have some way of defending myself if the situation ever comes to that.

I often cross paths with Sajra. He seems to be everywhere at once. Coming out of meetings with the king, heading to the kitchens, walking the gardens. His horde of attendants sticks to him like sap to a tree. Their watchful eyes dart from person to person as they follow the priest.

They don't miss much when it comes to the happenings in the castillo. Sajra certainly benefits from all the information. What he does with it, I can only guess.

At night I eat alone in my room and plan for the next day. It's time to focus on the Estrella. I've mapped out the majority of the castillo, memorized the guard's movements, their shifts, and what weapons they carry. I make a restless turn around my room, wringing my hands. Tension edges my shoulders. I only have the east wing of the castillo left to explore, and it's been nearly impossible to view the entire length of it. Atoc and his entourage crowd that side, and as a result more guards patrol it.

My mind races with possible excuses I could have for visiting the hall. There's nothing out of the ordinary to tour there except painting after painting of various animals.

I sigh. The paintings are my best option.

I pound on the door until the guard—Pablo? Pidru? Pedro?—opens it. "I think I'll explore the castillo today, instead of the gardens. I haven't seen all the paintings in the east wing, and they really are beautiful, don't you think?"

He shrugs. "His Radiance said seeing the castillo and its grounds were fine, provided you had a guard with you at all times."

I hide my smile. "Let's head there, then."

He points down a random corridor. I stride off, and then slow my steps and pretend to study the first painting I encounter. A detailed drawing of a llama. The guard stops at my side. I catch Atoc and his entourage at the end of the hall, climbing the stone steps that lead farther down the east wing. I lean closer to the painting, tilting my head ever so slightly to get a better view.

I wonder where they go every day. Perhaps to his office. The thought is tantalizing. What sorts of secrets could be hidden in his private space? The guard clears his throat and I straighten. I sigh and move on to the next painting, pretending to be enthralled by yet another llama. The guard clears his throat again, this time louder and a bit longer, and I smile as I lean forward.

This continues until Atoc and his entourage are walking toward us, deep in conversation, coming back from wherever they had gone in the east wing. They pass by without a look in my direction. I'm nothing, barely taking up space in his life. His indifference only propels me onward.

I can't properly explore the east wing with this guard breathing down my neck. Maybe I can bore him enough to leave me? I stop at the next painting and force myself to ponder every stroke. After doing this eight more times, the guard glances at me. "You'll stay on the first floor?"

"Yes," I say, then, "¿Por qué?"

He hesitates. "My son is sick, and I'd like to speak to the healer about giving him more té de maté. We only have a few hours left before the dinner bell. I want to catch him before he leaves the infirmary."

My chest tightens as I picture the little boy playing outside in the garden. For some inexplicable reason, it bothers me to hear about his illness.

"I'll be fine," I say. "I'm sorry your son is sick."

The words hang in the air, and I'm surprised to realize I mean them. I hate being sick. It means being trapped inside and not leaving my bed. Catalina insisted I was actually *doing* something by letting myself recover. I never felt that way.

"You're sure?"

I nod. "Go take care of your son."

"I won't be gone long. Just depends how long the line is." He still seems unsure. Stalling.

If only Catalina could see me now. Attempting to reassure a Llacsan guard whose name I can't quite place. "What's your name?"

"Pidru."

Of course. Rumi also mentioned the boy's name . . . what was it? I remember the child's face. Dark curly hair and laughing eyes, a pointed chin, and round cheeks.

"Achik," I say. "That's your son's name."

The guard blinks in surprise. "Sí. How do you know that?"

"The healer told me," I say. "How's he doing?"

"Some days are better than others. Today is a bad one. If you're sure—"

"Pidru," I say. "I'll be perfectly fine on my own."

"Ten minutes. At the most."

"Fine."

The guard nods, and after a small smile, he leaves me alone in the corridor.

I wait until he rounds the corner. Grinning, I continue my exploring, this time without stopping to look at the paintings. After you've seen one, you've seen them all. I can only take so many llama portraits.

I ramble on, making mental notes of how many doors I've passed. Most are bedrooms. I turn down another hallway and encounter the stairs heading up to the east wing. This is where Atoc ventures to every day, he and his entourage. Sajra too.

After glancing to the left and right, I bound up the stone steps, already thinking of possible excuses should someone catch me—I got lost, or I thought I heard something suspicious. A contrite attitude, perhaps a little sheepish, and I'll come out the other end unscathed. But my guard won't.

That brings me up short.

I reach the top of the stairs, and I look back the way I came. He'll get in trouble for leaving me. All he wants is to help his son and get him tea from the healer. Pidru might lose his job. I let out an impatient sigh. Where is this coming from? What do I care for a Llacsan guard? Didn't I just give myself a talk about staying focused?

My hesitation confounds me.

What matters more? The revolt or a guard whose name I just learned? He isn't family. He isn't an Illustrian. He'll stand against me if he knows my plans.

That answers that. I press on toward the east wing.

Several doors line one side and an iron railing lines the other. If anyone bothers to look up, they'll spot me skulking around. Moving quickly, I go to the first door and crack it open. A beautiful bedroom. The walls are a pale sky blue, and the bed could fit at least three people on it. A handsome chest stands off in the corner.

I pull open a drawer full of shirts, vests, and trousers. I spot darker-colored pants and tunics.

Don't mind if I do. I quickly tug the pants on under my long skirt and layer the tunics. The loose-fitting style of the Llacsans effectively hides my theft. I dart out of the room, hardly believing my good fortune. I have the makings of a perfect disguise.

Even during the day Luna watches over me.

Quietly, I poke my head outside the room, checking to make sure there aren't any guards patrolling. With a little smile, I leave the room as quietly as I entered it. I retrace my footsteps and veer toward the staircase. Pidru should be on his way back, but it doesn't matter.

I have what I need to explore the east wing tonight, thoroughly and without any distraction.

trece

I only have four weeks left before the wedding. *Four more weeks.* The realization sits in my stomach like a rock. Not even the savory smell coming from tonight's dinner of braised pork in ají amarillo with a side of llajwa calms me. By now Catalina must have received my message about Carnaval and knows when to stage the revolt, but if we don't find the Estrella, it's a moot point.

We need the ghosts to win.

The maid comes in late to clear away my untouched plate. "You don't like pork?" she asks.

"I love it. I'm not feeling well."

It's not exactly a lie. She frowns, concern flickering in her dark eyes. I tilt my head. Why the apparent concern? I thought she hated me.

"You must really be sick," she says. "It's not like you to leave food on your plate. You have a hearty appetite."

"I . . . Gracias?" It's the sort of thing Sofía would have said to me.

"I'll send for the healer," she says.

"¿Qué? No! Estoy bien," I say, scrambling out of the bed after her.

She shushes me and walks out.

I stare at the closed door in disbelief. Not only did I *not* want to see Rumi, I was suffering from nerves—not an illness. He'll see that immediately and assume I'm up to something, which of course I am. I have to explore the castillo tonight, and I can't have him coming in here, potentially spoiling my plan.

The temperature of my arms, neck, and ears soars to feverish heights. Resigned, I tidy up the room. I fold clothes, tuck my shoes neatly in the corner. I chew on mint leaves and then berate myself.

What the diablos am I thinking? Mint leaves?

I spit the leaves into the basin, light a few candles, and curl under the covers. I leave the balcony door open to allow Luna's moonlight to decorate the stone floor. Sinking into the pillow, I vow to keep the visit short. He'll check for signs of fever and then leave. Hopefully it'll dissuade him from thinking I'm up to something. He'll be cold and silent, angry to have been summoned by the Illustrian condesa. Maybe he'll demand I take something awful and forbid me from leaving the room.

Restless energy keeps me from calming down. I'm just about to throw back the covers when the guard opens the door. Rumi walks in, takes one look at me in bed, and frowns.

"You really are sick," he says.

I widen my gaze. "What?"

He comes up to the bed and settles a hand on my forehead. "You're flushed and a little warm. How are you feeling?"

I feel like I might die from embarrassment, and yourself? I move away, forcing his hand to drop to his side. "I'm fine. No need to trouble yourself."

The corner of his mouth lifts. "Why didn't you eat your dinner? It's not like you."

I shrug. "Not hungry. It happens sometimes."

He lifts a dark brow. Just the one.

"Does everyone think I'm some sort of cow?" I ask, exasperated. When he opens his mouth to respond, I hold up my hand. "Don't answer that."

"Have you been using the koka leaf?" he demands.

My jaw drops. "What? No. I've seen what it does to people."

His expression darkens. "Don't ever use it. Even with one use, you could become addicted. Too many people in this castillo already are."

"And you're the one who looks after them. That must be exhausting."

"Don't tell me you're concerned."

My voice rises. "Of course I'm not."

"I'll ask Suyana to make you té de maté," he says with a trace of amusement at my loud protest. "You don't have too high of a fever. Stay in bed and rest tomorrow. I'll let the king know you're ill."

Suyana? I'm about to ask, but it hits me that he might be talking about my maid. I never thought to ask her name. "If you knew me better, you'd know that's an impossible task. I'd rather swallow a hornet than stay in bed all day."

"If you knew me, you'd know to take my advice," he says idly. "It won't be so bad. You can weave—"

"Except I don't have any wool."

"You can read a book—"

"Except I don't have a book."

He looks at me.

My face flushes. I almost forgot. I did have a book, but I left it down in the dungeon.

I meet his gaze. "Do you think if we weren't at war, we'd be friends?"

He seems to seriously consider the query. "I honestly don't know. But if we can, it'd certainly bode well for the future."

I find I agree with him. Maybe it's not an impossible ask. Things would certainly be easier if Catalina had the full support of the Llacsans. I wonder what it would take. Would Rumi ever stand with the real condesa? A long silence follows. For some reason, I don't mind his company, despite the heavy stench of ragweed coming from his clothes.

"You should wash those," I blurt out.

He tucks his hands into his pocket, and the corners of his mouth deepen. "What now?"

"Your clothes. Do you have a pet skunk? They smell like you've been running around with one. I know there's a water shortage, but I think you could find a stream and a bar of soap somewhere."

I expect him to retreat behind his scowl and hunched shoulders. Instead he smiles, a fleeting and private smirk that's gone as soon as I catch it.

"A pet skunk. I like that."

"I can't believe your cousin hasn't kicked you out. It's *that* strong."

He smiles again. The expression transforms his face, softening the sharp angles. A single dimple appears in the middle of his cheek, just above his scruff. "You're welcome to wash them for me."

I don't miss the slightly teasing tone.

He doesn't either.

Rumi backs away from the bed as if it's on fire. I sink deeper under the covers, flushing. The brief moment tricks me. For a second it's like we're friends.

But that's nowhere near the truth.

"I think I've done about all I can for you," he says at last.

I twist the sheets around my fingers. His voice holds a new note. A little sad, maybe. He isn't talking about me being sick, I don't think.

"Rest, Condesa." He turns to leave.

Before I realize what I'm doing, I reach for his wrist. "Wait, healer."

We both glance at my hand in surprise. I've never willingly touched him before. I withdraw my hand, mortified. He peers down at me, blinking in confusion. The candlelight casts shadows across his angular face. He has a smattering of dark freckles across the bridge of his nose.

"Thanks for coming up," I mumble, and turn away on my side, my cheek resting on the pillow.

I pretend to fall asleep so I don't have to look at him anymore. And then I fall asleep for real. Hours later, I sit up with a start. I blink at the room, confused by the darkness. My dream was about setting a fire, and I remembered I didn't blow out the candles. But someone clearly did. I fumble for the matchsticks next to my bed and light one of the candles on the nightstand.

It's still dark out—perfect for exploration. I throw back the covers and my gaze lands on a book lying next to the candle. A mug of cold tea sits next to it. Leaning closer, I read the title in the flickering light. *Historia de las Llacsans.* Rumi had gone down to the dungeons and brought it back while I slept.

Instinctively, I look around for my basket of wool and find it full again. This time in blues and greens. I can't stop the smile on my face. There's plenty for more messages *and* to test my magic. I'll finally know if my tapestries can come to life.

A strange and unwelcome flutter passes through me, settling deep in my belly.

What reason does Rumi have to be nice to me?

This is the sort of thing that threatens my mission. I can handle surly tempers and cold hospitality. I can handle the Llacsans' hatred for me and the frank distrust in their eyes. But Rumi's random kindnesses? My guard Pidru smiling when I asked his name? He looked at me not as an Illustrian but as if . . . I'm just a girl. Even my maid, Suyana, has shown concern for my welfare.

They're getting under my skin.

I repeat to myself what I know: Atoc is still the wrong person to rule. Catalina will be a much better monarch.

I hold on to that as I put on one of the dark tunics I stole, leaving it loose and baggy to disguise my frame. Then I think about how to cover my face. I don't have much to work with. The pants don't fit me right either. I start to fold the hem but then get a better idea. I tear four strips of fabric from the legs and tie two of them together, making a loose-fitting wrap for my hair. Next I rip holes in the third piece for a mask. It falls over my nose and mouth, stopping at my chin. The fourth piece I store in case I need more fabric for later.

I open the balcony windows and venture outside. It's my best chance of leaving my room undetected. I'd checked the door, and while it was left unlocked, there's still a guard posted outside. A soft rain falls, enhancing the sweet smell of the eucalyptus trees. Cool night air pushes my curls away from my face, and thick swirls of dark clouds block the moon and stars. Because of the rain, Luna isn't visible. Will that hinder my plan? I need all the help and blessings I can get. Maybe I ought to wait for a clear night.

But I don't have the luxury of time. I have to find the enchanted gem. I peer over the railing—Madre de Luna, the balcony below seems *miles* from where I stand. The fall won't kill me, but I could certainly break a bone or three. The room below must be occupied, since the doors are flung open to allow the cool breeze inside. If I drop down—my stomach tightens at the thought— the occupant of that room might wake and scream for help.

But I have to risk it.

A small whimper escapes me as I swing a leg over. Pivoting, I face my room then pull the other leg over. I bend and slide my hands down the rail and drop my legs.

Beads of sweat trickle down my back. My room is on the third floor, and as my feet dangle, I sneak a quick peek toward the balcony below me.

My heart races. For a second I'm too dizzy to do anything but hold on to the railing for dear life. I let out a shaky breath. A mosquito buzzes by my chin and I flinch. My palms start to slide on the iron rail. I have to jump.

Ignoring the rushing in my ears, I swing out my legs, rocking until I have enough momentum. The time to let go comes and goes. My fingers don't want to release the railing, and the roar in my head increases.

I think of everything I've lost, and how far I've come. I picture Catalina and Ana; I picture Sofía. The hazy outline of my parents' faces. *Seize the night, Ximena.*

I let go.

The drop takes a second, but I swear it feels like a lifetime. My feet crash against the balcony floor, and I tumble sideways, landing with a loud grunt. The curtains rustle and tickle my cheeks as a breeze sweeps through. I brace for someone's cry— my fall was the opposite of graceful. But none comes.

Slowly, I get to my knees. Shooting pains move up along my right side, and my hip bone stings from the fall. There's no movement in the dark room. Maybe whoever's inside is a heavy sleeper?

With quiet steps, I pull back the curtain and go inside. My eyes adjust to the darkness. Peering toward the bed, I try to make out a shape.

But there's no one.

I fall to my knees, air whooshing out of me. Thank Luna there's no one in here—

The doorknob turns with a sharp creak.

I barely have time to press myself against the wall before the door opens in my face. A woman walks through, reeking of that popular Llacan corn liquor. She pushes the door closed and doesn't notice me as she stumbles forward. A sliver of slanted light draws a thin gold line on the floor.

"Match, match," she mumbles.

I reach for the knob, holding my breath. I grab the knob and pull, holding my breath as the patch of light grows wider.

The woman freezes, but before she can turn around, I aim a kick and clip the side of her head with my boot. She slumps to the floor in a heap. She's dead weight and I don't want to waste time moving her onto the bed, so I leave her where she lies, hoping she'll be too drunk or too high to remember a thing.

I make my way down the hall toward the stairs, blazing torches lighting my path, my steps quick and light. The library is on the second floor of the east wing, and I'm willing to bet Atoc's personal office is too. I just have to get to the other side of the castillo. This takes plenty of patience, as I have to wait until patrolling guards round corners.

At long last, I make it to the east wing in one piece. My footsteps thud against the stone floor as I pass the library. I keep going until I have to veer to the right, and there in front of me are tall double doors with lit torches on either side.

This has to be it.

I pull one of the torches out of its slot in the wall and open the heavy door using one of the iron rings. The room smells like tobacco and worn leather, mixed with the crisp outdoors. A variety of maps and paintings decorate the walls, as well as hanging pots overflowing with ferns. A large map of Inkasisa in black, white, and gold hangs behind a handsome wooden desk. It takes up the space of the entire back wall. I set the torch in one of the available slots and head over to the map, intrigued by the pins marking a variety of locations.

I trace the inky patterns denoting each region in Inkasisa with my index finger.

La Ciudad. The Altiplano and Tierra Baja. The Llaco Valley. Qullqi Orqo Mountain. The great Lago Yaku. I think only Manuel has visited each territory. Except for the Yanu Jungle. People never survive a visit to that place.

Each area is beautifully illustrated, with strokes of gold denoting rivers and lakes, roads and caves. The gold paint looks like the real thing, judging by the way it shimmers in the firelight. I know about the cave by Lago Yaku, the birthplace of the children of the Llacsan god Inti. Supposedly, that's where Atoc's ancestors came from. Centuries earlier they walked out of the entrance, dressed in all their finery, and settled Inkasisa.

The iron pins are scattered around the map, close to La Ciudad. Some are placed on the mountain, others on areas where there are well-known caves. There's even one embedded in the imposing watchtower of the castillo. A few pins are placed on forests. Thankfully not anywhere near the Yanu Jungle. Could Atoc have hidden the Estrella in one of the caves surrounding the city? What about in the mountain?

I take a step closer. If these are possible locations for the Estrella, then I've done it.

I've really done it.

I turn around and grab a loose sheet of paper from the king's desk. Dropping the quill's nib into a pot of black ink, I rush to write down all of the marked spots. I don't have the pretty penmanship the condesa possesses. Mine looks like a long scrawl drawn by someone who has enjoyed one too many glasses of singani. I splatter ink everywhere in my hurry to jot down all the places marked. I can't help my rush of excitement.

If one of these spots indicates the actual location of the Estrella, Catalina can send soldiers to check out the places farther from the castillo. I can certainly try to visit the locations in La Ciudad. I'll just have to determine how to sneak out of the castillo.

I fold the sheet into fourths.

Iron clangs against the door, and my breath constricts. I spin around in surprise, clutching the paper. A man dressed entirely in black from head to foot stands across the room.

My heart slams into my ribs.

El Lobo.

catorce

We stay like that, looking at each other as if we've discovered a new species of alpaca. The urge to flee makes my toes curl, filling me with nervous energy. But when else will I get a chance to be this close to him? I don't want to walk away without having learned something about him.

The vigilante stands a full head taller than me. Broad shoulders. Narrow hips. His eyes seem dark, but it could be the shadows from his mask. He tenses, and his chin ducks toward his chest. He wears gloves, and an opaque cloth covers the whole of his face. At his left hip is the infamous huaraca slingshot, attached to his black woven belt. Long-range Llacsan weapon. On his right is a sword. I have no way of knowing whether he's a Llacsan or Illustrian. Even under his tunic, El Lobo wears an undershirt that reaches up to his chin. Not a hint of either our tawny olive skin or the rich bronzed hue of the Llacsans.

Well, he certainly is thorough, I can give him that much. I must paint a bemusing picture for the vigilante. After all, I'm dressed like him.

"Words fail me," he says in a heavily accented, gravelly voice.

I tilt my head to the side. The accent matches that of a Lowlander; it has a singsong rhythm like those from the neighboring country of Palma.

"Well?" he asks. "Are you going to tell me who you are?"

I shake my head.

"Of course not," he mutters, sounding amused. "Are you an enemy?"

I shrug. I honestly don't know. His antics against the throne jeopardize our precarious situation. If he's an Illustrian, he ought to know better and publicly align with us. Why not come forward? Why not offer to work together? Instead he chooses to run around the kingdom creating merry hell for Atoc's army. A bristle of annoyance pulses within me. All of our plans for the revolt depend on having the element of surprise.

"How much love do you have for the king?" he says in a rough voice that sounds like two stones scraping against each other.

I hold out my hands so that they're parallel to each other. Slowly, I bring them together.

"You worship him. No wait, you merely tolerate him," he says as my hands draw closer. When they touch, El Lobo lets out a low whistle. "You despise him. Now we're getting somewhere. Well, you're obviously an admirer of mine—"

I snort.

"No? Interesting. And you're not sure if you're my enemy," he muses. "Well, should we fight to the death and get it over with?"

It would be a quick match seeing as how I don't have my knives or sword. I can probably bruise him though.

He laughs. "What would you like to do about this little conundrum?"

How to nonverbally respond to this? I shift my feet and flicker my attention over to the door.

"I'm very interested to see what you have in your hand." El Lobo takes a step forward.

I automatically hold up my hand. The universal gesture that means stop.

To my surprise, he does.

"I'm also intrigued by your decision to stay silent," he comments. "You might actually be mute, or you might hate the sound of your voice." He lowers his own voice to a dramatic whisper. "But I think you're worried I might learn something you wouldn't like."

Again, I shrug. It seems neutral enough. His accent sounds exaggerated and has that forced, rock-like quality. Maybe he doesn't want me to learn anything about him either.

Which means he has his own agenda, and he isn't interested in sharing it. A rogue Illustrian? I don't like it. But if El Lobo is a Llacsan . . . well, I don't really know what to think. My time in the castillo has stirred confusing, interesting, and dangerous questions within me. At some point I'll have to sort through them all and get back to where I started.

"All right," El Lobo says. "Here's what we'll do. If you give me a moment to myself, I'll do what I came here for. I'll extend you the same courtesy. . . . Unless, are you finished? Just that one sheet of paper?"

I nod.

"Then off with you. Next time maybe we'll have an actual conversation and you can tell me why you're pretending to be me. I have my reputation to maintain—"

I never get to hear the rest of his sentence. Both doors of the office fling open. Four soldiers rush in. Swords drawn. I recognize one of the guards. He stands in the middle of the group.

Pidru.

El Lobo backs away from the door and nearly collides with the desk. I tuck the sheet into the band of my trousers. The guards creep closer. I open and close my fists, nervous energy making my skin tingle.

"Did you know there were two of them?" one of the guards asks.

"There's the missing torch," another says, pointing to the wall. I make a mental note to carry a candle for the next outing. That, and to find a damn weapon. I'll grab a dinner fork if I have to. And I think better about using the moondust—anyone who sees me weave will instantly connect the dots.

I glance at the desk. Stacks of paper. A wooden box filled with envelopes. A tin paperweight. Silver letter opener. Dark feathered quills.

Wait. The *letter opener*.

El Lobo has moved around the desk, heading in my direction. His movements are slow and deliberate. One of the guards shouts for him to stop moving. El Lobo complies. But it doesn't matter. We're already standing side by side, our shoulders grazing.

"Official offer to work together," he says in a low tone.

I move the toe of my boot to touch his. Out of the corner of my eye, I watch his chin dip a fraction of an inch.

"We outnumber you," Pidru says. "Come around the desk slowly."

I meet the vigilante's gaze. Amusement flashes in his dark eyes. We both move at the same time. I hurl the letter opener at the guard on the far left. It somersaults and sinks deep into his shoulder, knocking him off his feet.

Rounding the desk, El Lobo charges the two men on the right. They step back, blocking the vigilante's advance.

That leaves Pidru for me.

I don't want to hurt him. Not after hearing about his son.

He jumps forward, the tip of his blade jutting toward me. I dodge to the left. I need to knock him out with something. There are only piles of paper. Frantically, I try pulling open drawers, but they're locked. Grabbing the paperweight, I hurl it at his head.

The weight clips his temple. Blood trickles into his eyebrow. I run around the desk and kick the guard I'd thrown the letter opener at in the stomach. He folds his body in half with a loud grunt.

"You're *unarmed*?" El Lobo cries.

He's already knocked out one of our attackers with the desk chair. El Lobo scoops up the guard's fallen sword and throws it at me, handle first. I catch it with my right hand and turn just in time to block a thrust from Pidru.

He advances. I stop each jab, my wrist quivering as steel meets steel. His foot comes up and connects with my side.

Wheezing, I counter the next thrust. I'm out of practice. Slow. But Pidru's girth works in my favor. He lunges with the sword. I sidestep out of the way, take advantage of the opening, and rake the tip of my blade from navel to shoulder.

Pidru grunts and touches his stomach. His fingers come away bloody.

He roars and lunges, an ugly twist to his mouth.

I whirl away and my back slams against a hard surface. El Lobo. I feel the muscles in his back move as he fights.

"Want to switch?" he asks, amusement threading his voice.

Do I want to *what?*

I don't have time to protest. The vigilante spins us around, gripping my waist. I blink and readjust my position to face the oncoming assault. I kick and land a hit on El Lobo's guard. He releases my waist and spars with Pidru. The other guard charges.

I block and counter. My arm burns from the weight of the sword. My hand shakes with the effort to follow through. But when the guard leaves himself open, I don't waste the opportunity.

One step forward. Direct stab under the ribs. His eyes roll up until the whites show, and he slumps to the ground. The blade slips out of him.

My mask sticks to my cheeks, hot and damp from the sweat trickling down my temples. Swords clang behind me. Startled, I turn as El Lobo advances on Pidru. The older man gives a valiant effort, but his movements are slower.

I can't watch. The doors to the office are still flung open. My feet want to carry me through. My heart must want the same thing because in seconds I'm there, one foot inside the office and the other free.

Pidru doesn't have any fight left in him. His shoulders sag. His blade moves wildly and without control. El Lobo shifts his weight. Preparing for the next hit.

"Don't kill him!" The words rip out of me. I barely remember to disguise my voice.

They both turn toward me. Pidru clearly stunned, sweat

drenching his tunic. El Lobo's blade freezes mid-slash. Even I'm surprised—I just saved a Llacsan guard. I back up a step. I don't have time to consider what I've done.

I run.

My footsteps echo down the long stone hall. I duck under doorways and hide around corners, timing my every move in order to evade the guards patrolling the corridors. But I still have to contend with the tall sentry standing in front of my door. I peer around the corner, and sure enough, he's there, leaning against the frame. His head dips and then jerks upward. The telltale signs of someone trying to stay awake.

I have to get inside. Quickly. It's only a matter of time before more soldiers arrive. Someone will have noticed the missing guards patrolling the hallway. I'm an enemy sleeping under their roof, the first one who will be questioned. I have to make it inside my room before more guards are summoned. Something brushes against my leg. I glance down and smile. A cat. I follow its intense stare to a group of chickens clucking at the other end of the hall, and an idea sparks.

The third floor is one big square. My idea will only work if the disturbance is loud enough to ensnare the guard's attention, and if I run fast enough around the square before the guard returns to his post. I suck in a deep breath and take off my boots.

Now or never.

I knock over two smaller pots just as the cat hisses and bolts down the hall. The clay pots make a resounding crash against the stone. The chickens squawk and the cat emits a loud screech. I sprint on my tiptoes down the hall, skirting around the flustered chickens squawking and flapping their wings in a rage.

The guard shouts in alarm as I round the first corner.

My calves ache but I stay on my tiptoes. Doors pass by in a blur. I round the second corner. My boots thud against my thighs as I pump my legs. Just one more turn. A stitch roars painfully to life in my side. I ignore it as I round the last corner. There's no guard! My lungs are on fire, but I don't let up the pace.

Four more doors to go.

Three.

Two.

I reach for the knob and swing my door open, careful to close it gently. Ripping off my tunic, I throw on a brightly striped shirt that hangs to my knees. Trousers come off next. I prop my boots neatly against the dresser and stuff the dark clothes into my pillowcase. The folded sheet of paper I stuff deep into my right shoe.

My heart thuds sharply in my chest. Snapping the covers back, I scramble into bed with my sword tucked underneath the pillow.

The door opens.

I shut my eyes, feigning sleep. Force my breath to even out. Slow and steady. The effort hurts. My body thrums with energy and it doesn't want to be quieted.

"She's been in here the whole time," someone says.

That'll be the tall guard stationed at my door.

"What happened down the hall—"

"Nastiest chicken and cat fight I've ever seen," my guard says. "Broken pieces of clay scattered everywhere. And the feathers! So many—"

"I saw the feathers," the other interrupts, his voice dry. "Are you telling me you left your post?"

My breath catches at the back of my throat. I squeeze my knees together.

"Not long enough for her to have done anything."

The sound of footsteps entering the room makes me want to cry out. But I force myself still. The strain of pretending to sleep overwhelms me. I want to fling back the sheets and grab the sword hidden underneath my pillow.

But I remain motionless.

"Heavy sleeper," one of them comments. "You stayed by the door the whole time? Other than to see the fight?"

"The whole time. Healer stopped by earlier and left tea. Said the condesa wasn't feeling well."

"Which she didn't drink."

"Maybe she doesn't like tea," my guard says idly.

"Probably thinks it's poisoned."

They move away from the bed, their footsteps fading as they head to the door.

"We had another visit from El Lobo tonight."

"When?"

"Just now. Rumi is tending to the survivors; he might be able to learn what else they saw. The rest of the family is searching the grounds, and the captain has men on every floor. Did you hear . . ."

The voices cut off when they shut the door.

My breath comes out shallow and hitched. What if one of the guards identifies me to the healer? I push the thought away. No sense in worrying over something that may not happen. My mask covered every inch of my face. The murmuring stops.

Then it's the deep quiet of night, interrupted only by the echo of my racing heart.

CAPÍTULO

quince

The next morning my maid—Suyana—comes in early, opening the curtains and balcony door, inviting sunlight's harsh attack. I need Luna and her cool moonlit rays. Not this sweltering heat and dry wind. I even prefer the rain. There's something about warm weather that makes things worse. I'm already in a perpetual state of anxiety.

Another court day.

Atoc will be intolerable and unpredictable because of the events from last night. He might take his anger out on me—or worse, one of the guards might have drawn conclusions about my identity. If there's even a hint of suspicion . . . I suppress a shudder. I don't want to let anyone down. I don't want to be thrown into the dungeon and rendered useless again.

I don't want to fail.

Suyana pulls my hair into two thick braids, muttering about the knots she can't untangle. After being stuck underneath a sweaty mask for most of last night, my hair looks like a charming home for parrots this morning.

"What did you do?" Suyana asks, holding up the end of a braid where my hair poofed out like a cloud. "That's *one* knot."

"I must have tossed around in my sleep," I say quickly. Which is partially true. I prayed for sleep, but the whole night I couldn't stop my mind from churning. Any moment, I expected the door to open and guards to clamor inside, shouting for my arrest. "Are we almost done?"

She pauses mid-grumble. "You're a funny girl, Condesa."

I hand her a navy ribbon. "What have I done now?"

"You don't act like a condesa," she says, tying up the end of one of my braids. "Every morning you make your own bed, pick up your clothes. When a plate of food is before you, there's nothing delicate about your table manners. You eat like a starving wolf. You don't like dressing up or painting your face. I can barely get you to sit still long enough to brush out the tangles in your hair. And I've never seen you look at yourself in the mirror. It's strange."

My heartbeat slips in and out of rhythm. The fear of being discovered as a fraud roars to life, ravenous and gnawing me to bits, tearing into my skin. Her list of imperfections are all wholly myself, wholly *Ximena*, and said so casually, oblivious to my inner turmoil.

I hope.

I work for a nonchalant tone. "It's strange I don't fit into the box you made for me?"

The smallest of smiles. "Everyone makes boxes. It's human, I think. You made one for Llacsans."

It isn't a question. I hand her the next ribbon. The anger I carry for the Llacsans has been my closest friend ever since I spent time on the streets after my parents' deaths. It's fueled me. Motivated me to survive. Anger carried me to the castillo gates.

And now? Do I feel anger toward Suyana? I thought about my plea to spare Pidru's life. Definitely not the actions of an angry girl. Definitely not the actions of an angry girl posing as a decoy spy.

That's when it hits me.

I'm no longer angry with *all* of them. Just Atoc and Sajra, and for very specific reasons. Not because they're Llacsans, but because they're corrupt. My realization feels important somehow.

I turn to face her, and nod. I want her to know that I heard her. "Yes, I did put you all in the same box. But that doesn't feel right to me anymore."

"Just as it doesn't feel right to keep you in the one I made for you," she says. "You're ready to face the king, Condesa."

Suyana leaves with a soft smile.

It should have made me feel better. The first real smile she's given me. Sincere and a little shy. But it's a lie. She smiled at the decoy.

The real condesa hates all Llacsans.

Juan Carlos comes to fetch me for court. He leans languidly against the door frame, a smile that I assume most find utterly attractive stretching his perfect mouth. My hair has been tamed, I'm wearing rouge on my lips, and the dress must fit right given the way he's studying me from head to toe. "You look very fetching. The loveliest girl I've ever seen."

How he manages to utter such ridiculous nonsense with a straight face is beyond my understanding. It takes a special kind of person, I guess.

"I don't care for your compliments."

He laughs. "So you've made clear. ¿Lista?"

I let my nod speak for me since I don't trust my voice to remain steady. My fear has caught me by the throat. Then we're out the door, the same tall guard from last night trailing after us. We march to face the king, and whatever mood he'll be in after last night.

At least they won't find the folded piece of paper detailing the possible locations of the Estrella. I snuck it down my dress in case Atoc demanded all rooms searched.

But they'd still find the sword and dark clothes.

My hands suddenly hurt, and I glance down in surprise. I'd been clenching my fists, my nails digging half-moon imprints into my palm. Juan Carlos lifts a dark brow in my direction. "You seem like you're in a bad mood." I flex my hands. "I mean, worse than usual."

"Have you ever seen me in a good mood?"

"I don't think I've seen you smile—not even once," he says. "Watch out for the eggs."

I sidestep a pile of just-laid eggs, lying about as if it's normal to have food on the floor. His words unsettle me. Catalina would have charmed this guard by now and sucked his secrets from him with her almost guileless manner and pretty grin. "You give your smiles away far too easily."

"Is that why you don't care for my company?" he asks, completely serious.

His words startle me to a stop. "It's because you're Llacsan, you—"

Laughter flickers in his dark eyes, spreading to his lips, and then he throws back his head. His shoulders are shaking and he props himself against the wall to steady himself.

My mood sours like rancid lemon juice. "Is this all a game to you?"

Juan Carlos straightens from the stone wall. There's still a hint of a smile plaguing his lips. "Of course not," he says. "But that's what makes it fun."

That's when I feel it. A sharp prickle at the back of my neck, a sudden awareness that this boy isn't as lighthearted and foolish as he seems. I bet my life he knows everything that goes on inside the castillo. With his agreeable manners and quips, lazy smile and affable personality, he gives off an almost studied air of harmlessness that makes him unthreatening and approachable. People must share their gossip with him, allow him to take them into his confidence, and blabber all manner of secrets and weaknesses. His shrewdness is deep and unassuming and thoroughly unrecognizable.

Juan Carlos is a natural spy.

He takes my arm and nudges me along until we get to the bottom of the staircase. Rumi is waiting for us. There are dark bags under his eyes, and I remember how he spent last night: tending to the guards I'd wounded. No wonder he looks like he didn't get much sleep. At our approach, he sends me a cursory look that lasts mere seconds. Juan Carlos keeps pace behind us. We walk silently toward the throne room until Rumi reaches out and rests the back of his hand against my temple.

I flinch, but I don't move away from his touch. It feels rude, somehow. I catch the scent of burnt leaves and wet dirt hovering around him and wrinkle my nose.

"No fever," he says. "I was surprised to hear from Suyana that you were up and well today."

Clearing my throat, I pull away from him. The distance between us grows by a foot. I breathe easier with the extra space.

"What was all the commotion about last night?" I ask.

He pauses. "We had an intruder. Did you hear anything unusual?"

I make a face. "I think I heard a chicken fight."

"Did the noise wake you up?" Juan Carlos says from behind us. "Draw you out of the room, Condesa?" His tone is coaxing and suggestive.

"How could I have left?" I ask. "There's a guard stationed outside my door, right?"

"So you didn't want to discover the source of the noise? It happened in front of your bedroom door."

Rumi studies us, a slight frown marring his features. He looks from my face to the guard's, and the corners of his lips tighten.

"I stayed in bed," I insist, bristling. His interrogation needs to stop. I pin him with a stare, rifling through ways I might change the subject: "Why are you named Juan Carlos?"

He blinks, clearly surprised. "What?"

"That's a common Illustrian name."

"My mother named me," he explains. "An Illustrian."

Well. Isn't that interesting? He chooses to fight for Atoc despite his background. We could use someone like him on our side. He's standing shoulder to shoulder with the healer, and again I'm struck by the similarities. About the same height, dark wavy hair, bronze skin, and wide-set dark eyes. His face is less angular, rounder, like a hazelnut.

Rumi tugs my arm and forces me to resume walking. "We're going to be late."

"Did they catch the intruder?" I ask Juan Carlos.

Rumi bares his teeth at me. "That's none of your business, Condesa."

But Juan Carlos shakes his head as we approach the double doors. "El Lobo has been sneaking in and out of the castillo for a long time. He's clever, and he fights better than most. His skill with a huaraca is unrivaled."

His words sound like a compliment. I narrow my gaze and try to picture Juan Carlos dressed in black. Could *he* be the vigilante? He's certainly tall enough. Broad shouldered enough. And he knows how to use a sword.

Fascinating.

"It's only a matter of time before the army catches El Lobo," Rumi snaps. "The capitán already has a few leads. And the guards from last night are bound to remember something."

My mouth goes dry. Sentries swing the tall double doors open. Juan Carlos stays outside while Rumi leads me inside to my fate. Once again, guards walk me down the aisle to their waiting king. He's dressed in a red-and-gold short-sleeved tunic and dark trousers, his ornate headdress an array of warm hues that set off the richness of his copper skin. No Estrella.

He stares into my eyes, his face cold and haughty.

Reflecting on last night, I think twice about being insolent. I have to survive. I'm no use to Catalina if I'm locked up or dead.

As much as I hate it, my behavior needs to be exemplary. But the flattering words catch at the back of my throat. The guards force me onto my knees.

"Condesa," he says with a sneer.

I lick my lips and swallow; my mouth feels full of cotton. "Your Radiance."

His fingers snap, his gold rings glinting. I'm brought to the seat on his left. When I sit, he takes ahold of my hand, threading his fingers through mine. My stomach churns, and I lean away from him. He smiles, clearly enjoying my discomfort. I think of Catalina and don't move my hand.

You have to be her, I remind myself. *You can't drop the mask, not ever.*

"Stand up, Capitán," Atoc snarls.

A tall man at the front of the aisle rises, a sword strapped to his side.

"What news?" Atoc asks, his voice a soft purr.

"Two of the guards are stable thanks to the healer's efforts last night," he says with a slight wobble. "We'll begin questioning today. I'm sure one of the intruders was the masked vigilante, Shining One; the other was dressed in the same manner. It could be a brother, perhaps."

My hand starts to sweat in Atoc's grasp. I pray to Luna he won't notice.

"How did they get in?"

"We're looking into all possibilities," the capitán says. "A thorough search of the grounds and gates don't show a forced entry."

The priest steps from the pillar's shadow. "Interesting. The intruder could have been let inside by someone." Then he pierces me with a pointed look, his dark eyes glittering. My body tenses.

"It's possible," the capitán agrees. "Or the intruder was already inside the castillo."

Sharp whispering and nervous glances are exchanged among members of court. Atoc releases my hand. "And the condesa's whereabouts?"

I focus all my attention on the capitán. *Don't show them anything.*

"In her room," he says. "With a guard stationed outside."

"I want more guards on every floor," Atoc says, his voice drenched in disappointment. He would have loved to catch me in the wrong, I'm sure. "Patrolling the grounds and halls."

The capitán bows his head. "As you declare, Radiant One."

"Tell me what's been done about the Illustrians crowding La Ciudad," Atoc says, and this time I can't keep myself from flinching. "Have they been arrested?"

The capitán nods. "The ones we can catch, but dozens more sneak into our city every day. It's my suspicion that there are some households offering them places to stay."

"No one would dare," Atoc says. "Where are you keeping the felons?"

My fingers are slick with sweat at this point. Catalina hasn't regained control over our people and is still letting them put themselves in danger. What in Luna's name is she doing? If she can't oversee and manage the Illustrians, how will she reign as queen over Inkasisa?

She can't.

The treasonous thought echoes in my head. I want to drown

out the words, but they're too insistent. Catalina is our only option, the rightful heir, and a whole world better than Atoc. She will simply have to learn, that's all. Desperation can make a great teacher. But my unease remains, no matter what I tell myself.

"They're kept in the city jail, Your Radiance," he says. "Though we're nearly at capacity. Will the dungeons house them?"

Atoc waves his hand benevolently. "If there is room. You may sit, Capitán." He calls out to the guards standing by the double doors. "Bring forth the prisoners."

I straighten. What prisoners? Illustrian prisoners? I grip the gold armrest. The door opens, and two Llacsans in chains are brought forward. They wear leather sandals, and though smudged with dirt, their clothes fit well. The mark of a good seamstress.

The herald steps forward. "Behold! His Majesty, King Atoc, ruler of the High and Lowlands, devoted servant of Inti, enduring forever—"

"Enough!" Atoc exclaims, his voice ringing in the hall, high and metallic. "Move on to the charges. I don't want to look at their faces longer than I have to."

The priest steps forward. "Shining One, these men stand accused of dragging your enduring name through the mud. Their publication blackens your reputation and dares to question your decrees. I am your humble servant and will carry out your justice." He bows low.

"Do you deny these charges?" Atoc demands of the two men. They're silent.

"Answer His Majesty!" Sajra roars.

"We do not," one of the Llacsans says, rubbing his throat. He's standing slightly in front of the shorter Llacsan, as if wanting to protect him from Atoc. His dark eyes flicker to mine, and then back to the king.

It's a look that lasts only a moment, but the Llacsan's face is seared into my mind. The expression is a mixture of pride and fear. I lean forward, almost of my own accord. There's a haunted look in the Llacsan's eyes. My hand itches to comfort him. To offer some encouragement for his bravery.

"I am magnanimous," Atoc says softly. "Don't I hear the petitions of my people? Tell me what your complaints are."

It's a horrible trap. Everyone knows it, especially the Llacsans in chains. But the taller Llacsan steps forward, his eyes blazing. "Our newsletter describes the events and times of Inkasisa. It's a truthful account, and if you're unhappy with what's written, consider changing your methods."

Atoc's body is coiled tight, like an anaconda waiting for the moment to strike. "Go on."

Stop talking, I want to shout. *Be silent, fool.* I don't want to hear his words, because I know, I *know*, Atoc's fury. I've seen it, and I'm afraid of it.

But I remember the overwhelming feeling of wanting to help Ana even as I knew it was futile. Despite the danger, my protest had burst from my lips, from my heart. Because words empowered by justice can never be silenced.

I sink back against the cool throne. This man will be heard, consequences be damned.

"Crime pollutes the streets of Inkasisa," the journalist says, "invited by the production of the koka leaf. Neighboring countries have sent their criminals, the worst of them, to buy, barter, and steal for the drug. Anyone with even the most modest of means is at risk for kidnapping and robbery. It's not safe for a grown man to walk the streets at night. Women are terrorized, assaulted, and murdered. But you won't stop the export or production of the koka leaf." The journalist's voice rises. "There will be a day when even you won't be safe from our neighbors."

The crowd shifts and murmurs, listening and protesting silently, folding their arms and lifting their chins. My heart sinks and sinks until I swear it's hit the floor. This man is doomed. Both of them are.

"The Llacsans planting the seed aren't paid well and most starve," the shorter Llacsan puts in. "But your family and their friends have become extraordinarily wealthy. They have the best homes, the best land. None of your promises have been kept—we are not safe, we are not equal, we are not free. We've exchanged one tyrant for another."

"Is that all?"

The journalist pales. "Is that not enough?"

There's a long silence. No one speaks. I stare at Atoc's profile, willing him to be reasonable.

"Both of you will be stripped of your properties," Atoc says coldly. "You are never to set ink to paper again. Take them away."

The guards yank at the Llacsans' arms, but the tall one speaks again. "Your people are starving. You are not the same king we fought for!"

"Silence!" Sajra growls.

"We're hungry. We—"

Atoc gestures at Sajra. "Cut out his tongue. I don't want to hear him speak again."

Acid rises within me. I turn away as the priest takes one of the guard's blades and approaches the Llacsan.

"Please! We have families to support! We only ask that you—"

The Llacsan lets out a smothered cry. The sound of the blade cutting off the tongue poisons the air. A gurgle follows, something splatters onto the floor. The man sobs, groaning as he tries to scream. The other Llacsan gasps, huffing air as he cries.

"Sajra," Atoc says calmly. "See that both can't ever write a word again."

The priest bows and turns to the Llacsans, his arms raised. I watch as their hands become pale, the blood leached from their fingers. Both pairs of hands blacken, then shrivel and curl into themselves as the Llacsans scream, fat tears leaking from the corners of their eyes. Sajra barks an order and the guards stride forward. With four quick slices, the useless hands are chopped off.

They fall onto the floor. *Thud, thud, thud, thud.* Dead and wasted things.

I stand up abruptly and scramble off the dais, loud exclamations following in my wake. I barely make it to one of the pots before I vomit. Through the haze of my nausea, I hear the king demand the Llacsans' arrests and imprisonment in the dungeon. The words barely register.

The door opens, and they're dragged down to the dungeon, moaning and crying as they go.

Clutching the clay rim, I steady my breathing. Someone takes away the pot, and I'm left on the floor, my ruffled skirt bunched around me.

A soft hand drops to my shoulder. Rumi. I can smell him. He lifts me up, and I wobble. His hand reaches around my shoulders. I feel his soft breath near my ear. The long line of his body presses against my side.

"Do not touch my betrothed," Atoc says, eyeing Rumi's arm.

Rumi tenses, and his hold on me tightens. And then he releases me. Cold air sweeps in where he stood. The strange smell on his clothes leaves with him. I suck in air.

"Come sit, Condesa."

I obey, trembling. The moment I sit, Atoc reaches for my hand again. This time I try to resist, but his fingers cling to mine. Blood stains the stone at our feet. The hands have been taken away.

I sit numbly through the rest of court. Every now and then Atoc's index finger traces my knuckles. A soft caress that threatens to send me back to one of the potted plants.

He's touching me to unbalance me. I'm sure if it.

Atoc orders more farmlands destroyed to make room for koka leaf crops. Then he organizes a committee to handle the preparations for Carnaval. It's to be the biggest festival yet. The loudest. The best parade to ever dance the streets of La Ciudad.

In short, it's going to be a spectacle. At the heart of the celebration, the royal wedding.

Mine.

Three seamstresses are brought before us to show off their potential designs for my wedding dress. Each one holds its own neutral color scheme and fair share of ruffles and flowery stitching. It's the embodiment of beauty for every Illustrian.

I'm strangely touched. It's clear they worked hard on the designs, and the effort impresses me. It isn't easy to create something out of nothing, and the fact that they'd chosen white doesn't escape my notice either.

One of the seamstresses hands the drawings to Atoc, who pores over each. He doesn't ask for my opinion. When he finishes, his lip curls. He tears up the sketches, and the women standing before us flinch.

"I want the dress and the suit to match," he says. "In the Llacsan style."

Madre de Luna. He really wants to eradicate all of our traditions, our way of life, our culture.

The seamstresses nod meekly and promise to deliver something by next court.

Atoc stands. We all follow suit. Court is over. I try to leave, but Atoc grasps my arm. "Enjoy the dress," he says. "And you need not bother giving me a wedding present. A son will suffice."

"A son?" I squawk. Nothing could have prepared me for the immediate terror that assaults me. Fear clutches my heart, and I push against it until I can find my anger. I hold on to it like a shield.

"The son you'll bear me," he says. "You'll do this for me, unlike my first wife."

His first wife. I know all about her. She was fifteen when Atoc took her as his bride. He was in his early thirties. Disgust roils inside me like a churning hot spring.

I jerk my arm away. "You won't touch me."

"For now," he concedes. Then he smiles and walks down the aisle, his procession following after him.

Later that night I'm finally alone in my room. Suyana has come and gone with dinner, and Juan Carlos is stationed outside my door. Sickness clings to my belly no matter how many cups of té de maté I drink. My pulse speeds up as visions of the Llacsans' withered, shrunken hands turn my insides upside down.

I take deep breaths, forcing myself to think of the mission. Of Catalina. Atoc can't be king, but I still remember my treasonous thought from earlier. Catalina cares too much about what people think of her; she's more interested in being their friend than their leader. At least currently, she isn't fit to rule. But she's still our best hope, and she's smart. With the right teacher, she'll learn to be an effective queen in time.

My gaze lands on the piles of bundled wool, and my shoulders relax. There's the answer. Weaving will calm me. I snap the covers back and scramble out of bed. After dragging the loom closer to the balcony doors, I gather the wool.

Each possible location for the Estrella has to be thoroughly searched.

The clouds break, and Luna shines her silver rays. Moonlight touches every corner of my room. I weave thread after thread, turning strands into art, turning art into a secret message. I only use keywords and pray to Luna it'll be enough. This time I keep the size of the tapestry manageable, depicting a colorful lizard.

After three hours, I finish. I stretch my sore back and stiff fingers.

The tapestry winks silver in the moonlight as I drape it over a chair. A slight movement makes me blink. I lean forward, and the lizard flicks his tail.

Madre de Luna. It *moved*. How is this possible? When I saw the bee's wing flutter, I thought I must have imagined it. But this—this *thing*—looks as if it's getting ready to jump off my tapestry. His legs are bent, and it stares at the edge.

"Luna," I murmur. "What is this?"

It flicks its tail again and inches a half step forward, bumping into the message part of the tapestry. "Oh Cielos. You're really moving. Wait . . . just stay there, why don't you? You're really scaring me."

It comes as no surprise that the thing ignores me. The lizard takes a step backward, its tail skimming the tapestry's edge. My breath catches in my throat. Is it trying to get off the tapestry? Can it *do* that? It takes another step, then another, until it reaches the last row—*and then it leaps.*

I jump back as it skirts underneath my bed. Now what? My heart slams as I slowly drop to my knees. I lift the blanket and squint into the dark. A pair of silvery eyes gazes back at me. I swallow a scream.

"Come here." I reach out to the lizard, praying to Luna it won't bite off my finger. "I won't hurt you."

It moves toward me and takes a tentative step into my open palm. As I stand, the lizard's tail curls around my hand.

"Incredible," I say breathlessly. "You're . . . alive."

The lizard curls deeper into my palm, his woolly eyes shut. It's *sleeping*. In my hand. Madre de Luna! I bend closer, parting my lips in surprise. Every stitch remains the same. It's an animal— but not. A woven thing that breathes air and moves like a reptile. I made it and now—Wait. As I turn toward the tapestry, I let out a little laugh. There's a gaping lizard-shaped hole. An easy fix—I'll simply add in a new pattern.

Nothing like this has ever happened. I mean, I've been weaving stars and constellations all my life. And yes, they glimmer and shine like the night sky. But they never . . . moved.

My knees quake. What if this is part of my Illustrian magic? Part of Luna's gift? My moon thread breathes life into my creations. Did I do something differently? Then it hits me.

Color.

Beautiful, vibrant, messy, forbidden *color*.

Cielos! What else can I do? I ease the sleeping lizard onto my pillow. "I'll be right back. I just need to finish the tapestry."

My new pet doesn't stir and I smile. I go back to work and fill in the hole. As I weave, concern presses against me. How am I going to send this message? Atoc won't allow me to bestow yet another gift onto a merchant. I finish the tapestry and immediately start another, my fingers flying across the loom. I want to create more animals; I want to see if all my creatures can come to life. I'll use up every last scrap of wool in my room if I have to.

The breeze ruffles the curtain from the open balcony. Luna's light makes crisscross patterns on the floor. I take a deep breath and turn the wool into moon thread. The silver light from the thread makes me squint. I ease the wool over and under the warped threads. A frog takes shape. I choose the poisonous breed—the one that scares me the most. One touch is all it takes for the venom to do its lethal work. But this frog has my moon thread. It's a friend.

The moment the frog has all four legs, it leaps off the tapestry. Laughing, I jump to my feet as frog and lizard circle each other warily. And suddenly they're running around each other as if playing a game only they understand.

My fingers itch to create more and more. I'm breathless and happy and I forget the Llacsans, forget about the Estrella. It's the happiest I've been in a long, long time.

Two hours later an anaconda curls around my feet, a sloth falls asleep on the foot of my bed, three little ants rest happily on my pillow, and a llama nibbles the corner of my bedspread. They all have the moon thread somewhere on their bodies, on ears and paws, a leg or a tail. The sloth and llama slowly stretch, the wool lengthening until they become regular-sized creatures. I've never seen this kind of moon magic before. What a gift from Luna. And they're for me. Not for the condesa, and certainly not for Atoc.

Me. I love them.

Stretching, I glance down at my nearly empty basket. I have enough supply for one more message to Catalina. I want to ask her about the discontented Illustrians roaming the streets of La Ciudad. I want to know if she has a plan, or if she's at least thinking about a solution.

But the question remains: How will I get the messages out of the keep? I throw a disgruntled look over to the tapestry I'd woven earlier and rub my brow in frustration. Part of me wishes I could transform into a bird and just fly out—

Madre de Luna.

I scoop up more wool, turn it into moon thread, and get to work. The head of a parrot appears beneath my fingers. On the body of the bird, I weave my message about the possible locations for the Estrella. Finally I add its claws and wings.

I want the bird to fly to the fortress and deliver my message. The parrot's wings twitch. I gasp in delight, stumbling to my feet and knocking over the stool. "Come on," I whisper. "Show me what you can do."

The bird peels off the tapestry and hops to my arm.

"Can you fly?" I ask the parrot. It turns a baleful eye in my direction. A smile tugs at the corner of my lips. This one has personality. "Can you understand me?"

The parrot flutters its wings as it grows to full size. Its claws dig into my skin. Spreading its wings, it soars away from me, and I whirl around on the stool, following the bird's movement. It flies close to the balcony.

My heart races as I fling open the doors and drop to my knees. Moonlight covers me from head to foot. The bird nips lightly at my skin.

"Luna," I say breathlessly, clenching my eyes. I need her help. Can she light a path to the castillo for the bird so it won't get lost?

I wait for a sign. And wait some more.

Luna reveals herself to us all the time. In small ways, in big ways. She pushes the constellations into new positions to communicate with us. Her moonlight revives and heals, and she speaks to those devoted to her. Her magic blesses us with extraordinary gifts.

I open my eyes and look at the parrot, then motion toward the night sky. Urging it onward as I cling to the hope that it will fly to the Illustrian fortress.

"Don't let me down, bird," I say. "I'm counting on this getting to Catalina."

It nibbles at my finger affectionately and soars out and away. I stand on the balcony as if transfixed. The bird glides high into the inky night.

It flies in the direction of home.

The next afternoon, Juan Carlos takes me to the gardens. He seems to know when I need fresh air, and the realization irks me. We walk to my favorite bench and he leaves me there, watching carefully from under the shade of a toborochi tree. The stone is hot beneath my long skirt, but I ignore the press of its heat.

One of the castillo's side entrances opens and out comes the healer, carrying bottles of dried herbs and walking toward the army training grounds. He tips his head back, shutting his eyes, letting the sun warm his face, and something flutters within me. Vaguely uncomfortable. I almost call out to him, but I bite my lip.

It doesn't matter. He sees me and stops from across the garden. We stare at each other for a moment, and then his toes pivot in my direction. He lazily cuts through the garden, his eyes on mine until he's standing a foot away from the bench.

"You'll melt out here if you don't seek shade," he says. "Your face is turning red."

"Buenas tardes to you too." I motion toward the glass bottles in his hands. "What do you have there?"

"Dried lavender," he says absently. "Seriously, you should get out of the sun. You'll burn—"

"Stop worrying," I say.

Rumi looks over my shoulder and meets Juan Carlos's gaze. "You're supposed to be watching her."

"I *am* watching her."

"I meant—" Rumi breaks off with a quiet laugh, his face flushing.

Juan Carlos chuckles as if there's some joke between them. The healer gently places the bottles onto the cobblestone, the glass clinking against the hard rock, and sits next to me. We sit in silence for several long minutes. I'm enjoying the honey and mint scent too much to go back inside the stifling castillo.

My gaze lands on the watchtower, several stories high. Assuming my parrot reached the keep, Catalina has read my message by now, and she'll be able to check out the distant coordinates. Only I can search that tower.

My fingers curl into a fist. I'll do it tonight. I have the disguise.

"You haven't said a contrary or sarcastic thing in ten minutes," Rumi says suddenly. "Are you feeling ill?"

"Can't I be—I don't know—deep in thought?"

He exhales and some of his exasperation escapes with his breath. "It's hot. Come with me to the fountain."

Said fountain is in the middle of the garden courtyard. I glance at it and then back to him. "I'm comfortable where I am."

He stands and holds out his hand.

I roll my eyes but let myself be dragged toward the fountain. "You're so bossy."

"I swear to Inti," he says, letting go of my wrist. "You try the patience of a saint."

"You aren't a saint, Llacsan. No matter what your mother might have told you."

For some reason this makes him smile. Warmth spreads throughout my body as if someone has draped a cloak around my shoulders. We sit on the fountain's edge and dip our fingers into the water, hauled in from a lake nearby. He drips some of it onto his face and neck. I frown. Outside the castillo, everyone else has to pay for the water from small lakes and streams. In here, we have more than we need. Enough to fill fountains. I wonder if the Llacsan journalists wrote about *that* in their publication.

"What's that expression for?" he asks.

"Honestly?"

"I didn't know you could be."

My gaze narrows. He's teasing me. "Then I'll keep it to myself."

"No," he says softly. "Tell me."

Somewhere in our interactions, he's lost that constant look of contempt. Still impatient and annoyed with me from time to time, but it's no longer a visceral hatred. He's not hostile or watching me distrustfully as one would an enemy. We're different, but that only makes our conversation deeper. I don't mind that he challenges me. I wonder when exactly that happened. He's not what I expected, and part of me finds him interesting. Catalina says that people are like books. Some you want to read and enjoy; some you hate before you've even read a word.

Rumi has become a book I want to read.

"Why didn't the Llacsans in court protest the treatment and arrest of the journalists?" I ask.

His lips part in surprise. "Why does it matter?"

"I'm trying to understand . . . everything."

Rumi studies me. "His Majesty can make any decision he wants. It's his prerogative. Besides, they acted against the throne. It's treason. If His Radiance didn't check every offense, there'd be chaos and dissension."

I smother the spark of annoyance rising within me. His reply comes out like polished marble. Not one scratch, and too smooth. Is he really so besotted with his king that he can't see clearly? Especially after the Llacsans' torture?

Of course not. He's up to something.

"But he represents all of you," I say. "Llacsans. I would—"

"Technically speaking, His Majesty represents *everyone* in Inkasisa. Not just the Llacsan half." He frowns. "More than half, actually. If you count all of the different tribes in the Lowlands."

"Who aren't technically Llacsan," I point out.

"But native to Inkasisa," he challenges. "Peoples born and bred out of this land. Unlike you."

"I was born here."

"Yes," he agrees. "But instead of coming to learn and live with the natives, you worked against us. Taking over and changing everything."

Irritation shoots through me. "It was a long time ago—"

"You belong to the new Inkasisa," he continues as if I hadn't spoken. "A way of life we were never invited to share. A way of life that damaged us. One where we were forced to work beneath you, rather than alongside. Your queen created misery but had the nerve to call it peace. The king wants to take things back to the way they were—before the Illustrian plague."

I shift on the bench, angling away from him. A peculiar feeling of guilt washes over me. One that I try to quash. The treatment of the Llacsans disturbs me, but it isn't as if my life has been easy either. Because of them, the revolt, the king's earthquake, I lost my parents.

"What is it?" Rumi asks. "Let's have it out. Whatever you're thinking, I want to know. Otherwise . . ."

"Otherwise what?"

He shakes his head slightly, as if physically clearing his thoughts. "What I said obviously distressed you."

"Of course it does. I'm not a monster," I say. "It's just . . . Sometimes I feel as if you're trying to tell me my life is easy. And it's not. After the revolt, I had no one for months. I lived under a doorway. Poor and hungry."

"I've never assumed your life was easy, Condesa. What I'm saying is that it's been easier than *mine*. What was your life like before the revolt? Did you have a roof over your head? Did you ever go hungry? Were you allowed to go to the public school?"

I squirm. "Sí."

"Yes, what?" he presses.

"Yes, I had a home," I mutter. "I could go to school."

"I did not," he says. "*Everyone* was affected by the revolt, but for Llacsans, this was on *top* of living under a ruler who denied us institutional power. The only people who benefited under the former queen were the Illustrians. Growing up, you were free from oppression. I was not. This is why Inkasisa can never go back to the way it was before—for *four hundred years*."

His words sink in. He isn't saying that I haven't had to make sacrifices, but for centuries Llacsans suffered while Illustrians flourished. The revolt begins to make sense to me. Which only sends more questions whirring inside my head that I don't want to answer. The biggest being: What does this mean for Catalina, who *does* want to revert Inkasisa to the way things were?

What does it mean for me?

"Is that what you want, Condesa? To rule like your aunt?"

The truth nearly bursts from my lips. *I'm not the condesa.* I don't want to speak for her. I want to have this discussion as Ximena. But that's impossible. I need to turn the conversation away from me before I say something truly idiotic.

"Do you think that's what El Lobo wants?"

Rumi shrugs. "I think one thing is very clear: He's at odds with my king. That makes him an enemy to the throne."

Yes, that much is clear. But El Lobo has also gifted what he's stolen to the Llacsans. He definitely stands for something. Like the Llacsan journalists.

Rumi gets to his feet. "I have to tend to the guards who survived El Lobo's attack. The capitán wants them lucid for questioning."

"Have you learned anything?"

He glances down at me, looking faintly amused. "If I have, why would I share it with you?"

I keep my face neutral. I'd give anything to listen in on that conversation. I want some hint, some *warning* as to what will come next. Any one of those guards could have seen something.

"Let me take you back."

"No need." I gesture to the approaching Juan Carlos. "The infantry is here."

I throw Rumi a wry smile as I stand. The whole way to my

room, our conversation sits heavily in my heart. This isn't an act of my imagination—Rumi *has* been different. Less hostile. Now when he disagrees with me, his tone remains even. Aside from his unapologetic loyalty to his cousin, our exchange was almost pleasant. Enlightening, even.

He isn't so bad when it's just the two of us talking. Atoc brings out the worst in him. Bumbling, idiotic, and embarrassingly effusive in his praise for the usurper. He tries too hard to win Atoc's approval. Everyone knows it and his king takes advantage of it.

It's hard to watch. I like the person Rumi is without an audience.

Juan Carlos opens my bedroom door and waits for me to walk inside. But I stand transfixed, my attention on the lone figure standing at the end of the hallway. One of Sajra's attendants. The eggplant-colored robe covers every inch of his body, and a hood obscures the upper half of his face.

When he's sure I've spotted him, the man moves out of my line of sight.

"Condesa?" Juan Carlos asks. He jerks his chin toward the open door. "Your dinner will be up soon. It's your favorite."

His words surprise me. "How do you know what my favorite is?"

"Anything fried is your favorite."

He grins the moment a smile stretches across my face, but it fades as soon as I catch the priest's man still lurking at the corner. I walk into my room, shuddering. That had been deliberate. The priest wants me to know I'm under his watch. The air in my room feels thin, as if I stand miles high on a mountain cliff. My

Llacsan dress clenches around me, as if I'm caught in a fist. What does Sajra's threat mean?

I am someone he won't let go unnoticed.

Darkness descends and Luna's moonlight washes over me as I change into my disguise and I strap the sword to my belt. On a whim, I take my three little woolen ants and tuck them into my pocket. I'd been thinking of bringing some animals with me on my adventures in case they prove helpful. Better to start small. Then I throw open the balcony doors and look down.

Hello, old friend.

Sighing, I throw a leg over and face my room. The animals leap from the tapestries, their hiding places during the day, and come to watch my progress, creeping out onto the balcony as if they want to go with me. "Sorry, amigos," I mutter, looking over my shoulder as I turn around. "I'll be right back."

I pray to Luna I'll find the Estrella hidden in that damn tower.

Chanting reminders to myself to keep my knees loose, I drop to the empty room's balcony, and then climb over the rail and drop again before heading straight for the entrance of the watchtower.

A torch blazes near the tall iron entrance. Orange and yellow light bathes a yawning sentry standing next to it. The guard lazily casts an eye around the garden before leaning against the doors, his arms folded across his chest.

I reach for the small canvas bag I took from my room. It's filled with moondust. Choosing the right moment to use it will be tricky. I can't be seen using it, or else I'll draw suspicion. The guard has to look like he fell asleep while on duty.

Massive potted plants flank each side of the door. I tiptoe over and hide behind the sprawling greenery. Quickly, I blow the moondust in the sentry's direction. All it takes is one breath.

The sentry yawns again and I smile into the night. A palm frond tickles my cheek. Frogs croak their eerie song. In seconds the guard slumps to the ground.

I pull the door open and peek inside. Darkness shrouds the entry room. I bend over and then hook my hands through the guard's underarms and haul him inside before his snores draw the attention of other patrolling guards. It isn't easy, and even harder to do without cursing myself into a frenzy, but I manage the task, sweating the whole time.

Once inside, I wait for my eyes to adjust and at last catch sight of a dim archway. I take cautious steps toward it. My breath comes out in huffs—it's sweltering inside this circular room. I steadily climb each step. There are cracks in the stone, and rays of moonlight shimmer inside the tower like shafts of mercury.

When I reach the top, there's a single wooden door with a heavy cast-iron lock waiting for me. My breath catches as I palm the handle of my sword. What if the Estrella is hidden inside? I know, *I know*, that it won't be this easy, but my heart flutters as if it were a bird rustling within a cage, yearning for freedom.

But first, the lock. I dip my hand into my tunic pocket, pull out the three woolen ants, and place them onto the lock. "Do your worst."

They scramble into the hole and the lock falls to the stone floor with a heavy, ricocheting clang. I collect my bugs, stuff them back into my pocket, and push the door. It swings open, creaking loudly from the rusty hinges. I step inside, blinking in the dim room, and I'm brought up short by a sputtering candle propped on a three-legged stool that looks precariously off-balance.

Someone has sealed shut all the windows with heavy wooden planks. There's a narrow bed, a small dining table, a couch, and a writing table. A basket of multicolored alpaca wool sits at the foot of a large loom.

What is this?

A sound comes from behind me and something heavy hits the back of my head. I drop to my knees, my vision swimming. I can't stop myself from falling forward.

The world blinks to black.

When I wake, the first thing I feel is the cold stone under my shoulder blades. Then it's a dusty pillow that props my head off the floor. I sneeze. My mask is lying next to my fingertips. I blink, my gaze fuzzy, when a scorch of heat burns my arm. I wince and reach for the spot.

"Oh, damn it," someone says. "Sorry, so sorry. Now I've gone and dripped wax on you. I've already knocked you unconscious too. Lo siento."

My vision crystalizes. There's a girl hovering over me, long hair framing her face. She's frowning and poking me with her bare foot.

"Will you make it?" she demands. "Please don't make me scream for help. Talking to my brother is the *worst*, and I'd rather not if it can be helped. Why don't you try sitting up?"

"Stop doing that," I say, wriggling away from her when she tries to poke me again. I do sit up, feeling the back of my head and finding a bump the size of a small lima near my left ear. "What did you hit me with?"

She holds up a massive tome with hundreds of pages squeezed between the covers. "My brother's biography. It's practically a murder weapon."

My gaze narrows as I try to read the title. There's a painting of Atoc on the cover, but it looks nothing like him—it hardly does the size of his nostrils justice.

Then it hits me. I scramble to my feet. "You're his sister!"

"Of course." She chucks the book onto the cot and turns to face me, hands on her hips. "You must be my future sister-in-law. I'm terribly sorry for your bad luck."

I let out a startled laugh. "How do you know I'm the condesa?"

She merely shrugs, but there's a mischievous glint in her honey-colored eyes. The look sends a ripple of panic through me. What else does she know about me? I take a step forward, reaching for my sword, but I come up empty.

"I've hidden it."

I scowl at her. "How do you know who I am?"

She smiles, and I remain scowling as we examine each other. Princesa Tamaya doesn't resemble her brother. Which is to say that she's very beautiful. Glossy black hair, high cheekbones, and dark slanting eyebrows. My age, but more sophisticated and refined. She wears her threadbare cotton wrap as if it's the finest gown in all of Inkasisa. No wonder Rumi is in love with her.

I feel unaccountably murderous.

"Bienvenido a mi hogar," she says, sweeping her arms wide.

I'm forced to look at the room in a new light. It's dreary and dark, and utterly wrong for her. I don't know her at all, but anyone can see she thrives around people. Yet she's locked away from all the world. The princesa of Inkasisa. Why would Atoc keep her trapped up here?

She eyes me shrewdly. "Dismal, isn't it?"

"Regrettable."

"I don't have much in terms of refreshment," she says. "As you can see, I'm sometimes forgotten up here."

The only thing on the table—aside from the one candle—is a half-eaten bowl of cold, unflavored quinoa. I'd be bitter about that too. "You don't get any visitors? Not even your brother?"

Her words are said with a hint of bitterness. "Especially not him."

"Why are you locked up?" I ask. This is Atoc's *sister*.

She motions for me to have a seat.

"Hasn't your betrothed mentioned it?" Instead of sitting next to me, she paces the room. Despite her polished exterior, she's a ball of barely contained energy, even in the middle of the night. Stacks of books litter the stone floor. The princesa uses her foot to push them away in order to clear a path for her pacing. She has a weaver's needle tucked behind her ear. The pockets of her robe are stuffed with wool.

"No one mentions you," I say. "Well, no one except Rumi."

The princesa smiles. "I haven't spoken to him in ages. How is my old friend?"

"Well, I guess. Smelly."

A startled laugh escapes her. "Smelly? What do you mean?"

"I mean he really ought to clean his clothing. The whole court smells it. I even said something to him—"

"You talked to him about how he smells? What did he say?"

I shrug. "I forget. Something contrary. He's really bothersome."

"Bothersome," she echoes. "Interesting. I've always found him to be polite."

"That's because he's in love with you."

Princesa Tamaya throws her head back and laughs. "What an idea!"

I smile, half surprised by the easy nature of our conversation, and half amused by her denial of Rumi's feelings.

"Nobody mentions me? Not even my brother?"

I shake my head.

She throws a scowl my way. "So he still doesn't know what to do with me."

I open my mouth to respond but catch myself in time. Is it possible she doesn't know her fate? I'm certainly not going to tell her. I can only imagine how well that conversation would go. The princesa observes me. She smiles again, this time a grim sort of smile that endears her to me. Maybe because she's just as trapped as I am.

"He's changed," she says shortly. "My brother."

"How so?"

"He lost his childhood love in the revolt," she says. "It made him angry, bitter. All of his energy turned to governing Inkasisa. The throne became everything: his family, his love, his best friend. Soon all he could talk about was ensuring his legacy. He stopped talking *to* me and talked *at* me. My brother used to sneak into La Ciudad to buy me orange rinds dipped in dark chocolate. He'd tell me stories while we ate them under the shade of a toborochi tree. We haven't eaten them together in a long, long time."

"That doesn't sound like the man I know."

"Have you visited his museum yet?"

"What museum?"

"The one constructed in our village near the mountain. It cost thousands of notas to build. It has the bed we slept on when we were kids, all of his old clothing, his cacho playing set, painting after painting of him on a horse, on the throne, or with a slingshot." She lets out a mirthless little laugh. "It even has his old chamber pot."

My stomach churns. "That's disgusting. I haven't heard about—"

"It's not open to the public yet. I think he means to announce the grand opening during Carnaval."

I settle back into the cushions, my eyes following her as she paces up and down the length of the room. This girl is like a caged parrot. Desperate to flee and soar the skies.

"I don't particularly care to talk about your brother," I say. "Unless you're dying to."

"He makes for an atrocious topic of conversation." She sits down heavily on the couch. "I admit, I'm surprised to see you here. I haven't seen anyone—outside of my guards, I mean—in *weeks*. I've been wondering what you'd be like."

"How do you even know about me?"

"Don't be an idiot," she says with a laugh. "Just because I'm locked away doesn't mean I don't have access to the outside world. Spies planted in the castillo and throughout La Ciudad.

I also have many resourceful friends. I think you even met one of them the other night."

My mouth drops open. "El Lobo? He's your confidant?"

She winks at me. "We're getting away from the topic, I fear. Tell me about yourself."

I avert my gaze, buying time to consider what and how much to share. It's clear there's bad blood between the princesa and her brother. . . . Perhaps opening up to her might be useful. Another ally against Atoc, and there's her connection to El Lobo to consider too.

"What do you want to know?"

"Anything! What do you like to do? What are you afraid of?"

"That's very personal. And specific."

"Have mercy on me. I'm alone most of the time," she says coaxingly.

"I like to stab things. Heights really bother me. I need coffee every day, and I'm not that excited about getting married."

The words are out before I realize what I've said.

Everything I mentioned describes *me*—not Catalina. I forgot that I'm playing a role. But the princesa has a way about her that feels familiar, like walking into a house that is cozy and inviting. It makes me want to relax. Which is dangerous. I can't afford to slip up again in her presence.

"Considering the groom, it's not surprising," she says dryly. "And I love coffee too. Atoc refuses to give me some. I think he's hoping I'll sleep all day and not cause any trouble."

"*Do* you cause trouble?"

She looks at me intently. "When the occasion calls for it. How old were you when the revolt happened?'

"Eight," I say. "I only have one clear memory from that night."

Princesa Tamaya doesn't press me for details. Part of me wishes she would, and a larger part wonders why she asked the question at all. Now I want to ask her what *she* remembers from that night. If she remembers the ghosts. If she remembers how many Illustrians died at their hands. If their deaths made her sad . . . or if she'd celebrated with everyone else.

"Do you remember what your life was like when an Illustrian queen sat on the throne?" I ask.

If she's surprised by my question, she doesn't show it. She tilts her head back and shuts her eyes. "I wasn't allowed to go to school. My parents didn't have a lot of money. There were more of us back then, and lots of mouths to feed. I remember being hungry."

"You must have been pleased with the victory."

She lifts a dainty shoulder. "Was I? We lost my parents, and two brothers. I was the baby of the family and was sent away to live with an aunt. I don't think even Atoc celebrated that day."

I avert my gaze and trace a pattern on the pillow with my finger. I've never thought about what that day must have been like for the Llacsans. It's easier to focus on what we lost and what they gained. Beyond that, anything else makes the solid ground I'm standing on wobble. I want to remain standing . . . not topple over and forget where I came from.

"Are you going to tell me why you're here, Condesa?"

Her question was inevitable, but I haven't decided what to tell her. She seems to hold contempt for her brother, but that doesn't mean I can trust her. The vigilante is one of her loyal friends, and he's about as trustworthy as a convict's wink.

Princesa Tamaya leans forward, an impish gleam in her eye.

"Or perhaps I can *show* you?"

I blink.

She strides to the handsome wooden loom. Using her foot, she drags the stool over and delicately sits, her knees spread apart. She inhales deeply and pauses for a long moment, as if waiting for inspiration to strike. I drum my fingers on the cushion as the minutes drag. What is she waiting for? I'm wasting my time. The Estrella can't be hidden here. At last she seems to settle on an idea and then proceeds to warp the loom, readying for a new tapestry.

I get off the couch and stand behind her, peering over her shoulder. Her elegant fingers fly across the loom, from one end to the other, and within minutes the bottom of the tapestry is done. I've never seen anyone weave faster than I do, but she's working the loom as deftly as if it were part of her.

"Recognize her yet?" she murmurs.

I bend and peer closely at the tapestry. I gasp—*Madre de Luna.* The image is of a girl with long, curling hair, dark eyes and brows. In her hands, she's holding a shimmering gem encased in a bracelet.

It's *me* grasping the Estrella.

Princesa Tamaya slowly pivots on the stool and looks up at me with a curved smile. "Well, well, Condesa. You're more ambitious than I've given you credit for. Looking for the Estrella, are you? Wanting to have your revenge against Llacsans."

Which is *exactly* our plan.

I step away from her. "How—how—"

She smirks, getting to her feet. "I was *very* popular at parties. Useful bit of magic, isn't it? Of course, no one liked being the subject of one of my tapestries, but they certainly had a laugh when it was someone else."

She read my mind—my desires—through her weaving. "Explain how it works," I demand. "Thoroughly."

She arches an elegant brow, fiddling with her weaver's needle. "No, I don't think I will. Suffice it to say that what you're looking for isn't here."

"I gathered."

Princesa Tamaya taps her index finger against her chin. "I'd bet all of my good health you don't know what the Estrella actually is."

"Oh, I know," I say softly. "It's a weapon. Don't forget that I've seen *them*."

"And yet here you are, seeking the gem. Do you know who the ghosts are, Condesa?"

"No. What does it matter?"

"It matters because they're Llacsan. Miners who were forced by your people to empty our mountain of its silver for four hundred years." Her voice drops to a sorrowful whisper. "Men, women, and *children* died to satisfy the greed of the Illustrians wanting to line their pockets with the precious metal. It's their souls that are trapped inside the Estrella. It's our people you want to use, Condesa. Just like your ancestors before you."

The ground seems to vanish beneath my feet, my stomach plummeting as horror sinks its talons into me. No one told me. But what's worse, I never thought to ask about the gem's origins.

"The Estrella is actually the reason I'm in here," she says almost nonchalantly. "I tried to steal it."

My jaw drops. Whatever I was expecting, it absolutely wasn't that. "You tried to steal the Estrella? ¿Por qué?"

Princesa Tamaya opens her mouth, but immediately stops. She tilts her head, her gaze narrowing, as if listening intently to something. I don't hear anything, but that doesn't stop her from marching to one of the covered windows. She must have done this before, because the wooden plank gives easily, swinging upward, allowing her to peer into the night.

"I thought I heard a shout," she says. "Perhaps you ought to leave, Condesa."

"What? No. I'm not leaving until you tell me about the Estrella."

She looks over her shoulder at me. "I think you may be needed elsewhere. There are several prisoners in the dungeon who won't live past tomorrow."

She must be talking about the Llacsan journalists—the ones who faced Atoc and were forever maimed by the priest.

"And what?" I ask. "You want me to set them free?"

"Yes." She steps forward and places a light hand on my arm. "There are also Illustrians down there. Atoc's ordered their execution, Condesa."

I swallow and look away. I couldn't possibly risk saving them. If I were caught, my entire mission would be jeopardized. "How do you know about the captives?"

The realization comes at me swiftly, like an arrow cutting through the sky. One of her spies told her. Maybe even El Lobo himself. And she's asking me to help him. Because his mission is to save everyone and their mamá también—*except Ana*, I think sourly and unfairly. He's attempting a rescue.

"It's your choice," she says. "But either way, we're done for the night. Fue un placer, Condesa."

I'm thoroughly dismissed, but another question sits burning on my tongue. "Can't you escape too? I can manage the lock . . ."

For all her openness, there's something guarded about Princesa Tamaya, but looking at me now, her eyes wide and earnest, I feel her sincerity as if it were hands and arms I could touch. "That's very kind, and I appreciate it." Her voice drops to a determined whisper. "But I can't run away from this. I *will* not run away from my brother."

"But—"

She retrieves my sword from beneath her cot, hands me my mask, and gently pushes me toward the door. "Remember, it's your choice whether you help him or not. It'll do wonderful things for your character."

I wasn't aware my character needed improving, but I let her push me out the door and onto the dark spiral staircase. My woolen ants go back inside the lock, and as it clamps shut once more, I'm unable to keep myself from feeling like I'm making a colossal mistake in not helping her escape.

CAPÍTULO

diecisiete

By the time I reach the last step, I've made my decision. El Lobo couldn't rescue Ana, but he still fought to save the Illustrians captured with her. I couldn't save Sofía or Ana, but here's my chance to help. It's risky, but I can't let anyone else die if there's even a chance I can rescue them. Who knows what else might be in store for the prisoners trapped under the castillo? Would Atoc submit them to Sajra's ghoulish blood magic?

I creep through the gardens, ducking behind tall shrubbery in order to evade the patrolling guards. Running in a crouch, I sneak into the castillo using the side entrance. Thanks to Rumi, I have another way to the dungeons that doesn't involve tiptoeing through the main corridors. The dungeon entrance is on the other side of the castillo foyer, down a short hallway, and through an iron door that leads to a long flight of descending steps.

Walking on the balls of my feet, I cross the room, careful to look over my shoulder for any signs of movement. I reach the hallway and press myself against the wall, expecting to see another guard standing watch in front of the door.

I'm right about the guard, wrong about his standing watch. The sentry lies on the ground, slumped sideways. His leg holds the door open. Blood pools around his smashed-in skull.

El Lobo's doing, no doubt.

I carefully step over the body and pull the door open. I make it halfway down the stone steps before the scuffling reaches my ears. Shapes move in the flickering light of a single blazing torch. Two men fight, their grunts audible from where I hide in the semidarkness. The room is large, with rows of cells lining the far wall. I can't discern exactly who is in which cell, but I can just make out the shadowy shapes of two prisoners in each. At least two of them are the journalists. The other four prisoners must be the Illustrians who Princesa Tamaya spoke of.

There's a loud whistling noise—El Lobo fights the guard with a slingshot. A sharp crack splits the air. I slink farther into the dark corner by the stairs. The scents of blood and sweat fill my nostrils. The victor of the fight comes into view.

El Lobo.

Question after question crowds my mind: How does he know about the prisoners? Does he have a spy in the castillo? Madre de Luna, was he at court like me, watching their horrifying torture? My skin prickles as a new question pops into my head.

Does the vigilante work in the castillo?

Juan Carlos's face hovers at the forefront. He kept watch outside the hall's entrance during the sentencing of the Llacsan writers. He would have seen the prisoners dragged into court and back out, wounded and bleeding, and missing both hands.

I don't have more time to dwell on the man-in-black's identity. El Lobo snatches the key from the iron nail and opens one of the prison doors. In the lambent light, two captives stumble out of the cell. They are missing their hands—it's the Llacsan journalists. One of them sobs, loud hiccupping noises. Dried blood covers his chin. He's the one who lost his tongue.

El Lobo places a reassuring hand on the man's shoulder. "We have to hurry," he says in his low, accented rasp. "Stop your tears and help me get you out of here."

The shorter Llacsan helps his friend toward the stairs. The remaining prisoners scramble to the bars of their cells, arms outreached, waving frantically at the vigilante. I squint into the dim dark of the dungeon and recognize the white clothing of my people.

The vigilante is leaving them behind. He's only helping the Llacsans—a telling choice. Is he one of them? My fingers curl into a fist. He's a breath away from their salvation. He ought to save them, too.

One Illustrian wraps his fingers around the cell bars, gripping it until his knuckles are bone white. His tunic and pants are smeared in filth. *"Lobo,"* he whispers. *"Por favor."*

The man in black urges the journalists toward the stairs and glances over his shoulder to the remaining four prisoners. My throat goes dry. He deliberates for one long moment before yanking the key from the first cell and opening the other doors. El Lobo rushes inside and helps the Illustrians to their feet. They're all too thin, with jutting cheekbones and deep shadows under their eyes.

"Why do you help us, too?" one of them whispers as the vigilante scoops her up in his arms.

"I wouldn't wish your fate on anyone," he rasps. "Up the

stairs, the rest of you. Hurry."

They move, and I trail behind them, my heart hammering in my chest. Would I have done the same? Would I have helped the Llacsan prisoners, or just my own?

I'm afraid of the answer.

I hope that I would have.

El Lobo leads them to the same side entrance I entered the castillo through. He gently sets the woman on her feet. Pulling out his sword, he attempts to push open the door, but the sleeping guard blocks his path.

He shoves the man out of the way and motions for everyone to follow him. The group heads straight into the garden. We're right below my balcony. I tilt my head back and catch the silhouette of the woven anaconda. It starts to creep over the rail, but I let out a low whistle while frantically shaking my head. It hisses, but mercifully retreats.

El Lobo leads the prisoners farther into the garden. I follow—and freeze. Six robed figures emerge from behind the thick tree trunks of the toborochi trees. Each carries a long, thin blade. Sajra's spies. Six men against El Lobo and the weak prisoners.

I see red. In seconds I've drawn my sword. I don't stop to think. I charge at the closest spy within reach. He spins in time to block what would have been a direct hit, but I manage to pierce his side.

El Lobo whirls around too, and the prisoners huddle behind him. He takes a step forward, brandishing his sword.

"No, you idiot!" I shout. "Get them out of here!"

There are too many of them. If he joins the fight, he'll risk the prisoners' lives. He can't take on these men. But I can. My body hums in anticipation.

I launch a kick at my attacker's temple and drive my blade into his heart without a second thought. These men are loyal to Sajra, who maimed the journalists. He wanted to keep them silent, destroy their ability to write their protests. I cannot stand for that. Another spy rushes at me from behind. I vault sideways to avoid the thrust. Pivoting, I land a blow on the man's shoulder. He aims for my exposed side, and I barely have time to dodge the blade.

With a hoarse cry, I slash at his head, but he ducks in time. My blade shears off the tip of his hood. Throughout all of this, the vigilante hesitates.

"Get them out," I snap, swinging my sword around. "Or this will have been for nothing!"

He curses and herds the prisoners deeper into the garden. The five remaining men circle me. I swallow my fear and hold up my blade. The whirring of a slingshot slices through the night. A round shape hurtles past me and crashes into the stomach of one of the men. He grunts as the force of the hit lifts Sajra's spy off his feet and flings him backward.

I lunge toward the robed fighter directly in front of me and thrust my blade into his thigh. Steel rips through muscle. Blood gushes from the wound. He drops to one knee, gasping.

Now there are three.

My arm muscles burn. I back away as they advance. The spy in the middle attacks first. Our blades clash, and we're nose to nose. His hood covers his head—but the cold smile that bends his mouth is in plain view.

I blink in surprise. A low chuckle comes from behind me. The sound sends a chill down the length of my spine, and my throat constricts. My sword clatters onto the cobbled pathway.

I drop to my knees and look around for the priest. This is his blood magic.

The attacker at my side flips his blade around. The hilt comes toward my head. For the second time that night, I slump forward.

And then I see nothing at all.

I wake up in a foul-smelling room. All the windows are shut, preventing the cool night air from ridding the stench of metal. My cheek presses against a scratchy wool rug. Pain throbs from a spot just above my right ear. Gingerly, I push myself into a seated position.

Open bottles of blood line wooden shelves. Diagrams of human body parts hang on the walls, along with detailed paintings of various wild plants and herbs, squat toadstools, and a flower with shimmery silver petals labeled *Killasisa*.

And sitting in a plush velvet chair in the corner of the room is the priest. He coldly regards me. "Interesting wardrobe, *Condesa*."

My hand flies to my face. He took off my mask. Panic roars to life inside me, all senses on high alert. How could I have been so stupid? So careless? I look for my sword, but it must still be in the garden and I'm completely out of moondust. I have no defense against the murderous priest.

"Imagine my delight," he says with a brittle smile, "to find His Radiance's bride is in league with El Lobo. King Atoc will be very pleased."

Terror claws at my edges. I'm having a hard time seeing straight, which doesn't stop the swirl of panicked thoughts in my head. Once Atoc learns of what I've done, I'm as good as dead.

"Since you haven't brought me to the king, I imagine you want something. What is it?"

He produces that acid smile again. "You're not as dumb as you look. I want the name of El Lobo."

"I don't know it."

"Don't you."

It's not a question.

"No," I say slowly. "I don't."

I rise, my knees wobbling. The room spins, and I grimace at the blurry outline of the priest. He stands before me. I try to move around him, but he latches onto me with his bony fingers. A simple twist, and I break free. But he bends his head toward mine; his words, uttered low in a soft anaconda's hiss, turn me to stone: "Just who do you think His Radiance will believe, Condesa? If he even suspects you're working against him, what do you think he'll do? Engagement or not, he'll torture the information out of you. He'll launch a campaign against the Illustrian keep and burn it to the ground. Whatever respect my king believes he feels for you will be gone. Whatever you're planning will be over before it has begun. Is that what you want?"

I swallow, my throat thick and dry like paper. "I *don't* know his name," I whisper.

His nails dig into my arm, but I force myself to remain still. The priest must be playing a game of his own. Why else wouldn't he have turned me in already? I have to ensure it remains this way. I can't go back to a cell.

"Do you want the throne?" I ask.

He bares his teeth at me. "Do you know El Lobo's name? Tell me, or we go to His Radiance."

I hesitate. Perhaps I could give a fake name—

"Condesa." He eyes me shrewdly. "Don't even think about it."

"I don't know," I say. "We're not in league—I was trying to free the Illustrian prisoners, but he ended up saving all of them. When your men showed up, I didn't think. I acted. That's what happened and it's all I know about the vigilante."

"I don't believe you," he says. "And you're wasting my time. There are ways I can rip the truth from you."

Sajra lifts his hands and I back away, horrified, the image of the Llacsans' shriveled, chopped hands haunting my dreams. I sweep both of my own hands behind my back.

"No. No. Wait. I—"

Sajra's laugh skips down my spine. He advances slowly, folding the cuff of his right sleeve and then his left. Precise, terrifying movements. There's nowhere for me to go, and I can't scream without bringing in more of Atoc's men. He's going to level me to the ground. Turn me to dust, shriveled up and useless.

"His name," Sajra says.

"¡No lo sé!" I cry out. "I don't know. I swear it."

"Wrong answer."

His awful magic does its work: My blood rushes under my skin, moving at a brisk pace, spreading out of my chest. I drop to my knees. My heart is trying to pump blood and failing, and I feel every hard-earned thump.

"Stop," I whisper. "I don't know it. You'll gain nothing by killing me."

"I don't believe you," he rasps.

Blood leaches from my heart. My breath comes in impossibly quick spurts as my lungs fight to replenish the lost air, and a cool fuzziness starts to sap the feeling from my head. I'm going to die in this disgusting room, utterly useless to Catalina, to my people. "I don't know," I say hoarsely. "I don't know. I don't know."

My body is a weak and shuddering thing. Seconds from becoming lifeless. I can feel myself drifting closer toward the ground, unable to keep upright.

"All right, Condesa," Sajra says. "You've managed to convince me."

I inhale deeply, my vision swimming. The words don't register, but sweet life-giving blood courses back into my veins. It rushes into my heart, my lungs, wild and forceful. Air comes easily. My heart thumps painfully against my ribs.

"You bastard," I hiss.

Sajra takes a seat in a leather chair, his face pale. I remember how using Pacha magic tires out the Llacsans. Maybe I could use this as an advantage. "I can still siphon your blood."

I'm sure he *can*, despite how tired he looks. But he stopped for a reason. This I know for certain.

"Your general is dead," he says almost conversationally. "Her magic shrouding the Illustrian bridge has vanished—of course I knew about her gifts, Condesa. Don't look so surprised." He leans forward, gazing at me with dark eyes that walk the line between black and brown.

"What do you want?"

"I want El Lobo's name," he says. "You have until Carnaval to bring it to me."

215

"Or you'll do what?"

He doesn't have to voice his threat. I can read it in every line of his face. If I don't bring him El Lobo's name, he'll unleash his magic on all the Illustrians hiding in the keep.

"No one will be spared," he says. "The women—"

I flinch.

"The children—"

I shut my eyes.

"No one will survive."

Tears drip down my face as I imagine the piles of dried and shrunken bodies. I can't mask the horror that pools within my heart. He'll murder all of them.

"You have two weeks," he says, lifting his finger.

My throat constricts. I can't speak, can't *breathe*. He whirls away, and my throat clears. I clutch the rug, fingers digging into the crevices, sucking in air. I'm still catching my breath when he calls for his guards. They help me to my feet and drag me back to my room, where I drop onto the bed.

My dreams are the stuff of nightmares.

dieciocho

The earthquake starts after the ninth bell. I've buttered my marraqueta and taken one delicious bite into the chewy dough when the floor pitches beneath my bare feet.

I clutch the bread loaf and wait. The breakfast tray shakes on top of the dresser. The clay plate rattles against the wood. I gasp and drop to my knees, squeezing my eyes shut.

This is how my parents died. Buried under rubble.

I shove the thought away, gasping for air, and curl myself into a ball. The mirror tilts and smashes, shards exploding in every direction. The bedposts slam against the stone wall. The ground lurches and I scream.

At last, *at last*. The world stills. I can breathe again.

I scramble onto my knees and fling the door open. Shouts and cries erupt from somewhere in the castillo. My guards are gone, and I race down the hallways, heading to the railing that overlooks the entry room two stories below.

Atoc lets out a violent cry. People rush away as he paces, his arms swinging wide. He snatches a painting off the wall and hurls it to the other side of the room. The frame splits when it crashes against the stone wall.

"Find them!" he shouts. "I want them back. I want them to burn. Find El Lobo!"

The capitán issues orders. Servants rush to clean up the splintered painting. Atoc must have found out about the escaped prisoners. In his anger will he attack the Illustrian keep? Make random arrests? Maybe—

"Time for you to go," someone says in my ear.

I spin to find Juan Carlos at my elbow.

"What's happened?"

"Have a guess," he says, yanking me from the balcony. He pulls me along even though I've stopped resisting. The door to my room opens with a snap and he shoves me inside. "Do you need anything before I shut you in here? You're always hungry."

"Espera," I say. "I can't leave?"

"Better you stay out of sight."

"Fine. But it will cost you."

"Uh-huh. Payment in fried food acceptable?"

"Yuca frita," I say. "With the cilantro lime sauce I like. But tell them to add more jalapeño. They never add enough. And more wool."

Juan Carlos nods before closing the door behind him. Within a half hour he's delivered everything I've asked for, and more. There's a lime-and-jalapeño dipping sauce for the yuca, and fresh jugo de piña to wash all of it down. He sets the tray on the dresser, cracking a disarming smile. I don't like that my first response isn't to give him the cold shoulder.

"Why have you been so nice to me?"

"Because my mother raised me right?"

"We're enemies," I say. "Remember how your people overran the city and kicked us all out of our homes?" My gaze narrows. "Are you spying on me for your king?"

Juan Carlos laughs, even as another quake lurches under our feet. "If I were, do you think I'd tell you?"

For some reason El Lobo pops into my head. The way that the vigilante stands and speaks reminds me of this guard. Shoulders thrown back, chest squared. They're the same height. Both have dark eyes. Once again I imagine Juan Carlos dressed in all black.

"I don't know. Would you?" I press. I want to keep playing his game. If I win, it might lead me to the identity of El Lobo.

"Absolutely not," he says. "I'd keep you guessing the whole while. Do *you* think I'm spying on you?"

"Yes. Otherwise I can't understand why you'd be this nice to me. I'm your enemy," I reiterate. "I'm your job."

His hand is light on the cast-iron doorknob. "I suppose it's because you remind me of her."

"Who?" My voice comes out breathless. I'm sure he's going to say the princesa, given the connection between her and the vigilante.

"Mi mamá."

Oh. His mother. Not the princesa. "What about me reminds you of her?"

"She was fearless," he says quietly. "And her temper was truly frightening. Mamá reacted first and explained later. She worshiped the heavens and was a potter. Like you, she loved to create things with her hands."

I clear my throat. "I'm not fearless."

"She hid her fear much like you do. Buried beneath an untrusting exterior. My father made her laugh all the time."

"And you too, I bet." I pause. "What happened to her?"

"How do you know something happened?"

"The pitch in your voice. The past tense."

He ducks his head. "Right. She died in the revolt."

"I lost my parents too. In the revolt." I don't know what makes me say it. Maybe it's the earthquakes and how they've brought my parents to the forefront of my mind. Maybe it's because I want a friend. It's a truth I share with Catalina. She lost her parents too.

Another earthquake rumbles, softer now. Atoc's magic must be taking its toll. Juan Carlos is staring at me with a glimmer of speculation. "Is that all, Condesa?"

At my nod, he leaves me with my thoughts. So many families were ripped apart that day. Gone in agonizing hours, minutes, days. Another war will shred more families. More children will grow up speaking about their parents in past tense.

I'm tired of it.

I'm not allowed to leave the room for the rest of the day. The castillo stays silent and gloomy until the moon glides into view. Restless energy courses through my veins. The lizard and frog huddle on the chair, gazing forlornly at me. I sense they're aware of my disquiet.

I fold every stitch of clothing. Make and remake the bed until the sheets are perfectly flat. I'm too agitated to nap. Too irritated to think. I'd give anything for one of my daggers and a target. But somewhere my people are reuniting with their loved ones. That's something, at least.

The problem of El Lobo weighs heavily.

As darkness descends, my loom beckons. I sit and take a deep breath. My fingers fly across the loom as I weave a jaguar and a condor. *What other dangerous creature can I weave?* My mouth twists into a grim smile. I'm clearly in some mood. It doesn't occur to me to be afraid of the creatures. They creep and glide around the room, sniffing and hissing as they explore. They make friends with the other woven animals.

I have quite the menagerie in my room now. Deadly, slithering, and the creepy-crawly. My kind of people. When guards walk too close to my door, they drop to the ground, flat and unblinking, or if they're close enough, they slide under the bed. The frog returns into its own tapestry, flattening and weaving itself back in place.

When I'm done with the tapestry, I venture out onto the balcony and keep watch for . . . I don't know what. Guards come in and out of the castillo gates throughout the early evening. They examine every inch of the garden and the side entrance. I wait for a guard to come for me. Someone must have seen me dressed as El Lobo, fighting Sajra's men. The priest's threat hangs ominously over me like a black cloudy night without any stars.

I rest my chin in my palms as I contemplate the guards scrambling below, looking for signs of disturbance. Three of Atoc's men search the watchtower, and for a moment I wonder if Princesa Tamaya will betray me. I discard the thought. Somehow I know she won't.

I have to go back to the tower and get her to tell me about the Estrella. Returning tonight would be too risky, but there's something else I can do. Atoc's study might have useful information about the princesa and her confinement. Perhaps there's a record of her actions against the throne, or a list of her possible associates.

At last the castillo falls into a deep sleep. I change into the dark clothing and a new mask fashioned from my leftover scraps, grab my bag of moondust and my sword, and make my escape via the balcony. Once I'm inside the castillo's main halls, I creep along the corridors, careful to avoid clucking chickens and shattered pots. Dirt lies in piles amid shards of clay. One more hallway to go.

I half run, half tiptoe, until I reach the corner and hide behind a tall leafy plant. I spread its leaves and peer around the edge. Two guards are stationed in front of the king's study. Maybe thirty feet away. Lit torches offer a dim visual. I'll have little success in taking the guards by surprise.

I press myself as close to the pot and its abundant leaves as possible and pick up a fragment of pottery off the floor. I steady my breath, but no amount of careful breathing can calm my racing heart. I say a quick prayer to Luna as I throw the pottery down the hall, in the direction I came from.

It makes a resounding crash. Both guards come thundering past my hiding spot. I sprint to the wooden double doors on the balls of my feet and yank on the iron door handle—

It's locked.

No.

"I'm afraid you'll need a key," says a low voice with a distinct accent and gravel pitch from behind me. I jump about a foot and then spin, clutching my chest.

El Lobo.

A sharp breath eases out of me. I point to the keyhole. Plodding footsteps grow louder with every second. The guards are on their way back. The vigilante pulls out an iron key and unlocks the door. We scramble inside just as the guards' voices become audible.

I softly shut the door, and darkness smothers the room. Last time I brought in a torch, and the guards noticed. El Lobo lets out a husky chuckle. He smells like the outdoors, woodsy with a hint of mint. It's pleasant and familiar.

"You don't come prepared for much, do you?"

I bristle and march away from the vigilante, fumbling my way in the dark as my eyes adjust to the dim starlight.

"No candles or matches," he muses. "No way of getting inside—"

"*You* have the key," I say in an undertone.

"Stole the spare," he says, quieter. "No weapon."

"I'm armed. I have a sword."

"That I gave you."

My eyes finally pick up the dark outline of El Lobo.

"I was right," he murmurs. "I did hear you correctly the other night. You're a girl." He saunters to the wall and leans against it casually, his ankles crossed and his arms folded. "If you insist on pretending to be me, you need to disguise your voice better than that."

My ears pick up a new note in his tone—wariness, as if he's stumbled upon something he doesn't like. "Black blends in with the night," I point out. "So unless you own the color, I wouldn't flatter yourself."

"Disguise your voice," he says in a steely tone.

"Careful," I say. "You're starting to sound like you care about me."

His crack of laughter startles me. "Now, that's funny."

"Well, what are you doing here, then? Don't tell me it's coincidence."

"It's not," he says conversationally. "I followed you."

"You followed—*What?* For how long?"

"I saw you in the corridor and became quite curious." He pushes away from the wall and lazily strolls over to where I stand, leaving four feet between us. His casual grace doesn't fool me. I've seen the boy with a sword. He might look bored, but from experience, I know he's alert. And dangerous. "I think it's time we have a chat, little wolf."

"Really."

He holds up a gloved hand and begins ticking off each question with his fingers. "Why are you running around the castillo dressed as me? Why did you come back to the king's study? Why did you help me free the prisoners?"

With each question his voice rises, battering my carefully constructed walls. I think of the priest's threat and my resolve hardens. This is the moment. The start of earning his trust. "I want to help you."

"You don't know anything about me."

"Yes, I do. You steal from the king's coffers and his food supply, but you don't keep any of it for yourself. You have access to the castillo. Maybe someone lets you inside. It's clear you have allies everywhere. But it's not enough. You need help."

"Is that where you come in?" he asks. "You want to join in the fight against the king? You're willing to risk your life to end his rule? To put others before you? To bring about change even though you may never live to see the fruit of your labors?"

Each of his questions is supposed to rattle my determination. But he speaks of my life without knowing it. I try to settle my rapidly beating heart. If I'm going to get information from the masked man, he needs to trust me. And that can only happen one way. I have to be honest with him first.

To a certain degree.

"We're a lot more alike than you think, Lobo."

The vigilante considers me, his head tilted to the side. Then he walks forward until he's inches in front of me. He meets my gaze. Dark eyes. The color of coffee beans. His hands are steady as he reaches for the bottom of my mask. The movement is soft, like a butterfly's wing. His thumb grazes underneath my left ear and sends a shiver down my spine. His fingers curl underneath the fabric. My breath catches, and I flinch when he grips the fabric tighter, but I don't resist as he tugs the mask upward.

It glides over my lips, my cheeks, my eyes. It falls quietly between us and lands on my boots. I don't bother retrieving it. I can't tear my gaze away from El Lobo.

His shoulders tense as his hands drop. Only his eyes are visible behind his black mask. And they see everything.

My cheeks burn. "I take it you're not going to do the same?"

"Well, no," he says. "I'm not an idiot."

"You took mine off!"

"I didn't actually think you'd let me."

This is going to be harder than I thought. Talking to a spitting llama would be easier. "I told you I want to help you move against Atoc."

"Why?"

I glance away. It's hard lying to him. This man saved all of the prisoners locked in the dungeon when he didn't have to. "We want the same thing. You don't want him sitting on the throne any more than I do."

"And who do I want sitting there? You?"

I detect nothing from his reply. Not a single note that leans toward support or contempt. I grind my teeth in frustration. I never did find out if he's a Llacsan or Illustrian—he's saved both. Maybe he's mixed, like Juan Carlos. There are many working in the castillo and living in La Ciudad.

"We don't have to answer that question tonight," I say. "What we both want is Atoc's removal. Can we agree on that?"

He nods.

Finally. Progress.

"If you tell me your plans," I say, "I might be able to help you."

I'm waiting for him to bring up the princesa and her role in all of this. I want to know about the Estrella; I want to know why she'd steal it. There's so much uncertainty, and I'm sick of fumbling in the dark.

He laughs softly. "Do you think I'd reveal my secrets to any pretty maid who asks?"

"And do you think it was easy for me to let you take off my mask?"

His laughter vanishes. "I don't know. Was it?"

The boy speaks in riddles! Does that mean he's on to my

ruse? That he thinks I'm merely acting? If he can see through me, then I'm in trouble. Luna take me, what am I going to do? He's impossible to read, impossible to navigate. I turn away, my eyes resting on the map and its marked locations. I need his name. Hundreds of lives depend on it.

I jerk my chin toward the back wall and strive for a nonchalant tone. "What do you think the pins mean? Places to launch an attack?"

He stands next to me in front of the desk, and we stare at the map. Our shoulders graze. At his touch, an unaccustomed flutter passes through me, faint and unsettling. His height reminds me of Juan Carlos. Or Rumi.

He could be either of them.

El Lobo turns his head and peers at me. "They're all the places Atoc has hidden the Estrella. I've checked every one but have come up empty."

I blink, hardly daring to believe my ears. "What did you say?"

"I don't like repeating myself, Condesa."

A cold shudder slides down my spine, and my mouth feels like I've swallowed spoonfuls of dry dirt. It's the feeling that comes moments before I lose a fight. "You're saying these marked places are useless."

"If you visited any of them, you'd find nothing left. Atoc burns the area to the ground after he's used the spot. He's become paranoid and rotates the location of the Estrella every so often—I haven't been able to pinpoint how often it's on the move."

My shoulders slump. Even if my parrot has reached the Illustrian keep, the message doesn't contain any useful information. I clench my jaw to keep myself from muttering a curse.

I've failed Catalina. This entire time, I thought—I believed—the Estrella was within my grasp.

Maybe he's lying . . . But no. His tone holds no malice, or any hint of deceit. His words are direct and laid bare for me to decide what to think of them. My gut tells me he's being honest.

Even so, it'd be foolish to take him at his word. Despite what he may think, I'm not a complete idiot. I'll have to ask him a question I know the answer to and see how he responds.

"All right, Lobo. Who tried to steal the Estrella?"

He slowly shakes his head, amused. "Because I'm in such a good mood, I'll tell you, nosy. It was Princesa Tamaya. Her antics against her brother are a fairly new development."

And look where it got her. Served on a platter to their sun god. "How new?"

"The-week-before-you-arrived-in-the-castillo new."

"That's why she's locked away."

"She's locked up because her brother knows he can't control her."

The mystery surrounding Atoc's sister confounds me. It's clear she knows more about her brother than either of us. I need to speak with her again, if only to learn why she tried to steal the Estrella from Atoc in the first place. Maybe there's a pattern, a clue, something. It's clear she's working with El Lobo, and I need to somehow earn *both* of their trusts.

The fate of my people is in my hands and I won't leave it to chance. I have to find out his identity. But the thought flusters me. How can I betray someone who's shown again and again that their intentions are to help everyone in Inkasisa, Illustrians and Llacsans alike?

What kind of person am I to even consider it?

An impossible coil. But I have no choice, not when there are so many lives at stake. El Lobo is staring at me, waiting for my next move.

"We have to work together," I say. "Let me help you rid the throne of Atoc."

"Forget it, Condesa."

I flinch at his tone. "He killed my parents. Even if that were all, it'd be enough. But it's more than that. He promised to look after his people, and he hasn't. I've had to sit and watch him make deal after deal, weakening our economy, destroying our fields, and raising taxes so high that no one can afford them. People have to pay for *water*. A commodity that should be free for everyone. I'm alone in the castillo with just my wits, trying to stop this madman from destroying Inkasisa. I'm desperate, Lobo. That's why I let you take off my mask. If you're going to laugh at me again, to hell with you and your cheap tricks against the king. Let's see how far that will get you."

I break off, breathing hard. I've never said anything truer. If he doesn't believe me now, he never will.

El Lobo remains silent. Watching. Assessing.

Damn it. What am I going to tell Sajra now? I can't make something up. The castillo is full of his spies. He'll know if I'm lying.

I pick up my mask and walk toward the door. My hand slides into my pocket to grab a bundle of moondust I can use to drug the guards outside.

"Espera."

My heart lurches. I face El Lobo and he crosses the room.

His dark eyes glitter in the faint starlight. He bends his head. His breath makes the cloth near his mouth move in and out.

"Never," he says in a raspy voice, "turn your back on a wolf."

I lift my chin and meet his unflinching gaze. I'm not afraid of him, whatever he might think.

"I don't know if I can trust you," he says.

"You'll never know if you don't bend a little."

A suggestive curve appears near his cheek. He's considering my idea, I know he is, but then he straightens away from me, shaking his head. I swallow my disappointment.

El Lobo holds out a gloved hand. "I want whatever drug you're using."

Rude question. But I answer anyway. "I don't use drugs."

"But you do," he says, his voice quiet. "I want what's in your pockets."

Has he searched my room? "How did you know?"

"The guard you drugged at the side entrance of the castillo. That was you, wasn't it?"

Oh. He's been watching *very* closely.

As if on cue, he leans forward until his masked face is inches from mine. "That's right, Condesa. I know where you lay your head at night. I know what bench you prefer in the garden. I know that you like your food spicy and fried, and which hand you favor in a sword fight."

I stiffen. His hand is still stretched toward me, waiting for the moondust. I drop the small bag into his outstretched palm. "Careful, one breath and you'll be knocked out for hours."

He pours a small amount into his palm as we suck in air at the same time. The moondust glitters in the candlelight, and his head jerks as if in surprise.

I give him a nod of reassurance and El Lobo turns on his heel. Without so much as a farewell, he opens the door and blows the powder into the guards' wide-eyed faces. They crash to the ground seconds later. El Lobo leaves me standing in the middle of the office, both guards propping open the doors with their bodies.

Because *that* isn't suspicious. "Imbécil," I mutter.

With an exasperated sigh, I pull on my mask and bolt down the hallway, careful to keep my steps light. After coming to a full stop at a corner, I scan the area for guards. Three patrol the hallway, and one heads for my corner. A cacophony of noise comes from somewhere outside the castillo. Frantic whinnying from the stables. The guards unsheathe their swords and race for the stairs.

I follow, keeping a safe distance.

Thanks to the clamor outside, most of the guards go to investigate. If there even is anything to investigate. Something tells me I have El Lobo to thank for the easy return to my room.

After shutting the door behind me, I lean against it, half listening to the commotion. My conversation with El Lobo swims in my head. I go over everything I know: El Lobo is a Llacsan who works in the castillo. That's how he knows where I sleep at night and how I like my food. That, or he has people spying for him. One of the cooks in the kitchen?

El Lobo is tall and broad shouldered. He knows how to fight. So far, those traits line up with everything I know about Juan Carlos. The vigilante could certainly be him.

But.

There's Rumi. Also tall, except I don't know if he can handle a sword. Besides, the night El Lobo and I fought together in Atoc's office, he was busy tending to the wounded guards. He can't be El Lobo. Not unless he can be in two places at once. Plus everyone would smell him coming.

¿Quién es El Lobo?

My stomach clenches. My admiration for El Lobo has risen, sure and steady like the sun, ever since he tried to save Ana and the Illustrians. His actions help the people of Inkasisa. He wears a mask—like I do. I can't help but respect his courage and conviction. I wish I could do more, like he's actually able to. To have the freedom to come and go throughout La Ciudad and even the castillo, working toward the betterment of everyone in Inkasisa.

But who is this stranger to me? I can't save one person if it means the deaths of hundreds of other people. He doesn't have my loyalty. We don't have *years* of friendship behind us. He's working against Catalina. The man in black is my enemy—I shake my head—I don't believe that anymore. Not all Llacsans are my enemies. I carry so many truths inside me, I fear I'll burst. I circle back to the one I know best.

I won't let any more Illustrians die.

Even if it means betraying El Lobo.

CAPÍTULO

Diecinueve

Now that I've decided to move against El Lobo, I find myself restless, tossing and turning in the lumpy bed every few minutes. What will happen if Sajra manages to capture the vigilante? Atoc will make an example of him. Publicly. His victories are never a secret. I sit up in bed, the sheets twisted around my legs, and rub my face.

I take a deep breath, craving a chunk of the darkest chocolate in existence. I get out of bed and light every candle in the room—no sense in trying to sleep at this point—and pace. I march the length of the room, up and down, my animals at my heels, jumping through my legs, playfully nipping my ankles and seeming to enjoy the exercise as they follow me from one end to the other. I absentmindedly stroke the jaguar's woolen head and my hand vibrates as he purrs. The llama spits woolly balls at the anaconda, who lazily flicks them away with its tail.

I toss one idea after another. And then it hits. My hands smack my cheeks. Why didn't I see it earlier? The solution is so simple. Find the Estrella. With it, I wouldn't have to worry about the damned priest and his blood magic. I'd have the power of a thousand ghosts at my beck and call.

If I succeed in finding it, no one can touch me or my people.

I march outside, throwing the doors wide as Luna's light washes the world in silver. My gaze snags on the heavily guarded watchtower. I have to see the princesa. She's the last one to have seen the Estrella, but how will I get to her? Since the earthquakes, more guards patrol every hallway. Sentries are stationed at the main staircase. On top of that, the capitán has brought in a slew of watchdogs. It's a damn menagerie with all the chickens and cats and dogs roaming the castillo.

I have to find another way in.

I flop back onto the bed. The anaconda slithers around me and I use its body as a pillow. Absently, I caress its soft skin. The jaguar sleeps by the bed, its tail flickering. It nuzzles my leg with its nose. I tally my animals—all but one are accounted for.

I want to send another message to fix my last one. But the bird hasn't returned. What if it never made it to the fortress?

Thoughts about the condesa make my heart ache, warping and twisting like thread gone awry on the loom. If she were here with me, what would I say? Could I tell her about the Llacsan writers and how their punishment affected me? Could I admit that my feelings are changing? I have to acknowledge the problem, or I can't fix it. If it even requires fixing . . . *Ugh.*

Right now I only want to think how Catalina would've laughed about the wedding dress fiasco. She'd remind me there isn't going to be a wedding, and I'm not going to give the usurper a son. Wedding present indeed.

Wait a minute. *Wedding present.* My body thrums. I sit up, pushing away the pillow, and look at the loom. There's the

slightest chance *flattery* could work. I have to play it just right—
but I have nothing else. It can't hurt to try.

Luna's incandescent light already illuminates the room.
I breathe in the silver shimmer, allowing it to wash over me.
Moonlight eases the tension off my shoulders.

I gather all my available wool and sit in front of the loom. My
idea will take the rest of the night. The animals perk up as I start
to weave, and I smile to myself. Maybe they think I'm creating a
new friend for them. But this is much more important.

I pray the work will pay off.

Suyana finds me asleep on the floor next to the stool. She shakes
me awake, and I force my eyes open. Stupid sunlight streams into
the room, and I wince from the glare. Luna's light never glares.

"What time is it?" My voice comes out as scratchy as llama
wool.

"Did you forget you had a bed?" Suyana asks, setting down
the breakfast tray.

I sniff. The warm and nutty coffee aroma mingles in the air.
Is there anything better than the smell of coffee in the morning?
She's also brought fresh loaves of marraqueta, a clay pot filled
with whipped mantequilla, and a jar of blackberry mermelada.
Sitting up, I rub my eyes as my stomach roars to life.

"You'll get wrinkles," she says in a stern tone.

I look at her balefully.

She smiles, shrugging. "It's what my mother says."

With a start, I remember my animals. Madre de Luna. What

if Suyana saw them? I jump to my feet, startling her. "Sorry. I thought—"

"You're acting strange. Well, stranger than usual."

I laugh, and it sounds awkward even to me. "Lack of sleep, I think?"

A tail moves slightly at the corner of my vision. It sticks out from underneath the bed. I jerk my gaze back to Suyana and slowly angle my body, blocking the jaguar from view. They didn't have time to hide back in their tapestries.

My eyes land on the cape slung over the dresser. I wove throughout the night, until my fingers cramped and my eyelids were heavy. It's my best work. A blend of white wool and the leftover gold and red thread Juan Carlos brought me. Half Illustrian, half Llacsan. I wove a pattern of the mountain and earth under a twinkling night sky, Luna's light threaded in each star. Suyana follows my line of sight and gasps. She walks over and gingerly touches the cape.

"I can't believe you made this." She holds up the tapestry. "It's beautiful work for an—"

She breaks off.

I stand up and pour myself a cup of coffee. "For an Illustrian."

"For an Illustrian," she agrees. "The cape will suit you very well."

"It's not for me," I say, taking a sip. "It's for the king. A wedding present."

I must have said it with a straight enough face because she looks over and smiles. "He'll be pleased. When will you give him the cape?"

"That depends," I say slowly. "Is he still at breakfast?"

"They're setting the table right now." Her eyes widen.

"Absolutely not—you can't go! It's for family only and you've never been invited."

"Don't Llacsans still have that custom of saying you're welcome with a gift?"

I'd once given my nanny a drawing on her birthday. The next morning, I'd found a crown of flowers on the table in front of my chair. A gift given in thanks for my thoughtfulness. Like the merchant who'd sent a slab of dark chocolate as his thanks.

"It's good manners," Suyana explains. "Why do you ask?"

"It was something my nanny taught me," I say. "Will you help me look presentable? I'll wear whatever you want me to, and I won't protest. I won't even care how many ruffles and ribbons it has."

A begrudging smile tugs at her mouth, and I know I've won her over.

The family dines on the first floor, in the prettiest part of the castillo. I remembered eating in that same room when I came to court with my parents as a child. A long, raw-edged wooden dining table stands in the center of the room. Plenty of windows and tapestries decorate the stone walls. Two guards stand on either side of the double-arched entrance. Even from here, the sounds of utensils scraping dishes and muttered conversation reach my ears. Other than the guards, I haven't seen anyone on the first floor. As if everyone knows it's off-limits unless you have an invitation.

The meal is a private affair. I'm the intruder. But I have to present the cape to Atoc in front of other Llacsans to ensure he'll follow tradition and offer me what I want in return.

A visit with his locked-up sister.

I tuck the carefully folded cape under my arm and smooth my long skirt. Suyana dressed me in a tomato-red ensemble—she insisted it's my best color—layered with a floral stitched vest that reaches my knees. She swept my hair up into a careless twist, loose curls grazing my cheeks and neck.

It was as if Catalina had dressed me. The condesa was forever modifying my outfits, taking pains with my unruly hair, and dabbing rouge on my lips. Fixing me up to look more like her. When Suyana had finished, I reached over and embraced her, surprising us both. She could get into a lot of trouble for helping me, but she'd taken the risk anyway.

I clear my throat and clutch the cape tighter. I smooth my skirt one more time before walking toward the arched doorways. My hands are clammy, and the castillo suddenly feels too warm and stifling. One of the guards blinks at my approach, casting a confused look toward the other sentry. I swallow hard, but my feet keep moving.

Twenty of the king's relatives are seated around the long length of the table. Pitchers of jugo de lima and naranja are on either end, and in between are platters of fried huevos and papas fritas tossed in smoked salt and huacatay sauce, bowls of marraquetas and the achachairu fruit, and small plates of queso blanco. When Rumi looks up from his heaping plate, he chokes on his jugo de naranja and hastily puts down his glass, the orange liquid spilling over the rim.

Gradually everyone turns to face me as I hover by the entrance. Atoc is the last to notice, having been in the middle of telling a story. He's the most relaxed I've ever seen him, here in the company of his family. He's dressed casually in a loose black tunic, dirt-colored pants, and leather sandals. He looks friendly and approachable and it disarms me. I know how to handle my enemy. But this Atoc is someone I haven't encountered before.

Maybe I'm making a mistake.

Atoc's gaze cuts to mine and he stiffens. "¿Qué haces aquí?"

I lift my chin. "Buenos días, Your Majesty. I've finished your wedding present. This was the only place I knew I'd find you. But perhaps it's too much of an intrusion. I can come some other time, if you'd prefer."

I don't dare look at anyone else, and I make sure not to take another step forward. The silence stretches until he beckons me with a crooked index finger. Plastering a smile on my face, I step into the room. Atoc remains seated, which means no one else gets up. It's just me standing near the head of the table, everyone staring at me as if I'm a mosca in their huevos. I hand him the cape.

He unfolds it, and the moon thread shimmers from the sunlight streaming through the tall rectangular windows. Someone at the other end of the table gasps. I barely notice.

"A fine gift," he says gruffly. Then he stands and pulls the cape around his shoulders. A perfect fit. "You're a talented weaver, Condesa. It's a nice trait in a wife."

Wife. It's the exact response I'm looking for, but my mouth still goes dry. I manage a nod.

He lifts a section of the cape and inspects the moon thread. "Astonishing. Your skill might be better than my sister's."

My heart thumps wildly. This is my moment—

"Don't let her hear you say that," someone cracks from the table. "She'll have your head."

Atoc glares at the male relative who spoke. I wring my hands, trying to figure out how to steer the conversation back to my gift.

"She's lucky to have *her* head," Atoc growls. "Tamaya needs to be humbled. Look at this! Have you seen her do better?"

No one contradicts him. I peek at Rumi under my lashes. All this talk about my weaving must upset him. But instead of a scowl, he studies me with a speculative gleam in his dark eyes. A faint smile bends his full lips.

Atoc turns to face me. "Gracias. In the future, approach the high priest should you need to reach me."

He sits as my composure threatens to crack. My smile suddenly hurts too much. I turn away from the family, but then Rumi loudly says, "I'm curious to see what you'll give her in return, Shining One. Do you think you'll be able to give her something better?"

I whirl around.

Atoc blinks in surprise. "The return gift, sí, of course. What would you like, wife?"

Now the label makes me squirm, but I somehow manage not to retch. I deserve something deep fried and smothered in chocolate for my efforts. "What can I have?"

"She'll make a fine queen," someone says at my roguish tone.

Atoc leans back in his chair. "My breakfast is getting cold. Make your request, and I'll consider granting it."

I pretend to think about it. "I'd like to meet the princesa and test my skill as a weaver against hers." Hastily I add, "Your Shiningness."

Rumi snorts. I guess that isn't an official title. How am I supposed to know? I hear a new one every day. All eyes snap to their king. I wait, my breath caught at the back of my throat.

He shrugs and returns to his breakfast. "Granted. She needs a good put-down. You'll meet her today. Now leave us."

The relief nearly makes me light-headed. "Gracias, Your Majesty."

"Where did you get the wool?" he asks gruffly.

"Some of it I brought with me," I say. "The other—"

"I've been bringing it to her," Rumi interrupts smoothly. "I thought Your Majesty would be pleased she practiced weaving."

There's a slight downward pull at the corners of the king's mouth. "Thoughtful of you."

Instinct tells me to back away. Atoc's gaze travels from my face to my toes peeking out from underneath the ruffled skirt.

"*I'll* see that you always have wool, Condesa," he says sharply. "You're excused now."

I glance at Rumi. His face slides into that bored expression he wears when he knows he has an audience. He tosses back more of the jugo and doesn't look in my direction again. I leave the room, unsure of the moment I just witnessed. But what does that matter? I've found a way to the princesa. If I can have even a few moments of uninterrupted time with her, she could tell me more about the Estrella and where Atoc might have hidden it.

It's only when I think about how awkward it's going to be with all of us in the room that a glimmer of an idea forms in my head. My heart beats faster.

I know how to find the Estrella.

veinte

That afternoon we all climb up the tower, except for Rumi, who mutters something about attending to the sick in the infirmary. Maybe he can't stand the sight of seeing his beloved princesa locked up. A servant rushes to my room to get my loom and wool. Our steps echo as we climb them, the king at the head of the line.

The priest follows close on my heels. I feel his eyes on me. Clammy chills seep into my bones. He's a cold shadow, touching everything and everyone around him. I shudder, remembering our deal about the vigilante. When we make it to the hallway before Princesa Tamaya's room, the sentry standing outside gapes at us. He hastily opens the door.

Princesa Tamaya stands by her narrow cot. At the sight of us all clamoring inside, her expression betrays her surprise for only a moment. She squares her shoulders, and her face slides into a veiled façade. It's nicely done, and I can't help but feel proud of her, even though I don't know her at all.

"Hermana," Atoc says coldly.

"Hermano," Tamaya says in the exact same tone. "To what do I owe this *incredible* honor?"

Her brother holds out his hand for me. I step forward, my mask firmly in place. By that I mean, I've managed a smile. It hurts, but it's on my face.

"We are here because my bride would like to pit her weaving talents against yours," he says. The cape draped across his shoulders winks in the candlelight. "I told my betrothed that I'd like to witness this contest for myself."

"A contest," she says, glancing at me.

I widen my eyes slightly, tilting my head in the direction of the attendant who carries my loom. *Please catch on. Por favor.* My entire idea hinges on her magic. Without it, I won't know where to find the Estrella.

"Sí," she says when her gaze lands on the loom. "A *weaving* contest. How delightful. It's been a long time since you've watched me weave, hermano." A slight smile stretches her lips and her chin dips once in an imperceptible nod. Relief brushes over me as if my fears were swept aside like yesterday's dust.

Atoc doesn't bother with a reply; instead he settles himself on the dingy couch. "You may begin."

The looms are placed side by side, a low wooden stool before each. Our baskets are filled with wool in a riot of colors. Mine are in varying shades of banana-peel yellow and honey, hers in deep shades of blue and red wine. I sit and gather my skirt and ruffles away from the loom.

The princesa does the same.

Our gazes clash and then we start to work, threading the strands over and under from one end to the other. Behind us, the spectators chat in low murmurs. I ignore everyone, pairing colors and trying to get a sense of what I want to weave. Any message is out of the question—it isn't night yet, so I can't use moonlight.

But this contest isn't about me. It's about the princesa and what she can do. I pause and turn to look at her tapestry. Her nimble fingers work the thread, and already she has a third of it done.

I'm fast, but she's faster.

"Tell me, hermano," Princesa Tamaya says over her shoulder. "How do you like your new hiding place for the Estrella?"

The temperature in the room seems to drop. Sajra shoots a quick look toward his king. The cold clings around my edges and I shiver. Atoc jumps to his feet, snarling.

"What do you know about it?" he says.

Princesa Tamaya merely smiles. "Just making conversation. It's been a long time since we've really talked."

"We're not talking about the Estrella," Atoc says through stiff lips. "Continue your weaving or I'll—"

"You'll do what? Lock me away from my friends? Take away all of my possessions?" She nods at my dress—another one of hers, apparently—and her mouth turns downward in scorn. "You've already done your worst, hermano."

A calculating gleam appears in Atoc's black eyes. "Not yet I haven't. Shall I have my priest handle that sharp mouth?"

Sajra's hands inch upward, eager and ready to pounce.

For the first time, the princesa's composure falters. Her jaw clenches as she shakes her head. Atoc settles back down, satisfied like a purring cat. Sajra looks as if he's been deprived of his last meal.

The princesa snaps around in her stool and takes up the threads. Her fingers fly across the loom and a scene emerges. Delighted cries erupt. Without thinking, I stand and peer over her shoulder. At the top of her tapestry, intricately woven rain clouds pepper the sky. La Ciudad is buried under heavy rain, while the misty lavender mountain looms in the background. Off in the distance, Lago Yaku roils under the gusting winds.

The scene is so lifelike, I expect to see the woolly clouds float off the tapestry, thundering and dripping water. I've never seen anything like it. Since childhood, I've been stuffed with truths the same way one stuffs their bags for traveling: I'm the best weaver in all of Inkasisa; I'm a skilled leader and an efficient fighter. Illustrians are better at everything.

But they were all lying. Ana, my parents, Catalina. I'm not the best weaver; that title belongs to the princesa.

I'm standing behind the princesa and she leans into me. My gaze narrows on her work, searching each row. As she continues to weave across the tapestry, her pinky finger glides over something buried in Lago Yaku.

A gem capable of mass destruction. The conjuring of murderous spirits.

The Estrella.

My knees buckle, and I hastily sit back down on my stool. My own tapestry is only halfway done. I half-heartedly pick up the strands of wool as Atoc makes a loud disappointed sound. He shoots me a disgusted look. The message is clear.

I've embarrassed him. No better than his sister.

"Is this the best you can do?" he asks.

I gesture to the princesa's work. "There's no competing with that. She's the better weaver."

"Then why am I up here, wasting my time?"

The urge to batter him over the head with my loom is overwhelming. I inhale and force myself to calm my blood's fevered rioting. When I reply, the words come out slowly. "You brought yourself. I didn't invite you."

Someone in the room sniggers. It's a quiet sound, cut off a second later, as if the person who'd made it realized how dangerous it is to laugh at Atoc.

"Stay up here, the both of you," the fake king snarls, my cape swirling around his shoulders as he marches to the door. His next words come out like a sharp bark from a guard dog. "Nothing to eat or drink for them. I don't care if they starve."

The door rattles when he slams it shut. Guards remain stationed outside the door. I look at the princesa grimly. My plan worked, but now I'm stuck up here. I wouldn't put it past him to keep me up here until Carnaval.

"Do you think the wedding is off?" I whisper.

"Hardly," Tamaya says. "He'll cool down and send for you soon. He's impulsive, but not entirely stupid. You can't die before he marries you." She reaches for me. "Sorry, but we have to hug. Do you realize what you've done?"

I nod. "I'm not entirely stupid either."

She laughs and embraces me, slightly trembling. "What will you do with the information I've given you?"

It's because I like her that I respond with the truth: "I don't know."

"Condesa, I think it's time we talk." She gestures to the couch. "Have a seat."

Because I'm locked up with her, I don't have a choice. I'm not ready for this conversation; I don't have the answers to her questions. I can't walk off in a huff like her brother did. I sit down beside her and take a deep breath. My time in the castillo has muddied my thoughts, and my mask has never felt so vulnerable. At the slightest provocation, I'm sure it'll fall away, leaving me exposed. Defenseless. *Ximena.*

"Why do you think Atoc wants to marry you?"

My brows raise. It's not at all where I assumed she'd start. "Because of our water supply."

The princesa shakes her head. "It might be one reason, but it's not *the* reason. He's been forgetting our upbringing, our values. Disappearing as he secures more money, more power. I don't mean to offend you, but in choosing you, he's forsaking *us*. He'd rather indulge in a power play than choose someone good for Inkasisa.

"My brother wants legitimacy from his oppressors, for them to respect and fear him. In marrying you, he thinks he'll *own* you—and by default, all Illustrians. He wants power, but his greed—so like your Illustrian ancestors—is twisting him into something else."

"You don't mean to offend me?" I repeat. "That's a gracious statement coming from a Llacsan."

The princesa gazes at me with solemn dark eyes.

"I used to think that all Llacsans hated Illustrians," I say.

"If it were true," she asks quietly, "could you blame them?"

The Llacsans revolted because of our mistreatment. So whose fault is it really that my parents are dead? How many of *their* parents died as we neglected them for centuries?

"No," I say firmly. "I don't blame them."

The words are out in the open and I can't take them back. I chance a quick look in her direction. I expect to see a triumphant smile. But the princesa merely tilts her head, curious. She's analyzing me, trying to sift through what I really think. What I really want.

I wish I knew.

"That's quite a concession," she says. "Condesa."

My chest tightens. I'm not her. I'm not Catalina.

"Do you know the story of the jaguar?"

I blink. "What?"

"It's the perfect story to describe my brother—the jaguar king who had everything: a kingdom filled with loyal subjects. But every day he'd look to the sky and was jealous of the birds that could soar to the heavens. The jaguar king wanted the impossible."

I remember the story. "He wanted to fly."

She nods. "He wasn't happy with the gifts he'd been given. He wanted more."

"Maybe he thinks by marrying an Illustrian, he might have their support?"

The princesa arches a brow. "Making you queen won't win their support. He could have had that without marrying . . . had he made different choices."

The words hang in the air.

The princesa pulls more wool from her basket. "Will your reign look different than your aunt's? And her father's? And his father?" I shift on the couch. *What does she mean by asking me this?* It feels like a test. One that I'll fail because I have to answer as Catalina. She wouldn't change a thing. The condesa wants our old way of life back.

"What would you change?" I ask.

"I would make the system fair," she says. "We all want the same things: opportunities and means for everyone to earn their bread; freedom of self-expression without consequences; for all children, not just Illustrians, to attend school—"

"What world do you live in, princesa? That doesn't sound like Inkasisa."

Her eyes blaze. "But it can be. Look into your heart, Condesa. I know you have your own ambitions, your own dreams and wishes. My heart is no different than yours. Why is it so hard to believe that even enemies may want the same things?"

I do believe her. And the realization shakes me to my soul. If I lived in that reality, then my whole life was for what? What about my parents? What about Catalina? Wasn't all of this— risking everything—for her? To put the right person back on the throne?

The princesa's eyes widen. "Don't you think it's possible? With the right person, can't you see it?"

Ximena the decoy can. Inkasisa needs a leader who'd unite them. If Atoc would have ruled like his sister wanted, perhaps we'd come to see things their way. But now the idea of another Llacsan monarch will only enrage everyone back at the keep. Atoc behaved in the exact manner the Illustrians had expected.

Corrupt. Power hungry. Ruthless. Ignorant.

Tamaya would be a much better ruler than Catalina—who barely has a handle on the Illustrians at the keep. I know this the way I know a well-thrown dagger always finds its target.

But Catalina? Becoming queen would make things right for her family. It'd honor her parents' memory. She will never give that up. Not for all the silver in the mountain.

My breath catches. Or would she?

"What if people can't change?"

The princesa gives a little laugh. "You don't believe that. You only have to look at yourself to see that it's possible. People change. For better or for worse, like my brother, they always do."

Her words sink in, faintly uncomfortable. I can't ignore that parts of me have changed any more than I can stop a river's journey downstream.

"I'm going to trust you with a secret," Princesa Tamaya says, leaning toward me. "Something only a few people know. People loyal to me. You don't show much, but even I can see that you're coming to understand who we are. I'm not your enemy."

"I believe you."

Luna save me, but I really do.

"I don't want to find the Estrella to have power over Atoc." She takes a deep breath. "I want to destroy the Estrella."

My jaw drops. Destroy the most powerful weapon in Inkasisa?

"A power so evil shouldn't exist," she says. "No one ought to have it. Not Atoc, not you, not even me. I want you to think about my plan—don't discard it simply because it's not what you'd do. Really think about what's best for Inkasisa. I promise you, that's *all* I want."

Her sincerity, her passion for Inkasisa is as tangible as a warm blanket wrapped around my shoulders. Her words only confirm my instinct about her—I like the princesa. I didn't expect to, but I do. In another life, we might have been friends.

The thought wars with my sense of loyalty and duty. It fights against the love I have for Catalina and Ana, and my dead parents. I don't want to be a decoy anymore. I want the luxury of having my own thoughts and opinions govern my decisions.

"If you decide it's the best way forward, I need you to find El Lobo and tell him where the Estrella is hidden. He'll destroy it."

"Are you sure he's trustworthy?"

Her eyes flash. "Condesa, he's made more sacrifices for Inkasisa than anyone I know. I trust him with my life."

"Why don't you tell him yourself?"

She shakes her head. "Atoc has more guards posted—it's too risky for him to sneak in like before. He can never be caught. Too much depends on him."

But I don't trust the vigilante, and I'm about to say so when the door snaps open. It's Juan Carlos and another one of my guards, come to fetch me. "His Majesty wants you back in your own room, Condesa. Sorry to spoil the party."

His eyes flicker to Princesa Tamaya and then quickly away, as if he's been scorched. We both stand and the princesa walks me to the door. "Remember what I said."

I nod. For some reason I have the strangest feeling that this will be the last time I'll see her alive. She gives a determined air, as if nothing will stop her from succeeding. I admire her for it. I know what it's like to yearn for a win.

It's realizing that I want to let her that stops me cold.

Dinner is waiting for me when I get to my room, but not even the sight of crispy pan-fried papas and the garlic-rubbed sirloin roast tempts me to take a bite. Princesa Tamaya wants to destroy the Estrella. I want to reject the idea outright. Having that kind of power offers what can't be bought: control.

But it never occurred to me that we could win the war against Atoc without fighting a bloody battle. It never occurred to me that we could get to the other side with our consciences unblemished and families intact. Unleashing the Estrella on Atoc and his army, his court, his followers makes us no better than him. Does the princesa have a point?

And now that I know the Estrella's location, what am I going to do about it? It won't take but an evening to weave the information and send it to the condesa. But that idea doesn't sit well—for a reason I'm afraid to think about.

Suyana comes to collect the dirty dishes. She takes one look at the plate and frowns. "You didn't eat all of your food. Don't tell me you're sick again?"

I pull off my socks. "I think I'm just nervous. Don't call for the healer. It's only worry and stress."

She nods as she wipes down the dresser. I expect her to pry, but all she says is: "A bath will help."

Once again, she surprises me. Instead of questions, she offers comfort. I appreciate the gesture, even if the bathwater usually arrives cold. When I say so, Suyana only smiles and carries out the tray. Later there's a knock and the water is delivered. My fingers nearly turn to ice when I touch it. The water might have come from the snowcapped mountain.

Then Suyana is at my elbow. "How hot do you like it?"

"Caliente," I say. "Thank you, though."

She smiles again and dips both hands into the water. Nothing happens. Her hands are submerged but not a single bubble appears.

"It's all right—"

"Now touch it," she says, her voice shaking a little. "See if it's better."

Carefully, I dip my index finger into the tub. I pull away with a sharp hiss. "It's hot!" Her face wears a pronounced grimace. "Suyana, I—Suyana? Are you all right? You look a little pale. Do you need to sit?"

She sinks onto the bed. "Sorry, it makes me weary."

"What does? Your magic?" I ask. "Do you always feel that way?"

She nods and points at the little bundle she'd brought with her. Inside is a towel and a bar of soap. "You should enjoy the bath while it lasts. I won't be able to heat it a second time."

I hold the bar up to my nose. Eucalyptus. I peel off my clothes and climb in, moaning in delight. My first hot bath in four weeks. Divine. A twinge of guilt mars my enjoyment. The

Llacsans living in La Ciudad barely have any water.

"What did you think of the princesa?" Suyana asks.

I scrub my toes. "I liked her better than I thought I would."

"I think most like her better than the king."

I keep my expression neutral. "Do you?"

"It's hard not to like the princesa. She's vibrant and full of life. Consistently optimistic. She remembers everyone's names. And I always liked how she asked about my mother. I was sad the day King Atoc locked the princesa up. Sad, but not surprised." Suyana folds one of the towels. "She fought with the king over everything. His decisions, legislation. When she tried to talk him out of marrying you, he'd had enough, I think. It was the biggest fight they had, and it happened during court."

"I see," I say, accidentally dropping the soap. This cements what I thought: If she'd been queen instead of her brother, Inkasisa would have been all the better for it. "Did she have any friends in the castillo?"

"She has that way of making everyone feel like a friend," she says. "But she's particularly close to Rumi."

"I think he's in love with her."

She frowns. "You think? But he's so—"

"Smelly, I know!" I sit up in the tub. "What is that stench hovering around him like an angry swarm of bees?"

"He works in the infirmary," Suyana says, giggling. "All manner of herbs and mushrooms are stored there. We've all tried to tell him, but he doesn't seem to mind."

"Of course not," I mutter darkly. "Rumi's accustomed to it. He's so odd. And the way he acts during court! As if Atoc bled rainbows."

"King Atoc," she corrects. "Rumi's always doted on His Radiance. We're all used to it."

I lift an eyebrow.

"Mostly used to it," she admits. "Some days he's more ridiculous than others. Half the time I want to tell him to quit slouching."

Laughing, I sink back into the tub.

Suyana stands. "Is there anything else you need for the night?"

"This was plenty. Gracias."

"I hope whatever is bothering you leaves you alone enough for a good night's rest."

It's only after she leaves that I realize the extent of what just happened. I enjoyed a hot bath because of her. At the expense of her own energy, too.

I'd made a friend without trying. Without manipulating or forcing it into existence.

I stay awake until midnight, unable to keep thoughts of Catalina and her reign from jumbling inside my head. The lizard is curled up on its favorite spot on the pillow, nestling close to my head. Both the jaguar and condor rest by the balcony doors. The llama has somehow managed to squish himself into the wool basket. The frogs never seem to stay still, constantly hopping from the bed, to the chair, and onto the dresser.

I've never had a pet before. And these odd, colorful creatures belong to me.

They slowly drift to sleep, lulled by the whistling wind fluttering the curtains, the stray dogs barking in the night. The lizard climbs onto my chest as by candlelight I read the book Rumi lent me. It's not just a history of the Llacsans, but of the Illari and hundreds of other small tribes in the Lowlands. Inkasisa is home to thousands of indigenous people, and Illustrians came in four hundred years earlier and turned everything on its head.

Before us, they'd built fortresses and roads, had armies and used the stars to navigate.

The stars. We claimed the stars for our own.

I close the book, a sense of dread flooding my body. I can't think of a single recent building designed and built by any of the tribes. When's the last time they created the things they'd been famous for? We stifled, buried, and stomped on them as if they were hormigas.

I settle into the pillow, my eyelids heavy. I want to stay awake, but sleep comes unbidden and unwanted.

The next time I wake up, I'm not alone.

I sit up with a jerk. That prickly feeling of unease courses through my veins like blood.

"You're a light sleeper," says a familiar voice from the corner of the room.

My eyes settle on the chair and the dark bulk sitting in it. I blink, waiting impatiently for my eyes to adjust. "Obviously not if you were able to get in here without me detecting you."

"You know, I actually felt bad about waking you," he says, faintly amused. "Clearly my chivalry was misplaced."

"Who ever said you were chivalrous?"

"Now you're just being mean."

My eyes finally adjust to the dark. A quick scan of the room reveals that my animals are deep in hiding. Probably underneath the bed or in their tapestries. I squint at the corner of the room where my chair is propped against the wall. El Lobo's slouched, his long legs stretched in front of him, his ankles crossed. His hands are folded behind his head.

"Did you fall asleep in here?" I ask, suspicious.

"For a little while," he admits. The mask obscures the smile on his face, but I hear it anyway.

"Long day working? I forget—you tend the gardens, right?"

He laughs softly. "Nice try."

"Maybe you spent too much time near the stove?" I press.

"You wouldn't want me near a stove."

Again, I hear the smile in his voice, hovering in the air like a glittering star. Not a cook, then.

"Perhaps you had a hard day training?" I ask. "Right, *Juan Carlos*?"

El Lobo startles, as if I'd prodded him with a stick. He shakes his head, chuckling. "I'm afraid I don't know who that is."

My intuition spikes like a fever. He isn't telling me the truth. Maybe he isn't Juan Carlos? Or maybe he's just trying to throw me off? Maybe he's a gardener or a cook?

"Why are you here?"

"You visited the princesa today," he says, all traces of laughter gone. "I thought perhaps there might be a message."

I curl the sheet higher until it's tickling the bottom of my jaw. "How do you know? You weren't there."

Or were you, *Rumi*?

"The outcome of your competition spread throughout the castillo. It wouldn't surprise me if half of Inkasisa knows of your defeat. How does it feel to lose to a Llacsan?"

"Strangely, I don't mind." I don't need to be the best at weaving. It's enough to know how to make something beautiful.

Which is not the answer he's expecting. He blinks long and slow and it seems vaguely familiar. That minute tilt of his head. The color of his eyes. Every interaction shows me a glimpse of the boy who sometimes surfaces beneath his black mask, like how he made sure I had a sword to defend myself, or when he tried to help me when I fought the priest's men. If I support Princesa Tamaya, we may even become friends.

What a terrible friend I'd make. If I can't find the Estrella, I'll have to betray him.

"What do you think of her?"

I stand up and march to the dresser. The night air gives me goose bumps. As I pull a long-sleeved tunic over my head, I watch El Lobo. His gaze centers on my every move. I settle back onto the bed and snuggle under the sheets. "I like her," I say. "She's different from what I'd pictured."

"What did you picture?"

I make a face. "The female version of Atoc."

"She'd scratch your eyes out for that."

Yes, I'm sure she would. And I like that about her.

We sit in unguarded silence for a moment, and it feels companionable. Princesa Tamaya's words infiltrate my mind: Should I tell him the Estrella's location? He's here because I've had access and he's hoping there's been a new development. He's right: There is. But admitting it is a heavy decision. I need more information.

"Tell me something, Lobo," I say. "What would you do with the Estrella if you had it?"

He doesn't hesitate. "I'd destroy it."

Somehow I *knew* he'd say that. "Why?"

"The Estrella is a power that doesn't belong in the hands of mortal men—Illustrian, Llacsan, people of Tierra Baja, or even the mythical Illari hiding in the Yanu Jungle. *No one* should have it. Now it's your turn." He leans forward, elbows resting on his knees. "Why did you ask me that question?"

"Because the princesa wants to destroy it, and I wanted to know what you thought."

I've surprised him. He stands and paces the room—something I've seen the princesa do. "She's shared one of our secrets with you. ¿Por qué?"

"I think she wants to convince me she'd make the better queen."

"What do you think?"

I shrug. "No lo sé."

"How were you planning on removing Atoc from the throne?"

I shrug again. Just because I know of their plans doesn't mean I have to tell him everything. I may be confused, I may like Tamaya, but I'm not ready to betray Catalina.

"You were planning on using the Estrella," he says. "You've been searching for it this entire time. You'd do the same thing Atoc did all those years ago." He slices the air with his hand, his voice this side of angry. "We have a better plan, Condesa. After destroying the Estrella, we'll rip the throne out of Atoc's hands in a *bloodless* revolt and crown Princesa Tamaya queen in his place."

Bloodless revolt. Is such a thing possible? Guilt riddles me as I think about it—of what it would mean to turn my back on my upbringing, my duty. But I can't deny how tired I am of war, war, war.

"How are you going to lead a bloodless revolt with Princesa Tamaya locked up?"

His mask ripples as he smiles. "King Atoc has more enemies than friends, Condesa."

"Fine. Keep your secrets." I push away the sheet and climb out of bed again. "Here's one of mine: I know where the Estrella is. If you can convince me your plan is better, I'll consider telling you."

El Lobo sweeps me forcibly against him. Disbelief shoots through me as I let out a low yelp. He doubles my wrist behind my back with a sharp twist, and I wince from the pressure. "I can force you to tell me."

I slam my heel down on his foot and attempt to knee his groin, but he wrenches my wrist again and I gasp. The jaguar pokes its head out from underneath my bed and bares its teeth, silent and deadly. I shake my head, urging it to remain hidden. I don't want the vigilante to know all my secrets. I don't want him anywhere near my animals.

His whisper caresses my cheek. "You don't think I will?"

I tilt my head and glare up at him. My breath catches at the back of my throat. The narrow slits in his mask provide enough of a gap to make out his dark eyes. His stare betrays nothing— no flickers of guilt, or indecision. He's sure of what lines he'll cross. Harming me isn't one of them. "No."

The grip on my wrist eases somewhat, and I exhale. The man in black holds on to me, but it no longer hurts. Awareness creeps in. The hard feel of his arms around me. The incessant croaking of frogs in the garden. Luna's moonbeams crisscrossing the room. A breeze rustles the curtains. His black cotton shirt tickles my chin.

We're standing very close. The air between is charged with tension. El Lobo notices it at the same moment I do. He slowly drags his hand down the length of my arm, and then up again. A shiver dances along the length of my spine and a warm glow softens his gaze.

For the hundredth time, I wonder who he is. I've met the vigilante, I'm sure of it. Rumi or Juan Carlos. I know it in my bones. And I wonder if it's who I want him to be.

The thought comes unbidden and I'm not prepared to name what I feel. It's too new, too confusing. Too forbidden.

"Tell me where it is," he says hoarsely.

My voice comes out even. "No."

His attention shifts to my mouth. "You're a menace," he says softly.

His head tilts toward mine and the sudden flare of heat that rises between us startles me. I'm frozen, unsure. "What are you doing?" I whisper.

He pauses. His breath tickles my nose. "Damned if I know," he mutters. "All sense disappears when you're near."

I place a hand on his chest to stop his advance. Confusion clouds my thinking, which is exactly why I can't let him kiss me. If I don't know how I feel about the vigilante, kissing him would only conjure feelings that aren't supposed to exist. I don't know who he is and until I do, nothing can happen. I shake my head slightly. What am I thinking? Even if I do find out, it won't change anything. I have to betray him.

I *will* betray him.

"Why?" His voice is a whisper.

I search for a reason. Any of the hundred I have will do.

"I might recognize you."

He laughs. "Have you been kissing people?"

"No," I admit. "But it could happen."

Both hands drop to his sides. "Interesting. With who?"

This time I chuckle. The idea is laughable, and for a second I wonder if he's jealous. I've never made anyone jealous. It's a heady feeling and I'm suddenly out of my depth. Distracted from what I'm supposed to do. "That's not something you should be thinking about, Lobo. All you have to worry about is convincing me your plan is better than mine."

"I think I know a way to do that," he says in a brisk tone. All traces of warmth and laughter gone. "I'll come for you in three days. Get some rest, Condesa. You have dark circles under your eyes."

I gasp. Not because I don't think it's true, but because he has the gall to point it out. His mask ripples again, another smile. He slinks onto the balcony and jumps over the railing, as if three stories high is nothing but a single step between him and the ground. I walk onto the balcony and peer down. He's nowhere in sight.

Dawn approaches, the first victorious rays of sunlight streaking against the conquered night. I stare in the direction of the Illustrian keep. Catalina will still be sleeping this early in the day. With the wedding only days away, she's anticipating me to send her another message.

And I'm no closer to figuring out what I'm going to do.

More wool arrives with breakfast the next morning. It's rough to
the touch and has a hideous, stuffy smell, almost unusable. No
doubt Atoc's doing after my failure yesterday. I sit in the same
chair El Lobo occupied only hours earlier, and eye the yellow and
ocher strands miserably. The Estrella's location weighs heavily on
my heart.

"Not up to weaving today?" Suyana asks. "His attendant
told me the king was greatly pleased by his wedding gift. Why
don't you weave him something heavier? For winter, perhaps?"

"He says not to interrupt him anymore," I say, because I have
to say something. I could care less about Atoc and his demands.

I have the location of the Estrella—thanks to the magically
talented Princesa Tamaya. The wedding is *days* away. I could start
a tapestry tonight, send by pygmy-owl—or whatever bird tickles
my fancy—and Catalina could have everything she needs this
very night. I'd be handing her the throne on a platter, trussed up
like a heavily seasoned duck.

But weaving the message feels too final. It means a win for the Illustrians. It means Catalina on the throne. It means robbing the Llacsans of their voice. I'd be responsible.

My next exhale is long and unsteady. Suyana says something again, but her words sound warbled, as if she was trying to talk from underwater. "What was that?"

"Huevos y chorizo with locoto," Suyana repeats. "That's what's for breakfast. Eat something."

"I'm not hungry." She throws me a look of concern. I ignore it because there's no way I'm eating anything while my stomach is roiling like hot water in a kettle. "What's the plan for the day?"

"You have a dress fitting."

I make a face.

"Be kind to them," Suyana says quietly. "If His Majesty is displeased, they will lose their jobs."

She tries to put the breakfast tray on my lap, but I shift away. "Te comprendo."

"I don't think you'll be mean," she says, placing the food on the dresser. "I just thought it needed to be said."

"Because I'm an Illustrian?"

She frowns. "Because you're going to be his wife."

I have to force myself from shuddering. I finish with breakfast and hand her the tray. "I'll drown them with compliments."

Suyana smiles and takes the tray.

Three seamstresses prod me into a short-sleeved red-and-white dress. Patterns of golden thread are stitched onto the thick belt.

The full, ruffled skirt swishes around my ankles as I shift on my feet. Something in my pocket moves.

While the women busy themselves with cutting more fabric, I glance inside and almost cry out in surprise. My stupid lizard has snuck into my pocket. It would have been funny if there weren't three Llacsans hovering close by. I frown at the creature, urging him to be silent.

"Condesa, step over here," says one of the seamstresses.

I carefully climb onto the step that sits in front of a full-length mirror. I stare at the girl in the reflection. She's thinner than I remember, with pronounced cheekbones and collarbones, dark smudges under her eyes. The dress cinches at the waist. Catalina would approve.

I look unhappy, this side of gaunt, and no amount of pretty fabric can hide the panic curling around my edges like wisps of fog hovering over Lago Yaku. I don't recognize myself. Even my hands are soft from the lack of training. The muscles I'd worked so hard to sculpt. The mirror shows the person I resemble the most, and it's not me.

I look like Catalina.

Disappointment sucks me down into a quicksand of self-loathing. I'm only a copy of someone else. Just a decoy. I'm not really her. I'm not me. I don't know who I am or where I belong, if anywhere at all.

"You'll wear a woolen pom-pom necklace in blues and purples. I'm working on the headdress tonight. I'm sorry it's not ready for you to try on, but it'll be in the same colors as the poms."

"It's fine." I study the dress again, and I'm unable to stop the corners of my lips turning downward.

"Condesa, don't you like it?" one of the women asks, hesitant and careful.

"What's not to like?" I ask lightly. "It's beautiful."

The seamstress's shoulders sag with relief. "That's wonderful, because His Majesty—"

The door snaps open and Atoc storms inside with his many attendants. My mouth goes dry. I try to step down from the mirror, but he stops me by holding up his hand.

"Quédate." He loops around, slow like a condor hunting its prey. Goose bumps crawl across my skin. Atoc scowls as he studies the dress—every ruffle, every stitch. The impulse to run makes my feet twitch. I want to examine him in turn, see how he likes being regarded as a prized horse.

The women huddle off into the corner. For their sake, I force a smile.

"Isn't it lovely?" I ask.

He doesn't bother responding, but circles once more. He stops in front of me. "Lower the neckline," he says curtly.

I jerk my head down—the neckline is right under my chin. Exactly where I want it. "Absolutely not."

This time I get a foot down but Atoc grips my waist and hoists me back on the step. He glances at me with frank interest, heat in his gaze. "The sooner you learn who you answer to, the better your life will be. Stop fighting me."

"You may have everyone else bending to do your will, but I'm not some creature you can control."

His face turns to iron, hardening and immobile like the impenetrable wall of the Illustrian fortress. "Leave us."

The seamstresses scurry away without a look in my direction.

I want to call out, but I keep silent. This day was long coming. I knew that, at some point, he'd get me alone and his first move would be to put me thoroughly in my place.

My skin turns to ice, but I pull my shoulders back. I'm not going to let him scare me. I summon the fire I felt when I first arrived, before I'd lost Sofía and Ana. "I am the last royal in all of Inkasisa—"

A fist slams my belly. The hit is strong and fierce and for seconds I'm left in stunned silence. I topple off the stairs and end up on the floor, the stone scraping against the skin of my elbow. The lizard moves, its tiny claws scratching against the folds of my skirt, wanting to get out. I push my hand inside my pocket, forcing it still.

Atoc stares at me in fury. "I've told you, don't interrupt me."

I get to my feet, my knees buckling. We stare at each other for a long moment, my rage simmering, barely contained. I use it to lock away my terror until all that's left is my desire for justice.

"No one's ever told you," he said. "About my first wife."

An acid taste swells my tongue. I don't want to hear this. I don't want to know about his marriage to someone who was years younger than me. Long dead and all but forgotten.

"We were married for three years. She never gave me children. Do you know what I need in order to create a legacy, Condesa?"

I make my voice sound cold—colder than the snow gathering on top of our mountain. "Why ask the question if you know the answer?"

He leans forward. His hot breath brushes my cheek. There are deep lines at the corners of his eyes, carved into his skin from years of looking at the world in distrust. "I need children," he

269

says as if I hadn't spoken. "That's one of the things you're good for, isn't that right, Condesa?"

I know what my other uses are. Through marriage, he'll have control over my people and a steady water supply—thank Luna it'll never come to that. Not with my standing in his way as his fake bride. The scrape on my elbow is sticky with blood, stinging and raw. The lizard hisses, its long pink tongue sticking out of my pocket.

"Do you know how she died?" he asks.

"In childbirth."

"Is that true?" His tone is like a blade dragged against my skin. "Is that what you really think?"

"What—what are you saying?"

Atoc's stare holds. He reaches for the end of my braid and strokes the hair escaping the ribbon. "I'm saying she disappointed me. Be very careful, Condesa. I don't ever forget slights, and yours have been numerous. Embarrassing me in front of court. Insolent in front of my servants. I'm telling you: Watch yourself. Don't you want to live?"

I say nothing. He curls my braid around his hand, once, twice. He handles my hair like rope and he tugs, hard. I resist, and my knees buckle a second time. I'm struggling to remain upright. The part of my stomach where his fist slammed into me is sore.

"I'm not someone you can make a fool of," he continues. "I have sacrificed too much, have lost too much. I will have what I want, and I'll do anything to ensure my legacy." His dark eyes narrow. "We have that in common, I think."

Madre de Luna. For a second I can't breathe. He was right— here I was, a stand-in for the last royal in Inkasisa, willing to do whatever it took to guarantee an Illustrian victory. I'd risk marriage to my enemy, a future of my own—my *life* to make that happen.

Atoc's gaze drops to my bleeding elbow. He walks to the door and pokes his head out. There's soft murmuring as he talks to one of his guards.

"Tell the seamstresses to lower the neckline." He looks me over again, not missing a single detail, and adds in a gruff voice, "You look lovely."

Then he's gone. I sink onto the steps, my knees finally giving out completely, and examine my elbow. It's a scraped-up, bloody mess. I can't stop trembling, thinking of his plans for me. Thinking of his poor first wife. Thinking how it could have been Catalina in this room instead of me. My blood floods with panic. I lift shaking hands to my face, thankful I'm alone. To take off the mask. To let myself worry about my own skin.

The door opens, and Rumi walks in. He takes one look at me, sitting as I am, my wedding dress bunched around my legs, my arm close to my chest.

"Condesa." He squats in front of me, lightly touching the area around my wound. "I'll have to clean it. Come on—let's go to the infirmary."

He gently tugs me to my feet.

I gesture to the wedding dress. The fabric feels tight around my chest, as if I'm not getting enough air. "I have to get out of this."

He nods. "All right."

I blow out an exasperated breath when he spins around to give me privacy. "I can't get out of this dress by myself. Can you help me?"

Rumi faces me. There's a slightly dazed look on his face, but it's gone before I can comment on it. I turn around and look at him over my shoulder. "There's a row of buttons."

"Right." He swallows. "One second."

Then he crosses the room and peers up and down the hall, presumably looking for help. I've never seen him this uncomfortable before. Finally he returns to my side, wearing a resigned expression, as if he's about to endure the worst meal of his life.

He works swiftly, his fingers grazing my skin. "It's done."

After he's turned around again, his back toward me, I quickly step out of the dress and change into my striped skirt and tunic. I lightly touch his shoulder to let him know I'm ready. He tenses under my fingers and I hastily pull away.

I follow him out of the room, down the hall, and toward the east wing. "Did he hurt you anywhere else?"

"Yes," I say. "But it's fine. I'll have a bruise, but nothing is broken."

Rumi gives me a sidelong glance. "What set him off?"

Away from Atoc, my nerves begin to settle and I feel safer. "My general well-being, I think."

The corners of his lips kick up into a soft smile. We pass windows shaped into narrow slits. Outside is a closed-in courtyard, one I've seen but never visited. Llacsans are stomping koka stalks with their bare feet, turning the plant into a thick paste that'll then be smoked in tobacco pipes. The result is something toxic and highly addictive. I turn away from the sight.

"Atoc's personal stash," Rumi says with one squeeze of lemon juice in his voice.

I've stayed far, far away from the drug, but nearly everyone at court smokes their pipes daily, littering the halls and grand rooms in cloying smoke. I don't have to ask Rumi if he's ever tried it; his distaste for the drug radiates off him as we leave the stomping Llacsans.

"He's ruined our economy with the production," I say as we approach a long string of doors. Above one of them is a block of wood with a carving of plants.

"King Atoc was desperate," Rumi says. "I'm sure he thought it was a good idea at the time."

"Will you stop defending him, healer? Por favor. He's destroyed tens of thousands of farmlands for the koka plant. You can't convince me it was a good idea."

"Are you an expert in farming now?"

We stop in front of the infirmary. My hands are on my hips; his are folded across his chest. Rumi leans against the wooden frame, settling into the argument. I swear he's trying not to smile, as if sparring with me isn't annoying but . . . fun.

"Whether you believe me or not, His Majesty *did* have good intentions. The koka leaf grows well in poor soil and withstands the onslaught of pests and blight. It's lightweight and lasts a long time before rotting, which means it can travel long range across the mountains. It also sells for ten times more than, let's say, citrus. King Atoc needed a viable export to lend credibility to his name. Because of the koka leaf, we are just as wealthy as our neighbors to the east and west."

I hiss out a disgusted breath. How could he side with Atoc after what he just did to me?

"I don't care about his intention," I snap. "He's made addicts of his countrymen. With the majority of campesinos planting the koka leaf, food production has stalled. No more regular supply of rice, bananas, yuca, maize, or citrus. Food prices have soared. When's the last time you bought a loaf of bread? I can't believe you'd support this. I thought you had more sense!"

"Stop putting words in my mouth and head," he says. "I can speak *and* think for myself. Thanks."

"Wait, so you don't agree with Atoc?"

"King Atoc," he corrects me for maybe the hundredth time. "Of course not, idiot. My people have been using the koka leaf for centuries. In its pure form, I can create *forty* remedies. Chewing the leaf helps with the high altitude and provides energy for miners and farmers doing strenuous tasks. But because the koka leaf is so expensive, many Llacsans and Lowlanders can't afford a single stalk. I'm not saying I agree with his methods, but I understand why he took the easy path. That's *all* I'm saying."

"Oh." I clear my throat. "Sorry."

Rumi rolls his eyes and uses his shoulder to open the door to the infirmary. The first thing I notice is the smell. All manner of vegetation grows inside the room. Pots of basil and rosemary line the table next to clay bowls piled high with garlic cloves. Hanging from the stone ceiling are dried bundles of lavender and thyme.

The room smells a lot like Rumi's clothes. Well, a rotting version of them.

Afternoon sunlight streams in from the large rectangular windows, casting patterns on the floor. There are several empty cots in one corner, folded blankets neatly stacked on each. I recognize the intricate detailing in the geometric patterns and the depictions of parrots. Tamaya's work.

"It smells like you," I say.

An amused huff escapes his chest. "Thank you?"

I settle onto a wooden stool. It wobbles under my weight. Smoothing my long striped skirt, I study the rest of the hospital wing. Drawings of various herbs and plants hang on all four walls. One catches my eye—a tiny sketch, and though it doesn't shine like the other drawings, it's still the same flower as the one in the diagram hanging in Sajra's den.

"What's that flower?"

Rumi looks over his shoulder. "Killasisa. It's a legendary flower people have searched for throughout the years."

I'm about to ask him more, but he pulls out a clear bottle from one of the lower drawers. Vinegar. My stomach roils. He sees the expression on my face and a small smile creeps onto his mouth. "I know," he says. "But I have to clean it. If I don't, you'll get an infection. Then I'll have to cut your arm off."

"You're exaggerating."

He lifts a shoulder. "Am I?"

"Try not to enjoy this so much."

His smile grows wider. "It's too late for that, Condesa."

Rumi pours the vinegar on a clean white cloth and presses the dampened corner directly onto my wound. I clench my eyes and hiss out several curses.

"Do you want to visit El Mercado and have salteñas tomorrow?"

I blink. "What? With you?"

"Would you rather go with the king?" At my recoil, he sobers. "Sorry. Terrible thing to say. I think you need a break from the castillo. I can take you at eleventh bell."

His dark eyes are on mine, crinkling at the corners from

laughing. Chances to leave the castillo are rare and I'm not going to miss the opportunity—or turn down free salteñas. And I wouldn't mind his company. As soon as the thought enters my mind, I blush. He notices, and that little line forms between his brows.

"Yes." I look at my arm. "All right."

He pours more vinegar onto the cloth and repeats the process.

My eyes spill with tears. "You owe me at least three for this."

"I'll be done in just a moment." He blows softly on the wound. Then he takes the oily liquid right out of a cactus leaf and smears the mixture all over my messy elbow. "It seems like I'm always patching you up."

I look over his handiwork. The wound is cleaner, the blood wiped away. "You're a good healer, Rumi."

His eyes flicker in surprise.

"What?"

"You've never called me by my name before."

His pointing it out makes me flush. Of course he'd notice something like that.

I lift my eyes and our gazes lock.

He's focused on me, not my damaged elbow. There's bewilderment in his eyes, a question that I don't know the answer to. I sit there, unmoving, his hand a gentle weight on my arm. His skin is warm and soft. That line between his brows becomes more pronounced. Then I shift my attention to my elbow, pretending to be absorbed by his skill.

"I feel . . . confused," Rumi says softly.

My breath stops at my chest. "Why?"

A long moment passes. He removes his hand from my arm.

"Your elbow will be fine. Don't wipe away the mixture, and keep it from getting wet."

"Rumi."

He stands. "Do you want tea?"

I blink. "All right."

He walks over to the hearth, where a black kettle hangs above the burning wood, and lights a fire. Then he pulls down a variety of herbs hanging from the ceiling. My lizard pokes its head out of my pocket, and I use my index finger to push him down. "Be still," I mutter.

Rumi turns from the hearth. "Can you handle spicy?"

I give him a look. "Do your worst, healer."

He smiles and places a steaming mug of tea in front of me. I take a cautious sip. "It's good," I say. "What's in it?"

"It's my own blend. A little heat from the locoto pepper, honey, pinch of lavender."

Whenever he speaks about his herbs, Rumi comes to life. It's like he takes off an ill-fitting coat and the clothes underneath are tailor-made for him. It strikes me how confident he seems to be away from Atoc and the court that laughs at him.

I take another sip. The warmth of the tea spreads all the way to my toes. The sting from my elbow vanishes, and I take a deep, calming breath. "My arm doesn't hurt. Is this your magic at work?"

"More or less," he says. "I have a knack at herb lore, but I don't have to use it."

"You mean that you can heal people without all this?" I gesture to the general room. When he doesn't say anything, I take that as an affirmative. "Pretty useful on the battlefield."

"It takes too much out of me," he says. "Hence all this."

"Right, right." I take a deep breath. My thoughts are crammed with wanting to know what exactly he'd felt earlier. "So, we should talk about it."

He straightens. "It?"

"Your confusion."

His face flushes a deep, deep red. The silence stretches. I want to push him into an explanation, because I'm feeling just as uneasy, as if I'm about to walk across the Illustrian bridge all over again. Specific details stay with me long after I've seen him: the way his hair just grazes his broad shoulders, the deep corners that bracket his mouth when he's trying to hold back a smile, the freckles dotting his nose.

I shouldn't like him at all, but I do. I can't make sense of it. The feelings are new and uncomfortable and alarming. But most of all, I hate one detail that looms larger than the others: He's utterly decent. The kind of person I could respect and admire.

"Well?" I prod.

But the moment is gone. Rumi's expression is carefully blank, like a fresh sheet of paper, and he's leaning far away from me; any farther, and he'll fall off his stool. He glances at the clock. "I have to see patients. The infirmary is officially open for the afternoon."

I swallow my disappointment. It's just as well. Nothing good could come of having *that* conversation. We both know it, and I was foolish to push him toward an open flame, one that could burn us both.

A guard shows up to escort me back to my room. As I leave, I pass two Llacsans waiting to see the healer. One grips his shoulder, wincing in pain. The other—a court member, judging by his fine cape and boots—leans against the wall, his head tilted back, attempting to slow the dribble of blood coming out of his nose.

That night, after Suyana has come and gone with the dinner tray, I take a seat on the stool in front of the loom and consider my dilemma. I am duty bound to write my message to Catalina. Duty bound to tell her the location of the Estrella.

I sigh and take up the threads. Silver light winks and glitters as the moonlight turns supple in my hands, bending and twisting. I weave the message into a striped owl. Once Catalina receives this, she'll know exactly where to send her fighters to collect the Estrella.

As soon as I finish, the bird springs to life, stretching its full wings. It bounds off the tapestry and settles on my shoulder. All I have to do is open the balcony doors. But I told El Lobo that I'd hear his plan, and a bloodless revolt profoundly appeals to me. I don't like war, don't like the killing and the ripping apart of families and friends. If Princesa Tamaya and the vigilante can circumnavigate a battle, then wouldn't that help everyone? Taking down Atoc without lives lost seems like the best option for both sides.

And I can't help but feel they have a point in wanting to destroy the Estrella. It's only brought destruction and death. Maybe they're right: Maybe no one should have access to that kind of power.

What would Catalina do if our positions were reversed? She's softer and kinder than me. If I could understand—and potentially support—the other side, why couldn't she?

I need to speak with her. Because of Rumi, I have the perfect opportunity.

The balcony doors remain shut, and the bird seems disappointed, but I take up more threads and start a new tapestry. In a couple of hours, a new owl stares back at me, the words MEET IN EL MERCADO. ELEVENTH BELL woven across his wings. She'll know the place. It's the one we talked about over and over again back at the keep—the first place we dreamed of visiting after we'd won the war against the Llacsans.

The salteñeria.

Guilt nags me. Sneaking into La Ciudad will put her in danger, but the risk is worth it. I can only hope that after talking to both Catalina and El Lobo, I'll know what to do.

And whose side I'll be on.

veintitrés

When the tenth bell tolls, I'm dressed and ready for our visit into La Ciudad. Suyana outfitted me in a soft yellow dress and a shawl stitched with mint-green flowers along its fringed hem. I'm reading the book Rumi lent me, my nerves alive and fluttering like a swarm of delicate butterflies. I can't wait to see Catalina, even if I'm dreading our conversation. There's a chance she'll understand where I'm coming from. Maybe she's even seen something in the stars that will support my argument. Maybe Luna is as sick of war as I am.

The door opens—but it's not the healer. Juan Carlos strides in halfway to eleventh bell. He has a broad smile on his face. "Salteña time!"

I look over his shoulder, but there's no one else. "You're taking me?"

"Rumi said this was on your schedule today." He squints at me. "Don't tell me you've changed your mind?"

Of course not. I need to go into El Mercado. I wanted—had *thought*, rather—I'd have a different escort. But our conversation yesterday must have spooked Rumi. Perhaps he wanted to keep his distance because it was the smart thing to do. I should feel the same, and I do on some level. I shake off my disappointment, throwing up the wall that should have been there all along, and focus on the most important thing.

Meeting Catalina.

The sun is bright outside, but I don't mind the heat from its rays. Fresh air mingles in my lungs as they expand, taking in this little moment of freedom. Juan Carlos casts a lazy smile in my direction and gestures toward the stables.

"Lady's choice. On horse or on foot?"

I glance up toward the sun, pulling my bottom lip with my teeth. I want to walk, to drag the time outside, getting my fill of unfettered blue skies. But the eleventh bell will toll any minute and I can't miss the chance of seeing Catalina.

"Caballo," I say.

Juan Carlos nods and snaps his fingers at a stable hand. In moments we're riding toward La Ciudad. Inkasisa's hilly landscape surrounds us, shadows peppering its curves and jagged peaks, flecking the earth with secrets and hidden enemies. Beyond the misty mountain rests the azure Lago Yaku, hiding the most powerful secret of all. I turn my attention to what lies ahead, at the foot of Qullqi Orqo Mountain.

La Ciudad Blanca. It takes shape as we ride closer, the red tiles sitting on top of the white walls and glittering under the sun. The city sprawls beneath the lavender mountain like a servant at the feet of its brooding sovereign.

"Beautiful, isn't it?" Juan Carlos asks me.

There's no denying it. "Yes."

"Must have been hard living in a fortress all these years."

I side-eye him. "Still trying to earn my trust?"

He laughs but doesn't say anything else. I'm suddenly annoyed that my life is composed of secrets, that even the people in it aren't capable of telling the truth. And I'm the worst one of them all. We'd shared old wounds the other day and built something akin to friendship.

"It was hard," I say abruptly. "I remember what life was like before the revolt. My grandmother baked a lot and we always came into La Ciudad for salteñas in the early afternoon. My nanny liked to weave with me after dinner, right before my parents would tuck me into bed."

He nudges his horse closer. "My family owned a tavern. I learned how to make silpancho when I was seven. Even now I remember how the customers liked the crispiness of my potatoes."

"You cook." I chuckle. "Of course you do. What's your specialty?"

"I make the best sándwich de chola," he says with a proud smile. "Double servings of braised pork, locoto, and my queso blanco and tomato salsa. The marraquetas are toasted on the grill, extra butter."

He's passionate about food. Huh. Who knew? If I had any talent in the kitchen, I'd spend all my time concocting new dishes, not watching over a wayward condesa.

"Why are you a guard then?" I lightly place a hand on his arm. "You should have your own tavern."

His smile dims. "It's my dream, but it's too risky. Besides, I'm needed in the castillo."

"Too risky?"

He nods. "It's just me providing for my family. My father left us when it became clear my mother's family wouldn't accept him. I think he thought it'd be easier for us if he weren't around. But my mother loved him and the day he left, he took her smiles with him."

I frown. "Did your abuelos accept you?"

"There's not many people I can't charm, Condesa," he says with a wink.

"Now that I do believe." We reach the outer walls of La Ciudad and proceed forward, taking turns on the winding roads, passing homes, shops, and several inns. Carts ramble by, carrying various wares. Sentries patrol the cobbled streets. Many are stationed at the white temple near the Plaza del Sol.

The square teems with noise and people. Everything I miss and love, everything I crave and want after this is all over. We leave our horses in the public stalls, Juan Carlos depositing a single nota in the waiting hands of the stable master, and we walk the rest of the way to buy salteñas. Half of the plaza is being rebuilt after Atoc's earthquake shook the ground.

The square is dusty, and half buried under cracked stone and piles of rubble, and despite the general bustle of activity, the people walking around us resemble the nearly destroyed city center. Broken and badly in need of repair. Some have fresh cuts and scrapes, missing limbs and patched heads. They wear forlorn and stricken expressions, because they know just as much as I do that they can't trust the ground beneath them. Not with Atoc lording over us all.

And everywhere the scent of dirt and grime covers the people of La Ciudad. With the water shortage, there's no respite from cracked lips and dry elbows. No salvation from parched throats and bodies in need of cleansing.

"I'm surprised Atoc allowed this outing," I say as we walk avenues filled with people buying and selling whatever food is available: tomatoes and choclo, yuca and bags of beans kept in barrels.

"He's gone for the day," he says. "On a visit to the Lowlands."

Which is about a day's ride from La Ciudad. We walk past more shops, and through the windows I spot various wares for sale: fabrics, tinctures, and shelves overflowing with bars of soap. The corners of my mouth pull down. Perfect for empty bathtubs, since there's not nearly enough water for drinking let alone bathing, but there's plenty of everything else for sale. Items made possible by the planting and selling of the koka leaves. How long can we survive before we're invaded by our neighboring countries, intent on the massive plots of land dedicated to the drug?

Murals of Princesa Tamaya decorate the walls, each collecting an assortment of wildflowers in honor of Atoc's imprisoned sister. Now that I've seen her, I can attest the murals depict her accurately.

A movement draws my attention. The tail end of a woolly anaconda snakes around the feet of unsuspecting vendors. I squint, and the creature must sense my gaze because it stops and peers up at me through silvery eyes—*my moon thread.*

It followed me to La Ciudad! With something like a cheeky expression on its woven face, it slithers into the shadows, vanishing without a trace. What on earth is it doing all the way out here?

"Condesa?" Juan Carlos asks.

I shake my head. "Sorry, I thought something fell from a stall."

He resumes his careful study of the plaza, looking for potential threats. I study the plaza too, suspicion flaring. Sure enough, my animals are scattered all around. Frogs hopping in and out of pots. Lizard on a windowsill, enjoying the bright sun. Jaguar weaving throughout the crowd, silent, and the llama spitting woolly balls at unsuspecting shoppers.

When they catch me staring, they slink into the darkness, almost *sulky*, and vanish completely out of sight. But I still feel their presence. Ever watchful.

We approach the salteña stall. Juan Carlos turns to me, eyebrows lifting. "How many are you going to devour? Your appetite is legendary in the castillo."

Something catches my eye, through the long line of people waiting to buy the savory pastry, past the other stalls selling choripán—a figure waiting in the shadows, hiding underneath a wide-brimmed hat and colorful Llacsan clothing.

Catalina.

She nods from across the gulf between us, then disappears into the alley next to the shop.

I return my attention to Juan Carlos. "Dos, por favor."

"Only two?" he scoffs. "You'll regret it. I'm buying you four."

When it's our turn to order, Juan Carlos marches to the seller and I make my move. As he's asking for eight salteñas, all spicy, I take a small step backward. Then another. The chatter swirling around us rises and I melt into the crowd, embracing the long arms of La Ciudad, disappearing so fully, I'm sure even the other guards who've been silently tailing us are thrown when I vanish.

Catalina sees me at the mouth of the alley and hurtles into my arms, the hat flying off her head. I latch onto her.

"You're here," she says, her face flushed. "You're really here. When I got your message, I couldn't believe it. Flying *birds*, Ximena?"

I shiver at the sound of my name. "I don't have much time. There's a guard—well, several—and—" My voice breaks. Now that I'm seeing her, the expression of relief on her face, gazing at me in adoration, I find the words I need to say are lodged at the back of my throat, unwilling to shatter the bright moment of seeing her, my friend. My condesa.

"What is it?" Catalina asks. She grips my arms. "I know about Ana. I've had spies planted in the city ever since you left. I know you were there, and"—she shrugs helplessly—"that you couldn't do anything to save her."

I take a step away. There's a hint of accusation in her tone, or maybe it's a question. As if she needed to hear from me that saving Ana wasn't possible. A flutter of unease passes through me. "Atoc was never going to release her. The messenger I killed was his cousin."

"Is that what you wanted to tell me?" she asks.

I shake my head.

Catalina stares at me, at the space I created between us. "Why isn't Sofía with you?"

"Gone," I whisper.

She sags against the alley wall. "When?"

"That first day."

Her voice cracks. "We have to tell Manuel."

"Has he sent word?"

Both hands cover her face as her shoulders start trembling. Her reply comes out mumbled. I almost don't hear it. "There's been nothing."

"Catalina," I whisper. Her hands drop to her sides. "I want to tell you—I want to ask you—something. I wouldn't have brought you here if it wasn't crucial."

Her tears carve silvery tracks down her cheeks. She takes a fortifying breath and then nods.

The moment has come, and my throat feels dry. "This is so important, and if I don't get the words right, any hope of peace might be gone."

"Peace?"

I tell her about Princesa Tamaya. About her plan to destroy the Estrella, about her intentions of uniting Llacsans and Illustrians with the hope of a stronger Inkasisa. I tell her about the lives we could save if she relinquished her designs for the throne. If she walked away from the rebellion we've been planning for most of our lives.

As I talk, her face becomes leached of all color. She's using the wall to keep upright, her hands gripping the stone. I skip telling her of the friends I've made within the castillo. I bypass all mention of Rumi, of Suyana, and present the argument as coolly and objectively as I can.

But she breaks down anyway. Sobs wreck her body. I reach for her, but she shoves me away.

"You want me to forget about what I've lost?" Catalina whispers. "Ignore the horror of what happened to our families?

Everyone I loved has *left* me. They've even turned you against me, and I have no one."

"Catalina," I say. "Stop. I haven't been turned—I've been *informed*. Do you want another war?"

Her fists cover the tears leaking from her eyes. "I hate them. I hate them."

She isn't hearing me.

"Do you even want to be queen?" I press. "Think about it. The amount of responsibility on your shoulders? You'd have the whole country looking to you. Imagine the pressure of getting it right. Do you really want to lead us?"

She takes a step back, drawing away slowly as if I were a predator. "How can you ask me that? Of course I want to be queen."

I shake my head. "I don't think you do. I think you're doing this for them—for the family you've lost. But it's not what you want. Not really. To be a queen, you can't be everyone's friend."

"Luna. *What are you saying?*"

I have to make her understand, even if I hurt her. She needs to know what it will take to lead Inkasisa. "If you're queen, not everyone will like you. Tough decisions are part of the job, and you won't be able to please everyone. Catalina, you're too soft. Too kind and sweet and impressionable. Inkasisa needs someone with iron in their blood. That life isn't for you. I love you, you're my best friend, and I *know* you. If you forget the throne, you'll be free to be the person you're supposed to be. Can't you understand what I'm saying?"

She flinches with every word, cowering against the wall. I know she believes the truth in what I'm saying. "And you think this Tamaya will make a better queen than me?"

I force myself to push the words out, knowing how this will hurt. How it will hurt us both. But she needs to know how I feel. Me, her *friend*. Not a decoy. "I do."

"No," she says, straightening from the wall. "*No*. This isn't you. They've destroyed my friend."

"Catalina," I say firmly, "no one can tell me what to think."

She takes a deep, shuddering breath. "Then you're not the person I thought you were. You're a traitor. A *rat*. I won't give up. If you're not with me"—her voice cracks—"then you're against me. Is that what you're saying?"

I shift tactics. "You've always tried to plan the revolt around fewer casualties. This is your chance to save lives. Take it and step aside."

"I can't give up," Catalina whispers. "My whole life has been about winning the throne. What will everyone say if I just quit?"

"I think they'd prefer to be alive." I splay my hands. "This is the better way."

Her expression shutters and I know I've lost her.

"I'll lead the revolution on my own," she says. "I don't need a decoy anymore. No more leading from the shadows. I am the condesa. You'll see how much iron I have in my spine. You may not believe in me anymore, but I do. I'll show you. I'll show you all."

She dries her tears and picks up the discarded hat, calmly brushing off the dirt. Without another look in my direction, she walks to the other end of the alley. Her shoulders push back, as if preparing for battle, and it's that gesture that splinters my heart.

Luna. Please let her forgive me.

La Ciudad waits for me at the other end of the alley and I

veer toward it, wiping the tears clutching my eyelashes. When I step into the sunlight, Juan Carlos is across the plaza, sword drawn, his neck muscles tight as he searches the crowd. I make it easy for him and step into plain sight, pretending to admire a barrel full of salted and dried fish at the first stall within my reach.

He's at my elbow in seconds. *"Condesa."*

I look at him innocently. "I think I'd like something else to eat."

He scowls. "Where did you go?"

I shrug. "I wandered off. I've been trapped for weeks and wanted to take in the sights."

"Do you really expect me to believe that's what happened?" He takes my arm and hauls me away from the stall, away from the plaza, and back toward the stables.

"No," I say. "But maybe I just wanted to see if I could do it."

"Do what?" he asks.

I take one last look at the disappearing plaza, at its noise and people living free of invisible chains. "Escape."

CAPÍTULO

veinticuatro

On the night El Lobo is supposed to come, I pick out the least ruffled dress in my arsenal and put it on carefully, making sure its hems lie exactly right. Chewing on mint leaves, I straighten the room, making the bed and wiping the dresser of any accumulated dust. I braid my hair and put on rouge the way Catalina taught me.

For some unfathomable reason.

I try not to think about it as I open the balcony doors, letting Luna's light flood the room like an untamed river current. I try not to think about it as I sit in front of the loom, getting lost as I weave moon thread into a new tapestry. My basket of wool is nearly overwhelming; every day more of it arrives. Soon I'll have enough to outfit every person in the damn castillo. Or to populate the whole of Inkasisa with woolly animals.

Time flies as I weave, and the world disappears and I don't care to join it. All I want is to choose the next color, the next pattern to create something new and beautiful that's just for me. But Catalina's words whisper in my mind, loud and insistent.

Traitor. Rat.

Tears rise from the depths of my wretched guilt. I angrily scrub my cheeks. Catalina is my best friend. But she's utterly wrong. I fight to remember that, even as my reasoning feels hollow. I take a fortifying breath and strengthen my hold on the wool strands. My animals jump back into their tapestries and watch me as I work.

"You're really talented," someone says from behind me.

I turn to meet the accented voice. He's lying on my bed, as comfortable as a pampered cat. Dressed in his usual black ensemble, he reminds me of the perfect night. The kind of night that makes you want to get lost somewhere. The kind of night that invites adventure and misbehaving.

He climbs off the bed and faces me as I stand. We stare at each other, and the silence stretches between us. There's something in the air that heightens my senses, or maybe it's the vigilante himself. He fills up the room, impossible to ignore, a tangible energy that fascinates me as much as it confuses me. Is he who I think he is?

"Do I know you?"

He blinks. "Yes."

This time he doesn't disguise his voice.

Luna. I've *heard* it before. My heart hammers in my chest. My next question is obvious—*Who are you?*—but he anticipates it and gestures toward my nearly finished tapestry. He doesn't want me to ask. I picture my guard, and then the healer, under the mask. Because he must be one of them. The height, the width of their shoulders, the dark eyes. He could be either of them.

"It's beautiful. Who's it for?"

"This one's for me," I say. "Who are you?"

He shoots me an exasperated look. "Can I trust you, Condesa? Because I don't think I can."

His admission doesn't bother me. After all, I *can't* be trusted. That's the sorry truth. And even sorrier is my wish that I can trust him. Maybe I can. At least with something small but important.

I clear my throat. "I want to show you something."

"What is it?" His voice holds a note of wariness that makes my heart stutter. As if he knows I'm about to cross some imaginary line we've drawn to protect ourselves from each other.

"It's a secret," I whisper. "One of my secrets anyway. Out of all of them, it's my favorite, I think."

"Are you sure, Condesa?" he asks, his shoulders tense.

"No," I say with a shaky laugh. "But the point is that I want to share something with you that's real. Something about me, something personal and—"

"Show me."

I draw a long breath, my body trembling. I've never been this vulnerable with a stranger. A *literal* stranger—his mask guarantees that. He could find a way to use my secret ability against me. But hearing him call me by Catalina's title sits heavily in my stomach. I want him to know part of the real me. Something that doesn't belong to her, something only I can do. I want someone to know Ximena Rojas—even this stranger who's pushed his way into my life in a manner I didn't expect.

I head to the tapestry hiding the serpent. "Come out," I say, my voice firm. "It's fine; he's a friend."

I must look like an idiot. After all, I don't know if my creatures understand a word I say, but in my heart, they do.

Nothing happens for several long seconds, but then the anaconda slithers from the tapestry, growing longer and stretching until it's full-bodied, and then it heads straight for the vigilante.

El Lobo jumps about a foot.

"It won't hurt you." I frown. "I don't think."

"Shouldn't you know for sure?" he asks, backing up a step. "They can swallow whole cows."

I pet the snake, the wool soft under my fingers. Its silver eyes gaze at me with apparent fondness. Then it turns its head toward the vigilante. "I made it. With my weaving."

"What do you mean 'with your weaving'?" he asks hoarsely.

The rest of the animals come out of their hiding spots: the jaguar and the condor, the sloth and the parrot, the fiesty llama and the frogs. "I weaved them in my tapestries using—using a special thread—and they came to life. Remarkable, isn't it?"

The vigilante takes a step toward me. The jaguar stills. I make shushing noises at it and reach a hand over to its ear. "It's all right."

"This is—I've only seen this kind of talent in Princesa Tamaya. I never thought anyone could . . . This is . . ." He pauses, shaking his head, as if sorting his thoughts. "And the fact that it's *you*. I hardly know what to think."

I take his hand and bring it to the jaguar's head. The animal stiffens but relaxes under El Lobo's tentative fingers. Soon it's purring.

"That's my secret," I say.

He slides a look my way. Then he crouches and reaches to pet the anaconda. Moments later the rest of the animals come out to properly greet him. El Lobo gently lifts the sloth into his arms.

"Why did you make a sloth?"

I shrug. "They're cute?"

His mask moves as he smiles. "I *love* sloths."

The creature nestles closer, digging its face into the crook of the vigilante's neck.

"I think the feeling is mutual," I say. "They all look so fierce in their own way, clearly not part of this world. It's amazing to see them interacting with another person." As an afterthought, I add, "You're the only one I've shown them to."

El Lobo digs an index finger into the folds of the sloth's woolly skin. "Why me?"

He knows why. Because I care about our friendship, however tenuous and fleeting it may be. I care about his opinion of me. And a small part of me knows that he cares just as much as I do. I count him as a friend. One of the few I have inside this castillo. "Don't be an idiot."

Despite everything, he laughs. "You're not one to be coy, are you?"

We settle onto the bed, and the creatures follow. The entire surface is covered with woolly tails, paws, wings, and a hissing tongue. They blend in with one another until it becomes too hard to discern which animal is which. Except for the sloth, who remains in El Lobo's arms.

"I'm supposed to be convincing you why our plan is the best for Inkasisa," he says softly. "But here I am, covered in all of this, and thinking you're not what I expected."

"I know the feeling."

"Do you regret showing me your secret?"

When it comes to my enemies, I've tried to avoid thinking

about what we have in common. I haven't wanted to see them as friends with families they want to protect and cherish. But now I've seen all those things in Suyana and Rumi and Juan Carlos. They've become friends, people whose company I enjoy. Even look forward to.

"No, I don't."

El Lobo sits up, gently removing my animals. There's a new light in his eyes, as if he's decided something.

He holds out his hand. "Come with me."

A chance to leave the castillo? There's really nothing to think about. I ask him to turn away so I can change into my darker clothing. When I'm finished, he turns back around and pulls an extra black mask from his pocket.

My mouth drops open and he shrugs, almost sheepish. "I brought it in case . . ."

"In case you thought I could be trusted?"

"Oh, I don't know that." He blows out a quiet breath, and I almost don't hear his next words. "But I want to."

My blood races warmer in my veins as I take the mask. The intimate way he's gazing at me is hard to ignore. I slip the disguise over my head. "Ready."

"Where's the sword I gave you?"

I grab it from beneath my pillow and tuck it under my belt. "At some point, I'd like mine returned. They took all of my weapons when I got here. Luna knows where they are now."

"What bastards."

I laugh. "Where are we going?"

El Lobo motions for me to follow. "You'll see."

I shut the doors behind me. We climb down the same way I did the night I visited the king's office. A literal jump to the balcony below mine, and then again. Forcing myself not to look down, I keep up with El Lobo. When we reach the ground, he leads me straight to the gardens. I spot the sentry at the gate, standing beneath a blazing torch. El Lobo jerks his head to the right, past the iron entrance, and we venture deeper into the garden, until we get to the very back corner. Hidden behind toborochi trees, their trunks wide and thick, are overturned crates. The corners of the gate are tall, square-shaped stone towers.

"Do what I do," El Lobo whispers.

He steps onto the tallest crate, then uses the brick on the gate to climb to the top of the wall, using his feet to hoist himself into a sitting position on the stone.

"Your turn," he calls down softly into the night.

The wind sends a shudder of movement through the branches. The low hum of insects rings steadily in my ears. The gate is at least ten feet high. Waving away a mosquito, I step onto the crate and reach for the crossbar. My fingertips barely graze the iron.

El Lobo reaches down and grasps my hand. He keeps one foot on the iron gate as leverage and then pulls me up. I'm able to get my left foot on the crossbar, and with his help I'm hauled onto the flat surface.

"No time to admire the view," he whispers as he points out another sentry. We scoot along the flat surface of the wall and turn the opposite way. El Lobo jumps first, and I follow. He catches me around the waist and sets me gently down onto my toes.

"There has to be a better method to sneak out of the castillo," I say, panting from the climb and subsequent jump.

He chuckles warmly. "I'm open to suggestions."

I speed after him. Crossing the cobbled street, turning right, down three blocks and then to the left. With every step I take away from the castillo, the heavy weight on my shoulders lessens.

Freedom. It hits me every single time I leave.

I recognize streets and alleys, shops and taverns. The city belongs to the Llacsans, and he takes me deeper into one of their poorer neighborhoods, the bumpy road dark and crooked. He stops once we reach a courtyard lined by stone arches. None of it looks familiar. In the center are overgrown bushes and tall palm trees. El Lobo takes my hand and leads me to the darkest corner of the square.

"I'm about to do something incredibly stupid," he whispers.

His words don't penetrate at first. But then realization hits and I'm aware that something's changed between us. He's come to a decision—a decision that might hurt him. My hands are shaking. "Lobo."

He drops my hand, reaches for his mask, and hesitates. I understand his unease—I feel it too. Part of me wants to learn the truth, and the other half is terrified of what I'll do with the information. Knowing his identity will bring us closer, and I crave the intimacy like a bird yearns for flight. I want his trust, I want his friendship, even though it means his ruination.

Do I dare let him do this?

I have to. What if I don't recover the Estrella?

I'll endure his hatred, the loss of what could have been, the end of our friendship. I'll suffer it all if it means saving hundreds of Illustrian lives. He'll never forgive me, but then, neither will I forgive myself. Once again I hear Catalina in my head.

Traitor. Rat.

He grips the bottom of his mask. The dark fabric creeps upward. Little by little, his face comes into view: a strong jaw. Scruffy beard. Thin lips. A blade of a nose and sharp cheekbones.

I *know* him.

It's Rumi.

My hand flies to my mouth. This entire time it was my enemy, my almost friend. The smelly grump. Not Juan Carlos. Rumi, the healer. Every single one of our encounters flashes through my mind. The first time I laid eyes on him. The night he lent me the book. Our conversations and fights, and the times he carefully wrapped my wounds.

My mind tries to connect one thing to the other—

"How can it be you?" I ask. "The night in the office! You showed up and tended to the guards."

Rumi leans against the wall, his arms folded, a lazy smile on his lips. "My room is in that wing. I ducked in, changed, and came out looking *very* alarmed."

"I thought you were Juan Carlos—"

"No," he says slowly.

"You don't like me."

"I didn't at first. You didn't like me either." Rumi pushes away from the wall. He tilts his head and smiles again, but it doesn't reach his eyes. The silence grows heavy. What is he thinking? He's too still. I know that court smile. All charm and no heart.

"Don't tell me you're disappointed," he says smoothly. "If you are—"

"Be quiet," I say. "I'm several things right now, but disappointed isn't one of them."

"Tell me."

I keep blinking, as if trying to make sure this is real—that it is *him*. Rumi who stood up to me and cared enough to tell me when I was wrong. Rumi who has no love for the king of Inkasisa. The last makes me exhale with profound relief. He hates Atoc as much as I do.

He stands at his full height, towering over me. Dressed in black as El Lobo, he seems more like himself than Rumi the laughingstock of court.

"I hoped it was you."

Whatever doubt existed flees from his troubled eyes. He lights up brighter than all of Luna's stars put together.

I'm in so much trouble. It's clear he might be too, and I wonder when it all became different between us. What brought him to this moment? I want—no, I *need* to understand. "Tell me why you took off your mask."

"Don't be an idiot," he says, volleying back.

"Spell it out for me."

His face is open, without guile, and utterly sincere. "Because we're the same. You're loyal to your own." I flinch, but he doesn't notice. "A fighter, willing to risk your life. Passionate and feisty, but a learner, too. You've surprised me. Our conversations are the brightest part of my day." He pauses. "And I think you're so lovely. Does that answer your question?"

I flush to the roots of my hair. In two steps Rumi stands in front of me, maneuvering me until my back is pressed against the wall. He removes my mask and leans forward, his face closer and closer. His arms are on either side of my head, and there's no looking away from him. I place my hands lightly on his shoulders. His lips brush mine, his fingers curling into my hair, pulling my head back. He looks down into my face, giving me time to decide.

I shouldn't let him near me. I have what I need to save my people, and I can't cross this line. Kissing him wouldn't be right. What does it say about me if I let him do this? I stare at my hands, willing them to push him away.

But I'm done lying to myself. If tonight is all we'll have, so be it. My hands slide up to the back of his neck.

He kisses me, his lips firmly pressing against mine, warm and sweet and thorough. We float between worlds, between two sides of a war, and the promises we've made to others. Everything fades away. I only feel his tight grip on my waist and his fingertips splayed against my lower back. His tongue softly parts my lips and it's impossible to think of anything but what he tastes like.

Impossibly right.

We pull apart, and Rumi has the look of someone who's just been told a precious secret. Like he's honored to have been trusted with something so vulnerable. His forehead is pressed against mine and we breathe the same sweet air.

"I want you to know the truth about me, Catalina," he says. "We'll never make it if there are secrets between us."

I nod, but my stomach clenches. If there was ever a time to reveal the biggest secret I carry, it's this moment. But I can't make myself say it. The ramifications are too much for me to take in—I've only just discovered how he feels about me, and to tell him the truth means losing him.

I don't want to lose him. Not tonight. Because in my heart I know this won't go the way I want it to. He'll hate me when this is all over.

Rumi kisses the tip of my nose. "What are you thinking?"

I meet his gaze. "This might end faster than you think."

He smiles gently. "We'll see."

Rumi leads me to a shadowed doorstep. Above it hangs a sign painted in the old language along with a faded sketch of a bird.

"What is this place?"

He raps three times—two quick taps, and the third long. Then he looks down at me and leans forward until his nose tickles my cheek.

His breath brushes my ear. "Everything."

veinticinco

The creaking door opens, revealing a tiny sliver of soft, flickering light and a thin slice of an older woman's face. A Llacsan. She wrenches the door wide, her grin spreading from ear to ear. Noise from within the tavern spills into the dark courtyard. Loud chatter, clinking glasses, and chairs scraping against the stone floor.

"Rumi," the Llacsan says. "We weren't expecting you tonight."

Then her gaze lands on mine, and her grin melts away as if she's wax and I'm open fire.

"Who's this?"

Rumi drops a heavy arm across my shoulders and tugs me closer to his side. "A friend."

I swallow. Her lips tighten, and she smooths back her graying hair. With her free hand, she grabs the crook of Rumi's elbow and ushers him inside.

Me she leaves on the doorstep.

"Taruka," Rumi says, half amused, half exasperated.

"Hmph," is all she says.

"Say hola, at least—"

"Shut the door behind you," Taruka says to me. She leads Rumi deeper into the tavern. He looks over his shoulder and mouths an apology. In a daze, I follow, taking in the vibrant room. The clay-hued walls are lined with curtain dividers, separating the tavern into a dozen private spaces. Each has a table with bench seating on either side, as well as a eucalyptus candle on a shelf. A ceramic pot hangs above the rectangular tables, nearly overflowing with yellow flowers.

In the center of it all stands a circular dais where a pretty Llacsan girl dances. She sways and jumps, while three other musicians blow into their harmonicas. Across the room sits Juan Carlos, his shoulders shaking in laughter to whatever his companions are saying. His eyes land on mine and he straightens, attention immediately falling to the boy at my side.

Rumi nods at him and Juan Carlos smiles in return, then lifts his glass in a salute to me, winking.

"What's he doing here?"

"He's the only family I have left," he says. "A cousin."

I frown. "You mean he's related to Atoc?"

"No," he says. "I mean we share the same blood."

Taruka deposits Rumi into an empty cubicle and, with a scowl in my direction, indicates the bench across from him.

"Dos apis," Rumi says. "Por favor."

Taruka ruffles his hair. "You're the only one I know who likes to drink api after dinner and not with breakfast. I'll heat it up."

"What is this place?" I ask when she walks away. "And who is Taruka? I think she'd like to feed me to an anaconda, bit by bit."

"She's very protective," he says with a laugh. "And you're a new face here, don't forget. She'll warm up to you in time. My mother and Taruka grew up together. They were best friends."

I chance a look back to Taruka. She stands by the hearth, stirring a steaming pot. She glances in my direction, her brows scrunched together. The place teems with people, and many have their attention on us. Some seem curious, but a few don't try to hide their disapproval. Most are in the cubicles, but several stand around in groups. I scan every face. Some look vaguely familiar. In fact, I'm *sure* I've seen a few of them around the castillo grounds: a gardener who cares for the plants surrounding my favorite bench; guards who stroll the hallways; maids coming in and out of the kitchen area.

My heart thrums wildly. There are so many of them.

"How many spies do you have in the castillo?" I ask in an awed whisper.

Rumi lifts a brow.

"I wondered how you moved around the castillo so easily. I figured you had help," I say, gesturing to the crowd. "But not this much help."

This place isn't a random bar in the city—it exists for the cause, created around *Rumi*. It's more than a tavern. Rumi brought me to the rebel hideout.

The api arrives, hot and ready to drink.

"Umaq is here," Taruka says when she slides the drink in front of me. I take a sip, enjoying the tartness from the pineapple mixed with the purple corn. The cinnamon stick adds plenty of spice to the frothy beverage. Rumi drinks half of his in seconds.

"Tell him to come over," he says. "Juan Carlos, and the rest of the group too."

She nods as I take another long sip. Seconds later a shadow

falls across the table and I look up, expecting the face of a friend. But it's not my charming guard. I spit out my drink. Peering down at me, a cold smile on his thin, long face, is the man who tortured me, who gave the order to kill Sofía. Who threatened my people and demanded I betray Rumi.

Atoc's right-hand man.

The priest Sajra.

Outrage blossoms on his face when he sees me. "You fool! Why have you brought her here?"

"I don't answer to you, Umaq," Rumi says coolly. "And I suggest you welcome her."

I listen to their exchange in horror. This cretin put me through the worst kind of misery. I stand up and rush at him, my hands reaching, ready to claw his eyes out. Rumi wraps an arm around my waist and holds me back. I struggle against his grip, pushing my elbow deep into his stomach. Rumi's hold only tightens.

"Stop," he whispers against my neck. "He's one of us."

My heart thunders against my ribs. I stop struggling, stop moving. I'm numb with shock, disappointment. "Let go of me."

Rumi releases me. "Certainly."

He's watching me carefully, as if I'm a volcano about to shoot ash and hot lava. I seriously just might. The priest slides into the booth as if it's a forgone conclusion that I'll remain in his company, that I'll talk to him, that I'll accept this new development.

I clench my fists. "I'm leaving."

Rumi stands in front of me, blocking my sight of the priest. "Condesa."

I flinch at the title. What am I doing here? Maybe I was

wrong about all of it: my feelings for Rumi, siding with him instead of Catalina, thinking Princesa Tamaya belongs on the throne. *Luna*, that hurts. If she can align herself with someone like Sajra, then I want no part of their plans.

"There's nothing you can say that will convince me to stay."

Juan Carlos is now standing next to his cousin, along with a few more people I recognize. Court nobles dressed down. Guards not in uniform. I try to move past them, but Juan Carlos drops a hand on my shoulder.

"Wait a moment," he whispers.

I pull away. "Absolutely not."

Rumi is looking at me silently, considering. Then he turns to the priest. "What did you do to her?"

Sajra—*Umaq*—polishes off the last of my api. "What was necessary."

In his response, I hear condescension and superiority. He's valuable to them, and he knows how to exploit that.

Juan Carlos mutters a low curse. Atoc's nobles shoot me sympathetic glances. I barely notice. Rumi places both hands on the table and leans forward until he's inches from the priest. "What does that mean?"

"He tortured me," I say.

The priest smirks. Rumi lunges, swiping my abandoned glass and shattering it on the table. He holds up a shard against the priest's neck. "You weren't to touch her."

"How else were we to know we could trust her?" the priest hisses. "I did the work neither of you could do. But now that you've brought her here, it was for nothing. *Step back*."

"Rumi," Juan Carlos whispers.

"He—" Rumi breaks off, letting out as sharp a curse as I've ever heard from him.

"I know." Juan Carlos takes a breath and switches to the old language, speaking low and urgent until Rumi lowers the glass shard from the priest's neck. His cousin pulls him away so that they're standing shoulder to shoulder.

Rumi faces me. There's regret in his expression, but also rage, barely contained. "I'll take you back."

My face is carved in stone, refusing to betray the tumult I'm experiencing under my skin. The shock of seeing the priest, the disappointment of learning he's involved with Princesa Tamaya.

Rumi pulls me away from everyone's watchful gazes. "His part in our plans can't be replaced. He has Atoc's ear and influence. That didn't come easy or immediately, and replacing the priest would be tantamount to giving up before the real fight begins."

It's my choice. I can't stand the priest, but it's clear the people I respect in this room had no idea of the tactics he used against me. The horrible truth, whether I can stomach it or not, is that Sajra was right to suspect me. I'd made the decision to betray Rumi if I didn't get my hands on the Estrella. They'll never know how close I came to giving myself away. I hate the priest for what he put me through. I'll never forgive or trust him, but I can hear what else these people have to say. I owe them that much.

I sit in the booth and level a look at Umaq. "Stay away from me."

There's that brittle smile, full of ice. Little does he know of the fire deep in my belly.

I won't let him touch me again.

"For what it's worth, I didn't enjoy it," Umaq says.

I flick one of the shards of glass at him, and he snarls when it slices into his tunic sleeve.

I bare my teeth in a feral smile.

The rest of the group slides into the booth until we're all pressed together like books on shelves. More drinks are ordered, along with bowls of sopa de mani topped with roasted carrots and chopped cilantro, and it's in the commotion that the mood lightens, shoulders relax, the tight lines around their eyes disappear. Easy camaraderie returns and private jokes are shared.

I'm the intruder in their inner circle. I can feel their watchful stares as they assess me, the expression on my face, the way Rumi sits closer to my side. They are protective of him and looking at me as if I'm a potential threat, a weakness that might make their entire foundation sink.

In the hubbub, Rumi presses a soft kiss on the inside of my wrist. In front of everyone. The chatter hushes as my face inflames. Juan Carlos, sitting on the other side of Rumi, leans forward and gives a suggestive eye wag that only prolongs my blush.

Rumi blinks long and slow, staring straight ahead. That's his only reaction to his cousin's gesture. If possible, my face flushes even more. Umaq makes a sniffing sound, like a predator searching for blood.

One of the nobles, an older woman with lustrous graying hair, clears her throat. "As charming as all this is, I'd like to know why you saw fit to bring the condesa to the tavern."

It's as if cold water has been doused all over me. I'm still deceiving them. The truth sits deep in my belly, an indigestible lump.

Rumi needs to know who he's dealing with.

Tonight.

My pulse races, but before I can dwell on confessing, Rumi takes ahold of the conversation. Thoughtfully explaining how many rebels are hidden within the castillo, ready to pounce the moment Atoc's weapon is destroyed.

The Estrella. I'm the only one present who knows its current whereabouts.

"Without the Estrella, he's weak and surrounded," Rumi says to me. "We have soldiers in his army, servants and stable hands, and more nobility on our side than you can guess."

He takes both of my hands. My breath catches.

"But without the Estrella, I can't give the signal. There's no chance of success without its destruction. Condesa, tell me where it's hidden so I can destroy it myself."

This is the moment. The final nail in the coffin between Catalina and me. Turning my back on long years of friendship and duty. The second I give away the location, it's truly over for her and all the Illustrians hoping for her reign. The silence stretches, poking and stabbing between us as I mull over the decision. Catalina's heartbroken face swims in my mind.

"If I tell you," I say haltingly, "what will happen to the Illustrians under my watch?"

"They are welcome in La Ciudad," Rumi says. "None will be harmed. I consider them peoples of Inkasisa, our equals and allies."

Juan Carlos is uncharacteristically silent. The rest of them watch me from hooded gazes, their guards up and not daring to make a sound as I consider Rumi's explanation. I sense how important my next words are to them.

I shut my eyes. "You swear?"

His hands tighten around mine. "I swear to Luna."

My eyes fly open and Rumi is looking at me with a long, searing stare.

Atoc's reign will be over. No more threat of war. Tamaya as queen. I find the choice is easier to make than I thought it would be. "The Estrella is hidden at the bottom of Lago Yaku."

Rumi's smile is joyous and loud cheers erupt as he cradles both of my cheeks in his calloused hands and kisses me thoroughly. His happiness is a well deep within him, nearly overflowing. Conversation renews around us, and dimly I hear Juan Carlos talk about Tamaya's execution. I pull away from Rumi. He offers input about the princesa and the plan to save her from death, gesturing wildly and every now and again, glancing at me fondly.

But I shut out his words.

He doesn't know who he's really trusting with his life. Who he really cares for. He wants no more secrets between us, but I have one more that can hurt us. Under the table, I clench my fists against the top of my thighs.

Traitor. Rat.

We're outside in the cool night, walking back to the castillo, neither of us in any particular hurry. Luna is high above our heads, her slanting light guiding the way back to my prison. We all agreed that I needed to be situated in the castillo until the last moment. The wedding is in three days. Before then, the rebels will alert everyone in the castillo when the Estrella's been destroyed. Rumi's holding my hand; the other is placed lightly on the hilt of his sword. We're both wearing our masks, which almost makes what I have to say easier.

Almost.

With every step, the crack in my heart widens and splits open. My hand is clammy in his, but I hold on anyway, because it might be the last time. The thought traps my breath in my chest. My fingers curl into my palm. I can't let this go further, not without him knowing everything. "Rumi, I have to tell you something."

"Sounds serious," he says after a moment. "Can it wait?"

I shake my head. "It has to be said."

His pupils are black wells in a calm circle of deep brown, but his shoulders give him away. He tenses. "Tell me, Catalina."

I inhale a deep breath and force myself to say the words quickly. "That's not my name. It's Ximena. I'm the condesa's decoy."

He jerks away as if I've struck him. *"What?"*

"I'm not who you think I am."

He stands in a stunned stupor for a moment and then hunches over, as if to protect himself from the next hit. I reach out to touch his arm, but he steps away. The silence stretches, and I breathe deeply, trying to control the frisson of panic coursing through my body. My heart shoves against my breastbone.

He stares at the ground, refusing to meet my gaze. *"Explain yourself."*

"Rumi, look at me."

He slowly lifts his head. The cold, shuttered expression in his eyes threatens to do me in. I contemplate running, but my feet won't move. I owe him the truth. All of it.

"I'm Catalina's decoy," I say. "I have been since I was eight years old. When Atoc demanded her presence at the castillo, it was my duty to take her place."

Rumi narrows his gaze. "Why? To assassinate the king?"

I bite my lip. "To find the Estrella, but if that wasn't possible, then yes. I was going to kill him on my own."

"That's not all of it," he says softly. "Otherwise you would have done it by now. You were sent as a spy."

Once again I hear Catalina's words.

Traitor. Rat.

Is that all that I am? I can't seem to stop hurting the people I care about.

"You don't deny it," he says. "And you snared El Lobo; that must have been quite a triumph for you, Illustrian."

My blood is rioting. "Don't make this ugly."

"It already is."

"Rumi," I say, fighting for patience. "I've changed. But I wasn't the one you needed to convince. Catalina will never give up her right to the throne. She's going to bring down whatever army she has left during Carnaval. I know you won't believe this—"

"Very true," he says, deceptively calm.

"Rumi, *listen* to me." Once again I reach for him, but he won't let me near and I crumble. "I gave you the location of the Estrella. You, not her."

"You might have *lied*. This could be part of your plan."

"I'm not lying to you." A flash of indignation flares. "You kept your identity a secret too."

"You're comparing what *you* did to my behavior? We both took off our masks, and I thought we were on equal footing, but you still had one more trick up your sleeve!" He spits out a bitter laugh. "But fine. That's fair. We're liars, the both of us. All the more reason why I can't trust you." He pauses. "Or myself."

Something detonates within me, bright and warm. I worry that it's hope. He still *cares*.

"You were right after all," he says softly. "This was never going to work between us. Too many secrets."

It lands like a physical hit. I almost double over, but I force myself to remain upright. It's hard to hear his bitterness and disappointment. Hard to hear that it's over—even though it was inevitable. My eyes burn, but I will myself not to cry. I choke on the words. "What happens now?"

"You know everything," he whispers. "The princesa, the location of the Estrella. My identity. *Everything*. You can ruin us. Destroy everything we've worked for."

I shake my head. "I wouldn't do that."

"Is that true?" He leans forward, examining my face. "Not even if it meant saving your people?"

"That's not fair."

"I know," Rumi says in an almost gentle voice. It sounds terribly sad. He swallows and unsheathes his sword. "You're a liability. I can't—I *won't*—let you leave."

A weird numbness spreads over me. There's no going back from this. My hand moves to the hilt of my weapon. Seconds pass as I deliberate. And then I let it drop. I choose not to fight him. If I do, the consequences would be irrevocable. Stupidly, I cling to hope that he'll trust me. That he won't hurt me or turn me in.

"You know too much." He says it like he's convincing himself. As if he's gearing up for what he has to do, but not what he wants to do. In this moment he's both boys I've known.

Rumi, the healer.

El Lobo, the vigilante.

I don't know who will win.

Rumi holds up his blade and points it at me. He takes a step forward until I'm backed up against the stone wall. The blade presses into my skin, over my heart. I wince when the tip pierces my flesh.

"I haven't shared any of this with Catalina. She doesn't know where the Estrella is. I talked to her myself. Go to Lago Yaku—you'll see that I've told you the truth."

Rumi's control is seconds from shattering; I can see it in the way his hand continues to shake. The cool steel of the blade trembles against my skin.

"When did you talk to her?"

"The day Juan Carlos took me to El Mercado for salteñas."

"The day you disappeared on him," he says flatly. "We wondered where you went."

"I was trying to convince her to relinquish the throne. To let Tamaya rule Inkasisa. She refused, and I made my choice tonight when I told you the location of the Estrella. That's the truth, Rumi."

His face darkens. "Why should I believe you?"

My heart hammers wildly. I'm unable to speak, my feelings too raw for words. His blade hurts against my skin and he's asking me to risk my heart further when there's a risk he'll only destroy it. My revelation may not be enough to save what's between us.

"Give me proof," he says, almost, *almost* pleading. "Give me one infallible reason why I shouldn't kill you where you stand."

A flutter dances in my ribs. His nostrils flare, a dark storm thundering on his brow.

My gaze locks with his. "I've lied to you, and I'm sorry for hurting you. I've come to care about the people you hold dear. I'm rooting for everyone I met tonight, and I'll fight alongside you all. You say you want proof? I don't have anything concrete to offer, but know this: If I were lying, I wouldn't have told you my secret. If I were lying, I would *never* have sat down at the same table as the man who tortured me and murdered my friend if I didn't believe in your fight."

The blade's pressure lessens. "This is a mistake."

The words don't sound like they're for me, but a response to the internal conversation he seems to be having with himself.

"Rumi."

His sword clatters to the stone. "Go back to the castillo, Illustrian."

I ought to feel relief. He's letting me live. I should get out of his sight before he changes his mind. But I stand rooted to the spot, the wall supporting me. His decision stems from how much he cares about me, and I imagine this is how far he'll let himself go. He is loyal to his people, the princesa, the cause. Nothing more will exist between us, but he'll let me go, he'll give me this much.

It's not enough.

I don't look at him as I bend to pick up his blade. Wordlessly,

I hand it to him. He takes the handle, careful not to touch me. My heart stutters and cracks. I walk away, heading for the cobbled road that will take me back to my cage.

"Ximena," he calls softly.

I stop, but I don't turn around. My name on his lips makes the hair on my arms rise. A hundred guesses traverse my mind, surrounding what I hope he'll say next. That he'll escort me back to the castillo. That he's willing to trust me. That he believes me when I say that I'm on their side. I think all those things in the seconds between his next words.

"Don't make me regret it."

CAPÍTULO

veintiséis

The next day passes in a blur. Suyana seems to notice my restless-
ness because she sends me outside, confident the fresh air will do
wonders for my nerves before the wedding celebrations. I leave her
in the room as she tidies; it's a mess of finished tapestries and bundles of wool and discarded projects. The disorder should bother
me, but I'm unable to focus on anything other than what's to come.

Carnaval. Catalina leading Illustrians to battle. Rumi destroying the Estrella. Saving Tamaya before she's executed. There are
too many components in the plan, too many ways it can lurch
sideways. It's enough to make living in a mess bearable.

Juan Carlos escorts me to my favorite bench in the gardens,
where we're tucked away from everyone else. It's hot and sweat
drips down my back and curls at my temples, dampening my
hair. I scan the area, looking for Rumi, but I know I won't find
him. He can't trust himself around me. I drop my head into
my hands. I knew our friendship would end up here, but that
doesn't lessen the hurt.

He kept his identity a secret too. I stubbornly cling to that truth because I'd rather feel anger than pain. He lied to me. He can't be mad at me for doing the same. But a niggling doubt pecks at me like an annoying, hungry chicken. Up until last night, I was going to give his name to the priest. I had good reason, but it's a betrayal nevertheless.

I can only hope that when Rumi finds the Estrella, he'll trust me again. I lift my head and push my hair back from my face, and as I do, I catch sight of the person I don't want to see at all. I stiffen as Umaq crosses the garden courtyard, heading to his quarters.

"Who is he really?" I ask.

Juan Carlos glances at the priest. "A Lowlander. He's actually a priest—that's not fake. Atoc is a fanatic when it comes to rituals and traditions. Umaq's blood magic is pretty rare, and his installation in the castillo was easy." He looks over at me. "We have no delusions about Umaq. He yearns for money and chases the obscurest legends in search of it. His motives have always been for the advancement of his people, but for now they align with ours."

"I don't trust him."

"He hates Atoc as much as we do."

The priest disappears into the castillo, and I can't help shuddering. "Still."

Juan Carlos plucks one of the eucalyptus leaves and inhales.

"Will he go?" I don't need to clarify the question. He knows I'm asking about Rumi and his possible trip to Lago Yaku.

"He leaves tonight."

I exhale in relief. He's decided to go after all. "Will you go with him?"

He shakes his head ruefully. "He wants me here. I fought him, but he insisted."

Warmth takes root in my heart and blooms. *In order to keep me safe.* But my next thought is dampening. Rumi might have his cousin watching me in case I move against Tamaya. I lean back, using my hands to angle my body up toward the sun. "I'm not going to betray him again."

"I believe you," he says.

I snap my head in his direction. "You do? Why?"

"People are people." He shrugs. "We mess up. You took the chance to make it right, and that's all we can really ask of anyone. My cousin doesn't trust a lot of people, and he shouldn't. He can't afford to—not with so much at stake. His life, our princesa's, and mine. He carries our people's hopes on his shoulders. What you've done threatens that."

I think again about how close I was to betraying him last night. Obviously, the priest wouldn't have turned him over to Atoc, or hurt the Illustrians at the keep. But I didn't know that. I understand Rumi's caution. It's kept him alive all this time.

"Who knows? After finding the Estrella, he might come to your room and get down on his knees, begging your forgiveness."

I let myself smile as we head back to the room at fifth bell. But Juan Carlos is wrong.

Rumi never comes.

The day of Carnaval arrives and I haven't heard a word from Rumi. Juan Carlos is strangely missing, so I can't ask him what's happened. I don't know whether the Estrella has been destroyed. I push aside the breakfast tray even though there's enough dulce de leche to normally make my mouth water. My head hurts and my body feels stiff and heavy, as if I haven't slept in days. But I'm not tired. Panic rises with every heartbeat.

Instead of eating, I'm sitting in a hot bath, rose petals floating in the water, my head tipped back and resting against the metal rim. Atoc has granted one of the grander suites for me to dress in. Voices belonging to several maids drift inside the small bathing chamber—chatter about my lovely dress, the headdress I'll be wearing, and the fine leather sandals made especially for the wedding. There's jewelry to be picked out, several hairstyles to try, and makeup to put on.

It's all chains to keep me trapped.

I don't know what the rebels' plans are. Despite finding the Estrella, maybe Rumi has decided to leave me out of everything. Maybe he's decided he still can't trust me. That I'm too much of a risk. My nerves pick at me like carrion birds intent on their prey. And when the anger comes, I let myself feel it. He should include me. I deserve to know what's happening.

I chose the princesa.

My fingers curl around the edge of the tub. I can't wait another second. I have to see him if only so I can yell at him for keeping me in the dark. Dripping wet, I climb out and wrap myself in a thick robe. I coil my hair into a tight knot, and the water sluices down my back.

I pick up the small bundle of moondust I snuck inside the room and carefully pour a palmful. It's barely enough for all the waiting maids. They might be out for an hour at most. But I don't need that much time.

I blow all of it in their faces.

They slump to the ground, all three of them. Including Suyana. I pull off one maid's clothing and don her servant's attire—a simple black pollera, cream tunic, and plain manta—and hustle out of the room, carrying a tray laden with warm loaves of bread and a heaping pot of coffee. I keep my head down, but I'm not noticed, as the whole castillo is nearly empty. Everyone is either dressing or off at the temple to prepare for the ceremony.

I have one destination in mind, and I don't even know if he'll be there. When I get to the infirmary, I don't bother knocking. The room is barely lit and there's a metallic scent in the air. I wrinkle my nose. Blood. I set the tray down on an empty stool with a heavy thud.

Rumi's head jerks up. He shows surprise for a second, but his expression becomes as dangerous as the edge of a blade. After a long moment he returns his attention to what he'd been doing before I interrupted. A wobbly breath skitters through my lungs.

He's sitting on the table, shirt off, dragging wet strips of linen across a gash on his right side, under his ribs. The wound bleeds into the fabric, blooming red. I've never seen him without his billowy tunic that smells of rotting leaves. He's leaner and sharper than I ever imagined. Rivulets of water trickle down the planes of his stomach and the muscles that delineate them. He uses his teeth to cut another strip of fabric, barely wincing as he lays it on top of the gash.

"It's too deep," I manage. "You need stitches."

"What are you doing here?" There's no warmth in his voice. It's empty and frightening. The candles cast flickering shadows across his face.

My gaze narrows. "There's been no word."

His expression barely shifts. A slight tightening of his mouth. When he glances back at me, he's detached. Aloof. But I know when he's angry—the taut muscles in his neck betray him.

The air between us is poisoned. Something terrible has happened. "Rumi."

He stands, his shoulders pulled back and tense. "Where's the Estrella, Condesa?" He barks out a laugh. "Or whoever you are."

"I told you—the bottom of Lago Yaku." My hands tremble. "Princesa Tamaya said it'd be there."

His cold veneer shatters. "It wasn't there! You lied to me and played me for a fool. Don't try to deny it." His nostrils flare. "What's your plan now? Does the real Catalina have the Estrella? Is she planning an attack on La Ciudad? Gods, I hope you're happy with what you've done. Hundreds of people will die because of you. I thought you wanted peace."

"I do. How can you doubt that?"

"Because the Estrella wasn't where you'd said it'd be!" he yells. "After the other night, it's all become too clear. You've been spying on us, earning Tamaya's trust—"

My temples are throbbing. "She said it'd be there."

"How convenient," he says sarcastically. "Since I can't ask Tamaya because she's already at the temple, awaiting her execution!"

I flinch. She can't die. I can't let that happen.

"Well?"

I swallow, trying to keep my temper under control. "I'm not going to defend myself again, Rumi."

He steps toward me. "I trusted you!"

"I didn't lie to you!" The poison in the air infects my veins until they run feverishly hot. "Trust me, don't trust me. I don't care!" My voice cracks. I'm lying again, and he knows it. "I *don't know why* the Estrella wasn't there, but anything could have happened to it. Maybe Atoc could have gotten there first . . . or—"

My vision hazes. Rumi's outline becomes fuzzy. I'm not seeing him anymore; instead it's my mess of a room as Suyana tidied it up. Making the bed. Clearing the floor of discarded wool. Tapestries put in order. There was one that was missing.

"Catalina might have it," I whisper, my voice hoarse. "I weaved a message with the location of the Estrella but decided not to send it. I haven't seen the owl in my room for days."

Rumi sags against the table and reaches out to the flat surface to steady himself. His face is slack and pale.

Madre de Luna. I've ruined them.

All of them.

I walk to him until I'm inches away. I force myself to keep my hands at my sides. He won't want me to touch him. "I failed you. But I did not lie to you, Rumi."

A muscle in his jaw clenches.

The infirmary door slams open, the sound ricocheting within the small room. Four guards rush inside. They grab ahold of my arms and yank me toward the door while Rumi calmly watches, perched as he is on the table, his face blank, blank, blank. I expect him to defend me as they haul me out of the room. I expect him to intervene when they yell at me for disappearing and knocking out the maids.

Rumi does none of these things.

I'm dragged away, and my last glimpse is of him putting another strip of fabric onto his bloody gash of a wound. He's careful and competent and undisturbed. He doesn't look in my direction. Not even once.

I'm thrown inside the pigskin-colored room, the door clanging shut. I scramble to search for the owl, flinging aside my other pieces until I've reached the end of the pile. My animals retreat from my mad movements, and I can't blame them.

Only one of them approaches. The owl, which perches on my shoulder. Around its leg is a tied bundle. A rolled-up message meant for me.

My stomach pitches. I slowly untie the ribbon and unfurl the single sheet of paper.

Message Received.
I forgive you.

I slump to the floor and raise a shaking hand to my lips. Catalina thinks I've changed my mind. She thinks I'm back on her side, supporting her claim for the throne.

And she's forgiven me.

I can understand Rumi's rage. It looks bad. My thoughts rush at me like an angry flash fire clamoring for victims. I can't drive the look in Rumi's eyes from my mind. It was hatred, as startling and clear as the water in Lago Yaku. Shame claws up my throat. He thinks I've strung him along for my own gain. Played him like an instrument, hurting him as if he meant nothing to me.

Just a job. Part of my act.

But he's wrong. And I have no way of proving it.

I've lost him. I've lost Tamaya the throne. I've lost the best chance for Inkasisa.

I pull my knees to my chest. This is how Suyana finds me. Curled up on my side, barely able to hold back the flood of tears intent on drowning me. At first she comes in looking annoyed, but her expression loses its hardness when she sees the state I'm in.

"Condesa," she whispers. She shuts the door behind her and crouches in front of me. "What's happened?"

Everything hurts—my chest, my arms, my legs. I want to scream until I can't feel anything anymore, but the room doesn't feel big enough. Panic climbs higher and higher, like a crashing wave threatening to swallow me whole. "I've ruined everything."

Suyana grips my shoulders. "Condesa—"

"I'm not her!" I blurt out. "I'm her decoy. I'm her friend—I'm not even royal. I'm just a nobody."

She stares at me with a look I can't define. But it's not surprise.

I've lost my mind. The entire story comes out in quick bursts. My mission, the search for the Estrella, the planned revolt, my betrayal of the real condesa, the messages in the tapestries. I want it all out.

"Who do you want on the throne?" Suyana asks, her fingers digging painfully into my shoulders. "Who?"

I don't even have to think about it. "The princesa. It can't be Catalina."

"Do you swear?"

I freeze. The sudden fierce gleam in her eye steals my breath. Madre de Luna. She is one of El Lobo's hidden friends in the castillo. My personal maid.

"I've been stupid," I say. "You're his confidante."

She considers me for a long moment. "I didn't trust you, but then Rumi decided to count you in on our plans."

"Not anymore," I whisper. "And now Catalina has the Estrella."

The door opens again and the other two maids I drugged come in, wearing their black polleras and tunics and eyeing me reproachfully. I wish I could care. Suyana has no choice but to help me dress for the wedding. I'm tucked and pinned into the dress. Something is done to my hair, still damp from the bath I'd taken a half hour earlier. The feathered crown is carefully placed on my head. Someone hands me a mirror, but I barely take a look. I'm numb as Suyana laces me into the new sandals. Numb as they swipe rouge on my lips. Numb while the two maids I don't know offer perfunctory congratulations.

It's only when Suyana reaches for my hand and squeezes it that I register what's happening. The door is open, and guards fill the frame, ready to take me away.

I've run out of time.

Veintisiete

Atoc's family and wedding guests are waiting for me in the front courtyard. At the head of the crowd, Atoc climbs onto his horse to lead the procession. The gates are already open, and the cobblestone road to La Ciudad lies ahead. Several guards loiter by the crowd, scanning the area. I startle when I recognize the dark hair and tall frame of my friend.

Juan Carlos.

He's staring at me in contempt. He's as stiff as a board when helping me onto the horse, touching me as little as possible, as if I were garbage. Everyone files into a line, and the entire procession of about one hundred people rides into the city, Juan Carlos on the left, within talking distance. His back is straight enough that I worry it might snap.

As we draw closer to the outer wall of La Ciudad, I'm painfully aware that it's my fault Catalina will unleash ghosts on a rampage against all of these innocent witnesses to my sham of a wedding. Crowds gather on each side of the parade. Loud cheering blocks out the noise of the horses and carts carrying wedding guests.

"I know you must hate me, but you have to help me stop Catalina before it's too late."

His eyes cut to mine, the corner of his mouth lifting in derision. "I'm only here to make sure you don't get in the way, Condesa."

"Juan Carlos. Por favor."

But he remains stubbornly silent. I stare ahead in frustration. Even if I were to try to break free from the procession, I wouldn't make it far. I'm surrounded by guards and well-wishers and court members. The journey is endless. The sun sits high above us, bearing down on the top of my headdress. It must be close to noon.

We reach La Ciudad, its dirty white buildings and clay-tiled roofs looming above us. The décor for Carnaval becomes more pronounced as we snake our way deeper into the city. People wear their best and most festive—every kind of hat and braided hairstyle accented with flowers. There are streamers and jugglers, dancers practicing one of the many traditional Inkasisian dances. I recognize the avid stomping and hopping of the Caporales routine. Musicians strum their charangos. Many others do last-minute adjustments to the main float depicting the silver mountain. All of them are performers for the parade that will commence from the temple and wind its way throughout the entire city.

I take it all in as if I'm not the center of the spectacle. As if it's not my wedding. I can't stop thinking about the ghost army or Tamaya's execution. But when we arrive at the white temple, realization hits.

I'm getting married.

I cast a furtive look in the direction of the Illustrian fortress. Even now, Catalina could be making her way toward La Ciudad with the Estrella. Juan Carlos leaves my side and melts into the crowd. I lose sight of him until he reappears near the temple entrance.

He's found Rumi.

My heart careens against my ribs. He's wearing black pants and a matching tunic, but over the dark clothing there's a colorful vest. He and Juan Carlos stand shoulder to shoulder, their matching brown eyes skimming the crowd. When Rumi's gaze lands on mine, a bolt of recognition courses through my body. His lips flatten into a thin pale slash.

I look away. It's over; there's nothing else I can say or do that will convince him. A guard pulls me off the horse. By the time my feet touch the ground, I've swiped his dagger off his leather belt. I quickly tuck the blade into the folds of my dress. No one will be closer to Atoc than I am. If I can't stop Catalina from summoning the ghost army, I can at least take care of the usurper.

I won't marry him, even if the throat I cut is my own.

A flurry of movement catches my attention and I squint under the bright glare of the sun. It's Suyana, rushing toward Rumi and Juan Carlos. Two guards pull me toward the entrance, and I let them drag me up the white steps and to the grand temple opening. It's Llacsan designed and in the shape of a square, but we painted the structure white hundreds of years ago. My ancestors carved the moon and stars into the outer stone walls and added the two pillars flanking the entrance.

The last time I'd stepped inside was for my abuela's funeral.

I only remember two things from that day: the round opening inside that allows Luna's light to brighten the white floors, and how we'd eaten her walnut cake in her honor. I ate so much of it, I'd gotten sick.

I cross the threshold of the temple where Atoc waits before the white altar at the foot of the chamber. This room used to have gold and silver stars decorating the floor, but it's been covered by horrible green paint. Princesa Tamaya stands off to the side, dressed in plain clothing and guarded by three men. Her wrists are bound, her hair loose and tumbling past her shoulders. She's pale, but she still glares at her brother, her shoulders pulled back, her chin lifted high.

Atoc can't strip her of dignity. She looks every bit the queen. I'm sure of the choice I made. I'm going to kill him. For her, for my people, for Inkasisa.

My heart thrums wildly. Fear works its way into my hands and feet, turning my legs to wood. It snakes into my blood, transforming into a river of living fire. There's no escaping the panic bubbling in me. I fight to remain calm, but I stumble down the aisle, shaking uncontrollably.

I'm about to get married to my enemy. There's no one to help me and nowhere to turn to.

But then Atoc looks at me with a smile that drips oil. Confident of his success. Ready to lead Inkasisa to its doom with me at his side. To cause more pain to everyone I know.

Every inch of me blazes with scorching heat.

This is my moment. I grip the handle of the blade as I step in front of the altar. Ana taught me how a well-placed thrust can be lethal. I only have to be close enough. From a side door, Umaq emerges, dressed in his eggplant-hued robes. The crowd hushes and the ceremony starts—or it would have, if I didn't open my mouth: "Atoc, you're making a mistake."

Of all the things I could have said, I thought this would best ensnare his attention. His body shifts in my direction. The room is silent. No one seems to breathe. No one moves. Not one rustle of clothing.

"What?" he growls.

"I'm not marrying you."

"You are," he snarls. "This minute."

I smile. "I'm not the condesa. I'm her decoy."

He takes a step back, his jaw clenched. "You're lying!"

For the third time in my life, I reveal my secret. Utterly calm. My back straight, my tone steady and unwavering. I could face a firing squad and not even blink. "My name is Ximena Rojas. And Catalina Quiroga marches to the city with the Estrella even now. The ghosts are coming."

Loud gasps erupt in the chamber. People scramble and start talking all at once. The room suddenly feels like a too-fast carriage ride, the crowd and colors blurring together in a chaotic mix. Everyone remembers the carnage, the absolute devastation done by the ghosts. But this time they're on the wrong side. The sound of pattering feet reverberates in the room as some wedding guests flee.

I use the distraction to pull the dagger from within the folds of my elaborate wedding dress and flip the weapon in my palm, blade up. Atoc sees and barks something to the priest. But it's too late. I've already pulled my arm back to launch the knife.

Shooting pain races down my arm, and at the last moment

the knife leaves my hand at the wrong angle and clatters uselessly by my feet. My body isn't mine anymore. I glare at the priest. He'd torture me to save his skin. Until the rebels make their move, until Catalina shows up, he'll play his role dutifully. I let out a curse as my body trembles, unable to move an inch.

Atoc motions to Umaq. "Kill the decoy."

I suck in air. I'm alone against my fight with the false king. "You will not survive what's coming." I pitch my voice louder. "You have too many enemies."

"Wait, priest." Atoc's pulse jumps in his throat. "What other enemies?"

"There are spies everywhere."

His face darkens to a mottled red. "Who are you working with? The vigilante?"

"You shouldn't have turned against your own, Atoc," I say loudly. "You've lost the respect of your people."

Atoc's head jerks back. He casts a nervous glance around the room as if suddenly remembering it's filled with his nobles and foreign dignitaries. "Give me the vigilante's—"

"You've broken your promises."

"His name." Atoc jabs a finger in my direction. "Now."

Out of the corner of my eye, I catch sight of Rumi. He pushes forward until he's standing near the front of the assembly, dressed entirely in black. No one seems to notice him. His gaze flickers to Atoc and then back to mine. A frown pulls at the corners of his mouth, and his brow is scrunched in confusion, as if he's wondering why I won't give up his name.

I remain quiet.

Umaq uses his blood magic against my arms and legs. My

limbs start swelling, fingers plumping and becoming engorged. The pain rips me apart and I groan as I fall to my knees. My hands are in reach of the dagger, but I don't have control over my body.

"It will get so much worse," Atoc says. "His name."

"My secrets will die with me."

"Then you're useless. Get rid of her, priest."

Umaq takes another step forward and I brace myself against the assault. The hem of his robe brushes against my legs. The priest stares down at me and slowly raises his hands.

Then someone bellows, "Stop!"

I look over my shoulder and my heart jumps a beat. Rumi approaches the altar, his slingshot poised and ready, a stone in the leather straps.

Atoc's attention snaps to Rumi. "What are you doing? Drop your weapon. Who do you think you—*Dios.*" The last word escapes on a gasp. He's put the pieces together. Rumi's black clothing. The slingshot. *"You."*

Rumi's bitter coffee eyes glitter in the shifting shadows. *"Me."*

Atoc's guards circle Rumi as the ground starts to tremble. The false king vibrates with iron and fire, his hands clenched into tight fists, his knees slightly bent in preparation for the impending destruction.

Rumi takes aim as guards rush him, and the polished stone crashes into a pillar next to the fake king. Atoc is distracted by the attempted shot. Rumi has another stone in his slingshot. Juan Carlos is by his side, fighting two men at once. The rebels flood the temple, battling Atoc's sentries. Suyana joins the fight, wielding an ax.

Umaq releases his hold on me and blood races away from my swollen limbs. I give myself a moment for my body to right itself and then I snatch the dagger and lunge at the false king. The ground lifts and Atoc lurches to the side. The steel blade tears at the flesh under his arm and he howls with all the fury of an enraged jaguar. The false king snarls and reaches for me, but I stab him again with the dagger, tearing at his skin—

The earthquake tilts the floor beneath my feet.

It sends me careening to my side. My dagger spins away from my hand. Atoc is on me, kicking my ribs, my stomach, over and over—I try scrambling away, but the ground is rippling too hard, keeping me trapped between his feet and the trembling white stone. Atoc slams a fist at my face and the hit shreds my mouth. I cough up blood.

Suyana knocks the fake king off me, but another guard charges at me, sword raised high. He aims for my neck. I try scrambling away, but I slip on my own blood. My dagger is yards away from my reach.

The sword comes down.

Rumi roars. There's a sharp whistling sound. A rock strikes the back of the guard's head. Blood and bone splatter everywhere.

Rumi is upon me, pulling me to my feet. He thrusts a sword into my hands. There's no time for words, but he looks deep into my eyes and brushes his lips to mine. It's only for a moment, then he pushes through the crowd, slingshot circling high above his head.

Battle cries erupt around me. There are people everywhere—kicking and thrusting blades, grunting and launching their stones. Atoc's Llacsan guards are distinguishable thanks to their uniforms: black-and-white checked tunics, and around their calves a dark band stitched with multicolored feathers. The Llacsan rebels are dressed entirely in black. A nod to El Lobo. In the madness, I've lost sight of the people I know. Suyana and Juan Carlos. The fickle priest, Umaq. Princesa Tamaya. Rumi.

A Llacsan guard attacks my left side. I jump sideways, raise my blade, and block his strike. I wince—the movement jars my ribs and sends shooting pains down my side. My attacker snarls at me.

He's still snarling when I drive the point of my sword into his belly. Blood gushes from the hole in his stomach, but I've already moved on. I suck in deep breaths, trying to keep the nausea at bay. I spit blood onto the white stone. The metallic taste burns my tongue. My dress is a hindrance, and impatiently I tear the delicate fabric of the skirt, shortening it to mid-thigh. I kick off the delicate sandals. The white stone is hot beneath my feet.

The battle moves outside the temple and onto the open streets. I'm pushed along with the crowd, through the fighting and puddles of blood smearing the cobblestone. Atoc hollers for his guards, for a weapon, for a defense against the approaching fighters. They're mixed in with the Carnaval celebrators and street vendors, who desperately rush away. In every direction, spears and swords are raised. One of Atoc's guards hands him a whip.

Someone lets out a bloodcurdling scream. I search for the source, my hands shaking. It sounds like the princesa. I spot her at Atoc's feet. She's on her hands and knees near the entrance of the temple. A deep gash mars her cheek. Several Llacsan rebels surround her, their blades swinging madly in their effort to ward off Atoc. He cracks the leather whip at anyone who draws near to him.

My hands grip my blade harder as I race toward the false king. He spins to face me, a cold smile stretching his thin lips. Atoc's whip cracks and the leather wraps around my wrist, once, twice, three times.

I use the sword to cut the whip, ignoring the scorching burn. Something crashes into Atoc, and he's catapulted off his feet. A white woolly jaguar snarls down at him. I gasp as a parrot swoops and claws the fake king's face.

They're here! My animals. *Here*, in La Ciudad.

The anaconda slithers into view, hissing. The jaguar pounces, its front paws out and slicing into Atoc's chest. I coo at the parrot flying overhead. My frogs hop around my feet, ready to poison anyone who comes near.

"The princesa!" I yell. "Guard her!"

My animals curl around Tamaya. The jaguar looms above her, its teeth snarling. Atoc pulls out a dagger and cuts through the animal's skin. He lets out a shrill, triumphant cry. I snap my gaze back to my jaguar and gasp.

It looks over at me, blinking sorrowfully.

"No," I scream. "No—"

Dropping to my knees, I pull the jaguar close as it unravels in my bloodstained hands. "Lo siento, I'm so sorry."

The jaguar goes limp, scraps of wool falling onto the ground. Hot tears carve tracks down my cheeks. My friend is gone. Something I made with my hands, put a piece of my heart into when all the world saw me only as someone else.

I jump to my feet and scoop up my sword. I'm racing at

Atoc, my weapon high above my head. The ground twitches beneath my feet. Then it lurches, up and down, knocking me onto my back.

A harsh cry rips out of me.

No one can stay upright. Everyone crashes to their knees or onto their backs. La Ciudad crumbles, buildings breaking apart in chunks. The bell tower smashes to the stone floor. Chunks of rock smack people as they scramble to the middle of the street, away from the falling debris.

I'm transported back to the day my parents died. The earth had risen and quaked, uttering a deep and harsh sound from its depth. My parents were on the bottom floor of our house, hollering for me to come downstairs. But the walls were shaking. I went to the balcony instead—and lived when they did not.

Another violent shake wrenches the memory away.

"Ximena!" Juan Carlos crawls to me, pushing people aside. "Stand!"

He yanks me up. Over his shoulder, a guard raises a knife aimed for the back of his neck. I scream, shoving my friend aside, and thrust my sword deep into the man's belly.

Juan Carlos looks up at me from the ground, smiling. "Dios, you're terrifying."

Before I can respond, Atoc roars and forces the ground to split and crack open like eggshells. Gulfs appear. Juan Carlos nimbly skirts around the cracks, then takes up his sword against one of the guards.

The gaping holes in the ground force people aside, and as the crowd parts, Atoc comes into my line of sight. His gaze cuts to mine. The false king leaps over the crevices and crashes into me.

We stumble onto the ground, him on top of my chest. I can't breathe normally. His strong hands wrap around my neck. He squeezes. My vision darkens. Overhead, my parrot has my dagger and drops it within my reach, clattering onto the cobblestone. It's the faintest sound against the roar of the battle encircling us.

My fingers find the weapon.

I plunge the blade deep into Atoc's neck. It slides into his flesh like a key into a lock and I twist the steel. There's a gurgling sound. His eyes widen as blood gushes out of his mouth. Splattering on my face, stinging my eyes. It's hot and sticky, tasting sour and rotten.

The ground stops shaking. I shove him away, kicking at the dead weight pressing into my bruised ribs. *He's dead. He's dead. He's dead.*

My anaconda hisses and uses its tail to grip Atoc's waist, flinging him away. I turn to my side, coughing up the blood of my enemy. A soldier steps in front of me, his dirty toes encased in rough sandals. I duck away from his blade as the parrot dives and sinks its talons into the man's eyes. The anaconda wraps itself around his body, squeezing and squeezing until he turns purple. The soldier lets out a final warbled scream that rings in my head.

I lurch to my feet, yanking the dagger from Atoc's neck. My sword is buried in the belly of a guard, lost somewhere in the fight. Tamaya rushes to my side and helps me wipe her brother's blood off my face.

"You saved me," she says, breathless. She pulls me into a tight embrace. "Gracias, gracias."

My gaze snags on something over her shoulder. Something

that should have stayed dead and buried. "Don't thank me just yet."

She stiffens and pulls away, a frown marring her brow.

"The ghost army comes."

CAPÍTULO

veintiocho

The Illustrian horn blares a deafening bellow, heralding the advance of the spectral beings. Someone lets out a bloodcurdling scream and points toward the plaza. A twisting mass curves around the crumbling buildings and floods the street—not fog or smoke or vapor, but gnashing teeth and translucent clawing hands. The swirling bulk lets out a violent, collective shriek and the sound scrapes against me, blotting out my thoughts.

One by one, it separates into individual men and women. They encircle all of us, those left standing and wounded alike, standing shoulder to shoulder.

None can pass. We are trapped.

Tamaya latches onto my arm, her nails digging into my skin.

I barely notice. My attention is on the ghosts. Their pale skeletons are visible beneath their sharp silvery bodies. Carrying picks and axes, they're dressed in simple clothing, worn and grimy at the knees. As one, their transparent flesh darkens, obscuring their bones, transforming them into something resembling humans. Harsh sunlight makes their skin chalk white.

They study their surroundings with centuries-old eyes.

The anaconda hisses. Fear blooms in my heart and spreads like poisonous ivy. My dagger trembles in my sweat-slicked hand.

Tamaya addresses the ghosts in the old language. Her voice rings above the clamor, almost shrill. But it's no use—they raise their weapons and with a roar they barrel forward. A ghost separates from the group and races toward the princesa. I step in front of Tamaya and launch my dagger. It cuts through the air, spinning until the blade sinks into the spirit's gut.

The hit does nothing.

The spirit doesn't howl or slow down but yanks out my knife and raises it high. I quickly scour the ground for another weapon. The blade of a sword winks up at me, buried under a maimed body.

"Look out!" Tamaya yells from behind me.

I push at the fallen Llacsan, desperate for that weapon. The ghost reaches me. Its cloying scent assaults my nose. Rotten bones buried in mud and dirt for hundreds of years. A decaying carcass given the gift of hate and violence and life. It pulls me upright by my hair. I try to wrench free, but my attacker holds on and drags me away from the sword.

There's murder in its glowing eyes. I scream as its knife angles toward my heart.

A blur rushes at the ghost. The grip on my hair lessens and I kick and claw away from the spirit. Juan Carlos stands above me, his weapon swinging. I drag myself to the sword, still hidden underneath the dead Llacsan. I shove the body away and grip the hilt.

When I stand, it's in time to see the spirit slice Juan Carlos's throat.

My chest burns as I let out a guttural yell. My friend slumps to the ground, his eyes unblinking as his life's blood gushes from his neck.

Tamaya drops to her knees, attempting to stop the bleeding with her clothes. She's sobbing, keening. Her hands are stained red from Juan Carlos's slashed flesh.

Time slows. Sweat drips from my hairline, stinging my eyes. My veins are hot liquid. The clamor of the fight dims. Everyone is shouting, but I can't hear any of it. I can't tear my gaze away from his vacant gaze.

Juan Carlos is gone.

The ghost turns to the kneeling princesa and raises the bloody knife.

"Tamaya," I say, my voice hoarse. "Get up."

She slowly stands and once again I push her behind me.

The ghost advances.

And then, just over its shoulder, I see her. She comes into my line of sight as if she's always been there. She wears no cape, her head uncovered, loose hair running down her back. The Estrella isn't visible. She grips a sword in her right hand. It's much too heavy for her.

Catalina.

I tip my head back and scream with everything left in me. "Condesa!"

She whips around, sees the ghost's intent. "Don't hurt her!"

It immediately quits its advancement.

Tamaya comes to stand next to me, slack-jawed as Llacsans

continue to get killed. Catalina's gaze flickers between mine and Tamaya's, her eyes wide and confused. I catch the moment when Catalina realizes whose side I'm on. She clutches her chest as if I've stabbed her heart.

And in a way, I have.

Traitor. Rat.

I stumble toward the condesa, Tamaya at my heels. Illustrian fighters circle us, forming a protective barrier against the onslaught. I know each of them by name. I've trained and slept and lived alongside them at the keep. And now they follow Catalina—the real royal. Their friend. I was nothing to them. Nothing but a stand-in, a fake.

My hands are sticky with blood. I manage to latch onto her arms. "Call them off! Catalina, do it!"

She jerks back. *"What?"*

"Look around you!" I scream. "This isn't you—stop them."

"You sent me the location!" Her voice quavers. "I got your message. This is what you wanted . . ."

"I killed Atoc." I squeeze her arms as I search for the gem. She's not wearing it, but I know it must be somewhere on her. "No one else has to die. Give me the Estrella—we have to destroy it."

"Destroy it?" She looks at the princesa, disappointment carved into her features. "Is this about *her*? You still want her on the throne?"

"She's not your enemy."

"You both are!" she yells, charging, her sword raised.

I jump away from her jab. We might have been training. Except this is a stronger Catalina than I remember. She's enraged and hurt, governed by her emotions. They drive her every move. Tamaya keeps behind me.

"Ximena!" Rumi yells from somewhere in the crowd. He tosses me a sword, and I catch the handle in time to block Catalina's next thrust. She attacks with all the rage of the sun. Each of her moves leaves me shaking. Sweat drops down my back.

I'm out of practice, out of shape. My limbs raw and burning as if on fire. But that doesn't matter. Catalina fights as if reading out of a book. By the rules, without any variation—but she's upset, and her moves become erratic. Frantic jabs that slice air and not flesh. She cries out in frustration with every missed opportunity.

I block her attack and slam the heel of my boot onto her toes. She squeals and drops her sword. I raise the blade and keep it level with her heart.

The anaconda coils at my side, ready to pounce.

"Not her," I say sharply.

Illustrians swarm behind the condesa, arrows notched and ready to fly. I sense, rather than see, the Llacsan rebels line up behind the princesa and me. The whistling from their slingshots spinning in the air tears through the cloudless blue sky.

The ghost army stands ready to strike. There are so few of us left. Cut down by their indestructible force. No one will survive against the spirits.

Catalina can give the order to attack, but it will only take me seconds to kill her.

Madre de Luna. We're all going to destroy one another. Unless I can make Catalina see reason.

"Catalina, please. Stop this before it's too late," I say softly. *"Por favor."*

"I won't ever accept anything less than the throne. Pick up

your weapon and finish this," Catalina snaps. "Nobody move. This is between Ximena and me. Pick up your blade!"

I shake my head. "There's a better way. For all of us."

Catalina's eyes flicker past my shoulder. Her voice is oddly flat. "I never thought I'd live to see the day you'd want a Llacsan on the throne."

"I want the *right* person on the throne. Someone who wants a united Inkasisa."

"Condesa," Tamaya says. "You will be equal and treated with the respect you deserve. I'm not my brother, and I want what's best for all—"

"Stop talking," Catalina says impatiently. She turns to me. "I don't know who you are anymore. What about our people? My parents? Your parents? You're disgracing their memory."

"Maybe," I say. "But I'm doing this for all of Inkasisa."

Catalina is crying now. "Don't talk about Inkasisa—this is about you and me. We've been friends for ten years. This is a betrayal."

That stings. It's so much more than our friendship. But I'm out of words. I can only beg. "Give Princesa Tamaya a chance. For me."

"Why don't you give *me* a chance?" Catalina asks. She digs into her pocket and pulls out a thick silver bracelet. The ametrine gem sparkles in the sunlight, half amethyst, half citrine. The Llacsan rebels gasp behind me. The Illustrians tense, waiting for the condesa's signal. I can't drag my eyes away from the cuff. I lunge at her.

The Llacsans launch their rocks—

The Illustrians shoot their arrows—

The ghost army utters a high, hair-raising shriek—

Catalina cries out as we crash to the ground. Her hand holding the Estrella knocks against the stone. It rolls out of her reach—

I kick the condesa away and scoop up the bracelet. It's as cold as a corpse. I push through the crowd, looking for a crack in the earth. Catalina is screaming something from behind me. But I ignore her, ignore the fighting, the ghosts on their murdering rampage. I find what I'm looking for.

A hole in the earth that leads down, down, down to fire and heat, the center of the world.

I stop at the edge, holding my hand over the gulf.

"Ximena," Catalina says. *"Don't."*

A noise like a rushing river envelopes me. I can't hear anything except the howling in my head, in my heart. The cuff is heavy, a block of ice. I know the moment I drop it, the moment it touches the heat of the earth, it'll be gone forever.

I slowly turn to face the condesa. "This is the only way."

Her guards have their arrows aimed at my heart. The ghosts press closer until I can smell every one of their rotting limbs.

"Don't shoot," Catalina says. "She'll drop it!"

But I'm going to let go anyway. She sees it in my eyes. My fingers loosen their hold on the Estrella. Her lips form a cry that rattles inside my lungs, leaving me trembling. She'll never forgive me for this.

I let go.

The cuff drops and vanishes. I peer over the edge as I'm surrounded by Llacsan rebels protecting me from the onslaught of Illustrian fighters and enraged ghosts. Rumi is at my back, sword swinging at the spirits wanting my blood, my life.

But I watch for the Estrella until I know it's truly gone. I don't have to wait long. A burst of light forms miles below, almost hidden by the craggy dark walls of the earth. The ground shakes, jostling me forward. Rumi grabs the scruff of my wedding dress and jerks me upright, but I can't take my gaze away from the ball of light.

I exhale. The Estrella is destroyed. Gone forever.

The ghosts vanish in a gust of frigid air. It whips my hair across my face. Then comes a crashing noise like glass shattering against stone. A high metallic shrill leaves my ears ringing. The explosion, the magical rebound of bright silver light races up the jagged walls of the earth. I don't have time to move away.

The blast reaches me in seconds.

Pain explodes in my chest, my head, my heart, my bones.

I'm lifted off my feet.

Everything blackens as my head cracks against stone.

CAPÍTULO
veintinueve

Someone opened the balcony doors too early again. I wince and turn away from the sunlight, snuggling deeper into the pillow.

"Don't you dare go back to sleep."

I crack my eyes open. A handsome boy stares back at me. Dark sweeping brows. Thin lips bent into a smile. Freckles dotting his sharp nose. Eyes the color of coffee beans staring into mine.

"Hola, Ximena," Rumi whispers.

He smooths my sweaty hair away from my forehead. I try to sit up, and he helps me, his grip firm on my shoulders. Then he places another pillow behind me.

I look around my room in the castillo. It's exactly the same as I'd left it: loom tucked in the corner, clothes folded neatly on the chair. The anaconda sleeps beside the bed, snuggled next to the llama and the sloth. My frogs are lounging on an old tunic in the corner while the parrot and condor are perched on the balcony railing. My ants are roaming the top of my dresser.

They're all here except my jaguar. My heart cracks.

"What happened?" I ask softly.

Rumi lies next to me, and I glance down from my propped position.

"You've been asleep for thirty-six hours," he says. "The explosion launched you into the air and you landed on the front steps of the temple. There was so much blood."

I whistle. "Sounds serious."

His voice goes soft. "I used all of my magic to heal you. I would do it again without hesitating but . . ."

"Yes?"

"Please don't put yourself in that kind of danger again," he says, his voice dropping to a whisper. I almost didn't hear him. "Please . . . just don't. We were lucky."

My heart warms at the *we*.

It must show on my face because he pushes himself up on his elbow and presses a soft kiss to my lips. My pulse races. I want to ask him about our friends, about the last moments of battle, but I'm terrified of the results. Who else didn't make it? The words don't come and I look at him helplessly.

He reads the question in my eyes and answers. "The Illustrians surrendered. But Catalina refused to concede defeat. She's being held prisoner—"

I bolt upright. "In the dungeon?"

Rumi pulls me back so I'm once again lying on the pillows. "In a bedroom with guards at the door."

"Tell me everything."

He starts with the moment Suyana found him right before the wedding. "We couldn't stand by and do nothing about Atoc's order to execute the princesa, so we went ahead with our plan.

Even without the ghost army."

"What did Suyana tell you?" My voice catches. "Is she alive?"

He nods. "She said you were one of us. When Atoc tried to kill you, when you refused to give up my name . . . I couldn't let you die, and then you saved Tamaya and battled the condesa. I fought and fought knowing that I'd made the biggest mistake of my life. It was the hardest thing, giving you that sword and not being able to tell you how sorry I was."

I remember the brush of his lips. The look in his eyes. "I knew."

He closes his eyes and nods once. Then he reaches for my hand and kisses the back of my wrist.

"Then what happened?"

"I've been attending to as many people as I can. My cousin—"

I cup his cheek. He was my friend too. "I'm so sorry. I saw it happen; there was nothing we could do."

His eyes clench, his shoulders tense, fighting to keep the tears at bay. He breathes in and out, controlled breaths that soften the tight lines around his eyes. He reopens them to look at me. "So many perished. After the battle, Catalina was allowed a funeral for the Illustrians who died."

I wound the sheet around my fingers. "How many died?"

"Lo siento," he whispers. "Catalina told me to tell you, but I can't—"

My voice goes flat. "How many."

He ducks his head. "Fifty-two."

Tears drip down my face. Rumi wipes them away and holds me as I cry. She'll never understand what I've done. And because of that, she'll never be able to forgive me for it either.

"Te amo, Ximena," he says against my hair.

"Yo también."

Rumi lets out a contented hum. His lips are soft against my skin.

I pull away and wipe my eyes. "Then what happened?"

"Umaq is gone," Rumi says bitterly. "He left on a stolen horse with plenty of notas from Atoc's treasury. I'm told he's headed for the jungle."

The Yanu Jungle? You'd have to be out of your mind to enter. *"Why?"*

Rumi shrugs. "Who cares? I never want to see him again. I'll kill him if I do."

"Whatever lies in the jungle will do that for you."

"Dios, I hope so." His voice becomes hushed, careful. "Now all that's left is Catalina's hearing. Tamaya insisted you be awake for it. Are you up for it today?"

I sink deeper into the pillow and shake my head. I can't face her yet. "Mañana."

"Whatever you want," he says, his eyes soft.

"Will she be executed?" I ask in a quiet voice.

"I don't know, amor. I really don't know."

He pulls me close, and this time I don't ask for another distraction. I let myself cry.

I wake up in darkness, Rumi's arm draped over my side. I shift to face him and trace my finger along his profile. Moonlight streams into the room, and I can just make out the strong planes of his face, the sharp curve of his jaw. I drag my thumb across his brow.

"Hmmm," he mumbles. "Why are you awake?"

"Nightmare, I think," I whisper. "We're sleeping in the same bed."

He cracks an eye open. "That's what your nightmare was about?"

"No," I murmur. "I think it was about Catalina."

"I should have asked you if it was all right," he says, yawning. "To sleep here, I mean."

I smile in the dark. "It's all right. A little shocking, maybe."

"I'm your healer." The sheet rustles as he leans forward to plant a soft kiss on my cheek. "What if you needed me?"

"Of course," I say in a serious tone. "You're being a professional."

"Are you always this chatty in the middle of the night?"

"I'm worried about her," I say. "Where is she? I know she's awake. Catalina reads constellations whenever she can't sleep."

He sighs and rubs his eyes. "She's on this floor."

"Will you take me to her?"

Rumi sighs again. But he sits up and assists me out of bed. He hands me a robe and helps me put on my sandals. He takes my hand and leads me down the hallway, until we stop at the very end, where two guards stand watch.

"I'll wait for you outside," he mumbles sleepily. He squeezes my hand and sits on the floor, his back leaning against the stone.

"I need to talk to her."

One of the guards nods. "Whatever you want."

I take a deep breath and walk inside. Catalina stands on the balcony, her head tipped all the way back. Her index finger is raised and moving slightly, as if she's tracing the faint lines between the stars.

"I thought you'd come," she says.

I join her outside but stand by the door frame. "I wanted to say I'm sorry."

"Would you change what you did?" she asks, her voice hard.

"No," I say. "But that doesn't mean I don't care that I hurt you. I wish I hadn't."

She keeps her back to me. "I'm not going to accept your apology, so you may as well leave, Ximena."

"Don't you want to know *why?*"

"No," she snaps.

I nod, swallowing hard. There is so much I want to tell her, but not if she doesn't want to hear it. The words will be wasted. I want to talk with her, not *at* her. Turning, I take a step back into her bedroom.

Her voice rings out. "Wait."

I spin, hope blooming in my chest.

She still hasn't turned around. "*Fine.* Why?"

The hurt in her voice splinters my heart. I can't live in Catalina's world anymore—to go back to a time when Llacsans scraped by, barely surviving, when they were being pushed out of their homes, forced to live in the mountains as Illustrians stole the air they breathed and the earth they had walked upon for centuries.

How do I begin to explain all that?

"I asked you to abandon the revolt because Inkasisa needs a queen who will unite the people and bridge the divide. It doesn't need more war or oppression, or mistreatment of anyone," I continue, my hands splayed. "More lives will be lost if things continue in the same way as before. Mistakes will be repeated. There would eventually be another revolt—and this time against *you*."

Catalina grips the railing of the balcony, her shoulders slumping, and the proud veneer she wears crumbles. Her body trembles and her hand comes up to her face. I want to reach for her, but I force myself to stay still. There's no one fighting for her anymore. She's alone and she knows it. I need her to feel that—because maybe she'll realize how wrong it is for her to cling to the throne.

"That's why I betrayed you, Catalina," I whisper. "I wanted to end the war and not start a new one."

"Get out," she says. "Just get out."

Catalina turns around, and the look she gives me tears at my heart. Her eyes do all the screaming.

I cross the room, already trying to forget the expression on her face. But I doubt I'll ever be able to. Rumi stands when the door opens, and he holds out his arms. I walk into them, settling my cheek against the soft cotton of his tunic. He rubs my shoulders and then gently leads me back to my room.

"What can I do?" he whispers.

I shake my head. There's nothing. I've lost Catalina for good. Tomorrow will only make it official.

The next day, Rumi helps me dress, a wicked gleam in his eyes. He teases and flirts and kisses me until I worry my cheeks will remain red until the end of time.

I know what he's doing, and I appreciate the distraction. It's nice having him around. More than nice. Especially since he keeps up the habit of washing his clothes. When I say as much, Rumi roars with laughter.

"What's so funny?" I ask. "It was a serious problem, Rumi. That smell was giving me *grave* concerns."

That only makes him laugh harder. "Ximena, I wash my clothes twice a week. At least. I always have."

"No—"

"Yes," he counters. "I stuffed my pockets with a bag of herbs to create the smell. A special blend, my own creation. That's all that it was."

"Why would you do something so silly?"

"Was it all that silly?" he asks slyly. "Distracted you plenty, didn't it? People focused on the smell, on the slumping healer who made a spectacle of himself fawning over his precious king. Who would have ever thought the laughingstock of court was El Lobo? Certainly not *you*."

I purse my lips. It's clever, but I'll never say so. His ego needs to be kept in check.

Rumi lets out another chuckle and opens the door for me.

"Wait," I say, turning around. My animals stare back at me. I motion for them to follow. "I want the world to meet them," I explain. "It's time."

Rumi takes the sloth in his arms, and the lizard settles onto his shoulder. The parrot flies above our heads, followed closely by the owl, who came back sometime during the night. I latch onto Rumi as we head down to court, the condor, anaconda, and llama at our heels. No guards trail after us. That's a pleasant change.

"You're quiet," Rumi comments.

"I was thinking about how different this walk is compared to the first trip I ever made to court. Do you remember that day?"

He nods. "I didn't know what to make of you. And you were wearing one of Princesa Tamaya's dresses. I like the outfit you're wearing right now much better."

I'd chosen a simple white skirt—no ruffles—and a tunic with a low-slung leather belt. Very Illustrian, save for the vibrantly striped vest over the ensemble. The perfect blend of the girl I used to be with the girl I want to be.

"It suits you," he says, as if he can hear my thoughts.

Warmth spreads deep into my belly. He smiles and pulls me closer as we continue to the great hall.

"By the way . . ." Rumi begins. "There are quite a few Illustrians sleeping in the spare rooms and courtyard. Most decided to stay for Princesa Tamaya's coronation. She gave a great speech about wanting their help in unifying Inkasisa."

But did she convince them? They've spent years living steeped in their dislike—in their desire for revenge. Princesa Tamaya has a long battle ahead of her. The process of making the nation whole will take time and energy and a strong will.

I stop. "Can I see them?"

Rumi smiles, gently pulling me along. "Of course—that's why I'm telling you, you fool."

He laughs when I make a face. The doors to the throne room loom ahead, and I stiffen. Two sentries open the tall double doors to the great hall. As I pass by, they salute and grin wildly at the sight of my creatures trailing after me as if we're a parade. The llama spits a woolly ball at one of their faces.

At the foot of the room sits the princesa, a resplendent headdress with delicate gold weaving on her head. Her dark hair tumbles loosely around her shoulders.

At my entrance, she jumps to her feet.

"Ximena Rojas," Tamaya says, grinning. "And company."

Rumi hands me the sloth and gently pushes me forward. As I walk down the long aisle, Llacsans and Illustrians drop to one knee.

By the time I reach the dais, I'm sure my face is the color of a ripe tomato. The princesa bounds down the steps and embraces me, careful not to squish the animal in my arms. Laughing, she clutches her headdress to keep it from falling.

Tamaya fingers the animal's moon thread. "This is extraordinary magic."

"Yours is better."

"Is it?" She tilts her head. "Or are they both special in their own way?"

"If you say so," I smile. But I understand her meaning. It was never a competition.

Her gaze drops to the animal in my arms. "Introduce me to your amigo."

"This is Sloth," I say. "He's a snuggler."

"Bienvenidos." She opens her arms wide. "To all of you."

Catalina stands at the side of the dais, flanked by guards. She snaps her head toward the door.

I swallow back the lump in my throat.

"Ximena," the princesa says. "You saved my life—you and these wonderful creatures—and I will forever be in your debt. I can't thank you enough. You and your animals are free to live in this castillo as long as you want."

I duck my head. "Gracias."

"Will you honor me by joining my council of advisors?"

Sitting around inside and talking all day? I make a face. "I'd rather open a shop in La Ciudad. I want to weave silly things for people to decorate their home with. Tapestries and bags, maybe even clothes one day."

Tamaya blinks and then lets out a resounding laugh. "Done. Anything else?"

I glance at Catalina.

Princesa Tamaya's face shifts into a sad smile. "She will be given every chance," she whispers.

The chamberlain calls Catalina forward. She obeys, stone-faced, refusing to meet my eye.

"Condesa . . . " the princesa begins. "I want to come to some sort of understanding with you. I don't mind that you hate me. That is your right as a human being. But will you ever be able to accept me as your future queen? What I do mind is fighting the same fight, month after month, year after year."

Catalina lifts her chin. "I will not."

"Then you'll drink the koka tea," Princesa Tamaya says, and motions to one of the attendants standing by the dais.

Catalina sways on her feet.

"No," I say breathlessly. "No, por favor."

I drop to my knees. Catalina will never beg for her life. But I have no such qualms. She needs to live—or else she'll never have the opportunity to change. To learn. I want her to have the chance.

The princesa hesitates. "She's that important to you?"

I nod.

Princesa Tamaya's poised and serene expression wavers. "Then I'll spare her life, but she cannot stay here. Catalina, you are banished to the Yanu Jungle and will be escorted there immediately."

I gape at the princesa. The *jungle*? "She won't survive. She's been sheltered her *whole* life!"

Catalina stiffens, and her lips pale.

The princesa shakes her head. "That's my decision."

I turn away, struggling for composure. Damn Catalina's stubbornness! If only she'd relent. I stare at her, beseechingly. "Catalina . . . accept her as your queen. *Por favor.*"

Her face hardens. "I'll die first."

"I'll let you have a moment," Tamaya says.

"No need." Catalina whips around. She marches down the aisle, the guards on her heels. No words of goodbye.

I stare at the door long after it closes behind her. "Did it have to be the jungle?"

"I think she'll come out the better for it," Tamaya says thoughtfully.

If she comes out at all. What kind of horrors will she encounter there? She's never been left alone. But I'm not Catalina's protector anymore. I'm not her decoy. She doesn't even consider me her friend.

I wrap my arms around my stomach. The condesa needs to learn how to fight her own battles—especially the ones she creates for herself.

"I'm going to need your help in the coming months," Princesa Tamaya says. "As you, though. Not a decoy, or anybody else."

My gaze lands on Rumi as he approaches the throne. Every choice has brought me to this moment, and I know in my bones that I'm meant to stand here with the rightful queen of Inkasisa, in a castillo that no longer feels like a cage but a home filled with people who are like family. Rumi smiles at me and I take a step forward, meeting him halfway. He cups my cheek. The sloth burrows deeper into my arms. The birds fly around in circles, happy and free. I can picture Luna smiling down at me.

I've made the right decision.

I'm ready to be me.

Only me.

glossary

QUECHUA

Atoc—fox

Inkasisa—royal flower

Killa—moon

Rumi—rock

Sajra—evil

Sisa—flower

Suyana—hope

Tamaya—center

Taruka—doe

Umaq—traitor

SPANISH

Araña—spider

Azucar—sugar

Fuego—fire

Mentiras—lies

Desayuno—breakfast

Cafe con leche—coffee with milk

Hormigas—ants

Girasoles—sunflowers

FOOD

Achachairu: my favorite fruit from Bolivia. It's egg-shaped and tastes like lemonade

Aji amarillo: yellow hot pepper

Api: a breakfast drink made of purple maize, cinnamon, sugar, and water

Choclo: large kernel corn from the Andes

Cuñapes: Bolivian cheese bread made from yuca starch and queso fresco; usually served at teatime, in the afternoon

Huacatay: cream of black mint

Llajwa: chili sauce made of locoto, tomatoes, and onion; I add this to everything!

Locoto: chili pepper; key ingredient in llajwa

Maracuya: passion fruit. Drinking fruit juice in Bolivia is as popular as drinking fountain sodas, often more so. Popular choices are maracuya, durazno (peach), fresa (strawberry), and pera (pear). You can blend them with water or milk

Marraqueta: crispy, salty bread; a breakfast staple, often topped with dulce de leche

Mermelada: jam

Pasankalla: puffed white maize, coated in sugar; we eat this at the movies!

Quinoa: crop held sacred by the Incas, the "mother of all grains." It's our version of rice. I grew up eating it, and when it became popular in the States, I was thrilled to see it everywhere on menus!

Salteñas: baked football-shaped empanada from Bolivia, filled with beef, pork, or chicken, raisins, peas, and exactly one black olive and boiled egg. The juice is like a stew and made with gelatin. When baked, the gelatin slowly melts and turns into a soup inside the dough

Sándwich de chola: Bolivian street sandwich with pork, beef, or chicken

Silpancho: popular Bolivian dish in my mother's native Cochabamba. Base layer is white rice, followed by a layer of pan-fried potatoes, then a thin layer of breaded meat, diced tomatoes, and white onion. Topped with fried egg and parsley. A family favorite

Singani: liquor made from white wine grapes and produced in the high valley of Bolivia

Sopa de mani: another favorite from Cochabamba. Peanut soup served before the main meal at lunch. Usually topped with crispy potatoes sliced into thin matchsticks

Té de maté: my mom gave this to me whenever I was sick—a bitter tea that I never warmed up to, but it's a particular favorite in Bolivia

Yuca frita: starchy root vegetable, often fried and dipped into sauces

acknowledgments

I'm going to attempt to thank everyone, but the truth is that words don't feel big enough to demonstrate my profound gratitude. Just imagine me writing this letter to you all, with a box of tissues at my elbow, and the largest slice of carrot cake at my fingertips.

So many hugs and heartfelt thanks to my incredibly gifted editor, Ashley Hearn. You are an absolute gem of a human being—thank you for fighting for this book. Your guidance, input, patience, and tremendous work ethic made all the difference to this story's journey to publication. To the entire Page Street team, for all of your hard work and support: my publicists Lauren Cepero and Lizzy Mason, editorial assistants Madeline Greenhalgh and Tamara Grasty, editorial intern Kayla Cottingham, production editor Hayley Gundlach, managers Marissa Giambelluca and Meg Palmer, editor Lauren Knowles, publisher Will Kiester, and the wonderful sales team at Macmillan. To Meg Baskis, who gave me so much freedom for the cover design of *Woven in Moonlight*, thank you for trusting me!

Many, many heartfelt gracias to Mary Moore, for encouraging

me to write a Bolivian tale, and for finding this story a great home. To my sweet writer friends Margaret Rogerson, Adrienne Young, and Rebecca Ross for championing *Woven in Moonlight* and for writing the loveliest blurbs. I'm so thankful for each of you—for our friendship, manuscript swaps, and encouragement. You guys are in my bubble and always will be. Kristin Dwyer, I think the world of you, and I'm so thankful for the laughs and support. I'll never forget our life-giving conversation in my car, while it was pouring rain, right after I screamed about that spider hiding on the steering wheel.

Adalyn Grace, your sass gives me life. Thank you for calling me out when I ought to be writing, for the laughs, an amazing time at Disney, and for generally being awesome, supportive, and lovely. You are so wise beyond your years, and I swear you really could be a CIA agent. Joanna Hathaway and Kristin Ciccarelli, you two are such genuine, beautiful souls. I feel so proud to know you. Thank you for the love and encouragement on the earliest drafts of *Woven in Moonlight*. Lisa Parkin, sweet friend, I don't know what I'd do without you! I cherish our breakfast dates and conversations about life and books. Love you!

My incredible Pitch Wars family: the entire 2015 class, especially Megan England, Leah Mar, Jamie Pacton, Kat Hinkel, Rebecca Mcloughlin, and Michelle Domenici. Thank you so much for reading snippets of *Woven in Moonlight*! Sheena Boekwreg and Megan Lally—I don't know how I'd survive the publishing world without you both. Thank you for the many years of friendship and support, for all the wisdom, laughter, and amazing guidance. Thank you for reading everything I write, once, twice, a thousand times. Shout out to Jenni Welsh, Haley Kirkpatrick,

Bridget Baker, Fiona Mclaren, for the early reads and feedback. A million thanks!

So many hugs and thanks to my Nacho Libro/First Tuesday Club sweet friends: Brianne Kaufholz, Jessica Meyer, Samantha Robinson, Chrystal Merriam, Kristy Lee Lawley, Anna Ware, Rachel Aldrich, Melanie Snavely, and Kristin Pavlic. You all have a special place in my heart. Every wonderful writing- or publishing-related memory involves book club and all of your sweet faces.

To my sweet friends who aren't a part of the writing world, and for that I'm so incredibly thankful because you've all kept me sane: Patricia Gray, Elizabeth Sloan, Davey Olsen, Jess Pierce, and Jessica Meyer. Thank you for loving me so well, for the love, support and cheers, no matter how many all cap text messages I send (especially to Jessica, who gets them twice!). Elizabeth, thanks for reading the beginning and for making sure I sound professional in my bio. We may not have the same taste in stories, but I know you'll love this one. <3

To everyone who has been a part of this journey, however small—thank you! You know who you are, and I'm so thankful for every bit of support, well wishes, and encouragement. Thank you for sharing social media posts, retweeting updates and news, and showing up—virtually and in person.

My incredible parents, you both came to this country, worked hard and gave Rodrigo and I amazing opportunities to pursue our dreams. You've supported and encouraged every wish I ever had, and my artistic, sensitive heart will never forget it. Mami, Ximena was named after you and there's so much about her that was inspired by your bravery, love of family, and your passion for justice in Bolivia. I'm so proud to be your daughter. Papi, you have always believed that I'd grow up to be a writer (or a singer—but listen, you can't have everything. Plus, I can't sing). Mil besos a los dos, los quiero mucho.

To the TV show Jane the Virgin: I saw myself in every episode, and every time Jane Villanueva sat down to write. Thank you for existing—representation matters. <3 <3

To my sweet, amazing husband Andrew: you've read every story I've written, sometimes more than once, and from the very beginning when it mattered the most, never doubted I'd get here one day. I love you with all my heart. Your support, love, and encouragement has meant everything and it's made all the difference in my life.

And lastly but most importantly, to Jesus. Thank you for loving me exactly where I am, even at my messiest and farthest.

about the author

Isabel Ibañez was born in Boca Raton, Florida, and is the proud daughter of two Bolivian immigrants. A true word nerd, she received her degree in creative writing and has been a Pitch Wars mentor for three years. Isabel is an avid moviegoer and loves hosting family and friends around the dinner table. She currently lives in Winter Park, Florida, with her husband, their adorable dog, and a serious collection of books. Say hi on social media at @IsabelWriter09.